Father Melancholy's Daughter

Also by Gail Godwin

The Perfectionists
Glass People
The Odd Woman
Dream Children
Violet Clay
A Mother and Two Daughters
Mr. Bedford and the Muses
The Finishing School
A Southern Family

FATHER MELANCHOLY'S DAUGHTER

GAIL GODWIN

ANDRE DEUTSCH

First published 1991 by
André Deutsch Limited
105-106 Great Russell Street, London WC1B 3LJ

ISBN 0 233 98691 X

A signed first edition of this book
has been published by The Franklin Library

Printed in Great Britain by
St Edmundsbury Press, Bury St Edmunds, Suffolk

to my own Father Melancholy, the sorrowful but animating spirit who dwells within

ACKNOWLEDGMENTS

The author acknowledges with pleasure the extensive guidance and many useful suggestions of the Rev. David L. Bronson, Rector Emeritus of Holy Cross Episcopal Church, Kingston, N.Y., and of the Rev. Gale D. Webbe, S.T.D., former Rector of St. Mary's Church, Asheville, N.C., and author of *The Night and Nothing, The Shape of Growth,* and *Sawdust and Incense: Worlds That Shape a Priest.* I am also grateful to Dr. George Vas for help with neurological matters, and to Paul Plumer for providing me with the paramedical scenario. To Dan Starer, as always, I am indebted for his meticulous and comprehensive research.

FATHER MELANCHOLY'S DAUGHTER

I : MORNING

Although I did not know it then, my life of unpremeditated childhood ended on Wednesday, September 13, 1972. The weather
that day in Romulus, Virginia, was warm and sunny; the sky an
unclouded Shenandoah blue. I had been in first grade for three
weeks. The schoolwork I found easy, insultingly so. It was the
social side of things, the winning over of other children that was
going to demand my subtler energies. I was, and was destined to
remain, an only child, and was more practiced in the management
of adults.

That morning I had dressed by myself because Daddy had
Wednesday Mass and had gone next door to the church to "set up
shop," as he called it, and Ruth, my mother, was completely taken
up with an overnight guest, a woman she had known at boarding
school. The visit of this person had been anxiously anticipated by
my mother for reasons I failed to understand. From the moment
she had arrived the evening before, sauntering arrogantly up our
walk and making her arch comments about the rectory, I had
taken a dislike to Madelyn Farley.

I remember well the dress I put on that fateful Wednesday
morning. At Romulus Country Day School, girls were allowed to
wear jeans or corduroys by then, just like the boys, but since I was
the Rector of St. Cuthbert's daughter, I guess it was thought that
I should uphold the old ways a little longer. My dress was one of

several new ones that Ruth and I had bought over in Charlottesville, the nearest good town for shopping before Romulus built its
giant mall.

It was a blue and brown plaid of soft cotton, but with some
percentage of miracle fiber in it so it didn't have to be ironed,
and the reason I liked it was because it had these wonderful buttons all the way down the front. They were of a magical clear
amber color that changed according to the light and they were
shaped like little cats' heads, even with the eyes and noses and
whiskers etched in.

"Those are real buttons, Margaret," Ruth had said in the store
when I was insisting on this dress. "Every time you put it on, you'll
have to button them all the way down, and every time you take it
off you'll have to unbutton them."

"I don't care, I want it," I said. "I don't mind buttoning the
buttons."

"Well, just remember, I'm not doing it for you. I've got enough
buttons of my own to worry about." My mother had this way of
talking. She would say something that sounded simple and harmless in her light, melodic drawl, but underneath you often got the
feeling she was saying something quite different at the same time.

When I came down to breakfast on the morning of September
13, I was waiting for Ruth to see how well I had buttoned every
one of the little cats' heads, but before she could even notice
anything, the woman named Madelyn started acting chummy with
me, asking how I liked school.

"It's okay, I guess," I said. Not one of my brightest answers, but
I could tell she wasn't truly interested. The chumminess was for
my mother's benefit.

"Oh, come on now, Margaret," said Ruth, laughing. "You love
school." She sat in her accustomed seat in our breakfast nook, the
nook she'd had built into the recesses of an old-fashioned bay
window when we had moved into the rectory. The bay window
had once been part of the dining room before my mother had
talked Daddy into getting the vestry's permission to knock out a
wall. It was her favorite spot in the rectory, this breakfast nook
that she herself had designed and implemented. Here she drank
coffee, made her lists and wrote letters, often slipping out of her
loafers and stretching her legs out in front of her on the pale
yellow window-seat cushions corded with bright orange. Occa-

sionally she did watercolors of Daddy's garden, which was really many different gardens, depending on the season and the particular time within that season. Once she made me sit across from her, where the woman named Madelyn was now sitting, and had tried to do a watercolor of me. It was not a success, although I almost went crazy keeping still. I pretended to like it, because she was so unhappy with the way it had turned out. But she was right. It had made me into a blurry little girl with flat brown curls and eyes as undiscerning as a blue-eyed doll's.

Now, hugging her coffee mug secretively to her chest, as if concealing a small, warm pet that belonged to her alone, Ruth was bragging to the visitor about how well I could read. Her rings flashed in the morning sun. Though she had stayed up most of the night talking and laughing with her friend, she looked fresh and lovely, particularly in comparison to Madelyn Farley. My mother was a collection of pleasing colors, with her honey-smooth tan, aquamarine eyes, and the silky hair with its red and gold and even some bluish lights. Lately she had taken to wearing her hair pulled back severely with a tortoiseshell clip, ever since one of our parish ladies had told her she looked more like a college girl than a rector's wife. With the bright fall sunshine upon her, she seemed partly made out of silky, liquid light herself. It is right there, in that vivid instant of my appreciation of her, that I preserve some genuine feel of what my mother was to me, some essential Ruth-ness about her that has not become blurred by my father's and my subsequent romanticizings of her, or worn thin by our obsessive retrievals. It's not a lot, but it's better than nothing. It lives on in me, that glowing little moment of paradise, when I walk towards her light and her colors as towards a treat; I am sure of my welcome, sure of her esteem. Even the unlovely visitor serves a purpose by providing a contrast: that's what you might look like if you are outside the light, when you are only basking in it briefly before taking to the road again.

"Margaret could say her alphabet by the time she was three," Ruth was boasting to her friend. "And she and her daddy have been hitting the books ever since. You saw how the two of them couldn't wait to get away together last night for their reading session. You should have seen the look on her face when she came home from school the first day. She is the single child in her class who already knows how to read! I was a little worried at first. You know, that her classmates might resent her. But her teacher says she's handling it just fine. She's going to be smart *and* popular, it looks like."

"Well, why shouldn't she be?" remarked the other in her brusque, flat voice. "You were."

"Oh, come on, Madelyn. I made friends easily, but I was certainly not a brain. I was just a good memorizer and knew how to please my teachers. No, Margaret gets her brains from Walter."

The woman plunked down her spoon and bared her big, square, white teeth at my mother in a sarcastic grin. She had been eating some grayish mush that I assumed was the wet version of the "high-energy" cereal she had brought with her in the glass jar when she had arrived last evening in her silver Mustang with the New York license plates. "This ought to be refrigerated," she had told Ruth in her flat, clipped tones. "It's got raw wheat germ in it."

Now she shook her head scornfully at my mother. "Ruth, Ruth, Ruth," she chanted in her mocking way. "You haven't changed at all. What are we going to do with you?"

"Well," said my mother, blushing, "it's the truth. Walter's mind is formidable and she gets that part from him. Maybe he does push her a little, but she seems to like it. It makes them both happy."

"Walter's formidable mind is not the question here," challenged Madelyn Farley with a wry look at my mother. She was the first adult who had not reacted with awe at the news of my precocious abilities. In fact, I felt as if I were invisible to her at the moment. Totally focused on my mother, Madelyn Farley sat with her back to Daddy's fall garden of Michaelmas daisies, scarlet asters, and what he called his indomitable little nasturtiums. The same morning sun that glorified my mother shone cruelly through the visitor's short, wispy, tinsel-colored hair. You could see through to the outline of her scalp and picture how she would look if she were bald.

"Margaret, honey," said my mother, "why do you always shake out a mountain of cornflakes? You know you'll only eat a fraction of them."

But Madelyn Farley answered for me. "Because, when you pour the milk over it, you have the satisfaction of watching the whole mountain collapse."

This was exactly the way I felt about the cornflakes, only I couldn't have expressed it as such, but I didn't like Madelyn Farley any better for putting my feelings into words for me.

She sniffed my animosity. Trying her chummy act once more, she slid forward her jar of the "high-energy" cereal my mother had teased her about last evening when we had been carrying in her things from her car. "Would you like to try some of my cereal?" she asked in her scornful voice. "It reacts differently from your cornflakes. With mine, you pour on the milk and everything *swells up*." She bared her big white teeth at me in what she probably thought was a smile, but her eyes, a hard metallic gray, like her car, were mocking. She was too complicated, even if I had wanted to be friends with her. Also she appeared to be challenging me in some way, as though the two of us were in competition.

"No, thank you," I said politely, looking down at my collapsed cornflakes drowning in their milk. I pretended to be intent on eating them. Only a few minutes more and it would be time for Ruth to walk me to my school-bus stop. I reminded myself that when I returned from school this afternoon, this unsettling person would be gone from our lives.

She was on her way back to New York after working all summer in some outdoor theater in southern Virginia. First she had been supposed to come and visit at the beginning of the summer, but she got a late start from New York and canceled at the last minute. After my mother rallied from her disappointment she told us that the end of the summer would actually be better because then Madelyn could stay a few days. All summer Ruth prepared for this rescheduled visit of her old friend. She and Daddy discussed it and then she sat down in her breakfast nook and wrote a letter to Madelyn Farley telling her about all the things they would do. "I've got to tempt her," Ruth said. "Madelyn is always working, working, working. You have to talk her into having fun."

"You could use some fun yourself," Daddy said, "after putting up with me this past winter." He was referring to his most recent depression, but after one of his depressions was over my mother didn't like to talk about it. I think she hoped each one would be the last. So she made no comment and continued writing her letter to Madelyn. "You two could drive to the Peaks of Otter," Daddy went on convivially. He was full of benevolence and good ideas since his hope and energy had come back. His sonorous, rolling voice, which Dr. MacGruder, our senior warden, called "our pulpit treasure," had its old bounce in it once again. "Do take a few days off," he urged my mother. "You and Madelyn go somewhere and be schoolgirls together. It would do you good. Margaret and I will stay here and hold the fort."

"We were never *girls* together, Walter," Ruth corrected him. "Madelyn was an instructor at Miss Beale's. She was twenty-five at the time and I was eighteen. Even eighteen isn't a *girl* anymore. It would be fun to go off somewhere, but on the other hand I really want Madelyn to get to know you and Margaret. Also, she'll be coming from down there and she might not want to double back, even for the Peaks of Otter. Madelyn's not someone who likes to double back on herself. It's all straight ahead for Madelyn."

"My," said Daddy. "She sounds pretty fierce. Well, you tell her we'll do our best to make her comfortable."

Ruth sent the letter off and weeks went by without a reply.

"She's probably not coming," said my mother disconsolately. "She has her career on her mind. Besides, our lives are so different now."

But finally, in late August, came a picture postcard showing a play in production at the summer theater where Madelyn was working. The picture showed two actors in overalls sitting in front of a shack on an outdoor stage. They were made up to look like ancient hillbillies, but you could tell they were young men. Ruth was overjoyed to get the card and read the message aloud to us several times. "Madelyn says thank God this isn't one of *her* sets, and she can come to Romulus on September twelfth and stay till Friday the fifteenth. I had been counting on a week, but she's a very busy woman. I think I'll buy a new bedspread to replace that sickly green one in the guest room. We'll need it for the Bishop in November anyway, when he comes for confirmations."

"The Bishop is color-blind," said Daddy amiably, "but you go right ahead and buy a new spread that will pass muster with your friend."

But when Madelyn Farley arrived on the evening of September twelfth, she had hardly climbed out of her car and allowed herself to be hugged and kissed by my mother before she was announcing in her flat, clipped voice that she could stay only one night. She had to be on the road to New York the very next morning, she said, sounding very pleased with herself.

"Oh, Madelyn, I'm *crushed*. I've been looking forward to your visit for *months*. I even went out and bought you a new bedspread!" Though my mother spoke lightly, and was pretending to make

fun of herself, anyone who knew her well could tell she was genuinely hurt. "Oh, I'm so *disappointed*, Madelyn."

"So am I," the visitor had replied breezily, not sounding at all
disappointed. "But this new job came up. I have to work for a
living, you know." She pulled a glass jar of something out of a
canvas bag on the backseat of her car and handed it to my mother.
"This ought to be refrigerated. It's got raw wheat germ in it."

That's when Ruth had laughed and teased her. "Oh, Lordy, if
it isn't your same old 'high-energy' gruel from back at Miss Beale's!
You still swear by it?"

"I still swear by it," repeated the visitor in a mocking singsong,
which sounded as if she were trying to imitate my mother's way of
talking.

"You used to say at Miss Beale's that it was the source of your
secret powers," my mother said.

"Did I really? How arrogant of me." But Madelyn Farley
looked pleased to be reminded of this former arrogance. Slinging
a stuffed gray leather bag over her shoulder, she started ahead of
us up our own front walk. She wore dirty sneakers without socks
and rumpled khaki pants and a dark polo shirt open at the neck.
She was a pale, lanky person, and though breasts were obvious
beneath the polo shirt, she loped along more like a boy. She was
different from the grown-up women I knew. And she seemed
another species altogether from our church ladies with their constricted, mincing walks and their soft-spoken pleasantries. My
mother, who had changed dresses twice that afternoon while nervously waiting for her old friend's arrival, followed joyfully behind, carrying Madelyn Farley's large black portfolio, which tied
with strings on all four sides, as if it were the property of some
awesome dignitary. I was put in charge of the "high-energy" jar
full of dry grainy stuff that had to go into our refrigerator at once.

Just before reaching our front steps, the visitor halted abruptly
and scrutinized our house. "So this is the *rectory*," she said wryly. "I
had first thought a chilly gray stone, but this grizzled brick creates
the same mood. I expected the ivy, of course. All rectories must be
smothered in ivy. But I really have to congratulate myself for
imagining your Gothic Revival windows exactly as they are." She
spoke as if, standing there with her legs apart, hoisting her stuffed
gray bag, she was actually *making up* our home on the spot.

"Madelyn is a scenic designer," Ruth explained to me. "She
makes the sets for plays, so she has to pay special attention to

houses and things. I don't mean she actually constructs the sets anymore, do you, Maddy? Not like back at Miss Beale's. Now that Madelyn here is in the big time, she just decides how things will look and then other people build them. Madelyn has worked on Broadway."

"Mmm," rumbled Madelyn Farley sarcastically. "And the play closed after three performances."

"But that wasn't the fault of your *set*, Madelyn. I mean, you didn't write the play. And besides, this is only the beginning for you. I'm sure all kinds of directors saw that show and admired your set, whatever they thought of the play."

"Oh, Ruth, it's good to see you again," said the visitor in a slightly condescending tone. "I really don't know how I stayed away so long." She slipped her free arm around my mother's waist and the two of them stood there swaying back and forth, my mother smiling happily.

"Run on, sweetie," Ruth said to me, "and put Madelyn's jar in the refrigerator. And don't bang the screen door."

"I'm *very* pleased with myself for getting your Gothic windows exactly right," said Madelyn Farley, still swaying back and forth, hip to hip, with my mother.

"I never much noticed what our windows were," came my mother's vaguely wondering reply. "Except to sometimes wish they let in more light."

I went on into the rectory as ordered, but forgot and banged the screen door. The long, straight hall that went to Daddy's study and then turned a sharp left towards the kitchen *was* rather dark. And as I realized this, I felt the stirrings of a profound uneasiness. I could not have said why then, but I wonder now whether I didn't sense that this woman about to enter our house might indeed possess "powers" capable of changing our lives by making us see ourselves differently.

Daddy was in the kitchen, stooped over the cocktail tray that he was ceremoniously setting up for the visitor. His stoop was his most characteristic posture, not only because he was six feet three and always inclining towards shorter people but also because of his close-up style of attending to things. He was nearsighted and had to get right down to their level. Being small myself, I appreciated this: I felt he saw me not just in outline, the way many adults did ("Oh, there goes a child"), but in all my unique particulars.

In honor of the visitor, I saw, he had fastened his clerical collar in back with the gold stud Father Traherne, his late beloved mentor, had given him at his ordination.

"Whoa there," he said as I stomped past with Madelyn Farley's energy granules. "What kind of critters have you got in that jar?"

"They're not critters. It's some stuff she eats for *power* that's got to be refrigerated." I packed my voice full of disgust, to signal to him my feelings about the visitor.

"Oh, oh," he crooned affably. "Well then, I expect we'd better get it on ice, hadn't we?" His playful inflections conveyed to me that my opinion of my mother's friend had been registered. "But we'll be cordial to her, won't we?" he said, capping the top of my head with his large hand. It was all he needed to say.

Madelyn and my mother went straight to the guest room. Presently Ruth returned alone. "She wants to shower and change first," she told Daddy. "Oh, and she can only stay one night."

Daddy raised his eyebrows. "I thought until Friday."

"A new job came up and so she has to rush back."

"I see. Too bad she didn't phone. You've gone to so much trouble with your menus."

"Oh, well," sighed my mother, sinking down on the sofa and looking despondent, "she's not a lady of leisure like me."

"Busy people can find time to phone," said Daddy, "and you are hardly a lady of leisure."

"I'm sure she *meant* to phone," said my mother defensively, frowning at the air in front of her. "By the way, she doesn't drink cocktails, she said. Just white wine with a little ice."

"In that case," said Daddy, "I'd better open the white wine, hadn't I? But I only bought the one bottle, for our dinner. Should I go out quickly and get another one?" He looked at his watch. "Though I expect they're likely to be closed by the time I get there."

"No, it's too late," snapped my mother, exasperated. She rolled her eyes at the ceiling, the way she did after a tennis game with Elaine Major, when she would fling down her racket and do parodies of the Major before going off to restore her good temper with a shower. But now she was making a supreme effort to keep her good temper. "Oh, Walter, I'm sorry," she said contritely, after a moment.

"Sorry for what, my love? There's nothing for *you* to be sorry for."

"But the visit's starting off all wrong. I wanted you two to like each other."

"Well, I promise to try my best," replied Daddy amiably. "But I can't promise on her behalf that she'll like me."

He rose resolutely from his chair to go and open the white wine, and after watching my mother brooding to herself for a minute, I escaped to join him in the kitchen. Except when he was having his depressions, Daddy was the most congenial person I knew. He could smooth over any awkwardness with a winning phrase. Whereas Ruth, my mother, though she always looked graceful and assured, could at the same time emit devastating little dagger waves of displeasure when things were not living up to her expectations. She was also more impatient than Daddy and tended to give up on people and things more quickly. She and Daddy differed in another way, too: when something did not go well, she would roll her eyes and sigh and exclaim, "*I'm* sorry, it's all my fault!" But you knew she was expecting you to convince her it was not at all her fault. In contrast, when something displeased or disappointed Daddy, he would shake his head sadly and say, "Civilization is crumbling. The world as we have known it is going down the tubes." But you could tell he was really blaming *himself* for not being good enough or powerful enough to make things conform to his expectations.

The visitor finally made her appearance and was introduced to Daddy. When he dipped his long, black-clad body to her in an old-fashioned bow, she gave him a suspicious side smile, as if he might be poking fun at her, but he wasn't. He was one of those men who still bowed to women. Madelyn Farley had changed into dark trousers and a smocklike flowing shirt crammed with embroidered figures and symbols. I thought it was a preposterous thing for a grown woman to wear, but it did break the ice by serving as a conversation piece.

"What a wonderful shirt, Madelyn," said my mother as Daddy handed the visitor her white wine with ice in it. "Is it from some place exotic?"

"It's from all over, actually," said Madelyn Farley in her brusque voice. As she positioned herself in front of our unlit fireplace, her long fishy-white feet in their scuffed sandals poked in opposite directions. Her tinsel hair stuck up from her head in damp separate wisps from her shower. She was definitely the strangest person I had ever met. "A costume designer I work with made it for me," she said, rotating her wine glass upon the palm of her hand, causing the ice to make a little clinking song against the sides of the glass. She appeared to be listening to the song, holding us all in the palm of her hand as we waited for her to go on. "She cut out motifs she liked from scraps of old fabrics and tapestries and arranged them to please herself. It's a *collage*." She drew out this last word in her dry, mocking manner. It was the first time I had heard the word, and for a long time after that, I thought it meant the type of garment she had worn.

"Well, it's most interesting," said Daddy, who hovered alongside of her in front of the fireplace because he couldn't politely sit down before she did. "I believe your friend may have cut *that* one" —and he lightly tapped a dove with an olive branch in its mouth on Madelyn Farley's shoulder— "out of an old altar frontal. Yes, because here's some more of it in the same weave and colors." He indicated with his finger, but this time did not actually touch, two intertwined letters on Madelyn's breast pocket. "Yes, your shirt certainly is 'from all over,' isn't it? That's the Alpha and the Omega you've got on your front pocket."

"What is the Alpha and the Omega?" inquired Madelyn Farley, at last deciding to take a sip of her wine.

"Well, they're the first and last letters of the Greek alphabet," said Daddy. "But in Christian symbolism they stand for the all-embracing, the totality. That's what I meant when I said you were right about your shirt being from all over. On altarpieces and vestments, the Alpha and the Omega stand for Christ. It's His monogram."

"Oh, my," said Madelyn Farley. She raised her eyebrows at Daddy, then smirked down at her pocket with complacency. "I'm going to have to look into this church symbolism of yours. There are probably things I could use in my work."

"Ah . . . undoubtedly," murmured Daddy. Still standing beside the visitor who was obviously not going to sit down, he smiled ruefully down into his Scotch glass, as if confiding to it something more than he was prepared to say aloud.

"I hope you aren't offended," challenged Madelyn Farley rather combatively, "that I am wearing Christ's monogram on my shirt."

"Well, of course he isn't offended, Maddy!" My mother spoke up from the sofa, where she had been raptly watching this important opening scene being played out by her husband and her old friend. "*You* didn't know what it was. I myself didn't know until Walter pointed it out just this minute. And besides, well, my goodness, it's just a shirt your friend made for you."

"A very striking shirt," my father assured the visitor in his affable baritone.

Madelyn Farley, in her dark trousers, made him a little bow from the waist.

My mother had given a lot of thought to dinner, as well as to all the rest of the meals our visitor would not now be having with us, because at Miss Beale's Madelyn had been a vegetarian. Ruth had spent much of that day preparing an elaborate cold meal with a dazzling variety of meatless treats. My mother outdid everyone in the art of presenting food attractively. Even the parish biddies, who undermined her because they could not quite forgive her youth and good looks, found no fault with her table arrangements, which were both pleasing and audacious. She could carve a radish into a rose, or make a little scalloped basket out of a tomato, but she also combined old ingredients in new ways. "I never heard of anyone putting those little slices of yellow bell peppers on cucumber sandwiches," the biddies would remark, "but aren't they *colorful*!" "Imagine!" one of them would trill, "just imagine wrapping salami around a piece of honeydew! But so tasty . . . ! I can't wait to try it."

My mother would thank them graciously, then after they were gone she would do parodies of them: their corseted, self-satisfied walks, the effortless niceties that rolled off their tongues. "Oh, Ruth, Ruth, you must stop," Daddy would beg, the tears oozing from the corners of his eyes because he'd laughed so hard. "You are wicked, you know. You could have been an actress."

"God, Ruth, what a feast," said Madelyn Farley when we went to the dining room and she saw the table prepared in her honor. "And look how *pretty* you've made everything." But even when she was giving compliments, Madelyn Farley's voice retained its mocking edge.

"And there's not a scrap of meat in any of it, Maddy, I promise," said my mother, glowing proudly. "Even the pâté is made from a soybean recipe, though you can hardly tell it."

Madelyn Farley looked thoroughly perplexed for a moment, then laughed. "Oh, I'm not a vegetarian anymore. When you travel around in the boondocks the way I do, you soon learn to eat what the locals eat."

"Well, you'll be eating what the lucky locals eat this evening," said Daddy, standing behind Madelyn's chair so he could push it under her when she decided to sit down. "And I for one can vouch for its being mighty good."

When we were all seated, Daddy took my mother's hand; he extended his other hand to the visitor, who raised her eyebrows at him.

"We always say grace like this," Ruth explained.

"Oh." With her mocking smirk, Madelyn accepted my father's hand. She was sitting in my place and I had been moved to the end of the table, facing Daddy. It was necessary for me to stand up and strain forward in order to reach her hand and Ruth's so we could make the circle.

While Daddy was asking God to bless this meal and, in his usual conversational way, sort of filling God in on our activities of the day, Madelyn kept her eyes wide open, disconcerting me when she caught me in the act of watching her. I slammed my eyes shut and therefore missed seeing her face when Daddy asked God to guide and instruct our visitor in all her endeavors and thanked Him for bringing her to our house. I thought his petition was generous enough; the thanks part, I felt, went too far. Because I could tell Daddy didn't like Madelyn Farley any better than I did.

We all helped ourselves from Ruth's pretty platters. I was particularly proud of how I transported my deviled egg on the serving spoon without a wobble from the platter to my plate, and was sorry that nobody noticed.

"This is like some giant antipasto," said Madelyn, sliding a deviled egg onto *her* plate. "And what are those cocky little flowers you've stuck around the edges, Ruth?"

"Those are Walter's nasturtiums," my mother said. "He grows them bigger and brighter than anyone. With nasturtiums you have to know just the right time to put the seeds in. Not too early and not too late. Walter is an inspired gardener."

"I just picked up a few pointers from my mother," said Daddy. "Now *she* was the inspired gardener. She communed with her plants, and this was long before it became fashionable. She could feel when a plant was moping because it had been put in the wrong setting, even before it showed signs of languishing. She would dig it up and carry it around in a baking pan with some peat moss and ask it, 'What about here? No? Beside that tree? Oh, all right, over here . . .' "

"I take it she's no longer alive," Madelyn Farley interrupted him.

"Why . . . no," said Daddy. But he seemed slightly startled, as though he had to remember she was dead. "No, my mother died while I was in England, serving my curacy. It was very sudden. As a matter of fact, she was due to fly over to visit me within a few weeks. We were going to take the train to the Lake District, a place she had always wanted to see because of her love for Wordsworth, and then we were going on up to Northumbria, where some very interesting church history took place." He plucked a velvety yellow nasturtium from Ruth's platter and examined it wistfully, holding it close to his face. "But instead, I found myself flying home to her funeral in Chattanooga. But what about your parents? Are they living?" With customary adroitness, he had turned the conversation away from himself.

"My father is," said Madelyn. "Farley's too mean to die. He is the supreme example of the completely selfish artist." But she laughed gruffly and seemed proud of him. "When I was fifteen, we went to the Adirondacks one weekend because there was this view Farley had been wanting to paint. Actually, we were all three painting. It was a 'family outing.' " Her voice was thick with mockery. "I had my easel next to Farley's and Mother was painting out of her box. She was quite a good painter in her own right, but after she married Farley she reduced herself to miniatures. Anyway, there we were in the Adirondacks, miles from anywhere, and she starts getting these horrible stomach pains. It was appendicitis but we didn't know it at the time. Farley wanted to finish his painting, so he told Mother to lie down and take deep breaths and she'd feel better. So that's what she did, my long-suffering mother, she lay down at the edge of the woods and took deep breaths. And Farley finished his painting."

"You don't mean to say," my father asked Madelyn with some consternation, "that . . . that was the end?"

"The end?" repeated Madelyn, frowning. Then she laughed curtly. "No, no, she didn't *die* then, if that's what you mean. But, yes, it was the end, in a way, because she left Farley that same year. Eventually she married again. A wimpy little psychologist who was always asking her what she was thinking. But apparently neither of them noticed the little black spot on her thigh, and when her gynecologist finally did, it was much too late. Melanoma. She didn't seem to mind much. While she was dying, we had the first good talks of our lives. She told me, 'I loved Farley but I never liked him, and I like Don, but I could never, *never* love him.' Don was the psychologist."

"I see," said my father, who had gotten more than he had bargained for by asking whether Madelyn Farley's parents were alive.

"What made you decide to be a priest?" Madelyn Farley asked bluntly. "Or is that not a polite question?"

"It's a perfectly *good* question," Daddy said, "and I'll answer it as simply and directly as I can. God did."

Madelyn got the same expression on her face that I'd seen on it during the family prayer. "Okay," she conceded, "but I mean was there a sudden dramatic moment? Or did it happen gradually over a period of time?"

"Well, I assume it did happen gradually," Daddy began thoughtfully. "None of us suddenly becomes something overnight. The preparations have been in the making for a lifetime. Perhaps even for generations. But, there *was* a moment—I don't know if it will meet your standards for a dramatic one—when I suddenly knew. I was sitting on the sofa reading a magazine when something shifted slightly inside my head, sort of like clouds parting, and I thought, oh, well . . . of course."

"Walter, you never told me this about the magazine," said my mother.

"It hardly seemed worth telling," said Daddy, "but if Madelyn here wants to pin me down to one sudden *moment*, I guess that would have to be it."

"What was the magazine?" Madelyn wanted to know.

"I really don't remember," said Daddy. "The magazine itself wasn't very important, I don't think."

"Hmm. I wonder," said Madelyn Farley.

A kind of verbal jousting continued between them throughout the meal. The reason I am able to set down so much of it now—probably the reason I am able to set down *any* of it—is because, in the years to follow, Daddy and I would go over and over *and over* Ruth's last evening with us with the same obsessive fervor as the apostles undoubtedly went over and over *and over* the Last Supper. What one of us couldn't remember, the other supplied—or possibly made up. Only there were eleven of them—subtracting the betrayer Judas—eleven apostles to compare notes on the Absent One, to shore up his memory with their varying modes of perception. There were only two of us. And, at the time, I had been six years old.

Daddy would therefore have to provide most of the verbatim stuff during these reconstructive marathons that were to possess us, and oddly console us, for the next sixteen years. Six-year-olds, even precocious ones, don't pay much attention to the subject matter in the conversation of adults. Too many associations are lost on them. But maybe that's why they are quicker to pick up on feelings: sudden shifts in alliances, eddies of resentment, gusts of unsuppressed yearning. All these were present that evening in our dining room as Daddy's gallant voice advanced and retreated in response to the brusque sallies and jabs of our visitor. And my mother's light, musical drawl wove back and forth in a constant effort to harmonize them into some kind of unity.

"But tell me," Daddy said to Madelyn Farley, "how did *you* happen to become a designer for the theater? Was there a sudden dramatic moment, or did it happen gradually over a period of time?"

If she caught my father's teasing echo of her earlier question about his vocation, she didn't show it. She became quite serious and dropped her mocking tone. "It happened when I was ten. I had rheumatic fever and they made me stay home from school a whole semester. I was bored to death, until one day I picked up a couple of Farley's used pipe cleaners and made myself a little figure. Then it needed clothes, so I made it a robe out of some sterile gauze that I dyed by dipping in some blue watercolor pigment, and then I sprayed the robe with Mother's hairspray to give it body. Then I sewed sequins all over the robe and that's when I realized my little figure was a magician. I gave it a wand, a needle from Mother's sewing box, and as soon as it had that wand in its hand, that's when things really took off. Then it could start making the things it needed for itself. It and I became partners. It would wave its wand—I named it the Hot Wand—and I would know exactly what it wanted me to make next. I made it a forest first, on those pieces of cardboard that come in men's shirts—I painted a triptych, three scenes taped together—and then after my magician got tired of its flat forest, it waved its wand again and signaled to me I had to do better. I had to go three-dimensional

and provide it with a town. So I made it a town, with real buildings. It even had a church, Walter, you'll be glad to know, only it
was a bare, white New-England-y sort of church, not your ivy-
choked, Gothic, southern mode, but boy, that steeple was a bitch
to make. Before my convalescence was over, I had turned my
bedroom into this entire little town. It got pretty scummy in there,
and there was only a narrow path for me to go in and out, but
Farley and Mother were happy because I was absorbed and they
could do their own work. They heaped supplies on me from both
their studios. I got very fussy about verisimilitude and having
everything to the right scale. I was teaching myself the basics of set
design, although I didn't think of it in those terms, of course. I
was making a town for my little figure, that's how I thought of it.
I was responding to the Hot Wand. And as long as I was obeying
the Hot Wand, I was completely absorbed, completely myself,
happy. I still feel that way when I'm doing a set, although the
popsicle sticks and masonite scraps and airplane glue now translate into thousands of dollars worth of materials that arrive on
trucks, and I'm in real trouble if I'm a quarter-inch off scale. I
think that's one reason women designers have such a hard time
getting productions . . . the directors just don't trust them with all
that expensive, heavy *lumber* . . . but don't get me started on that!
The point is, when I'm involved in a set, especially when I'm
doing my sketches and models, I'm still as happy as a ten-year-old.
My face heats up and my mouth waters when I'm under the spell
of the Hot Wand, just the way it did when I was ten years old."

"That's wonderful," said Daddy. Both my parents were regarding Madelyn Farley with admiration and a sort of protective tenderness. It was the only time during the whole evening when
everyone seemed to be in rapport. At this point, so Daddy tells me
(I have no recollection of it), I made my single verbal contribution
to the occasion.

"Was your magician a man or a woman?" I asked Madelyn
Farley. "You just kept calling it *it*."

According to Daddy, Madelyn Farley had looked at me with
new interest and then said in her flat, mocking voice, "That's a fair
question, but I don't really remember it being one or the other. It
was simply an extension of me. Or I was an extension of it."

"Then it would be a woman," I informed her.

"Not necessarily," she replied coolly. "Art doesn't necessarily
have a gender."

"Oh, Maddy, you don't know how lucky you are!" my mother suddenly burst out passionately. "To *have* your Hot Wand . . . to be able to create something all your own like that!"

"Why, Ruth," said Daddy. "You are one of the most creative people I know."

"Oh, I don't mean flower arranging and playing piano for Sunday school when Milly Winchester is indisposed, Walter," my mother snapped back. "I mean real art, genuine talent."

"Your talents are genuine enough for me," replied Daddy with appeasing good humor. "And what about your watercolors?" He directed Madelyn Farley's attention to the two framed paintings of churches that hung above our sideboard. "Ruth did those on our honeymoon in Charleston," he told the visitor. "That's St. Philip's and the one with the portico is St. Michael's. I think they're lovely, don't you?"

"Well of course they're *lovely,*" said Madelyn, not bothering to look at my father and giving the merest of glances to the water-colors above her. "Everything she does is *lovely,* but I hardly think that's the point. *Lovely* is the art of pleasing others. Art is about pleasing yourself."

"Margaret," Daddy said to me then, replacing his napkin on the table, "how about some more of *The Water Babies*?" And, according to him, he and I left the table directly after this remark of Madelyn's and went off together for our evening reading session in his study. It was my favorite hour of the day, and I was not at all sorry to say good night to the visitor. I do remember that.

When I was seated on my pillow in the chair next to Daddy, *The Water Babies* open between us on the desk, we could hear the voices of my mother and her friend through the closed door. They were obviously going right on with the conversation we had abandoned. Neither Daddy nor I mentioned Madelyn Farley. Our tacit reticence consigned her to nonexistence.

But later in the evening when Ruth came to my room to say good night, I remember asking her about Madelyn, trying to make her tell me all about her. Why would I do that? Maybe I had perceived how preoccupied she was with her old friend, and my asking about Madelyn Farley seemed the best ploy to get her to stay with me longer. That would fit my personality as I know it today.

"How can you two be friends when she's so much *older*?" was one of my questions. This was of course disingenuous on my part.

I knew perfectly well that people could like people older than themselves. After all, Ruth *loved* Daddy and he was sixteen years older.

"Oh, she's not *that* much older," said my mother, slipping out of her loafers and swinging her smooth legs up on my bed in one graceful motion. "Only seven years, though of course that seems ancient to you now. When I was a senior at Miss Beale's, Madelyn came as an instructor for our drama department. It was one of those last-minute things. The job she really wanted had fallen through. But I'm glad it did, otherwise I would never have met her. She was just so different from anyone I'd ever known, and yet, I remember, as soon as I met her, I felt I'd known her all my life."

"*How* was she different?"

My mother crossed her legs neatly at the ankles. I loved her anklebones; they were so sharply delineated, as if they had been cut out by an exacting pair of scissors. Her legs were still a deep golden brown from all our afternoons out at the MacGruders' lake. This past summer she had finally succeeded in teaching me to swim, and at the Labor Day picnic I was able to surprise Daddy by thrashing in my primitive crawl all the way from the dock to the float. Physical things did not come as easily to me as mental things did. In fact, I was a coward when it came to hurling my body out into uncertain spaces. But Ruth had been determined that I should conquer that cold, murky lake and my dread of touching the slimy float, and I did it to please her. More accurately, my dread of losing her respect turned out to be greater than my fear of anything the lake could do to me.

"How was Madelyn different?" She repeated my question with relish. "Well, she knew what she wanted and she wasn't afraid to say so. It's just such a surprise, and a relief, when people come right out and tell you what they want, what they really think. And she wasn't afraid to change her mind, either. Oh, no. When she first arrived at Miss Beale's, Madelyn was engaged . . ."

"*Engaged?*" What man would want that strange-looking, sarcastic person?

"Yes, engaged to be married. I thought the whole thing was so glamorous and exciting. I mean, here she was, this sophisticated woman of the world, not all *that* much older than we were, who'd lived in New York and actually worked in London, and now she was directing us in plays and living in our dorm. She was also our resident counselor. You could go and consult her if you had a problem, or if you just felt lonely. In the evenings her door was always open a crack and she'd be inside, sketching in her inks and watercolors at her big tilted table with its fluorescent lamp. She was designing her wedding, just the way she designed our plays. She was engaged to someone she'd met in London, a man who'd worked in the theater with her. I would go to her room every evening to see her latest drawings. 'How's the wedding coming?' I'd say, and this always made her laugh. They were going to get married in some forest in England, at night, and the bride and groom were going to wear long velvet cloaks trimmed with fur. And nobody's parents were going to be invited. I had never heard of anything so grandly romantic and unconventional. And then, suddenly, one evening in the spring, I went to her room and she told me she had broken off the engagement. She told me she had suddenly realized she was more interested in the idea of *producing her wedding* than she was in the man. Wasn't that courageous of her? If it had been me, I would have probably gone through with it just to keep from hurting anyone."

"No you wouldn't," I said, shocked. "Then you wouldn't have met Daddy and you wouldn't have me."

Ruth laughed and roughed up my curls. "Oh, Margaret, you serious little thing, you. *Of course* I wouldn't have. I mean, he wasn't even my fiancé. No, all I'm saying is that I admired Madelyn for having the gumption to face up to her mistake and *do* something about it. Before it was too late."

Soon after that she kissed me good night in her special way, snarling like an animal and nuzzling my throat. It always made me giggle, even if I was in a sad mood. Then she said, "How do you want your closet door?" She knew I had to have it opened at a certain angle before she turned the light out.

"Push it open just a *little* more."

"About here?"

"Perfect."

She always strove to get it just right, as if she, too, had a witch and knew how fussy witches were. And yet I had never told Ruth about my witch, in so many words. I had told neither of my parents about the witch who lived in my closet, but I often had the feeling Ruth knew, all the same. Because she knew exactly how the witch liked the door to be.

After she had turned off the light and gone back downstairs to

Madelyn Farley, I think I lay for a while and listened to their voices. Because I can still evoke the sound of those distinctly different cadences. My mother's airy, hoping-to-charm rhythms; her friend's blunt, mocking ones. Ruth's musical laugh that went up and down the scale; Madelyn Farley's sharp, single-noted one, like a snort. At some point, Daddy must have come upstairs from his study. He must have paused outside my door, which was always left ajar, and I, as I was to do so many times in the years of nights left to us, must have simulated the innocent deep breathing of the fast-asleep child. He had enough to worry about, my father, even before Ruth left us. Nobody wanted to send him back behind his Black Curtain, into another depression.

I can hear his soft sigh, as I heard it so many times late at night, when believing me asleep, he passed down the hall to his and my mother's bedroom, which he persisted in calling "your mother's and my bedroom" to the end of his days.

"It's so odd, Ruth," Madelyn Farley was saying to my mother the following morning, the morning of September 13, 1972, the beginning of the Wednesday that changed our lives, "it's so odd for me to think of you as 'the rector's wife.' "

I hunched over my cereal bowl, taking dogged slurps of cornflakes gone mushy with milk. Even *their* consistency seemed altered for the worst for coming under her beady scrutiny.

"Well, it's odd for me sometimes, too," my mother amazed me by saying. "Nevertheless, Maddy, it's what I am." She set down her coffee mug rather loudly and stood up. "Finish up, Margaret, or we'll be late for your bus. Madelyn won't be here when you get home this afternoon, so you two say good-bye now."

Good-bye and good riddance, I shouted silently while shaking Madelyn Farley's hand. "Come back and see us again," I said aloud in the singsongy voice of a good southern child.

"Well *thank* you," she responded in her mocking voice, crunching my fingers between hers. "Best of luck to you, young Margaret." A final display of the large white teeth as she bestowed her complicated smile.

Ruth and I hurried past St. Cuthbert's. The church's windows were tilted open and a pungent whiff of incense wafted to us through the warm September air.

"Lucky biddies," murmured Ruth to me without breaking her

stride. "Smells and bells even on a Wednesday. Your daddy sure spoils them."

I had to walk fast to keep pace with her, and we had almost reached the corner before I realized with a shock we had not played our usual Wednesday morning game as we passed the cars parked in front of Daddy's church. It was a highly subversive game: you had to show you knew whose car each was by revealing something, not necessarily flattering, about the owner, or by imitating the way that person talked. But you weren't allowed to mention the name of the person.

"If he's promised me once to get this noisy old heap fixed," Ruth would growl in Mrs. MacGruder's ravaged smoker's voice as we passed the dusty green Mercedes with its rackety diesel engine, "he's promised a hundred times. But you know how it is with a physician. He's got time for everybody except his own family."

"There's that same old bashed-in box of Kleenex on her front seat," I would murmur triumphantly as we passed Miriam Stacy's staid white Plymouth with its VOTE FOR MCGOVERN bumper sticker.

"*Mmmm,*" Ruth would chime in, in her deceptively sweet "coffee-hour" voice. "Now, if she'd use a few of those in *church,* instead of leaving them on her front seat, she could have herself a nice *new* box by now." Miriam Stacy, a drab, self-righteous old maid who lived with her mother, was the person who had told my mother she looked more like a college girl than a rector's wife and had caused Ruth to pull her hair back with the tortoiseshell clip. Miriam's sinuses always drained as soon as Daddy began his sermons, but she never blew her nose, only sat bravely snuffling her fluids back and driving everybody crazy.

It was our closest time together, this Wednesday game Ruth and I had recently concocted for our walk to my bus stop. It was ours alone, even Daddy didn't know about our secret war of insolence against this steadfast handful of ladies for whom one Eucharist a week was not enough. When Ruth and I were playing it, she seemed more like an older sister leading me willingly into rebellion against Daddy's Wednesday flock. She wasn't being malicious—even at six I knew that; she was just letting off some steam. And even at six, I knew she had steam to let off. I also knew that she really was fond of Nan MacGruder; I had heard her say she wished her own mother had been down-to-earth like Mrs. MacGruder. My mother was younger than the average rector's wife, she was twenty-eight and Daddy was forty-four. Added to that was her irrepressible flair for mimicry, and even Daddy admitted that St. Cuthbert's pews were filled with promising material. Ruth's favorite targets, the ones that inspired her most animated performances, were the drearily sanctimonious (like snuffling Miriam Stacy) and the self-congratulatory—the prototype of the latter being embodied by Elaine Major, that paragon of energy, good sense, and accomplishments, and the very person to tell you all about it.

The first woman elected to the vestry, "the Major," as many called her, had raised two sons to prominence, one a brain surgeon and the other an Episcopal bishop. The list of her good works in church and community would be too long to fit into her obituary, I once heard Daddy say. She was always thinking up some new way to help others, only she couldn't resist lecturing her beneficiaries. At age seventy, she was still a tireless hostess, had her thank-you notes in the mail within twenty-four hours, and played tennis six days a week. When she found out my mother could play, she insisted on doubles at the Club every few weeks. Coming home from these command recreations, Ruth would fling her racket on the sofa. When Daddy asked her how it had gone, she would roll her eyes back in her head and then declaim in a hollow contralto exactly like the Major's: "It was *puh-fect*, as always," and then head for the shower. "Puh-fect" was the Major's pet word; another was "guls." As in "Why guls need this Women's Lib is beyond me. *I* managed puh-fectly well without it."

In our Wednesday game, Ruth always did her best number when we passed the clean yellow Audi with the decal of the Episcopal Church on its rear window and the Wilson tennis racket in its white cover on the spotless backseat. I would wriggle in anticipation as we approached the Major's car. We had an unspoken rule that no matter whose turn it was, my mother always got to do Elaine Major. Each time she did her differently, but every performance was inspired. I wish I could do justice to Ruth's impersonations of the Major. They made me cackle like nothing else. They weren't spiteful, though they came mighty close to the line sometimes.

"Yes, my cah is clean, as usual," she might begin in the Major's forcefully projected, complacent contralto. "It really doesn't take much effuht. I drop it off at the Shell station next to my sheltuh for unwed guls, and when I come out, it's ready for my trip across town to altah guild." What made Ruth's Elaine Major so enjoyable was the way she *held back* the spite, in order to capture the Major's sincere conviction of her own excellence. And Ruth's performance itself was so convincing. You really felt you were spying on the Major, watching her very same self-satisfied duckwalk, with the pelvis thrown back and long, skinny feet in their expensive shoes splayed outwards as they bore down on her next good work; you felt you were overhearing the Major's thoughts about herself. ("It's a puh-fectly simple mattuh of *planning,* that's all. If you *plan* your day, there's no reason in the *wuhld* to complain there's not time for everything you want to do. I was widowed early and I raised two wonderful boys single-handedly and en-tuh-tained my friends and performed my church and community wuhk and puh-fected my tennis game and still found time for my rich and rewarding spiritual life before I had ever *huhd* of Women's Lib . . .")

But today the Wednesday morning game had been forgotten because of the visitor Madelyn. Breakfast had gone on too long and made us late. Now we had reached the corner, where, at the end of the church property, the Italian-carved Christ figure, his torso twisted gracefully sideways, hung on his wooden cross in the midst of a thick bed of ivy. Already I thought I heard the high-pitched wheeze of the school bus as it crept in low gear down the hilly part of Macon Street, and I felt cheated. My mother had scarcely noticed me since we had hurried out of the rectory. Usually there would be time for us to stand together swinging hands at this pleasantly shady corner with its solemn little outdoor cal-vary and plan what we would do when I returned home from school in the afternoon. Sometimes Ruth would look up at the stone figure, which had been carved far away in Venice over a century ago, and she'd cuff me affectionately and tell me the story of how, when I was three years old, I had asked Daddy why the church had bothered to build a roof over the suffering Jesus since he was going to die so soon anyway.

"Well, honey, here comes your bus," my mother was now say-ing. She did not seem to be aware that we had missed both our game and our usual discussion of afternoon plans. I was vexed by her absentmindedness and so I decided to punish her. I resolved not to look back, or wave, as I climbed aboard the bus.

This was accomplished easily, more easily than I had imag-ined. Before I knew it, the yellow doors had swung shut behind me and Mrs. Abner, our morning driver, was greeting me in her pert, familiar way that made it sound as if she knew something about me that I didn't know she knew. She greeted all the children this way. And then I saw my best friend, Harriet MacGruder, granddaughter of our senior warden, Dr. MacGruder. Harriet excitedly patted the seat beside her that she was saving for me. Because of our church connection, and because the MacGruders were always doing things for us, Harriet treated me as if I were her personal property. I played along with her, because I knew our friendship pleased our respective families, but Harriet had begun to bore me a little. She was such a known quantity. Chloe Niles was the person I secretly aspired to, with her pierced ears and black gypsy curls and nonchalant, devil-may-care solitariness. Her green eyes watched me out of her poker face. I knew she was studying me, biding her time, as I went about my business being a smart and popular child with the right connections. Chloe was being brought up by an aunt who ran an inn for summer tourists at the top of Macon Street; there was some awful mystery about her parents. I was saving up inscrutable Chloe Niles like an exotic treat. She would reveal her history to me and me alone when I should finally bestow myself on her. This morning she was sitting on the long seat at the back of the bus, watching me expressionlessly as I swaggered down the aisle in my new dress with the cat's-head buttons to claim the seat Harriet was saving.

I was so intent on pretending to be oblivious of Chloe that I had already forgotten about my punishment of Ruth. And thus it was that I also forgot to look out of the window, as the bus pulled away, to check on the results of my handiwork: to see if my mother was standing there, truly repentant, anxiously awaiting my wave. Was she hoping that I would relent at the last minute and thrust my face towards her behind the window? Or had she accepted my snub as deserved and then rallied sportingly, thinking ahead to the extra-special smile with which she would welcome me that afternoon when the bus would return me to her at this same corner? Perhaps she was already preparing other treats as well, to atone for her morning's neglect.

I forgot to speculate. For the last time in my life, although I did not know it, I was enjoying the luxury of being so sure of her that I could afford to forget all about her.

II : AFTERNOON

The morning of Wednesday, September 13, became Wednesday afternoon. The yellow buses lined up in front of the school. Our afternoon driver was a grim young woman named Lucy Brush. Completely opposite from the pert and familiar Mrs. Abner of our morning ride, who called each of us by name and intimated in her cheerful matronly manner that she knew us better than we knew ourselves, skinny, stoop-shouldered, intense Lucy Brush didn't appear to regard us as individuals at all. To Lucy Brush we were a head count. As, one by one, we clambered importantly aboard, lugging our empty lunch boxes and scholastic paraphernalia, puffed up or cast down by our day's little glories or tragedies, Lucy Brush's thin lips moved slightly, toting us up. But her eyes behind the glare of her glasses, with their out-of-date harlequin frames, swept over us collectively, never seeking out or recognizing any special face.

Directly behind her, taking up the whole of a seat meant for two, sat her sister Devonia. Although Devonia's permanent-waved hair was gray, and the doughy flesh straining the seams of her tentlike pantsuit was definitely that of an obese older person, her younger sister treated her like a small and precious child. As soon as the bus was under way, Lucy Brush embarked on a kind of loving travelogue for Devonia's entertainment.

"Look there, honeybaby, see them nice purple flowers?" she

would sing out, tipping her own tightly curled, permanent-waved head back towards the beloved hulk who rode just behind her, but keeping her eyes sternly on the road ahead. "Looky there, Vonie, there's that skinny old yellow tomcat we seen yesterday."

For the most part, Devonia simply bumped up and down like a giant floppy doll, staring wide-eyed at the passing treat being offered her. But if something particular caught her fancy, she would blurt out its name in her scarcely human voice. It was an awful voice, like a foghorn and an animal cry spliced together, but the sound of this voice was the only thing we had ever seen to bring happiness to the face of grim Lucy Brush. Whenever Devonia produced one of her utterances, whether an echoing bellow to something Lucy had pointed out, or an announcing cry of something she had found all by herself, Lucy Brush's face softened and brightened and her tense, sunken mouth (she was missing some side teeth) lifted at the corners. "That's *right*, Vonie," she would croon, soft and pink with pleasure, "that there is one *black* crow." And her thin shoulders would pull back with pride, though she never removed her eyes from the road.

We knew, because our teacher had explained it, that Devonia, though older than any of our mothers, would always have the mind of a three-year-old child. She could not be left at home alone when her sister came all the way from Varnerstown to drive us normal, privileged children home to our comfortable houses. Varnerstown, our teacher explained, was a depressed area, and Lucy Brush's bus-driving job was the sisters' only source of income.

So, primed by our conscientious teacher, we knew better than to snicker or look repelled by Devonia, even though the novelty of her kept us fairly silent at first. "Three years old forever, just imagine it!" whispered Harriet MacGruder as we studied the back of Devonia's permanent-waved gray head and waited hopefully for her next outburst. "And she can't even be left alone in their house."

I wondered what their house was like. Did Lucy Brush have to undress that big woman for bed every night, untie her shoes the way Ruth used to do mine until I got big enough to do it for myself? I pictured Lucy giving Devonia a permanent, then giving herself one.

But it was harder for me to picture how their town could be depressed. "Depressed" was a word long familiar to me, but until recently I thought it only described something that happened to my father. Daddy got depressed and had "depressions." Sometimes they were just little, temporary ones, brought on by a disarranged day, or an unexpected surfacing of a parishioner's ill will, or somebody criticizing him, or the bad manners of a salesperson or someone on the phone. Or, occasionally, just an item on the evening news would stoke Daddy's melancholy certainty, always burning on its low blue pilot light, that the world was sinking daily to new depths of ignorance and brutality. These short-term flare-ups, or "mini-blues" as Ruth called them, trying to tease him out of them, usually lasted no longer than an hour or two, or maybe overnight. But both she and I worked very hard to forestall them, the way you treat a minor infection before it turns into something worse. I would be very good and quiet and talk to him about the things he liked. I would ask him to tell me the story about St. Cuthbert being dried by the friendly otters after he had been standing in the cold North Sea praying all night. Or I would make him describe some more how he grew up on the Dudleys' estate in Chattanooga.

The Dudleys were a rich family who had owned the foundry where Daddy's father, John Gower, had worked as a foreman. After John Gower drank himself to death, the Dudley family let Daddy and his mother Gene, which was short for Genevieve (my own middle name), live in the carriage house on their estate. Because the Dudleys thought so much of Gene Gower, they remodeled it into an apartment for her and Daddy; they let her furnish it as she wished because they trusted her taste. And all she had to do in return was take care of the Dudleys' gardens and help Mrs. Dudley, with whom she had been friends in high school, do her shopping and correspondence. Which Gene Gower would have been happy to do anyway, said Daddy, because his mother liked to create beauty and bring order and serenity to people's lives. I loved to hear stories about this grandmother I would never know. Daddy said I was a lot like her. "You are careful and mindful of others, like she was," he would say. "And you have her high forehead and her same serious expression sometimes."

I also liked—in a different way—Daddy's stories about Stewart Hampton Dudley. Stewart Hampton was the Dudleys' only son— the "son and heir," as Daddy called him. Stewart Hampton had been the same age as Daddy, and they had become best friends after Daddy had passed the "son and heir" 's initiation rites and proved to Stewart Hampton that he would neither be bullied nor hold resentments. And many boys in Daddy's position *would* have held resentments, because until Stewart Hampton decided he liked Daddy, he put him through some pretty humiliating trials. I enjoyed these trial stories, especially when I was hearing them over again and knew that Daddy was going to triumph. And Daddy enjoyed telling them, even in his depressions: how he, as the poor boy from the foundry, came to earn the respect and love of the boy in the big house, and how they had been loyal friends until Stewart Hampton had been killed in Korea.

My mother's way of dealing with a depression when it was in an early stage tended more towards teasing, though sometimes with a biting edge. "Oh, come on, Walter," she'd say about the vestry member who tormented Daddy the most, "can't you see Ned Block for what he is? Ned's just an old St. Cuthbert's altar boy whose emotional ties are back there in the forties with his childhood rector. Ned is almost *your* age, Walter, and he's still playing with lead soldiers. Doesn't that tell you anything? So why should it send you into the dumps every time he frowns your way? It's probably got a lot to do with indigestion, from the look of that face and stomach."

Daddy's other depressions, the big ones that could last for months, came on suddenly and often for no apparent reason. He'd just put his head down in his hands at breakfast and mur- mur, "Ruth, I think it's starting again." And Ruth would say, "Let me call Doc MacGruder and get a prescription, before it gets too bad." "No," he'd say, "let's wait. It seems I ought to be able to vanquish this thing myself." "Oh, Walter, are you sure?" she'd ask, sounding very *un*sure. "Let's give it another few days," he'd say, his normally rich and rolling voice already gone flat and dull, "because I can't help feeling that if I could just once get to the bottom of it . . . look the damn thing in the face . . . then maybe I could come out the other end triumphant."

"But meanwhile it makes you miserable, Walter. It takes so much out of you." She didn't say, it makes us miserable, too; it takes so much out of *us*. But I could hear it in her voice, the way I often heard her saying things underneath what she appeared to be saying.

"I know," Daddy would agree, "but, well, I can't help but feel I'm interrupting some process by settling for MacGruder's pills. Besides, they make me drowsy, or they make my mind go all

mushy. I mean, as long as I can do my work, maybe it is a deso-
lation I'm meant to go through. In order to help me see . . . well,
I don't know what. But I may never know unless I tough it out."

And he would tough it out for a while. He could even be
humorous about it, though it was his dark humor. ("Well, I coun-
seled eight needy souls today, and not a single one of them appeared to notice that their rector was gazing out at them through
the portals of despair. At times, you know, Ruth, one is downright
thankful for the self-absorption of other people.")

He somehow got his sermons written, only he had to start on
them Tuesdays instead of Fridays, and every word he wrote down
was written without hope or pleasure, every sentence reexamined
and found wanting. "This is all counterfeit," he would announce,
dragging out of his study to wave the two yellow pages at my
mother. He held them by the tips of his fingers, as though they
had been dipped in something awful. Then he would sit down in
one corner of the breakfast nook and hide his face in his hands
while Ruth would sit across from him in her corner and read over
the pages. He typed all his sermons, whether in or out of depressions, single-spaced, back and front, on second sheets he bought
at the stationer's for three dollars a ream. Actually, he tore each
sheet in half, so it made two small ones, which could fit easily side
by side on the pulpit lectern. He'd read page one, then page two
next to it, then turn both pages over and there would be three and
four. That meant that page three had to be on the back of page
one and page four on the back of page two. I remember how
impressed I was, the first time he showed me his system. The four
half pages, single-spaced, he told me, made a twelve-minute sermon. ("And that is enough sermon for anybody." "And page four
always has to be on the back of page two, or it won't work out," I
would remind him. "That's right, my smart girl," he would say,
pleased.)

Ruth, moving her lips silently as she read, would go through
Daddy's latest sermon while he sat with his face buried, waiting for
the worst. But the worst never came. "But this is very good, Walter," she would say. "I don't believe you could write a bad sermon
if you tried."

"Oh, come on, Ruth. You don't have to flatter me. It's worse
than bad. It's fraudulent. I felt nauseated the whole time I was
typing it. Disgusted by my own presumption."

"Well, I'm sorry, Walter, but it doesn't read like a fraudulent sermon. You say a lot in a very *un*presumptuous way, if you ask me. And you *did* ask me, didn't you? It may have nauseated you to write it, because of the way you've been feeling, but the sermon doesn't show it."

"Ah, then that's the work of the Holy Spirit, I guess."

"Well, whatever, Walter. All I'm saying is, whoever wrote it, it's *fine*. It's more than some of them deserve."

But when he stopped sleeping, Ruth called Dr. MacGruder and ordered the pills. During Daddy's depression the previous winter, after he had given in and, after a few days of drowsiness and "mushy mind," the medicine was making him feel better, he laughed ruefully during supper one night and said somewhat bitterly but with the beginnings of the old resonant bounce in his voice again: "You all will be relieved to hear that the Black Curtain is lifting. Thank you both for putting up with me. These mashed potatoes are creamy and delicious, Ruth, and the ham is tasty, and I have a new book from the library I'm looking forward to reading later."

"Oh, honey, I'm really glad," said my mother. "Have some more ham." She looked so relieved she was close to tears.

But then he had spoiled it by adding wistfully, "I just wish . . . Well, I can't help wondering what it would have been like if I'd held on a bit longer with*out* the medicine and seen it through on its own terms. I mean, St. John-of-the-Cross didn't gulp down a pill every time he felt another sleepless Dark Night coming on."

"St. John-of-the-Cross didn't have a wife and child, either," my mother shot back. Then, looking ashamed of her outburst, she amended in a lighter tone, "And besides, how do you know for sure he didn't take something to keep himself going? I'll bet anything he dragged himself right over to the monastery infirmary, or herbarium, or whatever they called it, and said, 'Oh, Brother Herbarius, I'm feeling another Dark Night coming on, but this time I plan to tough it out.' And Brother Herbarius, who was a jolly, fatherly old monk, who looked a little like Dr. MacGruder, said, 'Well, John, okay, I know it's important for you to get to the *bottom* of all this, but won't you just take a few of these nice leaves I'm going to crush up for you and make yourself a cup of tea with them when you're feeling *extra-specially* blue.' "

"Oh, Ruth, Ruth," said Daddy, laughing, his first hearty laugh in months, "you can do anyone. I can just see this Brother Herbarius. And you're right, he *does* look like Doc MacGruder. Sounds like him, too. You could have been a first-rate actress, or a mimic, or anything you wanted, if you hadn't decided to waste yourself on me."

My mother, who had been very animated and pleased with herself during her rendering of Brother Herbarius and St. John-of-the-Cross, turned suddenly *dis*pleased. "I wish you wouldn't talk like that," she said quietly to my father. "Because if you keep on saying those things, one day *I* am going to become depressed."

But after that night, spring began to come for all of us. As the days grew longer, Daddy's step got lighter, and his voice regained its multiple cadences and inflections, and he began to enjoy doing things again. He and I drove to nurseries all around the country-side in search of certain perennials he wanted for his garden. He hankered after things he remembered from his mother's gardens, which were, of course, the gardens belonging to the Dudleys after he and she had moved to the carriage house to begin their new life. ("Before Mother came, the Dudleys' gardens were nothing out of the ordinary, despite all that available money. The Dudleys just didn't have Mother's eye, or her green thumb. She would do the most amazing combinations—globe thistle and goosenecked loosestrife, for instance. I still see those spiky, blue globes floating above the waving white tassels of the strife. Though you've got to be careful with that gooseneck; it's invasive and the devil to get out, once it's established.") Sometimes he would stop the car on the shoulder of a road and we would dig out some prized wild specimen flourishing in a ditch and rush it home and replant it. He carried a shovel and an old roast pan filled with dampened peat moss in the trunk of the car for these excursions.

And we'd go almost daily to the library again, because when Daddy's mind was functioning on all its cylinders, it needed plenty of fuel. We'd stagger out of the library, groaning under our respective armloads, and stack the plastic-covered volumes in neat rows along the backseat even though we knew they'd be sliding and sloshing all over each other as soon as we turned the first corner: children's books and gardening books and old memoirs and Victorian devotional books that nobody but Daddy ever checked out anymore, some of them so far gone that the librarian didn't bother to send them out to be re-bound. These old books held a special attraction for Daddy. He would hold them up to his nose and sniff their musty aroma, and was always delighted to find an antiquated bookplate pasted inside, with some old-fashioned name on it ("Edith M. Spofford—Christmas, 1886") or an inscription that set his imagination going about the person who had first owned it and the occasion on which it was presented, and by whom.

And once again in the evenings, he would hand my mother her cocktail in his gallant way, making her a little bow, and entertain her with anecdotes of current parish problems, the same kind of problems that, during his low periods, would have elicited from him a bleak, lethargic headshake or a gloomy sigh. Everything would have meaning again for the buoyant, charming man who had returned to us once more from behind the Black Curtain; everything processed by his senses came out stamped with his intelligence. He found sermons in the way his garden grew—or didn't grow, and he was able to derive useful insights from the astonishing variety of human behavior reported on the evening news, rather than letting it get him down. Everything connected and reflected upon everything else, was all part of God's plan again. The sheer variety and complexity of things was cause for rejoicing and stimulation for him, whereas in the dark days it was a reproach, a threat, a source of continual, low-grade exhaustion.

However, once a depression was over, Ruth did not like to mention it. Maybe she felt that bringing it up might bring it *back*. But Daddy was quite willing to talk about it if I asked him. In his good mood again, it interested him like everything else: it was something he could wrap his intelligence around and squeeze meaning from. Once last summer, when we were having our evening reading session in his study—we had been reading *Winnie the Pooh,* and an illustration of a black cloud of bees swarming around Pooh's head reminded me of Daddy's Black Curtain—I asked him, "Is your Black Curtain going to come back again?"

He perked up with approval, the way he always did when I said something he felt was penetrating, and he took time to formulate his answer. "It's not a question of the Black Curtain *coming back,* sweetie. The Black Curtain's always there. It's a place where I *go.*"

"But why do you go there? You know you don't enjoy it."

"I certainly don't," he said, laughing. "Oh no, I do not enjoy it, my Margaret. Why *do* I go there? I'm not sure I know, myself. It's more as if I *wander* there, or get led there . . . and suddenly, before I know it, I'm behind the curtain again and everything is dark. I can remember perfectly well what it was like, back in the world of light and meaning, but, you see, once I'm behind the curtain I can't find my way back. What's worse, I sometimes don't even want to. I don't have the energy to want. And when I do want to, I haven't the slightest clue how to proceed. I think to myself, if only I'd left a trail. You know, the way people make marks on trees to keep from getting lost in the forest? But somehow I never do. Or, by the time I think to do it, I've already lost the will to start. Now, the great mystics left trails. They knew how to go back and forth, to and from their state of pain, and each time they returned with something valuable, something that could help the rest of us. But I haven't been vouchsafed that ability yet."

"Can children go behind the Black Curtain?"

I had a vision of myself hurrying through a dense forest, an enlightened Red Riding Hood, knowing her way, telling no one where she was headed, and not stopping to pick any flowers, heading straight for the Black Curtain to release my father. "But however did you find your way here, sweetie?" he would exclaim, amazed and grateful as I flung open the heavy black folds, smelling damp and musty, just like some of those old library books he loved. "Oh, I just knew," I would reply wisely. "Did you mark the trail?" he would anxiously ask. "I didn't have to mark it," I would tell him proudly. "I just memorized it. Don't worry, I can get us both home."

While this vivid little drama was playing through my mind, my father, perhaps having second thoughts about the propriety of discussing his affliction so graphically with a child, was reassuring me that there was nothing to be frightened of: children were safe from the Black Curtain, the very nature of childhood kept them immune. I pretended to believe him and acted relieved. I felt I had to protect him from the knowledge that I could save him. The Black Curtain did not frighten me the least bit. It intrigued me, it provided a backdrop for my potential heroism.

That wasn't to say I was without fears of my own. For some time, I had been aware that the peculiar L-shape of my bedroom closet—one of the many construction anomalies in the rectory, which had been added on to and reproportioned many times to accommodate the needs of different families—was the ideal place for a witch to make her home. This witch, who lodged in the back part of the L, was lonely, cunning, and powerful if the conditions were right. I knew she was biding her time for the moment when the conditions were in her favor. Then, under cover of night, she would dart around the corner, whoosh past all my dresses and blouses and skirts on their hangers, and creep stealthily across my cotton, braided rug to claim me. The sensation of this horrible moment when she would actually lay hands on me and drag me back through the crooked closet into some unimaginable domain of her own, I endured as well as induced every night. It had become a ritual I forced myself to undergo in order to guarantee that I would wake up as myself the next morning; it was a sort of negative "Now I lay me down to sleep," only it had rules attached: I had to lie *completely still* under the covers, facing the wall, keep my eyes shut tight, and breathe deeply and regularly, as though I were asleep. As long as I did this, she could not touch me. She might stand there and rage at the nearness of her prey, but she was powerless to lay a finger on me as long as I gave her no sign of acknowledgment. But one ragged breath, a movement of my body, an open eye, and I belonged to her forever. There was also an additional hardship I had set up for myself. The closet door must *always be left ajar at night.* If I were to close it, she would know I was trying to keep her out: not that I could, for she could pass through doors. Also, if I closed it, she might not get enough air, and though the lack of it would not kill her—she could never die—it might give her a headache or put her in a vengeful temper and she would change all the rules and burst out at me. I would be fair game.

"No, my Margaret, children never go behind the Black Curtain," Daddy was saying gently. "It's not their element, so don't you give it another thought. Besides, it's just a manner of speaking. There is no real Black Curtain. It's only a metaphor. You remember what a metaphor is, don't you?"

"It's when you say something is like something else so you have a better picture of it."

"Well, *almost.* But you wouldn't use the word 'like.' If you used the word 'like,' that would make it something called a 'simile.' A simile is more obvious. 'My love is like a red, red rose' would be a simile. Whereas, if I said, 'the bloom is off the rose,' I might be talking about more than just that rose. I might be using the rose picture to describe something that was past its prime, or wasn't so perfect anymore. Do you see what I mean?"

"I *think* so." I didn't want to damage his belief in me as a precocious child. The truth was that a lot of what Daddy said went over my head, but I had every intention of catching up eventually.

"And you won't fret over that old Black Curtain talk, now will you?"

"No, sir," I reassured him solemnly. "I know it was just a metaphor."

Meanwhile I continued to elaborate on the appealing scenario of me rescuing Daddy from his place of pain. Behind the Black Curtain would be a descent into . . . what? I saw luridly lit chambers, like the inside of a giant's brain. Only with wet walls. Something like Luray Caverns, where Daddy had taken us last spring when he had started feeling good again and was thinking up family excursions. Only, in my scenario, there would be real dangers and lots of opportunities for getting lost. There would be no drawling lady tour guide in crepe-soled canvas shoes and flowered blouse and denim wraparound skirt that barely made it around her barrel-shaped middle. While Daddy and I had lingered at the dankest, most awesome spots, pointing out to each other the frightening shapes we saw in the giant limestone icicles, Ruth, who said underground caverns made her shudder, had cheered herself up by chatting with the guide about that lady's attempts to diet.

"See, Margaret, just up there where that stalactite and stalagmite melt together? Doesn't it look like the face of an angry man with bushy eyebrows?"

"Yes, and there's the head of an eagle on his eyelid."

"I declare, there sure is, honey."

"And on the *other* eyelid, there's a *snake* with two heads!"

"I see him, too," said Daddy, "a twin-headed serpent."

"I've tried the Scarsdale, I've tried that Hollywood fruit diet," the guide was telling my mother as they sauntered on ahead of us down the damp stone pathway through the caves, the guide switching on timed spotlights along the way to light up the next noteworthy formations, "but *nothing* seems to work. I'll lose thirty pounds, then gain back thirty-one."

"Oh, I know!" agreed my mother who was beautifully slim. "After my daughter was born, I went on a diet and couldn't lose an ounce. Finally, after I'd been denying myself for days, I said to my husband, 'Dammit, I'm *hungry*,' and we went out to this new German restaurant in town and ate like pigs, and the next day I discovered I had lost two pounds."

But when I would fling open the Black Curtain and descend into the chambers of my father's depression and walk alongside him naming each of its demons and confronting their dreadful visages until he would allow me to lead him back into the light, there would be no guide, no companion other than myself. Thus I pictured it in my fantasy. It would be all my responsibility. And though the task would be daunting, I would conduct myself as a hero. There wouldn't even be Ruth around, to lighten things with her humor and sociable self-put-downs. Much as I required her company, there was somehow no room for my mother in this particular fantasy.

How strange to think that at six years of age I was innocently concocting a script that would turn out to be the next sixteen years of my life.

Lucy Brush, our driver, was transporting her cargo down the final streets of our return journey from school. There were few of us left on the bus. As I was one of the last people to be picked up, I was one of the last to be dropped off. That being so, I tried to come up with some mathematical analogy that would explain why if the bus was full when I got on, it should be empty, except for one little boy, when I got off. It seemed to me that all things being equal in the first instance, they ought to match up the same way in the second. These were the kinds of things I enjoyed puzzling out when there was nothing better to do.

But that Wednesday afternoon of September 13, I was, I remember, preoccupied with the sticky human problem of how to keep Harriet as my best friend while wooing dark little Chloe Niles, who had something murky in her background. I wanted the predictable Harriet, but I also craved uncertainty and strangeness. However, I knew enough about the way society works to understand that tact and secrecy and some double-dealing would be required of me if I was to have them both.

Harriet had just been dropped off in the Riverview Heights section, where she lived with her grandparents, our friends and patrons the MacGruders. Harriet's parents, the junior MacGruders, were in the Foreign Service. Currently they were serving at a hardship post in a small backward country of volatile politics and no adequate school for young American children.

After my loyal wave to Harriet from the window of the bus, there remained six more stops before Fern Hill Manor, the gloomy old green Victorian house at the top of Macon Street, where Chloe Niles's aunt, Mrs. Radford, rented out her extra bedrooms and bathrooms to tourists visiting the Shenandoahs between April and September. Mrs. Radford referred to these paying visitors as her "guests," and was strict about what kind of person she permitted to spend a night under her roof. She did not allow smoking or drinking, either in bedrooms or dining rooms, though she did provide a "smokers' porch" for the unregenerate puffers. Young couples were not encouraged to sign the guest book at Fern Hill Manor, because this being America where one couldn't ask for passports, as Mrs. Radford lamented to Daddy, how could one be sure one wasn't abetting an illicit union? Mrs. Radford used highly rhetorical phrases like that. Tripping up and down Macon, to and from the neighborhood grocer, primly pulling her little aluminum cart behind her on its squeaky wheels, Mrs. Radford dearly loved to waylay Daddy and pour out her misgivings about the current morals at Fern Hill whenever she was lucky enough to catch him crouched at the corner of our street, picking through the thick ivy at the foot of the crucifix in search of litter. Hearing the squeak of her wheels, he knew he was in for it and always struggled gallantly to his feet. Ruth and I would watch him from the windows of the rectory, his stoop very pronounced as he bent to receive Mrs. Radford's litany of her guests' suspected crimes, his fingers fastidiously clamping the day's take of shiny candy wrappers and paper cups (in which he deposited the smaller detritus of cigarette butts, flip-tops from beer cans, and sometimes other things).

"Oh, Reverend Gower," Ruth would say to him when he returned to the house, "what vile new aberration has one sniffed out up at Fern Hill Manor? What forbidden odor have we detected wafting through the dry-rot now?" She could really do a number on Mrs. Radford, perfectly mimicking Chloe's aunt's plummy tones and high-flown language.

"You could have been a famous actress, Ruth," my father would say when he had stopped laughing.

"Oh, yes. And a famous painter and a famous everything. According to you, Walter, people would think I am throwing my life away merely being here with the two of you."

After the school bus had deposited Harriet at the house in the Heights, where her grandmother waited in hiding behind the tall yew hedge because Harriet had a big thing about not being "met" like a baby, and after I had waved from the window, as befitted a

best friend, I knew I had those six stops left in which to pursue
Chloe Niles before she was dropped off at Fern Hill Manor at the
bottom of the mossy, cracked stone steps where no one waited for
her at the top.

The time was ripe because today she had chosen the seat directly across the aisle, and even while Harriet sat beside me I had
been rehearsing openers for a later conversation. My hope was
that soon after the bus left Riverview Heights, Devonia Brush
would be stimulated into uttering her remarkable foghorn-animal
outcry, and then I could look over at Chloe Niles and we would
exchange a pitying glance. After that, it would be natural for me
to say something that would lead to my drawing out of this little
loner who was such a fascinating mixture of attraction and taboo.
("Sounds like an unholy mess," I'd overheard Daddy say to Ruth.
"And what confusion for the little girl, being shunted so abruptly
between *un*-holy and holier-than-thou," my mother had said. "It
would almost be better if she were a complete orphan.")

Chloe's mother was dead, that much had been volunteered by
Mrs. Radford, her mother's much older half sister, who made it
clear by her bunched lips that there was more to be said, but she
wasn't saying it. But Harriet said she had heard Mrs. MacGruder
tell someone over the phone that Chloe's mother and some young
man had asphyxiated themselves together in Mr. Niles's garage in
Florida. But apparently Mr. Niles was still alive and well and living
in Florida. Why didn't he want his daughter with him? Why didn't
he ever come and visit Chloe? She had been with her aunt ever
since she was three. I could not imagine my father being able to go
three years without seeing me. I couldn't imagine him going even
three days.

Two stops later, with only four to go before Fern Hill Manor,
Lucy Brush was letting off Brian Vesey of the rotting teeth at the
drugstore—his mother worked for the pharmacist and let Brian
read comics and eat candy bars until time to go home—when
Devonia spotted a stockboy coming out of the liquor store next
door. He threw some empty boxes on the sidewalk.

"Boy . . . throw away . . . GARBAGE!" bawled Devonia ecstatically.

At last. I turned swiftly towards Chloe Niles, who was already
looking steadily at me.

"Have all your *summer guests* left now?" I blurted out. Then I
went hot all over because I had forgotten to shudder at Devonia

first, providing a natural opener. Also, the way I had said "summer guests" sounded as though I were mocking the way Chloe's aunt said it.

"That's *right*, Vonie baby," Lucy Brush crooned indulgently, "that boy is throwing out some garbage."

Belatedly for Chloe's benefit, I rolled my eyes in the direction of the pitiable sister. But Chloe Niles didn't sociably follow my example, as Harriet would have.

"All of 'em are gone except for Mr. Harty," she said. "When he leaves, I can have my room back."

"Oh, then where are you sleeping *now*?" Compared to her, I sounded overexcited and too familiar.

"In the tower," said Chloe. "You know where the tower is."

She made it sound as if I had devoted my whole life to gazing up at the spooky little cone-shaped tower that jutted up over Mrs. Radford's "smokers' porch."

"I *think* I do," I replied coyly. "The one right above your aunt's porch."

"That's the only one there is," said Chloe. "I hate it in the summer, it's too hot. But I like to go up there in the winter. I can see all the way to downtown when the leaves are gone. I can see the roof of your church. Did you know some tiles are missing?"

"I'm sure my father knows," I said airily. "He'll have to take it up with the vestry and then they'll have to vote money out of the operational fund to fix it."

The bus stopped to let off the Gregory twins. I pretended to be very interested in watching them straggle down the aisle and hop down the three metal steps into the sunshine. Chloe Niles needed to be put down a notch. I was supposed to be the patron here.

"I'd like to sleep up there in the winter," Chloe went right on, "but it doesn't have any heating ducts."

"Mmm," I murmured. What did she think she was, an expert in architecture? I continued to watch the twins, staring straight past Chloe Niles's black gypsy curls and little gold stud earrings at the spectacle taking place through the window on her side of the bus. The Gregorys' untidy big sheep dog bounded joyfully over the sparse, weedy lawn, jumping up and slavering all over the two girls, almost knocking them down. They were unidentical twins and they were not very tidy. Nothing about the Gregorys was very tidy. They were allowed to wear the same jeans to school every day and their hair got washed only once a week. Their mother, who

also wore jeans all the time, was divorced. She had come to have
counseling sessions with Daddy several times, although she didn't
go to church.

Devonia was in seventh heaven as Lucy Brush drove away
from the Gregorys. "That big dog . . . HAPPY!" she bleated, wriggling her fat shoulders in the tight polyester and making little
gurgling sounds.

"That's right, honeybaby," sang out stern Lucy Brush, shifting
into the low gear that would take us up steep Sunset Circle and
into short Wiggins Drive where Georgie Gaines's greedy father
was ruining the landscape with his developing. Only two more
stops and we would be at the top of Macon, and Chloe would get
off at Fern Hill Manor. Time was too short for me to stay on my
high horse.

"Still, it must be fun to be up there on the *cooler* summer
nights," I suggested magnanimously.

"I wouldn't exactly call it *fun*. I like my real room better, because there's places to stick things up."

"Stick things *up*?" My voice rose to an alarming squeak.

"On the walls, silly."

Chloe Niles was not going to be easy, the way Harriet Mac-
Gruder was.

"Oh, you mean posters and things." I let her rudeness pass.

"Things I like," she said mysteriously.

The bus stopped to let off two more children and then turned
into Wiggins Drive. I was deciding whether to ask what kind of
things she liked, but wasn't sure my pride could deal with another
insult.

"As soon as Mr. Harty goes, I'll stick them all back up," she
went right on, as if she didn't need my side of the conversation.
"You won't be able to tell he was ever in that room if you come
over."

"I *won't*?" I sounded exactly like a stupid girl in our class, Sally
Ann Jenks, who got so excited when anyone was nice to her that
she cocked her head to one side and chirped. She had a long neck
and bright, feverish little eyes. Harriet had nicknamed her "the
Dodo Bird."

"Nope," said Chloe. "Except maybe to smell his mouthwash for
a couple of weeks."

Georgie Gaines, who was fat, heaved himself off the bus at the
entrance to Wiggins Drive. His father the developer had torn

down the old Wiggins estate that once had lorded it over the whole hill, and built a series of houses that all connected. Only they weren't really houses, but something new called condominiums. People had to buy them from Georgie's father and then pay monthly fees to him for as long as they lived. Daddy said Mr. Gaines was an opportunist and had no sense of the interconnectedness of things. During the construction of the houses, he had caused two landslides and was getting ready to deforest another hill for some more houses, which would probably cause a third. Mr. and Mrs. Gaines lived in the corner condominium, the fanciest one, but Mrs. Gaines did not come out of the house to meet Georgie, though her new red Jaguar was parked outside.

If you come over. Chloe's artless invitation took away the thrill of its unexpectedness. I had been working up to asking her over to the rectory, but in a more roundabout, face-saving way.

Now she was getting up to leave the bus, wriggling seductively into her backpack and sticking out her left wrist ostentatiously, to show off her gold bracelet with its little gold-chain safety catch. I was about to praise the bracelet, though I'd heard my mother say children shouldn't wear expensive jewelry and certainly not to school, but I decided I had said too many nice things already. In trying to please, I had forgotten to twinkle with my own mysteries.

"Well, see you," said Chloe Niles nonchalantly, giving her backpack a final twitch as Lucy Brush slowed for Fern Hill Manor.

"Guess so," I said, not meeting her eyes. I watched the backs of her legs go down the aisle. Already at six, she walked with a womanish sway. I did not look out the window after her.

How complicated it was, getting to know somebody. It made me tired. It was with a bounce of heart that I looked forward to my corner stop. Ruth would be waiting for me beside the little crucified Christ in his shelter. She would have thought up things for us to do this afternoon. We might take a bus to the Nature Center and watch the otters slithering and sporting in their pond. Or walk downtown to Walgreens and pick out some pretty paper napkins for the next coffee hour, and then sit together on the high stools at the soda fountain and have Cokes and cheese crackers. I could relate my exchange with Chloe on the bus and Ruth, as she always did, would pick up on the things that bothered me without me having to say them. She was good at this undercurrent stuff that went on between people. "Oh I remember this one time," she might say, "when I was just about your age, that I made a complete fool of myself. There was this little girl I wanted to like me . . ." And she would go on to relate some stupid thing she had done, describing it so vividly I could see it like a movie in my head. She would make me laugh and feel better about myself, and also give me some ideas how to be more successful at this kind of thing.

The bus had begun its grinding descent down Macon. I gathered my things together. Inside my backpack was a phonetics test marked 100 by the teacher that I would present to Daddy when he came home tonight after making his visiting rounds. I noticed that my new blue and brown plaid dress that Ruth and I had bought over in Charlottesville was crumplier than it had been this morning, but the little cats' heads, every one of which I had buttoned myself, were as perky as ever. I would unbutton them again tonight, in Ruth's presence, so she wouldn't be sorry we had bought it. And then, the next time I wanted something she had doubts about, I would say, "Remember that dress with the cats' heads all down the front? *That* worked out okay, didn't it?"

Such were my thoughts as the bus rumbled down Macon. Yes, I do recall them. I have met people since who have told me they could remember exactly what they had for dinner the night someone died, or could describe for me the scene they were looking at just as someone said or did something that changed their lives. I was thinking of my dress with the cat buttons and how I would unbutton them in front of my mother that evening, when Devonia, suddenly straining alertly forward in her seat, bawled out: "THAT MAN . . . *HURT!*"

"Where?" shouted the only other child left on the bus. "Is it an *accident?*" he demanded hopefully, scrambling up on his seat to see outside the big front window of the bus.

"Sit down back there, you," snapped Lucy Brush. "There ain't any accident." Then, switching into her soothing croon: "No, Vonie baby, ain't nobody hurt. It's just the preacher picking up trash."

I looked out the front window as the bus slowed for my stop, and sure enough, there was Daddy in his clericals, down on his knees in the ivy, stretching a long black-sleeved arm towards something that lay at the foot of the cross. He did look like someone crumpled in pain and imploring help from his Savior, if you didn't know what he was doing. I was glad that Chloe Niles had already gotten off the bus. I didn't care about the little boy so much. Everyone knew he was a hyperactive child.

But Daddy pulled himself up fast at the sound of our approach, and by the time the doors swung open to bestow me to my home turf, he had completely reassumed the figure of the Reverend Walter Gower, whom anyone would be proud to have for a father.

"How are you all today?" he asked Lucy Brush and her sister as he deftly pocketed a dirty squashed paper cup and handed me down from my bus like a princess.

"About the same, thank you, sir," replied grim Lucy Brush, already closing the doors.

I was flattered that he had come to meet me; he was rarely free at this time of day. But why hadn't she come?

"Where's Ruth?" I asked when he had kissed me.

"Well, I like that. Aren't I good enough?"

"Well, *yes*, but . . ."

"So how was school today? Anything particularly noteworthy to report?"

"No, nothing really *noteworthy*." I slipped my hand into his to show him I was glad he had come. As we walked slowly homeward alongside St. Cuthbert's neatly trimmed boxwood hedge that my father liked to do himself, I bumped my hip affectionately against his leg.

I was pretty certain I knew what had happened. Ruth was punishing me for not waving at her this morning; she was showing that she, too, could play hard-to-get. I could hear her saying to Daddy, "Walter, if you're not doing anything, could you go down to the corner and meet Margaret's bus?" Pretending to be in the middle of some household task. And now she was most likely positioned just behind the curtain of an upstairs window, looking down on this scene to see how I would take it.

Self-conscious as a little actress, I prolonged our mother-daughter game of coquetry by stopping suddenly on the sidewalk and taking out my phonetics test with the perfect score. Up there behind her curtain, she would be wondering, *Now what is so important that Margaret had to stop right in the middle of the sidewalk to show her father?*

It was through her eyes, from the window above, that I saw my father and myself resume our companionable stroll, he now hold-

ing the mysterious paper at arm's length in front of him, because
he didn't have his reading glasses with him, and moving his lips.
From up there she wouldn't be able to hear the silly sounds he was
making as he walked beside me, putting himself through my phonetics test. He was going through every single sound on the test
paper, relishing his own thoroughness—even seeming to want to
prolong it.

"It was pretty easy," I finally had to interrupt him, wanting his
attention for myself. We were almost to the rectory's front walk,
and except for asking me how school was, he had said nothing
directly to me. "But not all *that* easy," I went on. "It's *hard,* when
you already know how to read by the way things *look,* to have to
break the words down again into all those little *sounds,* just to
please the teacher."

This was precisely the sort of remark that always got a smile
out of him. But instead of smiling, he simply stopped in his tracks
on the sidewalk and repeated my last phrase in that automatic way
people do when they haven't been listening at all.

" '. . . all those little sounds to please the teacher . . .' " he echoed. Absently, he handed me back my perfect paper. "Your
mother has gone off on a little vacation. I talked her into it. I
thought she needed to get away for a bit."

I thought I hadn't heard him right. "You mean she's not in the
house?"

I looked up at the window where I had assumed she had been
watching us. It seemed a terrible thing he was saying. Even more
terrible when, all the time he had been walking along mouthing
those "ah"s and "nnn"s and "ow"s so enthusiastically, he had been
saving up this thing to say.

"No, I expect she and Madelyn are past Washington by now,
depending on the traffic."

"She and *Madelyn!*" I repeated incredulously.

"Yes, well, sweetie, Madelyn is not your or my ideal of a
charmer, but she's your mother's old friend. They can talk and
laugh together and be girls again. Your mother needs that. It's
been rough on her, especially last winter when I was in the dol-
drums for so long. Actually, the whole thing was my idea. I had to
talk her into going. She was worried about leaving you. I had to
convince her we'd do just fine together. She wanted to wait till you
got back from school, but Madelyn had to be on the road after
lunch. She has this new play, you know."

What had he done? I couldn't look up at him. But the strange thing was, I could still *look down on us from above.* I was still able to see us *as she saw us,* up there behind her curtain, watching him convey this incredible news. It was as though she, who was "past Washington by now, depending on the traffic," was also still here, so she could watch and see how sorry I was for not having waved from the bus this morning.

I don't recall anything of what happened immediately after, but my father told me later, after we had begun our reconstructive marathons, that I asked if she would be back by Sunday and when he said no, it would be more like a week or ten days, I turned into a little whirling fiend and started slinging my backpack at him and hitting his legs. He also told me I tore up my phonetics paper and stamped on the pieces. I remember nothing of any of this. We went out for a pizza that evening, apparently, and then there was a vestry meeting afterwards at the rectory. I remember the vestry meeting. Or at least I think I do. I remember it almost too well. The trouble is, I am the kind of person who can picture scenes created by other people's words.

Not all scenes, of course. I simply cannot picture myself whirling like a little dervish and hitting at my father's legs and tearing up my perfect paper. But apparently that's what I did.

> . . . A thousand ages in Thy sight
> are like an evening gone . . .
>
> —Isaac Watts, after Psalm 90;
> "O God, our help in ages past."

III: AN EVENING GONE

As some children become rapacious collectors of foreign stamps or rock star memorabilia or storybook dolls (Harriet MacGruder once threw such a violent tantrum over an out-of-stock Melanie Wilkes doll that her grandmother had to call the factory in California and beg them to airmail one to the house), I was to become a passionate collector of stories about runaway, or absent, mothers.

There was a fair number of examples in our own neighborhood and parish. The Gregory twins' divorced mother, who always wore jeans and sometimes sought counseling with Daddy although she wasn't a churchgoer, was a runaway mother, only she had taken the twins and the dog with her when she ran away. Before her big society wedding to Mr. Gregory, she had been a Romulus girl who had grown up in the same house where she now lived again, the one with the weedy lawn. Soon after the Gregory girls were born, she had realized that living with Mr. Gregory up in Rochester, where he worked for Kodak, was irrelevant and meaningless, and so, one morning after he had gone to work, she packed up her infant twins and the sheep dog puppy and drove back down to her mother in Romulus. The mother had since died, and Mrs. Gregory, who called herself once more by her girlhood name, Nita Cosgrove, had moved into her late mother's room, where she burned sandalwood incense and played Beatles records too loudly to suit the neighbors. She did other things that didn't suit the neighbors, either, which is what had brought her, in a fit of umbrage, to seek support from the Rector of St. Cuthbert's. How dare these bourgeois newcomers to Sunset Drive pass judgment on her life-style? She, Nita Cosgrove, who had made her debut in *Richmond* (meaningless and archaic as she now realized all debuts were); she whose family had built the first house on Sunset Drive and whose late mother had been a founding member of the Romulus Restoration and Rebeautification Society, one of whose first projects, the slandered daughter liked to remind my father, had been to have St. Cuthbert's stone Christ figure at the corner professionally acid-washed from its traffic-stained gray back to the pristine pearly state in which it had arrived to us a century ago from Italy.

And then of course there was the drastic defection of Chloe Niles's mother, who had shut herself up in her husband's garage with a younger man and turned on the ignition.

And strictly for the sake of my collection, hadn't even the complacent, well-cared-for Harriet been technically deprived of her mother for most of her childhood? From age six to nine, she lost her to the American Consulate in Djibouti; when her parents returned to live in Washington, Harriet didn't wish to leave her friends and continued living in Romulus, as did her little brother Ben, who had spent his babyhood in Djibouti. And when Harriet's father was made consul in Recife, both children initially went to Brazil with their parents, but then Dr. MacGruder died after trying to save a horse in a fire and our Mrs. MacGruder said her grandbabies were all she had left to live for, and Harriet and Ben came back to us in Romulus. Harriet, who was thirteen by then, confided to me matter-of-factly that quite frankly she was relieved to be back. Her mother could be a fun person, she said, but tended to be irresponsible and, just between us, she passed out too much on the sofa during the long Brazilian afternoons. Also Harriet and Ben had really missed Nana. No servants could make Nana's spaghetti sauce, even when you stood right behind them and told them exactly what to do next.

And the spring I was twelve and Daddy sent me over to help out in the afternoons at old Mrs. Stacy's while her daughter Miriam was mending from her hysterectomy, that entertaining old lady gave me a collector's item of a tale about her own aunt, the mother of two little girls, who had appeared to be a perfectly devout and happy wife and mother. Then, one autumn day, this woman had driven her small daughters in a horse and buggy over to a neighbor's house and left them while she went to town to do some shopping.

Only she hadn't gone shopping, this mother. Instead she had driven to a quarry, tethered the horse carefully to a tree where he could graze in the shade, and then loaded all her pockets and even the elasticized legs of her bloomers with stones, and drowned herself in the quarry. Nobody ever found out why. The day before, this aunt had put up fifty jars of fruit and vegetables from her own garden, cooked a delicious dinner for her family, said bedtime prayers with her two little girls, and—the grief-stricken husband had divulged afterwards—had satisfactory relations with him before going to sleep. There was just *no reason* for her to have done what she did, said old Mrs. Stacy, but sometimes in this world people were compelled to do things beyond reason.

I loved the story. It was something I could get my teeth into. *No reason.* And yet, there must have been some compelling *secret* reason, if only I could shake away the externals and get at it from the inside.

It continued to grip me even after Miriam Stacy, fully mended and returned to church, had her attack of conscience because of a reading from Amos 7, and took me aside right after the service. Bravely snuffling back her sinus fluids, which as always had started draining just as Daddy began his sermon, Miriam Stacy confessed to me that she had lain helpless in her bed and overheard her mother telling me an outright fib.

"My great-aunt *never* drowned herself in any quarry," Miriam Stacy assured me, her unctuous voice contrasting oddly with the glint of malice in her rabbity red-rimmed eyes. "Mother made the whole thing up out of whole cloth. Why, I remember *going to visit* that great-aunt in a nursing home when I was a little girl. She didn't drown in any quarry, she died at age ninety-three of hardening of the arteries! Mother does that. She makes up the most incredible fibs to suit the occasion. She does it just to *please*. I've been agonizing for weeks over what I should do. I even thrashed it out with myself in my journal. And then today when Dr. MacGruder read that passage where God shows Amos the plumbline and then your father pointed out in his sermon that prophets are sometimes called upon to tell unpopular truths, I felt I had been sent a clear message. I had to tell you, even though Mother would be *furious* with me. There was *no aunt* who drowned in a quarry. Just in case you'd been worrying, you know."

"Well," I said after a moment (using Daddy's upbeat "well" to stall for time), "I appreciate your concern. Thank you, Miriam." I gave this drab person, who could now never be anyone's mother, my best rector's daughter smile, worked up for just such occasions. The smile consisted of straight-on eye contact and a slight, soft upturning of the mouth, while I thought to myself some helpful phrase in connection with this person that would give "backing" to the smile while I dealt with my private feelings behind it. The phrase that helped with Miriam Stacy was one Daddy used when referring to those parishioners who really got on his nerves: "*also* a child of God."

"I knew it was the right thing," she said, patting my arm damply and trotting off to her car to reward herself with a honk on one of the Kleenexes she would have done better to bring into church.

"What was Miriam Stacy doing with you, over there by the bench?" my father asked afterwards. Uninvited by any St. Cuthbert's family today, we were enjoying a rare and cherished Sunday lunch by ourselves, out at Dorothy's Cafe on the highway, where we could order steak sandwiches, french fries, and Cokes—and apple pie a la mode for dessert if we felt like it. "Was she confessing her sins?"

"No, her mother's sins."

"Ah," said Daddy. "Then at least they were interesting."

"She said her mother made up that story. You know, the one about the aunt who drowned herself in the quarry. She said Mrs. Stacy makes up fibs just to please people."

Neither of us had to elaborate in words why Mrs. Stacy thought her story would please me. The sociable old lady had wanted to give me a gift of something worse than my own experience. My mother may have gone off one day and never come back, but she hadn't killed herself. We at least had the consolation of supposing that if it hadn't been for the accident, she might eventually have returned to us. After her "vacation" from us, she might very well have awakened one morning and come to herself, just as the Prodigal Son had, and said: "I will arise and go home to my husband and daughter."

"Mrs. Stacy does please people," said Daddy. "Even though she is nearly blind and unable to move about much anymore, she is an attractive, perceptive old lady. She's fun to be around, and she steals the show, what little show there is left to steal over there. Poor Miriam has her cross to bear." He fumbled around in the bread basket until he found the kind of roll he liked, and tore off a piece and buttered it. "The story's still every bit as good, though, Margaret. A vivid story can be far more illuminating than a dreary old fact. Our Lord understood that better than anyone. Don't let Miriam Stacy spoil the story for you."

"I won't," I said.

And I didn't. It remains one of the staples of my collection. I am still chewing on it, and it continues to yield tangy, if sometimes uncomfortable, revelations. I forget, over and over again, that the "real" aunt died at ninety-three in a nursing home. How could that faceless old husk in Miriam Stacy's drab, factual telling compete with the bright details of her mother's version? The horse and buggy bouncing the unsuspecting little girls and their doom-driven mother across the ripe autumn fields. And the fifty jars of fruits and vegetables, all those glassed-in colors from a summer's garden. And the cumulative stones, each one different from the next, all their roundnesses and sharpnesses clunking together and slowly filling out the white cloth of the mother's elasticized bloomers. And that delicate touch of the mother's courtesy to the horse, making sure he was in the shade and had something to nibble on before she went about the task of drowning herself. And the delicious final dinner of the night before—the family's Last Supper, though they didn't know it at the time, any more than we had. And then the bedtime prayers with the little girls and the "satisfactory relations" in the marriage bed. I could picture it all, even the satisfactory relations, these based on some spying Chloe Niles and I had done through her strategically drilled hole in the upstairs linen closet in her aunt's boarding house. Our unaware specimens had been a little old and stringy, and their coupling rather tired and perfunctory, but the spectacle had given me some definite thing to picture when I meditated upon this act that seemed to preoccupy so many people's thoughts in positive or negative ways.

I dwelt on the faces of the man and the woman in bed. Not the faces of the elderly couple performing their dutiful holiday embrace on Mrs. Radford's squeaky bedsprings, but the imagined faces of the father and mother in Mrs. Stacy's story. His was a complacent, ruddy, farmer's face, heavy-featured and somewhat obtuse. He was not at all aware of anything wrong with the woman who lay under him. Both of them had their eyes closed, even though the room was dark. Her face I saw as beautiful, though I couldn't make out any features. She was younger than her husband. In the darkness her skin glowed with a moonlike sheen as she undulated softly beneath him in this last ritual of a good wife's day. Her face showed no signs of any inner turmoil. Up and down they moved, performing their "satisfactory relations" like a couple in a dream.

The stories of absent or departed mothers in books counted, too. Why shouldn't they be part of my collection? They were just as vivid—sometimes more so. Daddy was right. It was the vividness that mattered. Whether or not they had actually happened in some real neighborhood was not the point. After all, they had been written down by real human beings, who drew on what they knew of real neighborhoods and life. And it was obvious from all these stories that there was a long precedent for absent mothers in the history of human experience.

Cinderella's mother, though married to a rich man, fell sick and died. Snow White's mother, pregnant with Snow White, was gazing out at the snow and pricked her finger with her needle. How pretty the blood looks, she thought. And died when Snow White was born.

Nancy Drew's mother had died when Nancy was three. This was told to you at the beginning of every Nancy Drew mystery, the information often not meriting a whole sentence of its own. The dead mother was the starting point for Nancy's life: after that, interesting things started to happen. Nancy, with the admiring background support of her successful lawyer father, and the excellent cooking of their faithful housekeeper Hannah Gruen, could get on with solving the endless succession of mysteries around her.

(It was not until I was in college, leafing through Benét's *Reader's Encyclopedia* in search of something else, that I learned that the author of Nancy Drew had been a syndicate of ghost writers assembled by one Edward L. Stratemeyer, who provided them with the outlines and ideas, though the *Encyclopedia* said he had written three of the Nancy Drews as well as nine of the Hardy Boys by himself. But it was the last part of the entry on Stratemeyer that really interested me. After his death, it said, the syndicate was managed by his two daughters, primarily by Harriet S[trate-meyer] Adams. Another father-daughter number. Where was *Mrs.* Stratemeyer when the daughters had been growing up? What part had *that* absent mother played in the creation of the Nancy Drew household? If indeed she had been absent. I chose to believe she had been, even if absent only in lack of influence upon her daughters.

Had Harriet Stratemeyer, like myself and Nancy Drew, been her father's mainstay, his intellectual and spiritual companion, his "little wife" in social obligations? The Stratemeyer household interested me far more than the topic I was supposed to be researching at the moment.

Jane Eyre's mother—ah, listen to this—had been *the wife of a clergyman.* She had married against the wishes of her friends. They considered the match beneath her. Her father cut her off without a shilling, and Jane hardly gets born before mother and father go visiting the poor in a manufacturing town and catch typhus and die. (What if I had lost *both* my parents? I would probably have had to go live with my mother's sister in Georgia, the notorious Aunt Con. My father had no living relatives.)

The heroines in the books I loved best had no mothers. Dorothea Brooke and her younger sister Celia are going through their dead mother's jewels at the opening of *Middlemarch.* And then there was Isabel Archer, in *The Portrait of a Lady,* whose handsome, ne'er-do-well father had taken Isabel and her sisters three times across the Atlantic before Isabel was fourteen. All we know about Isabel's mother is that she was Mrs. Touchett's "poor sister," and that Mrs. Touchett did not approve of the marriage to Isabel's father. Could women die of disapproval, then, in those less emancipated times?

Becky Sharp's mother was an opera-girl of humble French origin, but before her early death (Mr. Sharp beat her up a lot), she had bequeathed to little Rebecca the perfect Parisian accent that provided Becky with an entree to Miss Pinkerton's academy for young ladies, where she began her upscale trek. I secretly admired Becky's astute manipulations of people, and most of all I admired her energy, but a rector's daughter can't publicly proclaim she is charmed by a renegade. (I had somewhat the same problem when it came to Scarlett O'Hara—who also lost her mother fairly early.)

Jane Eyre I consistently admired the most. I say consistently because there was a period, my second year in college, when I was doing a paper on *The Portrait of a Lady,* when Isabel Archer represented for me the peak of valor and sophistication; I even approved of her going back to Osmond at the end, because it was a noble keeping-faith with her earlier, honorable pledge, even if it had been made to a villain in disguise. But then later, in a closer reading, I realized that her unhappiness might have been avoided if she had been aware that Gilbert Osmond was compelling to her because he was in many ways like her father.

When I was fifteen and a sophomore at Romulus High, Lady Diana Spencer, aged nineteen, appeared on television late one February afternoon, smirking shyly from under her choirboy bangs and flashing the sapphire and diamond engagement ring given her by the Prince; she walked beside him in flat heels, slumping to keep her height down, across the green palace sward while soft music played in the background.

That spring my classmates and I were obsessed with the future princess. Some of the girls rushed down to Rudolf's Hair Fashions to get "Lady Di" haircuts. Poor Sally Ann Jenks's was a flop. Literally. Her hair had no body. Harriet MacGruder declared it made her look more like a dodo bird than ever, with her long neck. (After several years of suffering under this unflattering comparison, Sally Ann Jenks had confronted Harriet fearfully but resolutely and forced her to look at the illustration of a dodo bird in *Webster's New World Dictionary:* "It does *not* have a long neck, it has a *short* neck and a big nose, and my mother says *you* could do with a little less nose and a lot more neck *yourself!*" "Oh really?" drawled Harriet in her most offhand, snobbish tone. But I was with her and saw mortification briefly flood her cheeks and neck. Yes, Harriet did have a very short neck. I hadn't noticed until then how short it was, but now I realized that Harriet had been aware of it for some time: Sally Ann Jenks, driven to attack, had shone a floodlight on Harriet's vulnerable spot. Yet, except for that single occasion, Harriet had won. Short neck or not, Harriet's personality was more compelling. She went right on calling Sally Ann "Dodo Bird," and making sarcastic references to her long, gangly neck. Such is the force of a strong personality. And those of us who followed her, for Harriet was definitely a leader, found her crisp neckless profile with its scornful tilt perfectly appealing and as it should be.

We even continued to think of the dodo as a long-necked bird.)

What captured our collective imagination that spring of 1981 was not that Lady Di was going to be the wife of the Prince of Wales ("Let's face it," said Harriet, "he has saucer ears, and she will have to watch her posture nonstop for the rest of her life"), but that this modern girl, so nearly our age and so accessible to our tastes, with her preppy, coltish looks and her unremarkable academic and job résumé that most of us expected to surpass, was our vicarious entree into a good old elitist tableau, complete with Ancient Privilege, robes old enough to be trimmed in the fur of animals on the endangered species list before anyone learned to feel guilty about it, crowns studded with priceless jewels like the ones in fairy tales, and legions of liveried servants so varied in function that they had a whole complex hierarchy of their own. Being socially enlightened children, we knew that we must not take such pageantry seriously, but it was awfully satisfying to watch, just as our parents faithfully viewed *Upstairs, Downstairs* week after week. We knew better than to want to be Diana; we were just hungry for some unabashed pomp.

But Diana interested me for a separate, personal reason. Hers was one more story that reinforced my own position. She, too, had been six years old when her mother had run away. The Viscountess Althorp had left her husband and three little daughters and three-year-old son for another man. This runaway mother had been thirty-one when she bolted. Three years older than Ruth. As each of these statistics became available, I fitted it where it belonged in my system of comparisons. Diana's mother had been married to Althorp thirteen years when she left home. Ruth had been married to Daddy only eight. But Diana's mother had left *four* children behind, one of them only three years old. I had to admit that was more serious: three more children had been hurt and one very young.

But on the other hand, Mrs. Shand-Kydd was not totally lost to her children. She had not been killed in a senseless accident within the year. She even got to ride in the carriage with Prince Philip on Diana's wedding day. Diana had gone off secretly to her mother's ranch in Australia just after Charles popped the question. I loved to imagine the details of that trip. Daughter and mother flung across matching beds, catching up on the past, each perhaps doing her nails.

"I know I wasn't a good mother," Mrs. Shand-Kydd might have said, "but haven't you done rather well without me!"

Then Diana might say, "I missed you, though. Did you miss us?"

And the mother would say, "It tore me apart. But I simply had to do what I did. I hope you will never find yourself in a similar position."

When Diana was fifteen, her father, Earl Spencer, had brought home a stepmother. And here I was, now also fifteen. Was this to be the year my father's bed would have a new person in it?

That summer I was so preoccupied in finding likenesses between Diana's family circumstances and mine that it was as if I myself brought Katharine Thrale into existence. She began coming to St. Cuthbert's during the long, slow procession of hot summer Sundays-after-Pentecost, when Daddy had to wear the green chasuble week after week.

Katharine's father, a retired Army colonel who collected rare maps, was losing his memory, and Katharine quit her job as librarian in a Jesuit college out west to come back to Romulus and care for him. A lapsed Episcopalian, she loved the old liturgy, and, having asked around town (the Colonel did not go to any church), was informed that St. Cuthbert's was the place for her, unless she wanted to drive all the way to Staunton. Daddy still clung exclusively to Rite One in the new *Book of Common Prayer*, the rest of whose revised contents had been a source of pain to him ever since the General Convention had voted them in two years before. He could wax quite bitterly on the 1979 revisions, and, fortunately for him, most of our congregation felt the same. He loathed the new, familiar "you"s in place of the "thou"s, and he hated what they had done to the Lord's Prayer. " 'Save us from time of trial' does *not* mean the same thing as 'lead us not into temptation,' " he kept reminding people, even when they were in complete agreement with him already. And he declared himself to have been personally robbed by the revised form of the Great Thanksgiving, which had been brutally shorn of his favorite phrase in the liturgy: "And here we offer and present unto thee our selves, our souls and bodies, to be a reasonable, holy, and living sacrifice unto thee . . ."

Taking away that phrase, Daddy said, was snatching from him his meaning both as a man and a priest.

I approved of Katharine Thrale the first Sunday she walked

into church. She was a noticeable person without being showy. New people to St. Cuthbert's usually entered our church swaggeringly or too humbly. It was either, "Look at me, here at last, bestowing my wonderful self on your little gathering," or, "I'm really nothing, please don't even bother to notice me." Though the "I'm really nothing"s frequently turned out to be the most blatant of "Look at me"s in disguise.

Katharine Thrale simply walked in on time, suitably dressed, knelt in the pew ahead of me, and said her prayers, keeping her back straight and not resting her bottom on the edge of the seat as so many women did. She was about forty, I judged, with neat, fine bones and a cap of gleaming black hair that she was letting go gray on the sides. Maybe this is she, I thought, remembering that Princess Diana had been fifteen, the age I was now, when Earl Spencer brought home Raine, former Countess of Dartmouth.

Katharine Thrale was easy to talk to. She neither preached nor posed, but simply volunteered information about herself and looked at you in a frank way that made you feel it was safe to volunteer information about yourself. She didn't push or pry and she didn't try to please, either. Though she was definitely, for me, in that category labeled "older woman," there was something girlish about her that made her seem like my contemporary. She and Daddy talked easily together from the beginning, but it was I who actually made the first overture. After church one Sunday I asked Katharine to have lunch with us out at Dorothy's Cafe. "We don't often have the chance to go to Dorothy's, because we're usually invited out for Sunday lunch by Daddy's parishioners," I explained. Then Daddy came over, still in his alb, and seconded my invitation. "I'd really like to," said Katharine in her straightforward way, "but Pop will be expecting me home. I don't like to leave him alone too long, because he forgets where he is sometimes, and then when he comes to himself he's very sad. But I *would* like to see more of you both. How would it be if I phoned you some afternoon, when Pop is resting? And then, if you're not doing anything, I could drop over to the rectory for a while."

"She seems an interesting person," Daddy remarked when we were settled into our customary booth at Dorothy's. "Not coy. I liked the way she invited herself to the rectory. You two get along, don't you?"

"I like her," I said, already imagining the wedding. Who would officiate? Daddy couldn't stand Jerry Hope, the trendy new rector

over at St. Matthias, who served communion to babies and flew up
and down the aisle during the Exchange of the Peace, hugging
everyone and even kissing some parishioners on the mouth. "I
just wish she would smile more," I added, not wanting to railroad
us into this thing precipitously.

"It can't be easy for her, watching her father disintegrate,"
Daddy said. "If my mind ever starts going like that, I want you to
dispose of me quietly and bury me under some needy perennials."

"The delphiniums, probably. They eat up fertilizer." I carried
on with the joke, though we both knew his name was already on
the headstone he would one day share with my mother out at
Romulus Memorial Cemetery. It was perhaps best that Katharine
Thrale hadn't come to Dorothy's with us, because we always went
straight to the cemetery after lunch on Sundays.

Katharine did phone us one weekday soon after that, and a
friendship quickly developed. She always came to us. Daddy did
try visiting at Colonel Thrale's once, but the visit was a disaster.
The old man thought Daddy, in his black clothes and clerical
collar, was a Jesuit coming to force Katharine to go back to her
library post at the Jesuit college and he first insulted Daddy and
then broke down and cried. Because her father was her first priority, Katharine could never stay with us for very long and we
could never make fixed plans for any kind of extended outing.
This lent an informality to her visits as well as an air of expecta-
tion. In a sense, she seemed already like a member of our family,
who had serious commitments elsewhere but who would drop in
when she could and was always looked-forward-to. Though
Katharine never, ever, dropped in without phoning first.

Often when she phoned us, Daddy was out, visiting people in
the hospital or counseling someone. But Katharine would come
anyway. She appeared to enjoy my company just as much as Daddy's. A devious person would have made it her business to charm
the daughter in order to win the father, but Katharine wasn't
devious. I think I actually made her smile more than Daddy did,
but she respected him a lot. When Daddy was present, they discussed the Gnostic gospels, which attracted and threatened them
both, or she would tell us about her vacations in monasteries.

Katharine had been a guest in heaps of monasteries. Just before her father had become ill, she had spent a wonderful week
with some Roman Catholic monks in New Mexico. She had a little
adobe hut by herself with only a kerosene lamp for illumination,

and the Abbot gave her a work assignment every morning just like the monks. The first morning, she washed all the windows of the refectory. Her brown eyes glowed as she described how, because every act of work, however small, was sacred, the sheets of newspaper were stacked just so and the window-cleaning tools were laid out for her as carefully as an artist's brushes, or surgical instruments. The second morning, she was assigned to help a monk do the laundry. They went down to the river, to a wash-house with an ancient Maytag wringer, and all around them were baskets and baskets of the monks' laundry. The monk put the clothes through the wringer, and Katharine's job was to hang them on the line in the sun. The work period was from nine until one, and as it got closer to one Katharine began to panic. There were still loads of baskets of dirty laundry. She began hanging things faster and faster, practically snatching them out of the wringer, until the monk asked her what was the rush. "We're never going to finish all these baskets by one," she said, almost in tears. "We don't have to," he told her. "Someone else will finish them. All that is required of us is that we work, steadily and for the glory of God, from nine until one, at our appointed task every day." That taught her a lot, Katharine said. She now tried to incorporate this attitude into her own life.

Another thing she had learned from the monks in New Mexico was how to make a wonderful incense from sage. It had such a clean, healing fragrance when you burned a small amount in a pottery bowl. Katharine showed me how to dry sage and mix in a little rosemary and tie it up in bundles to make the incense. She also taught me some rudimentary Greek, and later that autumn, after Georgie Gaines's greedy developer father had deforested another slice of Sunset Mountain and caused a landslide into the church property, flooding Daddy's Siberian iris beds, she introduced me to the art of dry walling. At her own expense, she had a truckload of bluestone dumped in the corner of Daddy's ruined borders, and before Harvest Festival she and I had completed a twenty-foot, curved, waist-high wall along the entire back slope of the rectory garden. I could have kissed Katharine Thrale the afternoon we finished that wall, sweaty and smelly as we were, if I hadn't observed that Katharine was not a demonstrative person. She was a firm handshaker but not a patter or a hugger, and I had seen her flinch once or twice during coffee hour, when one of the more outgoing St. Cuthbert members caressed or plucked at her neat person during the act of greeting. This reserve of hers might, of course, cause problems, I had conceded to myself, when it came time for "satisfactory relations" with my father, but I trusted in his tact when the need should arise. And anyway, at present, nothing could be accomplished in that department as long as Colonel Thrale retained exclusive claim on his daughter's nights.

That claim was terminated sooner than any of us expected. On a sunny afternoon in late October, Katharine was giving their lawn its last mowing for the season. It was one of her father's rare days of lucidity and they had spent the morning looking at his maps, he pointing out the ones that would fetch the most money if she ever decided to sell, and even giving her the name of a man at the Smithsonian who would be interested in buying them. When Katharine said she thought it would be a good day to cut the lawn, he didn't make his usual fuss about doing it himself, but told her she was a good daughter and poured himself a glass of iced tea and sat on the porch and watched her. He waved at her from time to time, when she was pushing the power mower close to the porch, and then she had to do the side yard, where he was out of sight, and when she came back to finish off the strip on the other side of the sidewalk she saw that he had gone inside. To the bathroom, she assumed, because he had left his glass of iced tea on the floor beside his chair. She went on and put the mower in the garage, her ears still vibrating from its racket, and took time to wipe it off with one of his old undershirts, and then, feeling happy with the job done and the smell of freshly cut grass and her father's calling her a good daughter, which more than made up for the abusive epithets he had been in the habit of showering on her during his "confused" days, she went inside and smelled the gunpowder. The empty presentation box for the Colonel's favorite Mauser—a DeLuxe model Parabellum, with ivory grips—was open on the dining-room table. The pistol and the body lay companionably connected and intact upon the carpet; the addled brains, which had shamed him so on the rare lucid day such as this one, were all over the room.

After the funeral, which Daddy conducted, Katharine went on retreat to a convent of contemplative Anglican nuns in Baltimore. She had wanted to go back to the monastery in New Mexico, but the monks had already promised their adobe guest hut to someone else. It was Elaine Major who came up with the convent in Baltimore. The Major knew the Reverend Mother there.

Katharine came back from Baltimore looking peaceful and young. She surprised Daddy and me by hugging us both quite warmly on her return. The next few weeks she was kept very busy sorting out her father's things. The man from the Smithsonian came down to look at the maps, pronounced ten of them treasures, and offered Katharine a fabulous price.

"Oh, damn," I said to Daddy, when Katharine phoned us with the news.

"Why so, sweetie?"

"Well, now she might think . . . I mean . . . that we're after her money." It was the closest I had come to saying what was surely on both our minds.

"You really care for Katharine, don't you?" Daddy asked then, gazing at me closely through his new trifocals. I tried to see him objectively, as a prospective bride would: he wore glasses all the time now, and his hair was a lot grayer, but the prospective bride had quite a bit of gray herself. Both of them were slender people, though Daddy needed to exercise more. Katharine would see to that. They might even do a dry wall together. The slope behind the sacristy could use some shoring up, since Mr. Gaines's bull-dozers had gouged out the hill directly above us to make way for another three levels of condominiums. And Daddy was still just as tall and eloquent and kind. What was more, he hadn't had a depression lately. If only we could catch Katharine before he wandered off behind the Black Curtain again.

"I like her a whole lot," I told my father. "I think she'd fit in here really well."

"Well, then," said Daddy after a minute, "I guess I'd better get on over there, hadn't I?" He looked at his watch. "We've left it a little late for tonight, though, don't you think?"

"It's not all that *late,* but since she just called about those maps, it might look like . . ."

"I get you." Daddy laughed. "And we probably ought to sleep on it, anyway."

We slept on it, and Daddy went over the next morning. He stayed a long time. What could they be doing? Or were they so blissfully happy together that they had forgotten all about me? I reconsidered what I had done. Had I worked against my own best interests by wanting this? And had I really wanted it? We had been doing very well by ourselves. It was just that if he was *going* to bring home a stepmother, as Earl Spencer had brought Raine home when Diana was fifteen, I wanted it to be someone I felt would suit us.

At last Daddy returned with a thoughtful smile on his face. He doesn't want to show all of his happiness, I thought; he's afraid I'll feel left out.

"Well?" I said.

"Well!" repeated Daddy, sinking into his chair. He raked his fingers through his hair, as he often did after some ordeal, and sighed mightily. Then he began chuckling to himself.

"What *happened*?" I demanded.

"Would you like it blow-by-blow style, or get-to-the-end-quick style?" We often asked this of each other when there was special news to report. Almost always, I would opt for blow-by-blow, because Daddy told a story well, and I liked the buildup and picturing all the details along the way.

Not this morning. "Get-to-the-end-quick," I said.

"God got there first," said Daddy, chuckling some more.

"What's *that* supposed to mean?"

"He beat me to it. When I got there, she said I must be psychic. 'I was just about to call you with the good news,' she told me. 'I've just finished talking to the Reverend Mother at Our Holy Mother up in Baltimore and I've been accepted into the novitiate. You and Margaret are the very first people I wanted to share my happiness with.' "

"You mean Katharine's going to become a nun!" I screamed.

"Sure does look that way," said Daddy. He didn't look too sad, but maybe he was covering up for my benefit.

"But . . . did you even ask her . . . about the other?"

"Well, not in so many *words*, but . . . you'll have to trust in my intuition, here, Margaret . . . I think she knew why I'd come. Something in my voice probably gave it away when I phoned this morning. It even crossed my mind, as I drove home just now, that whatever-it-was in my voice may have prompted that phone call to Baltimore."

"Are you saying you drove her into the arms of God?"

"I wouldn't say I drove her exactly. It was more like I prompted or reminded her. I think she's *been* there for quite a while already, only there were other things in the way until now. And we have to give some credit to the Major in all this."

"The Major? What does *she* have to do with it?"

"She was the one who suggested Our Holy Mother Convent.

Katharine didn't know there were contemplative orders for Episcopalians, and she couldn't see her way to becoming a Roman.
Then up she went to Baltimore, on the Major's advice, and found
the perfect home. Lots of windows to wash, too, she tells me. She
was poking fun at herself; she knows it won't be easy. She's twice
the age of the average novice, but she said the order encourages
women who have done some living first. Then they know what
they're getting into."

"With the money from those maps, she'll be able to buy a
lifetime supply of window washers for that convent," I said.

"And there's the house, too. She's putting her father's house
on the market," said Daddy.

We both went quiet, thinking our own thoughts. I was testing
myself, to see if I regretted losing Katharine. I even tested myself
about the money. Both would have been nice, but, then again,
who knew what changes they might bring. They might have
changed *us*. Chloe Niles had been ruined by her new stepmother
and some money. I had scarcely recognized her when she came
back from Florida to visit last spring. Of course, Katharine was
not anything like Chloe's brassy stepmother, and I was not Chloe.
Still . . .

"You know who's going to be the most disappointed of all
about this?" Daddy said finally. "The Major."

"Why? I thought . . ."

"The Major has intimated to me on a number of recent occasions that I couldn't do better than move Katharine Thrale into
the rectory as soon as possible. It's not fitting and proper, in the
Major's opinion, for us to bum around like two bachelors. You're
getting to the age where you need a woman to instruct you in
womanly lore."

"Did she say that, or did you?"

"Uh, the last bit is me, I guess. The Major would have gotten
'gul' into that sentence somewhere. All women are still 'guls' to the
Major."

" 'Gul-ish' lore," I intoned in Elaine Major's domineering contralto. " 'A nice gul to instruct your gul in gul-ish lore.' Such as
building a twenty-foot, waist-high dry wall."

"Such as that, indeed," laughed Daddy. "Oh, Margaret, you
reminded me so much of your mother just now. The way she
could do people. Remember her impersonation of Mrs. Radford?
She'd have me in convulsions. You know, honey, first impressions

are often the most acute, and do you remember, at the beginning of the summer when I asked you how you liked Katharine, you said you wished she would smile more? Well, that's exactly it. Can you imagine Katharine Thrale ever making us laugh the way Ruth did?"

I said no, I couldn't.

"The poor old Major," said Daddy cheerfully. "How shall I break the news to her that has so many good works in progress that sometimes one of them is bound to knock another one right off the agenda."

Thus closed the chapter on Katharine Thrale, who was the closest anybody ever came to becoming my stepmother.

All of which is to say: Ruth never came back. My mother never came back. She left the rectory with Madelyn Farley just after lunch on September 13, 1972, while I was still at school, and though she remained in this world until the following June, neither my father nor I ever saw her alive again. I have never been able to come across the name of St. Cyprian in the prayer book without equating him with her loss, because it was on his feast day that she and I walked together to the bus stop for the last time and I decided to punish her for forgetting to play our game.

She was living with Madelyn, in England, when she was killed. June 24, 1973, a Monday. The Nativity of St. John the Baptist in the Church Calendar. Six days after my seventh birthday. They had rented a house near Guildford, where Madelyn was scenic designer for a local theater's summer festival. It was in the evening, one of those long English summer evenings around the solstice when it stays light till ten. Ruth had driven the little minivan into town to buy chocolate for the two of them, leaving Madelyn behind to work on some sketches in the garden. She was on her way back from the tobacconist's, with two Cadbury's chocolate bars with orange filling, when she apparently forgot that she was driving in England. The road she turned into, driving on the wrong side, happened to be, by one of life's cruel coincidences, a road my father had driven on daily when he was serving his curacy in nearby Farnham. After he and my mother were married, he often spoke of taking her to that part of England and showing her all his favorite spots, and then afterwards they would travel to the north of England, to York and Durham and the Holy

Island of Lindisfarne; he and Ruth would complete the pilgrimage he and his mother never got to make.

Now, instead, he flew to England to bring Ruth's body home. I stayed with the MacGruders. Mrs. MacGruder and the Major went to the rectory and picked out a dress, the dark silk paisley with the mandarin collar that had called attention to her long-waistedness and set off the highlights in her hair. But when Daddy came back, he told them the coffin would stay closed, and so we hung the dress back in the closet, where it remained for many years because neither of us wanted to part with it.

Daddy and his vestry always met in the church crypt, where we had our coffee hours and Sunday school. But on the evening of the day my mother left with Madelyn Farley, after we came back from having our pizza, he wrote out a sign with a big Magic Marker and thumbtacked it to the church door: VESTRY WILL MEET AT RECTORY THIS EVENING.

"Why did you write *that*?" I demanded, as soon as I had finished sounding out the words aloud in the showy, "phonetic" way our teacher favored. "Why aren't you all meeting down in the crypt like always?"

"Because there's no one to watch after you tonight."

"I don't need anyone to watch after me. I'm not some three-year-old child. I'm not like Devonia *Brush*, or somebody."

"Well, of course not, but we have to consider how the thing looks, don't we? It wouldn't look right to the vestry if I left you all by your lonesome self when we could all be more comfortable at the rectory for just this one time. Now would it?"

"I guess not." He had said "just this one time," which meant he definitely expected her back before the next meeting, didn't it? But of course he did. The vestry met only once a *month*, whereas he had said she would be gone "at least a week or ten days."

To find out more about this sudden "vacation" from us that my father had talked Ruth into, later in the evening I did what children have done since homes have had staircases. I crouched at the top, out of sight, to hear how Daddy would greet each vestry member at the front door and how he would explain about Ruth's vacation.

The first to arrive was Mr. Pasco, of Pasco Plumbing and Electric. Ernie Pasco was always early to things, my mother said, because he was so amazed to have been invited at all. Mr. Pasco had been elected to the vestry only last winter. "What an inspired choice," Ruth said to Daddy. "Now we can get the new double sink installed in the church kitchen and, who knows, maybe somebody will just happen to mention that I would dearly love to have somewhere to plug in my hair dryer in the bathroom."

From my perch on the second step above the landing, I could see only Mr. Pasco's heavy, round-toed shoes, obsessively wiping themselves on our doormat.

"We're meeting over here tonight, Ernie," Daddy explained in his congenial, ball-bearings voice, "because Ruth is taking a little trip up to New York with an old school friend."

"Nice for her," came Mr. Pasco's fast, breathless reply, his shoes still scuffing zealously on the mat. "I hope she's been pushing that test button on the outlet I installed for her in the bathroom. She should push the little yellow button at least once a month. I explained it all to her, it's for safety's sake."

"Yes, Ernie, you very kindly went over it with us all. I'm sure she has been doing it faithfully."

"The wiring in these old houses," Mr. Pasco went on, his feet still vigorously engaged with the mat, "sometimes it isn't so good. But with these new outlets, she's safe. If too much steam gets in the bathroom, say she's taken a shower and then decides to dry her hair, and she plugs in the dryer and nothing happens, well, that's because the outlet is protecting her till some of the moisture goes away. What she has to do, see, is just wait a minute or two till it clears, and then she'll see that little red band showing and all she has to do is push the Reset button and she's back in business."

"Yes, well, it's certainly agreeable, Ernie, to feel so protected. We're much obliged to you." Daddy's feet walked beside Mr. Pasco's feet into the living room. I heard him ask the plumber, who was a member of the Romulus planning board, about some proposed rezoning law.

"If you all don't do something soon, Ernie, George Gaines is going to turn the whole of Sunset Mountain into his own personal giant mud pudding, dotted all over with atrocious mansard-roofed raisins."

"Ha-ha, that's a good way of putting it," Ernie Pasco said, laughing, and went on to say something about Mr. Gaines having friends in high places. Mr. Pasco hadn't even acknowledged my

mother's absence. He had made it sound as though she was standing naked in our bathroom at this very moment, waiting for the
moisture to go away so she could push the Reset button.

The next vestry member to ring the bell was Daddy's nemesis,
Mr. Ned Block. Privately, Daddy referred to him as "The Stumbling Block," which I at first had taken to refer to the stumbly,
sleepy way Mr. Block moved. He had a large head and stomach
and small feet, and he walked like a bear on two legs. But Daddy
meant it in the sense that Ned Block put obstacles in his way and
was always lying in wait to trip him up, constantly comparing
Daddy's ministry unfavorably to that of Dr. Hazeltine's, St. Cuthbert's former rector. Ned Block worked at Shenandoah Proper-
ties, a real estate firm owned by his uncle, but spent most of his
time playing with toy soldiers on his desk. His passion in life, if
you could ascribe any passion to him, was battle reenactments of
The War Between the States. He took frequent days off from his
uncle's firm in order to travel around the state participating in
them in his authentic Confederate officer's uniform.

Ned Block had been on the search committee for the new
rector after Dr. Hazeltine announced his retirement, and Daddy
had later heard through the grapevine that Ned Block had been
"lukewarm" when the other members of the committee decided to
issue the call to Daddy. His reason being that Daddy's "background" would prevent him from being totally at ease with the
typical St. Cuthbert's parishioner. Ned Block knew someone in
Chattanooga who had told him Daddy's mother had been a *servant*
of the Dudleys. This mistaken information regarding his mother
hurt and enraged Daddy more than anything else. But since it
had reached his ears through hearsay, he felt he could not confront Ned Block. To do so would be just the ungentlemanly type
of act expected of a person not "totally at ease with the typical St.
Cuthbert's parishioner." And because Daddy felt constrained out
of a fear of fulfilling his enemy's negative prediction about him,
the slur ate on him inwardly and caused him to emphasize, sometimes unnecessarily, what a close friend of Mrs. Dudley's my
grandmother had been, and how all the gardening and other
things she had done for the Dudleys, after she had moved into
their carriage house following the death of John Gower, had been
done out of her innate love of beauty and order and serenity, and
simply because it was a belief of hers that it was your duty to do
for others the things you did well.

"You're overreacting to that stupid rumor," Ruth would tell Daddy. "And what if your mother *had* been someone's servant? Some of the world's greatest people have been the children of servants. Many of them probably started off as servants themselves. My own mother, who was a hopeless snob, always enjoyed telling how some ancestor of ours who came over in the sixteenth century was an indentured servant."

"Having a sixteenth-century ancestor who was a servant is another thing entirely," Daddy said. "But aside from the servant thing—poor Mother, it would wound her so!—Ned is still luke-warm about me. He doesn't approve of me. I wish I knew why."

"*Because,* Walter, Ned is lukewarm by *nature.* He has to drive around the state and dress up in an antique uniform and shoot blanks out of antique cannons just to arouse himself. Ned is slow-witted and complacent and you've got too much sensitivity ever to be satisfied with yourself. *That's* why, Walter. It's no big *mystery.*"

Yet Daddy continued to think it was. It interested him to ponder it, it seemed to *please* him almost, the nagging suggestion that there was something wrong with him or his style of ministry, spotted by Ned Block alone and continually evidenced by Ned's indolent disapproval.

"Hello, there, Ned," I heard Daddy saying too heartily as he greeted his tormentor at the front door. "We're altering our procedure a little and meeting here tonight because Ruth is away spending some time with an old school friend from Miss Beale's."

"Oh, Miss Beale's," said Ned Block indifferently. I saw his small oxblood loafers with their tassels pad across our mat without a scuffle. "How long will she be away?" The loafers shambled on towards the living room.

"About a week or ten days." Daddy's narrow black shoes did a propitiatory dance of attendance in the wake of the tasseled loafers. "The Church Calendar's pretty free now, until Harvest Festival."

"What about Ember Days?" asked Ned Block languidly. "I always liked the way Dr. Hazeltine stressed the fasting on Ember Days. And then on Friday night, Mrs. Hazeltine always had a soup supper for the altar boys here at the rectory. It really filled you up, Mrs. Hazeltine's soup." Through the hall mirror I saw his bottom half settle into the most comfortable armchair. One tasseled loafer propped itself upon a tightly trousered thigh. A small, plump white hand reached down and stroked the red-socked ankle.

Immediately afterwards, their two pairs of wingtip cordovans doing polite scuffles on our mat, came Mr. Wirt Winchester and Mr. Harlan Buford, a trust officer at the bank who was always ready with a joke on himself. Ruth privately called him "Harlan Buffoon." About Mr. Winchester, a quiet, pock-marked lawyer with diabetes and a stutter, whom everybody affectionately called "WW," Ruth had once commented to Daddy, "WW's one of those people everybody can afford not to hate."

Right behind them, straight from his evening rounds at the hospital, came Dr. MacGruder.

"Ruth has up and left me," Daddy told the three men humorously. "She's run off to New York with a friend from Miss Beale's to have herself a little fun." He could say that because he felt sure of himself with these men. With Ned Block, he reminded me of myself with Chloe Niles.

"Glad to hear it," boomed Dr. MacGruder. " 'Bout time that gal had herself a good outing." His collegiate tan bucks with the red rubber soles, which he wore summer and winter, did an exuberant soft-shoe on the scratchy mat and loped confidently in. "Where's my pretty Margaret?" Aiming his voice up the stairs.

I shrank back.

"In her room reading," said Daddy.

"Pretty *and* smart," said Dr. MacGruder.

"Every time my Clara Jane goes on one of her New York junkets," sang Harlan Buffoon in his ingratiating drawl, "I have to take out a loan to pay off all the *junk*."

Sympathetic male laughter swept them on into the living room. "H-hi, Ernie. H-h-h-how are you, N-ned?" said WW, the kind of person everyone could afford not to hate.

The Major was next. "Well, Fathah, are you stahting a new precedent?" Her boat-shaped patent-leather pumps duckwalked into sight and performed a brief exhibition step on our mat. It struck me as bizarre every time I heard the leathery old matriarch call Daddy "Father." Her son the Bishop was older than Daddy.

"You're looking fit, as always, Elaine," Daddy told her. "No, Ruth has gone up to New York on a little pleasure trip with an old school friend, and that's why we're meeting over here at the house."

"But she'll be back by Satuhday." It was an assertion, not a question.

"Well, no, it'll be more like a week or ten days." Daddy's black shoes stood at attention before the Major's patent-leather pumps.

"But Ruth is playing tennis with me at my club on Satuhday morning," said the Major. "It's written down in my book."

"Well, you see, it was an impromptu decision, Elaine. Madelyn, that's Ruth's old friend, had to leave earlier than we expected and I talked Ruth into driving on up with her so they could spend more time together. Ah, Trevor, is that you out there in the gloom? The evenings are suddenly so much shorter."

" 'Lead, kindly light, amid the encircling gloom,' " a man's mock-weary voice sang slowly, off-key. Would Professor LaFarge's timely arrival save Daddy from the Major's displeasure over having her tennis game upset?

"Trevor. Fathah here is telling me that Ruth has gone off to New York with . . . what was the gul's name, Fathah?"

"Madelyn Farley. She designs plays," Daddy said. "She's worked on Broadway," he added.

The patent-leather pumps splayed emphatically to one side so as not to be dusted up by the Professor's sloppy yellow Wallabees. "Ruth never mentioned the gul to *me*. I hope she's not one of those women's libbers who will fill her head with puhfectly silly propaganda."

"Oh, Ruth's head is very much her own," said Daddy gallantly.

"There are at least six plays running on Broadway that I wish *I* could see," interjected the Professor's affected, weary voice. Professor LaFarge had a doctorate in Literature from Yale, but, because of some earlier career mishap, he now taught multiple sections of Freshman Composition at the community college. Daddy liked him better than Ruth did.

When grown people got together for a meeting, they first had to say a lot of useless things before they could talk about what they had really come for. Otherwise it wasn't good manners.

At last, I heard Dr. MacGruder declare that they had a quorum, which was Latin for when you had enough people at the meeting so you were allowed to call it to order.

Professor LaFarge read the minutes of the last vestry meeting in his mock-weary style. He read them as if he were poking fun at the way he had written them, but at the same time knew that they were superior to anything anyone else could have written.

Mr. Harlan Buffoon gave the Treasurer's report, interrupted twice by the Major. He tried to make everybody laugh and they did. When he had finished, Dr. MacGruder said jovially, "All our

problems would be solved, Harlan, if we'd be more like our Baptist brothers. Instead of giving till it hurts, we should keep on
giving till it feels good again."

Everybody laughed some more, but you could tell from the
way they laughed that Dr. MacGruder's jokes were more respected
than Mr. Harlan Buffoon's. Nobody, for example, not even Ruth,
would ever play around with Dr. MacGruder's name, would call
him "Dr. MacGoon," or something.

Mr. Harlan Buffoon read off a list of figures. The last one was
how much Daddy had in his Discretionary Fund. "But just you
wait," said the banker. "Wait till Ruth gets back from New York
with her packages and the credit card statements start pouring
in!" Everybody laughed, except for Elaine Major.

I got up and tiptoed back to my room, where Daddy had
thought I had been the whole time, reading to myself. I sat
propped back on my pillows, *The Water Babies* open on my knees.
I didn't like it much. It was an old mildew-smelling library book,
and except for the frontispiece, all the pictures were small and in
black and white. Also I didn't like the boy in it, although I knew
you were supposed to, and I couldn't say exactly why I didn't. But
my father liked this book because some clergyman in Victorian
England had written it, and Daddy had a partiality for books
about England, and especially books by English clergymen.

What interested me more, as I sat there "reading," was that I
could split myself into two Margarets. To an observer standing
just outside the open door of my room, I was a good child reading, or, as Dr. MacGruder might want to add, "a pretty *and* smart"
child reading. But then there was the Margaret inside of me who
was engaged in making sense of my world. This more important
of the two Margarets was tallying up the evidence from my staircase spying, while the Margaret with her eyes cast obediently down
on *Water Babies* provided the "front," so I could work in peace.

I still didn't like the idea of my mother's "vacation," but I felt
somewhat reassured by the vestry's reaction to Daddy's news. Except for the Major being miffed about the tennis, nobody seemed
alarmed that she had driven off to New York with Madelyn Farley.
Dr. MacGruder had been enthusiastically in favor of it, and even
Ned Block hadn't seemed to mind about her *going*, only about
Mrs. Hazeltine's long-lost Ember Days soup.

Daddy's voice floated upwards as he presented his list of fall
projects for St. Cuthbert's. It was curious, this business of being

rector. You were the star, nobody but you could wear the gorgeous vestments or administer the sacraments or preach the sermon, but at the same time you were always having to ask permission and plead for your spending money like a little boy and worry about causing gossip or offending people like Ned Block.

I slid down from my bed and wandered quietly down the hall to my parents' room. I thought I would check out their closet and see what she had taken. Both of my parents complained about their closet. "How did the Hazeltines ever cram *their* clothes into it?" Ruth would say, angrily scraping the laden hangers back and forth along the sagging rod to force a precious extra inch of space; "They were both such large people. They were each of them twice as large as we are." "Well, they probably each had half as many clothes as we do," Daddy would reply humorously. "Rectories are such funny places," Ruth had said once. "They seem to have been built to accommodate everyone but the present inhabitants. When Mrs. Hazeltine was giving me the grand tour, she told me the small dining room had been her cross to bear. *Small!* I thought. I'd like to take half of it and make more closets with the space. When I'm dumpy and gray and giving the next young wife *her* tour and bitching about the small closets and that weird misshapen one in Margaret's room, I wonder what she will be thinking. Probably, *Closets!* Who cares about *them?* I wonder what she *will* care about?" "I wonder sometimes," Daddy had mused, "whether there'll be a church left for any new young rector down the line. The way things are going."

She had taken her linen slacks with the jacket to match, her denim skirt and several blouses, but had left behind the handsome dark silk paisley with the mandarin collar, the outfit that everyone said looked so well on her. The trip to New York couldn't be very important to her if she'd left her best dress at home.

I went into their bathroom and climbed up on the toilet lid to check her cosmetics shelf. She didn't wear makeup, except a little powder "to keep down the shine," and lipstick. Both were gone, but she hadn't taken the perfume Daddy and I had given her for Mother's Day.

Her new bottle of cucumber lotion, that had cost her sixteen dollars over in Charlottesville, the same day we bought my dresses for school, was gone. "I really oughtn't," she had told the saleslady behind the counter. "It's much too expensive, but, oh! . . . it's so cool and refreshing! It makes me feel . . . I don't know. Here, Margaret, try some. What do *you* think?" She had pumped a generous squirt from the tester onto my arm. It took a long time to get it rubbed in. It smelled like just a lot of cucumbers mashed up, and I said so, making Ruth and the saleslady laugh. Then the saleslady said, "I always find that a clean, fresh scent can give you a new lease on life." And Ruth pulled a crisp twenty-dollar bill out of her wallet. "You've made yourself a sale," she said. "You want me to wrap it up nice for you?" asked the saleslady. "Oh, no . . . well, *yes*, why not?" said Ruth. "That's right, give your*self* a gift," the saleslady egged her on. The two of them were suddenly in cahoots about something. The purchase strangely elated Ruth. At home, she slathered it on her tanned arms and legs and down the front of her chest and behind her neck. I would catch her sniffing her arm at intervals, as though she and the lotion were communing.

I took her abandoned perfume from the shelf and climbed carefully down from the toilet lid. I sat on the bath rug and, anchoring the bottle firmly between my legs, pried loose the glass stopper. I laid the stopper on the rug and liberally patted myself with the perfume, then went through the whole rigmarole of putting everything back the way it was.

Enveloped in the rather ornate scent, I wafted back into their room and scrambled up on the high bed. This bed had once belonged to the man Daddy had admired most in the world, Father Francis Traherne, Rector of All Saints in Chattanooga when Daddy was growing up. Their friendship had started when Daddy was cleaning Father Traherne's gutters one autumn; it was largely because of Father Traherne's example, Daddy said, that he had wanted to become a priest himself. The two of them had remained close right up until Father Traherne's death. After the funeral, when Daddy was helping Mrs. Traherne clear out the rectory, she asked him if he would like Father Traherne's four-poster bed, as otherwise she planned to sell it. So Daddy had it shipped back to Falls Church, Virginia, where he was serving as assistant rector, and he had slept in it ever since, first as a bachelor and then later with my mother.

It was a big bed, as old-fashioned double beds went, and high enough off the floor so that I had to take a flying leap to catapult my top half over the edge. Then I would wriggle the rest of me on, and lie down in splendor, exactly in the middle, arranging my arms and legs so that an extremity pointed towards each of the four posters. There on my back in this outspread fashion, like the figure lashed to the wheel of fortune in those medieval illustrations, I would concentrate on feeling the white cotton bedspread with its raised, whorled patterns all along my underside, meanwhile taking big, self-conscious gulps of air until I achieved an expanded sense of myself. In such a state I often entered a realm of magical confidence; it would seem to me, as I lay spread-eagled across my parents' bed like a small but potent household god, that I was the one in charge of things around here and that I could make anything I wanted happen.

I was lying there in my magical position on Father Traherne's four-poster, bathed in my mother's perfume, willing her to be thinking about me, when the phone rang. I flip-flopped to Daddy's side of the bed to snatch it up.

"Oh, Margaret, honey, good," Ruth said. "I was hoping you'd answer."

I was so stunned by what I had wrought that I didn't speak.

"Margaret? Are you there?" There was some public kind of noise in the background. Her voice had a metallic echo.

"Where are you?" My own voice, faint and whiny, totally unlike a household god, dismayed me.

"Somewhere in New Jersey. We stopped to eat something. Madelyn wants to get to New York before—"

"Hello?" My father had picked up the phone downstairs.

"Oh, Walter, it's only me. I just wanted to—"

"Ruth! Where are you?"

"Oh, on the highway somewhere in New Jersey—"

"The highway? You mean you had a breakdown of some kind?"

"*No*, Walter. We only stopped for dinner. Madelyn wants to make it to New York by—"

"Wait, Ruth, I'm going to my study. Margaret, are you on the phone up there?"

"Yes."

"Well, you two keep on talking while I run to my study," said Daddy, and hung up.

"Actually, it was you I wanted to talk to anyway," my mother said to me. "I felt bad about taking off while you were still at school, but if we'd waited till you got home we would have had to drive all night. Margaret, are you there?"

"Yes."

"What were you doing when I called?"

"Nothing."

"You picked up the phone awfully quick. I'll bet you were on our bed."

As this was not really a question, I saw no use in answering. I was having trouble on my end, anyway. I felt constricted in my chest. And I was suddenly very angry. It wasn't fair for her to know where I was and meanwhile to be far away from me where I couldn't picture her.

"Where exactly are you?" asked Daddy, picking up the phone in his study.

"Oh, honey, just some restaurant that smells of coffee that's been brewing all day. And I'm calling on Madelyn's credit card so I can't talk long."

"Give me the number of the pay phone," Daddy said, "and we'll call you right back. I've got the vestry here, but they can wait."

"The *vestry?* Oh, of course, how stupid of me. They have to meet at the house because I'm not there. Margaret, I love you and miss you. Do you hear me?"

A contrary demon kept my mouth clamped shut.

"We love you and miss you, too," said Daddy. "Harlan thinks you're going to go on a shopping binge and wipe me out, and the Major's not too happy you forgot Saturday's tennis game, but everyone else things it's *fine* and I want you to enjoy yourself. Doc said it was high time you had a good outing."

"What did Stumbling Block have to say?"

"Oh, just some mutterings about Ember Days . . . Ruth, darling, *do* give me that number and let me call you back on our nickel."

"There's really no need, Walter. Madelyn's waving to me that our food's come. She's anxious to get on the road again. Margaret, I can feel you're peeved with me, but I'm not going to sleep easy until you say something sweet. What would you like for me to bring you back from New York?"

"I don't want anything," I said.

"Oh, well, then," said Ruth, sounding irritated.

"Just bring yourself back," said Daddy. "That'll be enough for us, won't it, Margaret?"

I was deciding what to answer, when she said, "Look, I'll phone again tomorrow when we're in New York, okay? Oh, and, Walter, will you please tell the Major that I'm puh-fectly contrite about the tennis game?"

"Will do," promised Daddy, chortling. "Margaret, aren't you going to say anything more to your mother?"

"Oh, she doesn't have to if she doesn't want to," said my mother, sounding suddenly tired of the conversation.

"Don't worry about us," Daddy reassured her. "We'll hold the fort just fine. The important thing is for you to *enjoy* yourself, Ruth."

"I'll try my best," she said, sighing, as if he had just assigned her a new responsibility. We all three hung up.

I climbed down off the bed and returned to my room. With great concentration, I unbuttoned the little amber cat's-head buttons of my dress, starting from the bottom, as I had been instructed, so that it got easier as you worked your way up.

(". . . Ruth . . . bite to eat in New Jersey," my father's voice reported buoyantly to the vestry downstairs, ". . . she and Madelyn . . . New York by tonight.")

He found me, after the vestry had left, sitting up in bed wearing my pajamas, *The Water Babies* open on my knees.

"Oh, oh. You haven't read *too* far ahead of me, now, have you?"

"Not too far."

He walked over to my window and stood looking out, hands clasped behind his back. His bare elbows jutted out at sharp angles below his black short sleeves. A last car engine revved up very efficiently. It sounded like the Major's clean yellow Audi, with the shield of the Episcopal Church on its rear window and the Wilson Tennis racket in its white cover on the backseat.

"Well, there they go, the corporate body of Christ, God help Him," said my father as the car purred off into the night. "What is that smell? Oh, I know. Someone has been using somebody's perfume. Why didn't you say more to your mother on the phone?"

"I couldn't think of anything." I turned a page in *The Water Babies*. The new pages had no pictures, not even one of the tiny black and white drawings. Suddenly I felt sick at the prospect of having to go word by word through all these old pages, even though it made my father happy. "I can't just talk when I don't know where someone really is."

"Ah, Margaret, you funny little girl," he said, coming to sit down on my bed. "You say such amazing things. I know what you mean. *Where someone really is* means more than just New Jersey, doesn't it? I just realized: this is the first time you have ever been separated from her. But you know she's carrying you right along with her in her heart. Only I'm afraid she's a little sad because you didn't have much to say to her. We'll do better tomorrow when she calls, won't we?"

"What if she calls while I'm at *school*?"

"But, sweetie, that's what I was telling you. She *knows* when you're in school. Just because she's in New York, or New Jersey, doesn't mean she's not just as much here, in her *love*, with you. She can picture what you're doing. She knows when you're in school and she knows when you get home. She carries you, and what you'll be doing, *with* her. Don't you understand that?"

"I *think* I do, but I want her really here. I may do something different tomorrow that she *won't* know about. Then she won't be able to picture it, will she?"

Daddy laughed and pulled me close. "I prayed God would give me an intelligent child," he said, "and here you are. Those things you do, those different things you're going to do tomorrow and the next day? The things *you* don't even know you're going to do yet? Well, those are the things you have to save up to tell her when she gets back. And *she* will have saved up all her new things, and won't you two have a bunch of things to talk about. I won't be able to get a word in edgewise, probably."

"But you'll have your new things, too."

"That I will," he agreed, though he didn't sound completely convinced of it.

"I think I may be too tired to read any more of this book tonight," I said.

"Funny, I was having the same thought, only I didn't want to disappoint you. After a vestry meeting, I feel cut up into ribbons and blowing every whichaway. All these personalities and their beloved, *conflicting* agendas! Let's see, how far have you got? Oh good, Tom hasn't seen Hartover House yet. I want to read that passage for you myself, it's so funny. But I'll be more entertaining tomorrow when I'm fresh."

He took the book from me and, after tucking me in, switched off the light and knelt down beside my bed and put his hand on top of my head. Then he launched into one of his conversational prayers where he brought in stuff from the day and made it mean other things as well. There was something about God carrying us in His heart and being able to love us and picture us, whether we were in Romulus or New Jersey or New York. He seemed to be attributing my mother's powers to God, or the other way 'round. He asked God to watch over Ruth in her travels, and to "bless and protect me, through Christ Our Lord, Amen."

"Amen," I said, "but you forgot about yourself. Please God, bless Daddy, who forgot to include himself."

"Thank you, my love," said Daddy, getting to his feet. "I needed that. Well, good night."

But instead of leaving the room, he lingered, prowling about. Then suddenly he stepped over to my closet and shut the door.

"Don't do that!" I shot up in bed. "It has to stay open."

"Oh, sorry." My father opened it again.

"No, that's too wide. It has to be halfway."

"Half*way*," he repeated solemnly. "Like this?" From the light in the hallway, I saw him step to one side and make a playful bow in my direction.

"No, a little more than that."

"A little more open, or a little more shut?" Humoring me.

"A little more shut, but not too much," I said patiently. He just didn't know how serious this was.

... Heaviness, gloom, coldness, sullenness, distaste and desultory sloth in work and prayer, joylessness and thanklessness,—do we not know something of the threatenings, at least, of a mood in which these meet? The mood of days on which it seems we cannot get rid of a dull or acrid tone in our voice; when it seems impossible frankly to "rejoice with them that do rejoice," and equally impossible to go freely out in any true unselfish sympathy with sorrow; days when, as one has said, "everything that everybody does seems inopportune and out of good taste;" days when the things that are true and honest, just and pure, lovely and of good report, seem to have lost all loveliness and glow and charm of hue, and look as dismal as a flat country in the drizzling mist of an east wind; days when we might be cynical if we had a little more energy in us; when all enthusiasm and confidence of hope, all sense of a Divine impulse, flags out of our work; when the schemes which we have begun look stale and poor and unattractive as the scenery of an empty stage by daylight; days when there is nothing that we *like* to do—when without anything to complain of, nothing stirs so readily in us as complaint. Oh, if we know anything at all of such a mood as this, let us be careful how we think of it, how we deal with it; for perhaps it may not be far from that "sorrow of the world" which, in those who welcome and invite its presence, "worketh death."

—*The Sorrow of the World,* with an Introductory Essay on Accidie, by Francis Paget, D.D., late Bishop of Oxford, 1912

... Agains this horrible synne of accidie ... ther is a vertu that is cleped fortitudo or strengthe, that is, an affeccioun thurgh which a man despiseth alle noyous thinges ... This vertu hath many species; the first is cleped magnanimite, that is to sayn gret corrage. For certis ther bihoveth gret corrage agains accidie, lest that it swolwe not the soule by the synne of sorwe, or destroye it by wanhope. This vertu makith folk undertake harde and grevous things by her owne wille, willfully and reasonably.

—"The Persones Tale," by Geoffrey Chaucer

IV: STUDIES

"*I*t's just me," said my father's melancholy voice through Mrs. Dunbar's downstairs telephone. "Did I disturb anyone? Am I calling too late?"

He always prefaced his calls with some such qualms, as though he could not imagine himself to be anything but a burden or an interruption. It was only nine, I told him, and Mrs. Dunbar, the lady whose commodious Charlottesville house I shared while attending the university, was in the living room, engrossed in *The Sound of Music* on the VCR her son Buddy had given her for Christmas.

"And what were you doing?" he demanded gloomily. "I probably interrupted your studying."

"I needed an interruption. I was about to go cross-eyed with Chaucer. It's such a hodgepodge, Middle English. It hasn't made up its mind whether it should be French or Latin or Anglo-Saxon."

"How is old Stannard?"

"Courtly and nearsighted as ever. He always asks about you when I go for my honors tutorial. I think he'd kind of like to be invited to Romulus again. Maybe after you're feeling better."

My father sighed. "I enjoyed him, too. I love having a good talk with a medievalist. We had fun that weekend, didn't we? When was it, last spring?"

"No, two springs ago. When I was a sophomore in his Medieval and Renaissance survey course."

"And you did that paper on St. Cuthbert that impressed him so."

"You helped me," I reminded him.

"Not really. We just talked over what you already had."

"You got me all fired up, Daddy. Don't you remember?"

"Hard to imagine me ever firing anybody up," came the doleful reply. Usually I could count on springtime to be my best ally in luring him out from behind the Black Curtain. But the daffodils had been out for several weeks, Easter was two Sundays away, and in mid-May was my graduation. From my landlady's living room came the opening burst of the Mother Superior's "Climb Every Mountain" solo, just before she sends Maria away from the convent to take care of the motherless Von Trapp children. Its juxtaposition with my father's downbeat speech rhythms only fueled my exasperation: as if lives could be uplifted and set on their ideal path in a mere moment, simply by someone bursting into the right song.

"I came across a reference to Chaucer just a few minutes ago," Daddy said. "I've been rereading Bishop Paget on acedia, and he mentions that 'The Parson's Tale' contains one of the most arresting descriptions in literature of the malady. I wish I had a copy of *The Canterbury Tales* handy. I'd look into it."

"I'll check it out tonight," I promised. "If it's anything good, I'll make a photocopy of the pages and get them off to you tomorrow."

"Sweetie, you've got enough to do."

"It's no trouble. The book is open on my desk right now. I'll be happy to, Daddy."

"Well, you're a good girl," he said resignedly, with a heavy sigh.

By "the malady," he of course meant his own: his Black Curtain, his acedia (or accidie, depending on which text he had been reading), his wanhope, his Dark Night of the Soul: he clung to the old names, the ones that still throbbed with religious implications. That he had been rereading his old standby Bishop Paget, I took to be an encouraging sign; it was tantamount, in these most recent years, to his desire for medicine. Since our dear friend and protector Dr. MacGruder had died, no physician had succeeded in getting capsule or tablet down my father's throat if it carried with it any promise of alleviating mental pain. And even from Dr.

MacGruder he had accepted, without fussing, only the nightly sleeping pill when insomnia started to interfere with parish work; *with* fussing, and much grumbling about wanting to be left alone to "tough it out," he had occasionally cashed in a prescription for what our old doctor was careful to proffer as "only a temporary elixir, Walter, for your *blues*, you know," only to find himself disgusted with his own capitulation each time he came face-to-face with the generic or trade name of the antidepressant, typed non-euphemistically on the label. Then, out the bottle would go into the garbage, and guilt for wasting money would be added to Daddy's already heavy burden. "It made me groggy and off-balance," he would complain to Dr. MacGruder. "I can't go reeling around town visiting my parishioners: they'll forgive me my melancholy—they've grown used to it; I sometimes think they get a certain satisfaction from the spectacle; it even brings out attractive touches of self-forgetfulness in them—but if I come lurching and pitching up their front walks like a whiskey priest, that'll be one provocation too many, and I need this job, I've got a child to support and get through college. And besides, Doc, I can't help feeling that if I could just face this thing down, right to the bottom, I will be shown . . . well, what I am *meant* to see."

Well, he *had* supported me; he *had* got me through college. And, more important, I had got *him* through. Although it seemed to me, sometimes eerily, that my childhood had passed away in one long, protracted day, for him my "childhood" must have been a daily rope of duty, something he could cling to, swinging back and forth over his pit of despair these past sixteen years.

Only, what next? Where did we go from here? When I graduated, would he let go at last and drop straight to the bottom? Once there, if the fall didn't kill him, would he be granted his wish of seeing what he was "meant" to see? And if he survived *that*, where did we go from there? In July, he would be sixty; at sixty-five, he would retire. And after we left St. Cuthbert's, what then?

"How is the Paget, this time around?" I asked him over Mrs. Dunbar's phone. By which I meant, how are you? Where exactly are you behind the Black Curtain?

"About the same," said Daddy, with another sigh. "The trouble is, I've marked up this book so, over the years, that it's hard to hear Paget through my own clutter. But I did just sit and look at his picture for a while this evening. That one on the frontispiece? What a homely man he appears to have been. And the strange

way he parted his hair! Yet Father Traherne never mentioned
Bishop Paget being homely. Father Traherne met him while he
was over studying at Oxford, you know. Paget was a busy man at
that time, he was in charge of six hundred parishes, but Father
Traherne said he was one of the most attentive and empathetic
people he had ever met. Speaking of Father Traherne, I had the
awfullest dream last night. When I woke out of it, there were
actual tears on my pillow."

"Do you want to tell me any of it?"

"If you've got a minute, I would like to hear what you make of
it. You have a knack with dreams, like your mother."

"I'll do my best," I said, bracing myself.

"It started off with me going from room to room in the rectory. Only, you know the way with dreams, it was and it wasn't the
rectory. I was looking for something I had mislaid, I don't recall
what. The thing was, as I went from room to room, I was certain
that someone had been in that room just ahead of me. I was
following, but, at the same time, this person was *leading me on*.

"Well, at last I came to my study. The door to it was closed, but
I knew I hadn't closed it. I knew someone must be in there, and
that it was the person who had been going through the house just
ahead of me. I didn't know who or *what* awaited me in there but
I knocked, and this frail, womanly voice called out, 'Come in.' I
thought, oh me, another tedious old lady who expects me to talk
her out of her misery, when I'm the one who needs someone to
talk me out of mine. But when I opened the door and went in, the
room was filled with this amazing light, sort of silvery greenish,
shimmery . . . I don't know . . . otherworldly, but it was also cool and
part of nature, like just after a thunderstorm.

"And there in my chair sat Father Traherne, wearing my old
sweater, the one you keep threatening to throw out. He had what
looked like a small brown parcel on his lap. I was so glad to see
him that the tears started up in my eyes. I went towards him, to
shake his hand, but he waved me back. He said, 'Yes, Walter, it is
I myself,' in a man's voice now, but very stern, reproachful even.
Then he held out the brown parcel and at first I thought it was
some desiccated infant Jesus doll, from an old Christmas pageant.
But, looking closer, I saw that it was a small, dead child, all shriveled and dried up, like a mummy. And Father Traherne said,
'Walter, I want you to help me bury this child.' He said, 'It's just
not seemly to sit here rocking its poor little carcass any longer.' "

My father's voice broke. Maria, in the next room, on Mrs. Dunbar's VCR, launched into a governessy-but-playful little number, to win over the aloof Von Trapp children. Who had, like so many of us, Lost Their Mother.

"Was there any more?" I asked.

"No, that was the whole thing. Isn't that enough?" He was at least trying to be humorous.

"Well, I guess the first thing to find out is, what aspect of it do you think caused the tears on your pillow?"

"Boy, you zero in, just like *she* always did. What made me saddest, though I suppose it ought to have been the dead child, was the way Father Traherne spoke to me. I mean, here he was, risen from the dead and come all the way to see me, and then, after I got over my fear at having some intruder in the house, and my disappointment when I thought it was a morose old lady come for counseling, and I was actually on the threshold of being comforted by my old mentor, to have him suddenly berate me like that . . ."

"But he didn't actually berate you, did he? You said he was *stern.*"

"Reproachful, too," Daddy reminded. "He was not pleased with me about that child."

"Who do you think the child was?"

"I suppose it was probably me. All my shriveled, dried-up possibilities. Even my old mentor, who cared for me more than my own father, had decided it was time to chuck me out. That's why he was wearing my old sweater that you want to put in the garbage. The sweater was a symbol."

"Hey, wait a minute. Who's supposed to be analyzing this dream?" My father could still shock me when he turned the full force of his own intelligence against himself.

"Sorry, honey. Please go on."

The terrible thing was, his analysis made sense. After all, it was his dream; he had produced and directed it all by himself. And what more natural dream for his downcast soul to come up with than this little masterpiece of self-hatred in which he managed to rob himself of his last remaining comforts: the memory of the good man who had believed in him and loved him, the refuge and autonomy of his study, and his favorite sweater that I teased him about. Of course I didn't really want to chuck it in the garbage, my mother had given him that sweater; it was just that during his depressions he wouldn't take it off long enough for anyone to wash it. Also, by association, he had made me into an enemy in the dream: Father Traherne, who wanted to bury the baby, was wearing the sweater that I "wanted to throw away." The beloved old mentor and the loyal daughter had joined forces to trash Walter Gower for not being good enough.

"Tell me more about that light," I said, snatching at the one (possibly) hopeful aspect of the dream.

"What light, honey?"

"That shimmery silver-green light, like after a storm?"

"Oh, that light," he said disparagingly.

"And also, listen, Daddy, what was the first thing Father Traherne said to you in the dream?"

"He said, 'I want you to help me bury this child.' "

"No, *before* that! When you entered the room and started towards him."

"Oh. He said, 'Yes, Walter, it is I myself.' "

"Well?"

"Well, what?"

"The phrasing, Daddy, the phrasing. '*It is I myself.*' "

"Ah. I see what you're getting at. Luke 24. Clever child. At least you know your Gospels; I haven't failed in that department, at any rate. But after the risen Christ said that, he invited the apostles to touch Him. Whereas Father Traherne motioned me to stand back. So the analogy breaks down right there, doesn't it?"

Now it was my turn to sigh disconsolately, and I made sure he could hear it through the phone. My father's joy in negative interpretations was defeating me. What would *she* have done at this point? Shamed him? Teased him out of it? But I could no longer truly hear either her voice rhythms or the words she might actually have used. By now, memories of both were too overlaid with all our retrospective commentaries on her. In fact, at this moment, I was entertaining the unwelcome possibility that it might have been just this chronic and deep-rooted disparagement of himself that had finally convinced her, as he himself was always telling her, that she could do better elsewhere. Nevertheless, *I* was still here and it was still my job to try to save him from himself, even if my style was less potent or amusing than hers would have been.

"I think you are looking a gift horse in the mouth," I said as reproachfully as I could. "And it's just not grateful of you."

"What do you mean?" He sounded genuinely astonished.

"Well, you can cherish your negative analyses all you like," I said, "but couldn't you just allow that maybe Father Traherne was sent to you as the most likely person you would listen to? Maybe he was sent to tell you it's time to bury your *depression*. Maybe he was saying it's not seemly to keep cradling it like a living child. And furthermore"—I dropped my voice for homiletic emphasis— "that *parcel* is coming between you and the healing touch of those who love you. It's keeping you from the living Light."

I stopped while I was ahead. I had learned a few tricks from my father's sermons.

"Do you really think so, Margaret," he finally asked in a pathetically trusting way. "Do you really think it was something I was *sent*?"

"You've said yourself that God needs materials to work with. I mean, you provided Him with the materials. You've been reading Bishop Paget, Father Traherne knew Paget, Father Traherne gave you that book. Oh, and something else I just thought of. Remember that priest who spoke about dreams at the Kanuga Conference we went to, how he said that you should look for aspects of yourself in all the characters in your dream? So you'd be not just yourself going through the rectory looking for something you'd lost, but you'd also be the unknown figure who was leading you on, and you'd be Father Traherne . . . the part of you who wants to bury that old outworn depression so you can partake of the light again, the light after the *storm*. But the way you *responded* to it is the big clue, Daddy. It got through to you, there were tears on your pillow when you woke up. The *feeling* is the proof, Daddy."

"There was certainly feeling," he conceded thoughtfully. "Well, bless you, honey. I didn't mean to ruin your evening. You're not worried about exams are you, with your perfect average?"

"Don't you know people with perfect averages are the ones that worry the most?"

He laughed. "I guess you're right. The way rich people are always worrying about their money. Speaking of rich people, greedy George Gaines has struck again. But I'm not going to bother you with it now."

"*What*, Daddy? Now you've *got* to tell me!"

"Oh, well, Gaines and the town are going after our corner. Where our little Italian Christ hangs."

"But why on earth would Mr. Gaines want our cross?"

"He doesn't want *it* as such. He wants . . . the town wants . . . to widen Macon Street. So that the affluent retirees living in his Sunset Villas condominiums won't have to endure bottlenecks at our corner. They get impatient, idling the engines of their Cadillacs and having to postpone their highballs while being forced to gaze sideways at Our Lord hanging there in his little bed of ivy."

"But, Daddy, they can't take our corner. It belongs to St. Cuthbert's. It's church property."

My father chuckled ominously. "Ernie Pasco says they *can* take it—eventually. You know, he's on the City Council now, and he used to be on the planning board. He's upset about it, but he's a minority of one. They can do it under the rubric of what they call 'an overriding state reason.' "

"But Macon Street is a *city* road, Daddy."

"Well, no, actually it's a county road. I've gotten very knowledgeable about these matters in the last few days, Margaret. 'Overriding state reason' doesn't necessarily mean the state. It just means the governing body concerned. In this case, our City Council. If the planning board decides slicing off our corner is best for the public good, they'll recommend it to the Council and they'll condemn our corner."

"You mean they can just take it? But they have to pay you something, don't they?" I was getting upset.

"Ah, honey, that's why I'm between the Devil and the Deep Blue Sea. If they *take* it away from you, they pay you what they think it's worth. But if we don't put up a fuss and cost him litigation, Gaines is willing to pay us thirty thousand dollars for the corner and the swampland in back. Of course, it's swampland because he *himself* flooded it seven or eight years back, when he was slicing away up there at the mountain. Remember my poor Siberian irises?"

"But the vestry wants to fight this, don't they?"

"Well, I'm ashamed to report, the response has been mixed. Of course the *Major* is furious, she wants to fight for our little outdoor Calvary to stay right where it is. Pasco is emotional and he'll fight, but probably not very effectively. Wirt Winchester is fence-sitting in his gentle nondescript way. Ned Block is abstaining from comment, to see what I'll do. That's his way of tormenting me. If I lose the corner, I'm damned, and if I lose the thirty thousand dollars, I'm equally damned. But the rest of them have made it pretty clear that if we had a thirty-thousand-dollar windfall, we could gussy up our moribund image. We could attract more of the young professionals and the rich oldies who are pouring into the area: people who expect social life and *programs* with their church fare. We could afford to pay a program director, like Jerry Hope has over at St. Matthias. Jerry Hope is so busy these days rushing around to all the activities his program director dreams up that he doesn't even counsel anymore. Since January he's had his own pastoral counselor, a trained psychologist. Father Bonner, I think I've mentioned him. Very much the new mode of 'specialist priest,' Bonner, but I like him. He's adopted me as his sort of mentor. He's determined to pursue a spiritual life and I really admire him for it. So many of these career-track priests can't be bothered because it won't show up anywhere on their résumé."

"Did Gaines really offer thirty thousand dollars?" I wasn't the least bit interested in St. Matthias's new pastoral counselor.

"That's what he told the Council, I have it from Pasco. Gaines wants it settled, he wants the road in. He's still got twenty-five or thirty villas left to sell up there. And the people who've already bought are getting teed off with the bottleneck. Thirty thousand dollars is nothing to a man like him, Margaret."

"Oh, Daddy, this is awful." I felt I should be able to come up with a brilliant suggestion that would save our corner and relieve his mind. But what would it be? The damage had already been done. But why hadn't the planning board looked ahead and seen the problem coming years before?

"The Major thinks we ought to try to get it registered as a historic landmark. The little Christ figure *is* over a hundred years old."

"You should get started on that right away."

"She's at work now trying to get a restraining order from a judge she knows, somebody her son went to school with. Not Charlie the Bishop, but Billy the brain surgeon. And then that would gain us time to look into the historic landmark status. The Major's also got some friend in the legislature who's been instrumental in saving old taverns and restoring mills and things."

"God bless the Major," I said, though I usually reserved the opposite kind of sentiment for her take-charge ways.

"Yes," said Daddy. "She's lady bountiful, but she's also shrewd as an old ward heeler when it comes time to call in her favors. This friend of hers in the legislature she's going to enlist in the cause

... it seems she helped send him through college for a while, when his father was having a bad time. And who knows what she did for the judge."

"Well, I wish she had bought Mr. Gaines a ten-speed tricycle, back when he was a poor little boy," I said.

"That one was worthy of your mother. That was just her brand of comeback. Alas, I fear George Gaines is one of those new honor-free mutants. The idea of human reciprocation is totally lacking in him; just full steam ahead, over everybody else's dead bodies. Over God's dead body, if it comes to that. But let's not give up hope. It may turn out to be a tempest in a teapot. I have faith in the Major, and I've put in a call to the newspaper editor. If we can just stir up some local indignation. Although in my present state, I'm not much of a stirrer-upper."

"Maybe I'll come home this Friday."

"But your Easter break doesn't begin until next week."

"I could come and go back again. It sounds like you need some moral support. Have you started your Palm Sunday sermon yet?"

"I've got the germ of one. To do with expectations. How people can turn against the person they've idolized, if their expectations are thwarted."

"That sounds interesting."

"Well, I don't know. But it's likely that the very people who waved their palm branches most ardently at Jesus were among the same rabble who were screaming 'Crucify him!' a few days later. They were expecting something different from what He had in mind, you see. Oh, if you do come this Friday, maybe you can help me stir up my sluggish brain on another topic. Father Bonner wants me to address a group of people who meet at his house."

"What kind of group?" Waiting for me upstairs were dozens more "eek"s and "I trowe"s of "The Knight's Tale" to plow through. But first I must look up the stuff about acedia in "The Parson's Tale" for Daddy. And also there was dear dependent Mrs. Dunbar who needed *her* fix, and ... oh, bother, if I went home Friday, I would have to break my date with Ben MacGruder and raise up *his* tempest of emotions.

"Father Bonner calls it a study group. They meet at his house twice a month in the evenings and he invites a speaker. It's all very ecumenical, but he likes to organize it around specific topics. None of this rap session stuff, I admire him for that. He's had a rabbi speak to them about the universality of the Joseph story, and some doctor from the state facility over in Staunton to talk about our attitudes towards the mentally ill. My subject is supposed to be on some aspect of the spiritual life. Anything I want, he says; only I've been so low I haven't come up with anything yet."

"When is it?"

"Next Monday evening. I don't like taking on extra things during Holy Week, but I hated to disappoint him. If only I had some *glimmer* of a topic."

I stared into the weak salmon-pink glow of one of Mrs. Dunbar's Victorian glass lamps in its wall sconce. Mrs. Dunbar's entire house swam in pink light; she believed it was flattering to a woman's skin. "What about your sermon on crosses," I suggested.

"On crosses?"

"The one that made Ruth fall in love with you when you preached at her college."

"That was a good long time ago, honey. I could never find those old notes."

"You could get out her letters and look up the first one she wrote to you. Remember? When she was talking about her conference with you? You could reconstruct it from there. That letter had *lots* about the cross sermon in it."

It did not seem unusual for me to be quoting back to my father a sermon he had given at my mother's junior college before I was ever thought of. I had re-created that week so often in my mind that I felt I had been among those St. Mary's girls during the Lenten Retreat of 1964. I had imagined all the scenes that had led to Ruth Beauchamp's subsequent seventeen-page letter to the handsome, diffident priest with the sad baritone voice that throbbed with conviction, after the Retreat was over and he had gone back to Virginia. Daddy had let me read all of the St. Mary's letters. I could go and get the pale green·stack of them out of his bottom desk drawer whenever I liked. What a pity that his letters to her had been lost somewhere between moves, but as he pointed out to me, "You can always reconstruct *my* side, because you've still got me around."

"Maybe I will go hunt out that letter."

"I should be getting to Romulus around three on Friday."

"Well, you come on then, if that's what you want."

*   *   *

As I put back the receiver quietly into its cradle, Mrs. Dunbar, who had uncanny hearing, sang out in her breathless little-girl's voice, "Margaret? Come tell me how your sweet father is!"

I stuck my head around the door. "He's okay. Don't let me interrupt your movie."

"No problem," she chirped, brandishing her remote-control gadget like a wand and eliminating Julie Andrews and her newly won-over charges from the screen. "I dearly love my new toy. Thanks to darling Buddy, I can have an intermission anytime *I* feel like it, and I don't get those tacky commercials. My children are so good to me. Just like you're good to your father. How are his *spirits*? Have you time for a cup of cocoa?"

"They seem a little better, thanks. Don't get up, I'll make it."

"I will so. It was my invitation." We went through this polite ritual every night. "My poor legs need the circulation. But I'll let you make it because yours always tastes better than mine." Gallantly, she stuffed her tiny puffy feet into a pair of malignly pointed snakeskin pumps and teetered ahead of me into the kitchen on their punishing spike heels. If she wanted circulation, she would have done better to keep her swollen feet out of those torture pumps, but Mrs. Dunbar had formalities by which she lived. Every evening I had known her she had come downstairs *dressed* (and that included girdle, stockings, high heels, and braided hairpiece) and she remained that way until she clopped upstairs to bed at night. She had never owned a pair of slacks in her life and still wore hats and gloves when she went out. She kept her stock of calling cards replenished and used them liberally, tucked into the flyleaves of books lent to friends, Scotch-taped to the jar lid of her peach preserves dropped off on someone's porch. During my four years in her house they had awaited me on my pillow on countless occasions: "Mrs. Rupert Chauncey Dunbar," topped with three or four Hershey's Kisses in silver foil, and a note dashed off in her childlike scribble on the back:

> Playing bridge over at Dottie's.
> Don't wait up for me!

> Your Daddy called. So charming! Nothing urgent he said.

Elaine Major had made the match between Mrs. Dunbar and me. I had wanted to commute to the university and live at home.

Other people did it. I wanted to get my education in peace and keep an eye on Daddy. But the way I had put it to him was, we just didn't have thousands of dollars to throw away so that I could share a dormitory room with some oblivious noodle who would sit facing me on her matching bedspread, surrounded by stuffed animals and painting her toenails. I had made him laugh and had all but convinced him when the Major butted in. In her eighties now, she still played tennis (though no longer every day) and was agile as ever when it came to advising people how to live their lives. The Major had just happened to know a "sweet gul" over in Charlottesville, a recently widowed lady knocking around in a big house; she didn't need the money, but would be so glad to have the company of the right kind of young person. It would be, crowed the Major, who considered the matter settled merely because she herself had proposed it, a "puh-fect" arrangement: this way I would not be denied the experience of a "normal college life."

It was her strategic deployment of this ludicrous phrase that won Daddy over. He worried about my having been shortchanged when it came to normality. "I want you to go over there to Charlottesville and live your young life," he had told me, standing beside my packed car on the morning I left. "You've been a good little parent to me, Margaret, but now I'm old enough to manage on my own," he had added gaily.

His gangly black figure with its stoop had perched on the rim of my consciousness all the way to Charlottesville; I never lost sight of him through my rearview mirror. As I drove towards my "normal college life," I kept tracking him back at the rectory. What was he doing right now? Dead-heading the Frikartii asters? Picking up a book to sustain himself? *Which* book? Autumn was the worst time for him, the season in which he began to sink. She had left us in autumn and now I was leaving. I had been insulted by his cavalier command to "live my young life." I had never been young, what made him think I could suddenly start now? But his whimsical image of himself as my child did not offend me. It was, in a sense, true, but it conflicted not at all with my admiration and respect for him. He just needed taking care of. I believed him to be a remarkable man. Despite his sorrow-haunted mode, dogged as he was by his frequent periods of low self-esteem, he nevertheless exemplified that phrase he loved so much in the old liturgy: he *did* offer his self, soul, and body to be a reasonable, holy, and living sacrifice, and people knew it. Even during the periods when his mind felt like molasses and his step was slow and his voice was thick with disbelief that he had anything to offer anybody, people still got sustenance from what he did and said. I had seen it happen and reminded him of it later, when he needed bolstering up.

"I was so depressed, I could hardly speak to Mrs. Stacy, lying there hooked up to all that breathing apparatus," he had confessed to me, after a visit to the hospital when that old lady was dying. "All I could do was just sit there in silence with her for about an hour, holding her hand. I felt like weeping and I'm sure she saw it." "But that may have been the very best thing you could do," I told him; "I mean, how many people do you know who would sit by anyone for an hour, holding their hand? And feel like weeping for them. That was probably the very thing she needed." "Wirt Winchester stammered to me after church that my sermon had touched him; I can't imagine how. I felt dead while I was writing it. I had to fight for every word I put down, and then overcome my disgust after I *had* put it down." "But Mr. Winchester didn't know that, Daddy. He only heard the result, and it wasn't dead at all." My father frequently worried, even during his exuberant times, that he was not good enough for the job, that one day some terrible gaffe in his ministry would come to light and we would be out on the sidewalk. Whereas, the truth was, and anybody but he could see it, he was beloved by many and respected even by his critics. According to the Major, Ned Block had recently remarked languidly to a group of parishioners that though Daddy would never have the *presence* of the late Dr. Hazeltine, you wouldn't find many clergymen today who always remembered to genuflect before the Sacrament as Daddy did, even when he was only opening windows or setting up before a service.

So here I was in Charlottesville, in my fourth year of making cocoa for Mrs. Dunbar, but also worrying about Daddy's nightmares and his upcoming sermons over in Romulus.

My landlady was somewhat like my child, herself. At first her determinedly chipper innocence had exasperated me, until I got to know her better and saw it as a rather brave defense against loneliness and fear of old age. And she was decent and kind. There wasn't a mean bone in her little body. And looking at it another way, she was the nearest experience to a grandmother I would ever have.

Though Mrs. Dunbar never stopped singing their praises, her

two children weren't all that wonderful to her. Although UPS brought several expensive presents a month from her son Buddy—everything from a battery-powered foot-warmer to a bread-making machine—he denied her the present she craved for the most: a spend-the-night visit from his eminent self. He had descended on her only about half a dozen times during my residence there, and always stayed at the Boar's Head Inn with his driver, a handsome young mulatto who waited outside in the car, nodding and jerking to the music on his headphones, while Buddy, a florid-faced executive who walked as if his belt were a notch too tight for comfort, went from room to room in the house with a melting drink in his hand, his fluttery mother following in his wake, checking to see that all the presents he had sent to her were on display and in good working order. Then the driver would whisk him away to the Boar's Head for a late-afternoon workout on the jogging track and a sauna, and he would return at dusk in jacket and tie to take a painstakingly dressed, eternally grateful Mrs. Dunbar out to dinner.

Dee Dee, her divorced daughter, who worked for a firm of decorators in Washington, visited us fairly often. But the object of *her* visits seemed to be to see how many times she could make Mrs. Dunbar cry. As I was considered part of the family, I was included in the discomfiting cocktail hours during which Dee Dee, sipping straight vodka through crushed ice, enumerated between hissing slurps all the ways in which her mother had failed her. Dee Dee spoke in a nasal snarl, from which every tendril of Mrs. Dunbar's billowy Tidewater accent had been cropped. The daughter was a complete contrast to the mother. A long, skinny malcontent with brassy, sliced-at hair, she never wore anything but trousers and, to Mrs. Dunbar's chagrin, frequently dispensed with any sort of support beneath her T-shirts. Though in her early forties, Dee Dee had recently had her teeth fitted with braces. She slumped or flung herself about in aggressively unladylike poses on the sofa, haranguing Mrs. Dunbar, who sat very small and still and upright in her wing chair, her plump stockinged feet allowing themselves the matching ottoman to relieve their edema. Her face would bunch tighter and tighter against Dee Dee's accusations, yet she never missed a stitch in her needlepointing.

"I was the one who had the overbite, but who got the braces? Darling Buddy, of course. I'll tell you one thing, Mother. Buddy may be your beautiful boy, but you'll never get a grandchild out of him, either."

"I wish you wouldn't *foreclose* on yourself like that, Dee Dee. You still might meet someone . . . And Buddy's still having fun. The men in our family marry late. Poppy was almost forty when he married me. Buddy's worked *so* hard to get where he is. Let him play the field a little."

"The field of *what*?" inquired Dee Dee with a nasty smile.

"I don't know what you mean, Dolores," the mother's flutey voice would be a-tremble now. But jab, *plok*, went the thick needle regularly through the cloth, never missing a beat. "I do wish you and your little brother were better friends. Buddy has nothing against *you*."

"Well, why should he?" retorted the daughter complacently, refueling with a hissy slurp of vodka through the splintered ice. "I have nothing against him either. There are just a million other people I happen to like better. But I wish you'd face facts for once in your life."

"What facts do you want me to face, darling?" Mrs. Dunbar would venture tremulously, the baby-blue eyes spilling over. But the needle still went bravely on, jab, *plok*, jab, *plok*, even as the first rounded tear detached itself and embarked on the slope down her bosom.

They would continue on like this until Mrs. Dunbar would be sobbing heartily, almost with a healthy enjoyment. And Dee Dee would glower at her handiwork with a loving fascination. The expression on her face as she watched her mother cry was the nearest I ever saw her come to tenderness.

And then, to my amazement—and some consternation—mother and daughter would make up. Dee Dee, without ever having gone the limit and *told* Mrs. Dunbar what facts needed facing, would untangle her bones from their sofa slouch and stride across the powder-blue carpet to aim an awkward little peck at her mother's wet cheek or the top of her braided hairpiece; then she would amble back to the kitchen to replenish her crushed ice and vodka.

And Mrs. Dunbar, sighing like a child after a hard cry, would proudly hold out for my inspection the needlepoint altar cushion or the pillow for somebody's baby, and smilingly assure me how *good* her daughter's visits were for her. "Dee Dee sharpens my mind. And goodness knows it could use some sharpening. And it does Dee Dee a bunch of good to let off steam."

Was this the way mothers and daughters behaved, then, when their lives had been permitted to ripen together through decades? I imagined myself in the body of a forty-year-old, haranguing Ruth for . . . what? If we had been allowed to grow older together, what faults would I have found with her? It was more probable that she would have found them with me. I couldn't imagine Ruth being old, like Mrs. Dunbar. I couldn't even picture her with gray in her hair. The realization came to me that if Ruth had lived she would have been about Dee Dee's age now. My mind boggled at the thought of having Dee Dee for my mother.

In Mrs. Dunbar's up-to-the-minute kitchen I got out two packets of Weight Watcher's Hot Cocoa Mix and put the kettle on to boil.

"Buddy would be mad we're not using his new microwave," said my landlady. "But you're like me. It tastes better when it's made on the stove."

"We don't know that for sure. We'll give it a chance one of these nights, as soon as I get time to read up on the directions." I took down her favorite mug ("Virginia Is for Lovers," a gift from one of her many friends) and selected one with the U.Va. crest for myself. As I performed the nightly ritual, she climbed on a high stool and, folding her small, beautifully manicured hands on the countertop, proceeded to follow my every movement with the rapture of a child at a magician show.

At times like this, when I was simply going about my business, doing whatever it was that presented itself to be done next (right now, tearing open the packets of cocoa mix and shaking the brown powder into the two mugs without wasting any or spilling it on the counter), a strange sensation sometimes came over me. It was as if another presence were allowing me to become aware of its unwavering attention on my behalf; for it was always there, this larger, luminous, and highly focused consciousness. It registered, ceaselessly, not only what I did and thought and felt, but also *all that I was beyond what I knew.* This "extra-consciousness" was not something that I could summon through my will or through sheer concentration or desire. On the contrary, its preference seemed to be for simple moments, moments of disinterest. And then suddenly I would be aware of it, aware *with* it that everything I did counted, and that the thing I was doing right at this moment was part and parcel of what I was going to become.

But what I was going to "become" in the more immediate sense of after graduation was still unknown to me. Despite the certainty that, unless I failed my exams (and possibly not even then), I would have a Bachelor of Arts degree and a charming, melancholy father who would probably remain a bachelor the rest of his life, I had no idea of what I was going to be doing this time next year. How had I allowed this to happen? The futures of my friends already hung in their closets, chosen professional costumes that they would soon take out and put on. Harriet MacGruder had been accepted at her grandfather's old medical school; she knew that she wanted to specialize in geriatrics. A girl in my American Civ. class would be starting to work the week after graduation at a TV station in Richmond. A boy in the Business School whom I went out with sometimes had told me proudly that he was already planning for his retirement.

"I wonder if Poppy and I *ought* to have named Dee Dee something else," Mrs. Dunbar was musing. She tilted her head rapidly from one side to the other, like a pert, worried sparrow. "Maybe she's right, maybe it *is* something to do with her name that is causing the child's unhappiness. She was going on about that last time she was home, remember, about Dolores meaning sorrows and aches and pains in Spanish. But I told her we had never even thought of the Spanish. It was the name of my favorite great-aunt, and a happier, more contented human being than Aunt Dee you couldn't have found anywhere on this earth. Who were you named after, Margaret?"

"St. Margaret, Queen of Scotland. And St. Margaret's was the name of the church where Daddy served in England." The kettle whistled. I poured the boiling water into the mugs, leaving that crucial inch of space at the top.

Mrs. Dunbar sighed and tilted her head so violently that her braided hairpiece slid sideways. "I do hope Dee Dee was just trying to get a rise out of me when she said that about going to court and having her name changed to Tanya. She was, wasn't she?"

"*Prob*ably." With a teaspoon, I stirred the hot mixture in each mug into an appealing-looking chocolate froth. Now for the culminating splash (actually, two splashes for Mrs. D.), which was, of course, the reason she preferred me to prepare the cocoa.

"Well, I hope so." She was repinning her hairpiece, her eyes cast demurely elsewhere as I took down the bottle of Jamaican rum from the cabinet. "Tanya sounds so Russian. We have no Russian blood. It sounds like, I don't know . . . somebody's big yellow dog. I thought about writing her this week and suggesting Dorothea, or maybe even Daphne. If she *is* serious, at least have it start with a 'D.' That way she won't have to change the monograms on her towels and sheets. Oh my, Margaret, that looks just delicious. I love a warm drink in the evening, even if it's warm weather, don't you?"

She accepted her evening's ration with a touching display of nonchalance. Mrs. Dunbar worried about two things concerning her person: one, that she would get fat and disgust her friends, and two, that she would become one of those women who drank alone and disgust her children. For a five-foot-three lady of sixty-nine, she put up a heroic battle against unwanted flesh; she and I together conducted a relentless market research for the most flavorful, least caloric combinations. As for the booze threat, she had made a simple rule and stuck to it faithfully: she would touch no alcohol unless someone else poured it for her. That way, nobody could ever accuse her of drinking alone, could they?

I pulled up a stool and sat across from her at the counter and listened to her chatter on while simultaneously thinking my own thoughts. So many absent presences hovered about us that Mrs. Dunbar and I together convened quite a large family. There were Buddy and Dee Dee, in fear of whose disapproval and rejection Mrs. Dunbar lived constantly; but balancing them in the benevolent middle distance was Poppy, the late lamented gentleman of this household who, for the twenty-one years he had taught in the Law School, had kept a spare necktie and jacket in every room of this house so he would always look presentable in case a student dropped by. And in my corner was my father and *his* retinue of menaces and models. And there was Ruth, *my* Ruth, what few true-seeming bits I still possessed of her.

"Oh, I can't help it, I know it is selfish of me," Mrs. Dunbar was saying now, her face happily flushed with the spiked cocoa, "but I do wish you were going on to Law School or graduate school here in Charlottesville. We haven't done at all badly together, have we? At first I worried you might be pining for dorm life, but you just fit right in. You've been like a daughter to me, Margaret. And much easier than Dee Dee in a lot of ways, though I don't mean to sound disloyal. If by some chance you *did* decide to go on for a higher degree here, we could turn the upstairs into a whole little apartment for you and I could move downstairs. But, of course, I don't know what your plans are, do I?"

"I'm not sure I do, either."

"You girls today have so many choices. In my day you got married or maybe if you were *real* brave you taught school or became a nurse. Nowadays girls can be jockeys or steelworkers . . . or even priests. Funny! I don't have anything against a female jockey—women have always been good riders—and I don't even mind if some girl sets her heart on a blowtorch and a hard hat, but I just can't go along with women priests."

"Daddy has trouble with it, too."

"I'm like your Daddy. I just can't look *up* to a woman priest. And I never know what to call her. I can't call her 'Father' and I can't call her 'Mother.' So she ends up being just 'you,' or 'Karen' or 'Linda' or somebody. And the vestments never fit women right in front, do they? Goodness, I'd better not talk this way in front of Dee Dee. The next thing I know, she'll be rushing off to enroll in a seminary just to get a rise out of me. She'd come home calling herself Father Tanya, and I'd have to call her that, too, wouldn't I?"

Soon after, I excused myself to go back to *The Canterbury Tales*. We brushed each other's cheeks good night. Mrs. Dunbar's skin was soft and smooth as a baby's: her reward for a lifetime's abstinence from sunbathing and her faithful nightly applications of Dorothy Gray's Cellogen Moisturizing Hormone Cream.

At the landing of Mrs. Dunbar's curved staircase, there was a six-foot, gilt-framed mirror, flanked by the ubiquitous pink lights in their sconces, and you could watch yourself rise into view, head, shoulders, torso, legs, and feet. I sometimes imagined that Ruth was waiting just on the other side of the mirror, watching me as I came into view as a grown woman for the first time. How would I look to her? Would she recognize me from her last view of me as a child? Sometimes I thought she would be pleased with the way I had turned out; other times I suspected she would be disappointed. It depended very much on how I was feeling at the time.

Entering my room, I met with such a density of pure meaninglessness that it knocked the breath out of me. *The Canterbury Tales* lay open on the desk under the reading lamp, exactly as I had left it when I had run downstairs to answer the phone, suspecting it would be Daddy. But I could not drag myself back to the desk. Instead I sank crosswise upon the same bed that had formerly supported the malcontented sighs and thrashings of the girl Dee Dee. This had been her room, and in a funny way I didn't mind the company of her psychic leftovers, especially at times like this. I lay on my stomach, my chin propped on my hands, and stared out the window directly ahead of me. I breathed in and out and waited for the feeling to pass. It always did. Though maybe as I got older it would last longer, and one morning I would awake to find myself behind the Black Curtain like my father. Whatever had brought this one on, the thing itself was at the opposite end of the spectrum from the luminous moment in the kitchen when, in the act of tearing open the packets of cocoa mix, I had felt myself to be part of an intended progression and blessed in the entirety of my endeavors: a feeling my father would attribute to being momentarily in the presence of God. Now I was in the presence of something as suffocating as the other had been exhilarating.

Outside was darkness, but I knew exactly where the branches of the old redbud, about to blossom, would be making their intersecting patterns against the crossbars and mullions of the window. I concentrated on how the tree would appear to me, its intricate, gracefully twisted shape, pregnant with hundreds of buds, when I wakened and looked out at it tomorrow morning. In Dee Dee's time, which was before I was born, the tree would have been much smaller and she would have gazed through the scrim of her ill humors at a different array of branches, if any at all had yet grown as high as the second floor. The miasmas of the young Dee Dee were almost comforting to contemplate when compared to the malign assault of futility that had been waiting for me in her girlhood room. To seethe with unfulfillment, to rage at slights, at least signified the presence of energy and desire. The thing I had walked into just now was the absence of all energy and desire. Nothing at all seemed worth doing. The idea that I could be part of any "intended progression," or the object of any "higher consciousness"'s unwavering attention, struck me now as mere childish fantasy.

What difference would it make to the dips and peaks and plains of the ongoing human landscape whether one undergraduate in the southeastern United States in the late nineteen eighties dragged her resisting body back into the waiting circle of desk

light and forced herself to puzzle out a few more pages of a tale
written six hundred years ago in scarcely recognizable English?
The man who had written it, famous as it was, had perished.
Shakespeare had perished; so had Thomas Jefferson who designed this university; so had the man Jesus, whose brief public
life had given countless people, my father among them, an occu-
pation. All these great ones had exerted themselves and then
perished, and the sun went right on rising and setting according
to schedule without them, and the current crop of living bodies
shuffled through the shopping malls of their lives, coveting and
spending and wasting and always wanting more, the more powerful and greedy among them tearing down whole mountains and
causing landslides and traffic jams because they wanted more,
more, more. What good was it to try to do anything? Christ had
died to prove that His kingdom was not of this world, and the
world had taken Him at His word. The majority of people dab-
bled in His kingdom when it suited them, but beware if His kingdom got in the way of the world, or even slowed down a few
Cadillacs en route to their condominiums.

It was enough to send anyone who really thought about it
behind the Black Curtain. Perhaps it could drive you mad, if you
were the type inclined to madness. In my second year at the
university, I had briefly known a girl who went mad, Lindsey
Hayes, a bright, flighty girl who couldn't seem to get herself together. Pieces of her flew in all directions, her hair, her fringed
silk scarf she wore around her shoulders like a gypsy shawl. Papers were always flying out of her notebook and fluttering to the
ground, and once she lost the rubber heel of a loafer as we were
walking past the Jefferson Rotunda. But I found her interesting to
talk to, though she did almost all the talking. She talked mostly
about her parents, she was obsessed by them. Lindsey had been an
only child until she was twelve, then her parents had divorced to
marry other people. Both new couples had children, and Lindsey,
who shuttled back and forth between their residences, told one
hilarious domestic story after another, stories in which she was
always the fall guy or the misunderstood outcast.

Then she disappeared from campus. I only learned what had
happened later from her roommate, with whom I took a class the
following year. Lindsey had gone over to the medical center to get
something to help her sleep. But once there, she told the doctor
on duty that she was pregnant and had AIDS and her insomnia

was because she couldn't make up her mind whether to have an abortion or bring a doomed baby into an already doomed world. She spoke so convincingly that the doctor was drawn into her dilemma and went off to schedule a test to see if she really did have AIDS. When he came back to the examining room she was raving: she had started a war between Russia and the United States, there was a price on her head. She became violent and had to be restrained. Her parents were summoned. She refused to acknowledge either of them. She berated the doctors and nurses, using much imaginative profanity, for not seeing what was obvious: that these two people were only posing as her parents; the real parents, who had disowned her, had hired these professional actors to impersonate them, and as soon as these impostors had sprung her from the hospital, they had orders to cut her up in small portions and bury her piecemeal around the Jefferson Rotunda.

The roommate told me that Lindsey was in a private clinic on Long Island. She had been diagnosed as schizophrenic and would have to be on some drug for the rest of her life. The drug made her gain weight and caused involuntary twitches, but otherwise she would lead a pretty normal life. The parents had been in touch with the roommate and she said both of them seemed to be genuine, caring people, not at all the way Lindsey used to describe them in those amazing stories. When Lindsey got out of the clinic, she was going to live with her mother's new family and be a day student at the local college. Lindsey was very grateful to both her parents, the roommate had said.

I didn't like to think of Lindsey as a heavy, twitching convalescent, drugged into "gratefulness." At least I wasn't mad or recovering from madness. It probably wasn't in me to go mad, certainly not on Lindsey's grand scale. And yet her madness had accomplished what may have been her deepest wish: to get "Russia" and "The United States" back together again, to force them to come flying to her side.

I felt stricken with the very opposite of grandiosity in my low moments. I felt pregnant with nothing, angry at nothing: simply impotent and without desire. Not only was there nothing I believed I could do, or wanted to do; I couldn't even think of anything to want.

What *should* I want? Ah, that saving *should*. I wanted what was best for Daddy, didn't I? That was the only answer that could reach me during these flattened states. But it was better than no answer at all. Perhaps my father was the key to my sanity. As long as he was around to worry about, I couldn't afford the vacation of going mad.

Even now, the thought of his need was pushing me up from Dee Dee's bed, a feat I had despaired of only a few moments ago, and propelling me towards my assignment. Not the assignment his phone call had interrupted, but the assignment that had come out of his call for help. No more of "The Knight's Tale" for tonight, sorry, Professor Stannard, I won't be shining for you, tomorrow; on to the back of the book, to "The Parson's Tale," to see what balm for my father's chronic wound I could extract from the text that Bishop Paget himself had found value in.

And as I laid claim to word after tendrilly old word concerning this ancient sin of "ydelnes and unlust" and what Chaucer, speaking through the holy and diligent parson, offered as antidotes to it, the angel of meaning returned to me in Dee Dee's girlhood room and showed me how all human experience, from the beginning of time, formed a connecting *living* membrane.

What I was reading now, written six hundred years ago, for instance: wasn't it describing, under the rubric *Remedium Contra Accidiam*, exactly what I was in the process of doing: willfully undertaking a task at hand in order to enfeeble wanhope and enforce the soul? I felt close to the writer of these archaic words that, once deciphered and absorbed in their full meaning, became welcome friends the next time around, became, more and more, their irreplaceable selves. Unlust! What a word we lost when we lost that one. I must remember to remind Daddy of this good word. Chaucer too must have known periods of depression; otherwise, how could he describe it so accurately from the inside out?

Daddy was probably in his study now, reading through the St. Mary's letters from my mother, revisiting favorite old passages before he settled down to the first one, the seventeen-pager that had been my assignment to him.

"*I don't want to be trivial,*" Ruth Beauchamp had written to my father from her junior college after the Lenten Retreat. That was *her* rubric, though it was buried midway in the sheaf of mint-green, deckle-edged sheets, filled to the margins on both sides with her open, trustingly readable slant. She had obviously felt safe in unburdening her soul to this man of God who had made such a deep impression on her and her classmates. Or perhaps, made bold by the belief that she would never see him again, she gave in to a rare extravagance of autobiography and confession: how she had never known her father (he had been killed in World War II a few weeks before she was born) and how she could never get over the feeling that her mother and older sister held her responsible somehow for turning their fortunes around. She had grown up embarrassed by her mother's and sister's social-climbing lies, yet she was constantly on guard with outsiders, worried that she herself might slip up and tell the "wrong truth" about something and bring her mother's and sister's carefully constructed pretensions crashing down on all their heads. She had deferred to her sister Connie, who was "the more striking sister," everyone said, and a thorough extrovert. It was not until high school that she learned that her big sister was not universally respected, and this totally shocking revelation had come to her in the worst of all places, while she was inside a toilet stall.

I heard some of the older girls talking and laughing about Con. They had come in after me and didn't know I was inside the stall. One of them called her "Connie Roundheels," and another girl asked what that meant, and the first one said, "You don't know? My brother says that's a girl with heels so round that the least push will put her on her back." I lifted my feet up out of sight and stopped breathing till they'd all left. I was mortified and angry! Not at my sister so much as at these girls for saying it. And suddenly I knew it was true, though I didn't want to know. If I admitted it, I would be on their side against her. I felt so divided. And from then on, I could never write natural letters to Con—she was off at college then. I mean I kept writing to her, but the letters just weren't the same anymore. I was holding myself back from her.

Next year, things got better, because I was sent to boarding school on account of Mother wasn't well. (I don't mean things got better because my mother was sick! I mean because it gave me a chance to start over, with new people.) Nobody at Miss Beale's knew Connie, or had a brother who had. At Miss Beale's I did real well in my studies and came out of myself for the first time. I was popular. I even acted in plays. Nobody was more surprised than I.

I'm not telling you this in order to brag, but what you said in that sermon about the ways we can choose to carry our crosses really hit home. You said we can just flat out deny we have a cross, or we can refuse to carry it, or we can *whine* and blame everybody else. Or, you said, we can just accept it and carry it in such a way that it builds our strength and serves as an example for others. You said we could incorporate it into our style and make that style a fine and splendid thing that can have meaning for ourselves and others. Well, I was on my way to doing something like that at Miss Beale's. It was like my home life was my golf handicap or something like that, but I had managed to transcend it by going on in spite of it. But down here at St. Mary's, I seem to have regressed. That's what I was trying to tell you—so inadequately!—during our conference in the Green Parlor. But I think I ended up just making you see me as a girl in grief over losing her mother. I may have even used Mother's death to get your attention. I wanted you to see me differently from the other girls, more serious . . . *I don't want to be trivial.* I want my life to add up, to mean something, only I don't know what yet. The truth is, which I haven't told anyone but you, my mother's death (after her miserable last years—she was an alcoholic) and my sister Connie's marriage to a man who thinks she's wonderful and can take care of her *have taken away my cross.* I can't believe I am actually writing this, but now I don't have to worry about upsetting Mother every time I forget to back her up in some fabricated story about our family. And Connie is safe now from those girls in the bathroom.

What I really wanted to ask you during our half hour in the Green Parlor was, what does a person do when her cross is taken *away* and the absence of it takes all the starch out of her? I wanted so very much to ask you did *you* have a cross and, if so, what was it, but I didn't dare. You sat there and looked so calm and *sure,* you seemed to be right in the center of what you had chosen to do with your life, and willing to share that certainty with anyone who asked for it, but I couldn't rise to it. I ended up saying everything trivial and went back to my room hating myself. You are too much for me. I wish I could be more like you. Yet meeting you gave me a little hope for myself, otherwise I wouldn't have had the courage to write this letter . . .

"And what did you do when you got the letter?" With this question I would lead my father, always willingly, into the retelling of his favorite story, the one I could never hear enough times; as I grew older, the mysteries deepened every time he told it.

"Well at first," he would always begin, "I didn't know who it was from. The last name of the envelope said . . ." And as he spelled out the letters, "B-e-a-u-c-h-a-m-p," I would call up the fascinating image of my father standing beside a mailbox in Falls Church, Virginia, where he was serving as assistant rector, and frowning down on the letters that spelled his future wife's maiden name, only he didn't recognize it because it looked different from the way it had sounded.

"In our conference, she had introduced herself as Ruth 'Beecham,' you see; whereas the name on the envelope read to me like the French pronunciation, 'Beau-champ.' I ought to have remembered from my time in England how these Continental spellings get Anglicized, but I didn't. Of course, as soon as I opened the letter and began to read, I knew exactly who it was. She was not a girl you are likely to forget. Only I never expected a girl like that would write to me."

"Why not?"

"Oh, the big age difference, for a start. She was barely twenty and here I was already an old bachelor of thirty-six. And also she was not the type of girl, well . . . that I would expect to notice me."

"What do you mean? What type are you *talking* about, Daddy?" These smug allusions to his own unworthiness angered me on his behalf, but I liked him to describe this type of girl.

"Well, the type who always went for Stewart Hampton Dudley. Back in Chattanooga, he was always bringing home these cool, streamlined creatures who fit right into the Dudleys' manorial surroundings. These girls had come from homes like that themselves. Whereas, I was the poor boy who lived in the carriage house. These girls didn't light up for me, because they knew from the start I could never move in their league; oh, I got invited to their coming-out balls, because I was a pretty fair dancer, and I knew I was supposed to keep cutting in on them, but it was Stewart Hampton who always brought them—and took them home."

"But she *wasn't* one of those girls . . . she said as much in her

letter. You know: how her mother and sister were always pretending to be more than they were socially."

"Well, but she had their movements and that streamlined quality. She had that same reserve. And also . . . well, she was just so
vividly lovely."

"So? Why shouldn't you be entitled to a vividly lovely wife?"

"But I wasn't thinking of her in that way, you see. Not in our
conference. I know she claims in her letter to have been somewhat
intimidated by me, but that didn't come across at all in our conversation, not at all. She sat there so lovely and poised and cool, so
completely in command of her person. Of all the girls who had
signed up for those half-hour slots with me in that Green Parlor
with those wretchedly uncomfortable sofas and chairs, she seemed
to need the least from me. Why, as we talked, I remember the
thought crossing my mind that this girl had only signed up for
this chat as a sort of gracious hostess gesture, out of respect to the
visiting preacher. To make me feel welcome, you know."

"But that's not *at all* the way it comes across in her letter! I
don't see how the two of you could have had such totally different
impressions of what was going on in that room. *She* said that *you*
were the calm, sure one, sitting in the center of your life. *She* said
you were too much for *her*."

"Ah, well," my father would concede with a sweetly baffled
look, as though he were faced afresh with this miracle of Ruth's
appreciation of him before he had ever aspired to her. "She did
tell me how grim her mother's last months had been. It's not a
pretty death, liver cirrhosis. But even while we were talking about
that, she was in perfect command of herself. She seemed to want
to talk about it, though I had no sense of her wanting or needing
anything other than a sympathetic listener. I thought she spoke
very well, there was certainly nothing trivial in what she said. She
didn't seem particularly broken up, only somewhat taken aback at
finding herself without any parent. She wasn't downcast or particularly solemn. In fact she said several funny things; you know,
those sharp little observations about people she was so adept at.
She was a respectful, amusing, lovely girl, but when she got up to
go and we shook hands, I thought that was that. She was something to appreciate, like a cool mountain stream or a rainbow, and
then you go on with your life. But her letter changed everything.
When it came, I knew I wanted her, if she'd have me."

"But you didn't propose right away."

"Nope, not right away. Didn't want to frighten her off. No, I lured her slowly, with passages from the mystics and the metaphysical poets. That sort of ambiguity is great in letters, when you're trying not to scare somebody off. She can always think you meant religion, when all the time you're talking about love. I couldn't go *too* slowly, though, because she was due to leave St. Mary's in June, and then the plan was for her to go and live with her married sister in Georgia and do her last two years of college down there. Naturally, I discussed it with my rector. Being a happily married father of three, he was all for it. He even pushed me some. 'Get on your charger, Walter, and go back down there and claim her,' he said, 'before she goes off to live with that Babylonian sister.' And so I did."

> . . . Who can deny mee power, and liberty
> to stretch mine arms, and mine own Crosse
> to be?

> —John Donne, "The Crosse"

V: CROSSES

And eight years and six months after she had written him the letter that won his heart, she drove away from us both in a silver Mustang with a houseguest who, as she had explained to me the night before, "was just so different from anyone I'd ever known": a woman whom she admired because "she came right out and said what she really wanted, what she really thought." A woman who "wasn't afraid to change her mind."

She let us down slowly, Ruth did. First it was going to be "about a week or ten days," as Daddy had told Ned Block. When she wasn't back by Harvest Festival, people began to question Daddy. Some did it coyly, like Miriam Stacy, who snuffled up to him after the Festival service, and inquired in her affected humble tone whether he didn't agree that this year's decorations "understandably" lacked a certain flair.

"I don't know what you classify as flair, Miriam," said Daddy, cutting right through her insinuation, "but I think the children's corn sheaves around the baptismal font are charming, and Clara Jane Buford certainly went beyond the call of duty with her window decorations this year. And Elaine Major's altarpiece of gourds and fruits was pretty spectacular, most people thought. If you mean by your 'understandably' that we missed my wife's artistic contribution, I would have to agree, but she's having herself a well-earned vacation."

The Major was more outspoken. "Tell that gul of yours to come home, Fah-thah. Four weeks is too long, and you know it."

"Ruth is having her first taste of independence," Daddy told the Major. "She went straight from junior college to me to motherhood. This time in New York with her friend will do her good. As a matter of fact, Ruth told me in our last phone conversation that she is helping Madelyn with the sketches for a new stage set."

"Too many guls today are confusing independence with irresponsibility, Fah-thah. And New York is the *wuhld's* stage set for these discontented women's libbers."

"Oh, I'm not worried about Ruth," Daddy replied loyally.

When our Bishop came in November to do confirmations, and Daddy explained that Ruth was staying on in New York for a bit to help an old school friend design sets for a new play, the Bishop, whose own wife was a reclusive sort who never accompanied him to any function she could get out of, merely nodded sympathetically and said, "You must miss her cooking." We took him out for lunch and dinner, and he slept under the new bedspread in the guest room that my mother, wanting to please Madelyn, had told Daddy she needed to buy for the episcopal visit, even though my father had reminded her that the Bishop was color-blind.

When she wasn't back in time to make the Advent wreath, or to be present when its candles were lit, even the indulgent Mac-Gruders saw fit to break their tactful silence; each came separately to Daddy. Dr. MacGruder mentioned an old colleague practicing in New York who was always happy to see him, and offered to "run up there" and "look in on" Ruth, who was staying with Madelyn Farley. Mrs. MacGruder (Daddy told me this when I was older) gently inquired whether there was any problem with the marriage and confessed that during the first years of her own marriage, she had undergone a "panic" and run away briefly to her mother, leaving the doctor and her small son to fend for themselves. But then she had come back to her senses and returned to find them getting along happily without her. "That was such a blow to my pride," Mrs. MacGruder told Daddy "that I never dared leave them again. I was afraid they might not miss me and I'd find myself out of a job!"

Daddy thanked Dr. MacGruder but resisted his friend's offer to run up to New York City and look in on Ruth.

"I can understand her not wanting to leave until those sketches are done," Daddy said. "She's gotten involved in this production

of Madelyn's. Of course she misses us, but I told her to go on and
see it through."

To Mrs. MacGruder, he said, "Ruth will never find herself out
of a job here. But we've all got to realize my wife is a creative
person, and if that means she has to go off by herself now and
then and paint pictures or design sets, or even act in plays, then
I'm all for it. Isn't that better than slapping the lid on and having
the energy erupt in other ways? The former rector's wife over at
St. Matthias, I understand, indulged in semiannual shoplifting
excursions. And the wife of my old mentor in Chattanooga spent
most of her afternoons lying in bed sipping sweet sherry out of
the bottle, though I must say when she had to get herself together
for a social occasion, nobody could fault her. I would far rather
Ruth go on *creative* excursions and come home to us invigorated
and refreshed than fester here at home in some of the many ways
clergyman's wives have been known to fester."

As Christmas drew nearer, there were long conversations between them on the telephone. "Of *course* you do . . ." I would hear
Daddy declare benevolently in the "encourager's" voice that he
had adopted for these long-distance sessions. "That sounds exciting . . . you both must be thrilled. Give her my best, will you?
Margaret and I are doing fine. We're holding the fort. We made
a mushroom omelet last night that wasn't half-bad. That's because
Margaret reminded me that *you* always sauté the mushrooms first.
I would have just dumped them in raw on top of the eggs and
then wouldn't we have had a mess."

My conversations with her were more problematic. As much as
I needed for her to come back, I dreaded our sessions on the
phone; I grew to hate them.

When my mother and I had been together, I was often aware
that she spoke to me on more than one level. As far back as I
could remember, I had been able to receive these latent communications of hers. The tone of them, I mean. They came across in
another medium than words. On the day that we were buying my
dresses for school, for instance, and she had said about the one
with the cat's-head buttons, "Well, just remember, I'm not doing it
for you. I've got enough buttons of my own to worry about," I had
picked up the ominous rumble of dissatisfaction. I knew, though
I couldn't have articulated it then, that she was not just talking
about buttons on her dresses, and it had cast a cloud over my
victory of getting her to buy the dress. The cloud had grown

larger in her subsequent exchange with the saleslady who talked her into giving herself the present of the cucumber lotion, telling her that a clean, fresh scent would give her a new lease on life. "You've made yourself a sale," my mother had said. Simple enough words. But they flashed forth from her with a surprising determination that made me distrust that lotion; it was as if she were going to use it *against* us in some way.

And now in our strained long-distance dialogues, I was picking up things I couldn't stand. The tone behind her words, however lovingly those words came across on the surface, was heavy with a demand I couldn't supply. It was as if, just below her voiced concerns for my welfare and her assurances of love, she were asking for my forgiveness or my *permission* for something. Each time I failed her, she grew colder and more impatient with me. And, conversely, my replies grew more sullen and resentful and monosyllabic; or, perhaps worse, full of a pretend-cheerfulness and self-reliance that was meant to wound her. Often I would feel she was trying to convey, in her subtextual way, information I didn't want to hear, messages she had tried to send Daddy, but that he either could not or would not hear. These attempts on her part enraged me the most. My throat would close up and something would start expanding inside my chest.

"Margaret, you would love the Christmas decorations in New York. Tiffany's especially, but of course Tiffany's is famous for its Christmas windows."

I hated the way she spoke about "New York," as though it were some dazzling new friend who interested her more than her old ones.

"There are little animated dolls . . . in every one of the windows they are doing something different. And there is a toy store, F.A.O. Schwartz, that you wouldn't believe. I was in there yesterday, trying to imagine which things would attract you the most. Oh, Margaret, I can just see your stern little face. Where are you? At which phone?"

"The one in the hall."

"Then you're not very comfortable, are you? There's no place to sit down."

"I like standing up."

"Oh, *well*, then." Her voice cooled by several degrees, but she grimly carried on with this little wooing session of hers. "Madelyn thought you might be ready for a paint set. Not a child's paint set, but a really good one, from an art store."

I didn't answer. *Madelyn* thought! What business did Madelyn have deciding what I "was ready for"?

"We're not communicating very well today, are we? I wish you could be here with me, right now. I would *make* you communicate. I would gnaw at your neck and make you giggle. If *that* failed, I would blow bubbles on your stomach."

Why should she tease and torment me like this? If she wanted to gnaw on me and blow bubbles, why was she wandering around a New York toy store with Madelyn?

"You know, Margaret, you and I will always be connected. You are my little girl. Nothing, nothing in the world, can break that connection, whatever happens. Do you understand what I am saying, Margaret?"

During the first few weeks she had left, I had broken down in several of our phone talks and asked her when she was coming back. At first she said soon, but she needed to sort some things out. When I asked her what things, she said things about herself. Then, in a later conversation, she said she wished I were a little older. Then, she said, we could talk about all this better. I did not ask what "all this" meant, because it made me feel funny, as if I might throw up or something. After that, I stopped asking her when she was coming back, although I believed—as far as I can remember, I *think* I believed—that she would come back. But it would not be the same. I think I knew that, too. She would come back bringing things that were new and strange, things inside her that were not about us.

When her Christmas presents started arriving, I opened none of them ahead of time, though always, in Christmases past, I had begged and been allowed to, just to keep the pressure down on my impatience.

"This one looks interesting," Daddy tempted me, picking one of Ruth's presents out of the pile and pretending to X-ray it with his eyes through the smart, unfamiliar wrapping paper. In past Christmases we had used the same papers over and over. It was for economy's sake, of course, but there was a satisfying feeling of continuity in the thought of brand-new, unknown gifts already making themselves at home in last year's papers whose stripes and designs recalled to you the predecessor gifts that had lain inside these same wrappings.

"Want to take a peek at what's inside?" Daddy said. "They have some very fancy stores up there in New York."

"No, I'd rather wait," I said. I didn't want *him* to get started on F.A.O. Schwartz.

"It's up to you, sweetie."

After a number of my refusals, he picked up a small, thin, square package with his name on it. "Maybe I'll open this one of mine," he said tentatively, as if needing my permission. "I'm really curious to know what it is."

Anyone could guess that it was a book, a paperback book, but as she had sent him only this one package I felt it would be mean of me to refuse.

"Go ahead, then." I shrugged, the accommodating little parent. Yet I felt a pang as he undid the brown and gold paper with extreme care, as if already saving the paper for what would be wrapped in it next year. Unbeknownst to him, he might be undoing a sort of magic bargain I had made when these presents started to arrive. If I opened none of them, if I left them lying untouched in their sinister out-of-town papers, *right up until Christmas morning . . . until Christmas AFTER MASS*, then she would have to come back. Even as late as Christmas morning, she could realize it was only right that this day should be spent with us. She could get on an airplane and be home in time for Christmas dinner. We were having it at the MacGruders, so she wouldn't even have to cook this year.

Would my father's inability to hold out until Christmas morning, Christmas morning *after Mass*, cancel my bargain? I hadn't included him in the terms when I made it, but would it still count?

"Oh, the metaphysical poets," said Daddy. With the appearance of satisfaction, he held up an orange paperback with a design of tiny black leaves on the cover. "This was very thoughtful of her." He riffled through the pages. "And she's inscribed it. 'To Walter, with love, from Ruth. Christmas, 1972.' " He held out the page so I could see her writing for myself.

"Does it have any pictures?"

It didn't, but he seemed happy enough with its thin paper and small print. It didn't seem much of a present, if you were only going to send one present. Perhaps she was planning to send a bigger one later.

"Nice selection of Donne . . . oh, and George Herbert's 'Easter Wings.' And printed in the proper style, too . . . look, Margaret, the poem's shaped like wings when you hold it sideways, see? Oh, and Henry Vaughan's 'The Night.' Listen, honey, listen to this:

> "God's silent, searching flight:
> When my Lord's head is fill'd with dew, and all
> His locks are wet with the clear drops of night;
>   His still, soft call;
> His knocking time; the soul's dumb watch,
> When spirits their fair kindred catch . . .

"Now, *that's* the real thing, my Margaret! 'When spirits their fair kindred catch'! This is a lovely little edition, really."

He flipped back and forth through the book some more, as though searching for something behind the closely printed poems. Some further message from her, perhaps? In years to come I would often see my father pick up this book and riffle through the pages with this same look of furtive hope. And though he was a lavish annotator of all his books, this little orange paperback was never to receive a single bracket or checkmark or star from his restless pencil. Had he been afraid that any mark of his might obscure one of hers if it ever did decide to float up out of the long baffling silence and manifest itself, like a small overlooked miracle, next to some revealing line or passage that would explain her actions to us at last?

Early Christmas morning she phoned us. She and Madelyn were spending Christmas in the Catskills, at the house of Madelyn's father, the landscape painter. "Old Farley is an old curmudgeon," Ruth told Daddy proudly. I was listening on the extension. "He snaps at Maddy and me and won't come to meals on time, but he's a genuine artist. I see where she gets her talent from." Then Ruth asked me if I liked my presents. When I didn't say anything, Daddy answered for me: "She hasn't opened them yet. I think she's been having a little game with herself. You know, hoping you'd be back in time to open them with her."

"I was not!" I cried out, humiliated. How had he known this? And, even if he had guessed it, why had he betrayed me?

There was a shocked silence from them both. Then Daddy said, "I think what she meant, Ruth, was that . . ."

"Let me be the judge of what my daughter says to me, Walter.

Oh, dear. This call is not turning out to be very Christmasy, is it? I'm *sorry*, it's all my fault. I just thought I'd call early, before you all went over for Mass. Margaret, I hope you like your presents when you do get around to opening them."

"There are some things under the tree for you, Ruth," said Daddy. "We should probably have sent them on up to New York, but Margaret felt strongly about wanting them right where they are."

My mother made an exasperated choking sound.

"We'll be having dinner with the MacGruders," Daddy went on congenially, as if Ruth might have been just down the street from us and he was only filling her in on the activities ahead for all of us.

"I will miss a good dinner," she said. She seemed to have regained her composure. "I am very partial to Nan's leek pies. She was always going to give me the recipe."

"Well," said Daddy, with maddening good humor, "you can get it from her when you come back. How about if we give you a call this evening, and Margaret can tell you about her presents?"

"We may be on the road back to the city by then. We're going to feed old Farley his Christmas turkey—I'm roasting it because nobody around here can cook— and then we'll probably try to beat the traffic back. Maddy's production starts in three weeks and there's still so much to be done. How about if I call you two tomorrow? That would be better, I think."

I was unable to eat at the MacGruders. I was afraid if I tried I would throw up, so I asked if I could lie down in Harriet's room. Mrs. MacGruder came up and bathed my forehead with a wet washcloth onto which she had sprinkled a few drops of some lemon-smelling cologne. She told me as she sat beside me on the bed that her own mother had bathed *her* forehead in this same cologne when Mrs. MacGruder had been a little girl and had felt under the weather.

"Oh, by the way," I said, when I felt better, "My mother said this morning that she's very partial to your leek pie. She hopes you will give her the recipe."

"Well, bless your heart," said Mrs. MacGruder.

Later Dr. MacGruder came in with his medical bag and listened to my chest with his stethoscope. "Now, I'm going to prescribe something," he said, very officially. "I'm going to prescribe a little, just a very little, of Nana's plum pudding with rum sauce."

It was after dark when Daddy and I got back to the rectory. Madelyn's mean old father would have eaten Ruth's turkey by now, and she and "Maddy" would be beating the traffic back to the city. Daddy helped me undress, though I could do it by myself, and he went across to my bathroom with me and stood in the doorway while I washed my face and brushed my teeth. I was feeling queasy again.

"We've got to remember that Ruth never knew her father," he said with sudden enlightenment, as if the thought had just descended upon him out of the air. "That's probably why she was taken with Madelyn's old father. And something else: your mother was not proud of her big sister."

"What does that have to do with anything?" I demanded crossly. I was sorry I had let Dr. MacGruder "prescribe" the plum pudding with rum sauce. It hulked inside my chest like an unfriendly animal, sending up its treacly breaths into my freshly toothbrushed mouth.

"Well, don't you see," said Daddy, "Madelyn is the big sister she can be proud of."

"But they aren't sisters," I protested irritably. "Why *wasn't* she proud of her big sister?" I had yet to meet my aunt Con, and this was, of course, years before I read about "Connie Roundheels" in the first St. Mary's letter.

"Your aunt Connie wasn't always . . ." Daddy hesitated, searching for words. "She wasn't always comme il faut."

"What does *that* mean?"

"It's French for behaving decently and properly. From what I gather, Connie was somewhat lax in that department."

I wished the pudding animal would come up or go down. I really didn't care about Aunt Connie, and although normally it pleased me to be the precocious student of Daddy's theories about people and learn new words from him, this French phrase simply added its burdensome volume to the one already bulking inside my chest.

"You're not looking so hot," said Daddy.

"I don't feel so hot."

"What shall we do?"

"It's that pudding. I'd like it to come up, but I don't think it's going to. It just sits there."

"Hmm. Maybe if you were to lie real still, it would settle down. Would it help if I rubbed your back?"

"That might be a good idea."

I got into my bed and he rubbed my back. After a while the pudding animal relaxed and gave me more room to breathe. But the bothersome comme il faut continued to shift and circle about: was it comme il faut to cook a Christmas turkey for a rude old man way off somewhere, when you had a husband and daughter and presents waiting for you under your own tree at home? Was *that* behaving decently and properly?

"I know what," said Daddy, sensing my restiveness. "I'll stay here beside you awhile and read to you. I'll read some poetry from the book your mother sent me."

He fetched his new treasure and settled into a reading position on top of the covers. Even when he sat upright against my headboard, his legs in their black trousers still stretched to the end of my bed. "Let's see, let's see," he muttered happily, turning the pages. "Donne is my oracle and George Herbert is my soul-mate, but this poem by Vaughan is incomparable . . . just incomparable." I snuggled down in the bedclothes and closed my eyes. I didn't care what he read; I only wanted his voice to roll over my burdensome thoughts and bring this weary day to its end. He read "The Night," the poem he had plucked phrases from on the day he opened his present.

His voice gathered momentum as it traveled through the stanzas. The poem washed over me like a night sea, rolling and retreating, striking in my brain a phosphorescent spark of meaning, leaving behind the occasional spume that formed itself into a picture, not necessarily connected to the poem. When he came to the part about "When spirits their fair kindred catch," I thought about the witch who lived in my closet.

> Were all my loud, evil days
> Calm and unhaunted as is thy dark tent,

My father's voice longingly caressed the lines, especially the ones about darkness and the night. It was as if he wished he could get there. It was where God lived, in all his deep and dazzling darkness, the poem said.

Her Christmas presents to me were a Fair Isle sweater with blues and browns ("my" colors), a pleated tartan skirt that went with it, a pair of red suede gloves lined with rabbit fur, and two books, *A Child's Book of Saints* and *Madeline Goes to Paris.* There may have been a couple more things, but I don't recall them. I have no memory at all of opening any of the presents.

I wore the sweater and skirt, but I couldn't wear the gloves: they were a size too small already. I still have *A Child's Book of Saints,* with its beautiful illustrations, but it always did puzzle me why my mother should have chosen it, since it is the fictitious and more sensational of the St. Margarets who is portrayed in the book. The one who was swallowed by the dragon, not the Scottish Queen after whom I was named. Or hadn't she noticed the difference? I hated the *Madeline* book as soon as I spelled out the first word of the title. My mother's friend spelled her name differently, but I didn't know that then, and even if I had, I could feel her influence behind the choice of that present. It was Madelyn, through my mother, trying to be chummy again.

Was Ruth letting us down slowly, or was she letting herself down slowly, as week followed week and the altar frontals and my father's chasubles changed from green to purple to white for Christmas, then back to green and then to purple, for Epiphany and Lent, on to red for Passion Week and white for Easter, and then back to the long green of Sundays after Pentecost, broken up by the occasional red for a martyr's day?

Maybe letting herself down slowly was the wrong figure of speech; getting her courage *up*, was that closer to what she was doing? At what point did she know she was not coming back, or was there ever such a point? My father held fast to his belief that she would have returned to us had she lived. The way my father saw it was that he had taken her away from her girlhood too soon, and this "vacation" from us was her sort of Junior Year Abroad, which she was entitled to. And he himself had put her up to it, he always reminded people. He took full responsibility for her going away. Not that he expected her to stay away for a full liturgical year, from green back to green so to speak, but if that was what she needed to restore herself, well then, that was fine with him. If she had needed longer, that would have been all right with him, too. Only the accident had intervened.

But weren't accidents God's will, too, I asked when I got older. No, maintained Daddy, God's will was that we should have the freedom to choose; otherwise we would just be His puppets. Unfortunately, in the process of our choosing, we sometimes ran into accidents.

In the process of our choosings . . .

What *was* my mother choosing during her time away from us? Was she choosing between ways of life, or was she choosing between us and Madelyn? The latter supposition led to a stickier question, which my father categorically squashed whenever the rumor reached him that anyone had been insinuating it. He squashed it head-on with Miriam, of whom he was not afraid, simply accosted her late on one Altar Guild afternoon when she was off in a corner by herself, polishing the brass candlesticks in sanctimonious contentment.

"My wife is not a lesbian, Miriam. At the risk of shocking your maidenly virtue, I have to assure you that, as her husband, I can assert this with full confidence."

"Oh, I never used *that* word," protested Miriam.

"No, of course you didn't," said Daddy. "*I* used it, it's *my* word, for which I take full responsibility, and let us hope it clears the air around here of vain babblings before they increase into more ungodliness. Now, *those* words, in case you're interested, Miriam, are from Timothy II. If you haven't yet chosen the text for your evening's devotional reading, you might look into Timothy II."

But Ned Block's "vain babblings," when they reached Daddy, were much more hurtful, not only because Daddy drew back from initiating any confrontation that might serve to bolster Ned's old argument that Walter Gower wasn't gentlemanly enough to be Rector of St. Cuthbert's, but also because Ned's innuendoes cast unpleasant aspersions on my father's late mother as well as his wife. It was Ned Block's understanding, via "mutual acquaintances" in Chattanooga, that the friendship between Gene Gower and her patron Mrs. Dudley had been quite close indeed, some said even closer than Mrs. Dudley's relationship with *Mr.* Dudley. Interesting, wasn't it, how a man might choose for a wife the same kind of woman as his mother had been?

"My poor mother," said Daddy when this inspired bit of poison arrived on our doorstep via our ever-producing grapevine, "she would surely turn over in her grave if she could hear such wicked slander. And Mrs. Dudley, too. I wonder if Mr. Dudley is still alive. I have a good mind to write down there and find out. But no, he was never really himself after Stuart Hampton got killed in

Korea, and, besides, to the best of my knowledge you can't sue somebody for slander on behalf of the dead. And it would only make more strife for us here. But Mamma didn't deserve this. Neither did Mrs. Dudley, who was pure generosity itself. She and my mother had been friends ever since first grade. And then they married into vastly different spheres and couldn't see each other on the same social basis anymore. It was hard, but Mother understood. John Gower worked in Mr. Dudley's foundry, so, as much as she might have wanted to, Mrs. Dudley couldn't have my mother to her teas and parties. But then when my father drank himself to death . . . now *there's* a parallel I might go along with, Ned Block: my father and my wife's mother both killed themselves with alcohol . . . the Dudleys lost no time is asking Mamma and me to live in their carriage house. Mr. Dudley liked and admired Mamma every bit as much as Mrs. Dudley. And Mamma and Mrs. Dudley went back to being best friends . . . they had so much to catch up on after all the intervening years . . . and Mamma *liked* doing their gardens and taking care of Mrs. Dudley's little notes and things . . . there was no question of anybody being anybody's *servant,* either."

"You have to face the possibility," Harriet MacGruder said to me, when we were in our late teens and discussing the mystery of my mother, "that they were not getting along. When Ben and I were down in Recife that boring *boring* year with my parents, they said terrible things to each other, things I wouldn't repeat. They hated each other so much they didn't sleep in the same room, only they didn't want the servants to know, so my father made up his bed in the bathtub of their suite. But *we* knew, and probably the servants did too because when my mother needed to go to the bathroom, which was often with all her drinking, she used Ben's and mine, which was at the other end of the hall."

"I know my father and mother slept in the same bed right up until the day she left," I told Harriet. "And I never heard them say terrible things to each other."

"Oh well but," continued Harriet undaunted, "it could have been a more subtle thing, like walking pneumonia. With walking pneumonia a person doesn't even know they've *got* pneumonia. That's why it's called that. They just keep walking around, feeling worse and worse. But then when it hits, it really hits. The convalescence can take *ages.*"

I mulled over this latest theory of Harriet's: Ruth extended vacation from us as her convalescence from her marriage. But after a convalescence, nobody chose to return to the sickness that *caused* the convalescence. So, in that case, she would never have returned to us.

"I don't really think it was like that," I told Harriet.

I'd thought about it all as much from Ruth's point of view as from my own. I came to *prefer* thinking of it from her side. That way, I could remain cool and dispassionate. Besides, it interested me to imagine it, like a story, from her point of view. It didn't even hurt.

I saw her year away from us as a journey of some kind. I mean an inner journey. At the beginning she may have taken it a day at a time. She probably, those first weeks (months?), felt strange to herself. Didn't know what to call what was happening to her; didn't want to call it *anything*. I just need a little outing, that's all; I need a new lease on life, as that lady who sold me the cucumber lotion promised it would give me. I just need a little vacation from *them*, much as I love them both; I need a vacation from wifehood, motherhood, from being "The Rector's Wife." I need to *collect* myself. Surely there must be a central character in me behind all these parts; surely there is more than being cheerleader to a melancholiac, swimming teacher, and afternoon entertainer of a child. I am those things, but where is the person behind it, the person who wants . . . what? I once wanted . . . what *was* it I wanted? Surely I must have wanted *something*.

She must have been leery about facing the world as a woman traveling with another woman, whatever her feelings may have been about Madelyn Farley. Everything in my mother's background would have revolted at such a comedown. The biases of her nineteen fifties' southern girlhood would have tugged mercilessly at her for even considering such a choice: leave the genial Rector of St. Cuthbert's and your six-year-old daughter, your own flesh and blood; leave your respected place in the community, your window seat that you designed yourself, with the yellow slipcovers banded in orange, your best dress in the closet, your honeymoon watercolors of the two Charleston churches on your dining-room wall . . . leave all this to become the companion of a mocking, charmless woman, to help her with her sketches and cook her father's Christmas turkey and fetch the fatal chocolate bars with orange filling to share with her. Crazy, that's what you'd

have to be, in the eyes of most people, if you were Ruth Gower
and you made such a choice. Either crazy or depraved.

Her own sense of the appropriate must have caused her some
squirming at the beginning. She must have had moments of in-
comprehension and remorse; there must have been mornings
when she woke up in Madelyn's New York apartment and was
baffled, perhaps ashamed. Asked herself, "What am I doing
here?" And then she would call us, and Daddy would say cheerfully, "That's fine . . . isn't that wonderful . . . you do what you
have to do, honey, Margaret and I are holding the fort." And I
would get on and dole myself out in grudging monosyllables or
withhold myself altogether, and she would hang up from these
calls and feel disoriented. Was everything all right, then? Nobody
was complaining, were they? Nobody seemed to reproach her or
even desperately miss her. Well, perhaps she'd go on with this
strange odyssey a bit longer, see where it led, see if maybe she
would wake one morning and look into the mirror and come
face-to-face with the central character, who would be able to tell
her what she'd been wanting all along.

I guess what I wished I knew was, had that morning ever
come? Did she ever get the satisfaction of looking into the mirror
and saying, "At last!"

"I just would like to know," I said to Harriet, "whether she felt
she was living the life she had to before the accident. They said it
was instantaneous, but if there *was* a split second when her life
flashed before her, well I hope she didn't die thinking the whole
thing had been a mistake."

"She undoubtedly thought of you," Harriet assured me with
her habitual supreme confidence. "*You* weren't a mistake."

"Well, but maybe I was. I mean, from her point of view, I may
have been."

"If you ask me, Margaret, you overdo the empathy thing. It's
not healthy. What about *your* point of view?"

"But we were talking about hers. You just said she undoubtedly thought of me. That I wasn't a mistake. And then *I* was
saying simply that I may have been a mistake in her overall destiny."

"You confuse me with your semantics," said Harriet. "I'm just
the straight science type. But why not just get on with your *own*
overall destiny?"

"I'm trying! But how can you finish with being a daughter when you don't know who your mother really was?"

"You never *will* finish being a daughter," replied practical Harriet. "You will be one when you're ninety and so will I. Not a day goes by over at our house that Nana doesn't say something about *her* mother. Every time she presoaks her underwear, Nana says, 'Mammy would be so pleased if she saw me doing this just the way she did.' But meanwhile, *you've* got to live, too, Margaret. You think about *them* entirely too much. I'm going to tell you something about yourself I bet you don't know."

"What?" (That keen mixture of dread and thrill when your best friend threatens to reveal you to yourself.)

"Okay. Do you know what you do, nine times out of ten, when we get together and I ask you how you are?"

"No, what?"

"You start talking about your father. His depression. His garden. His sermon. His memories of the seminary or that dead priest whose bed he still sleeps in. His memories of England. What some old gossip said to him. You talk about *his* problems, what *he's* reading. You never start off with how *you* are."

"But that *is* how I am," I told her, disappointed by her revelation. "I mean, those are the things foremost in my life."

"That's exactly what I'm saying. And it's not healthy."

"What do you call 'healthy'? Making a big drama out of my little ups and downs?"

"Yep," said Harriet complacently. "When you get to Nana's age, or your father's, you can start laying on the empathy. It's attractive for older people to show interest in others. But now . . . well, watch out that it doesn't become a form of escape."

"From *what*?"

"Oh, you know," said Harriet. "Your deep, dark self."

When Daddy flew to England to bring back my mother's body, he saw a great deal of Madelyn, of course. Everything had to be done *through* her. It was Madelyn who picked him up from Heathrow in a rented car. It was Madelyn who took him to the hospital morgue. It was Madelyn who drove him along the road into which my mother had turned, driving on the wrong side.

If Daddy had ever gotten to realize his dream of going to England with Ruth and showing her all his favorite spots, they would have had to drive on this very road in order for him to have

taken her on his old rounds. They would have had to use this road
to get to the church where he served; or to drive past the house of
the old widow who had rented him rooms. ("I had assumed I
would have my evening meals with the old lady, but she sent my
dinners up on a tray and ate in the dining room by herself. At first
I thought it was because a curate was too lowly for her, but, no, as
it turned out, she thought *I* was too exalted!")

He would also have driven my mother along this road to reach
the ruins of the ancient hilltop chapel, to which he had bicycled on
many an afternoon, taking a sandwich and a book to read. They
would have parked the car and hiked to the top of the hill that
had been a sacred place long before it had become a Christian
shrine. ("The local people claimed the present chapel had been
built on the site of a former pagan temple to the goddess of the
river that flowed just below. Your mother would have liked that.
Oh, I had splendid afternoons on that hill. The bacon sandwiches
. . . nobody can make bacon sandwiches like the English. And the
first summer I was there, I discovered an old edition of *Kilvert's
Diary* in a secondhand bookshop. I was so delighted by the parallels: one hiking young clergyman sitting on top of a sacred hill
reading the diary of another hiking young clergyman from Victorian times.")

He would have driven my mother back and forth along this
road to get to the other roads that led to the homes of his former
parishioners who were always inviting him to tea and pressing
gifts on him. ("I was given everything from a sack of goose
feathers—to make myself a pillow!—to jars of homemade black-
currant wine—sour but potent, especially when you're too poor to
afford anything better. Oh, they lavished their bounty upon me,
whatever their bounty *was*. A curate can do no wrong, you see,
because he has no power. And curates come and go, like beloved
or eccentric nephews, on their way to somewhere else, whereas
the rector stays and stays. *Paterfamilias, semper eadem.* My rector
was a particularly dour fellow anyway. He just didn't like people;
sometimes when he was supposed to be greeting his congregation
after the service, he'd suddenly turn his back. And he hated talking on the telephone and going to the hospital. He did give excellent sermons, only nobody listened because they didn't like him.
And he could mend and embroider. He had taught himself to sew
so that he wouldn't have to endure the parish ladies fussing over
him. He started off by mending his vestments, then he bought a

machine and made some curtains for the rectory, and by the time I met him he was deep into crewel embroidery. He would copy medieval figures and emblems from the stained-glass windows of churches. It relaxed him, he said.")

Daddy claimed his two years in England had been the happiest time in his single life. Everything appeared to him rinsed and shining. All the corners of his days were filled in, as they are when someone has found the work that best suits his disposition. Each small household chore of the church not only made perfect sense in itself ("Keeping the little stone stoup filled with holy water, for instance . . ."), but reverberated with correspondences and significances. ("You see, if you don't put enough in, then somebody won't get some: and it's likely to be just the person who is most in need of it, who will read an omen, or reproach, when his fingers hit that dry bottom. On the other hand, if you fill it up too high, the water sits there, week after week until the sides of the stoup get slimy, and you simply have to wait it out. And I loved blessing the water beforehand. Still do. 'I adjure thee, O creature of salt' . . . 'I adjure thee, O creature of water . . .': it just seemed such a privilege, being able to put on the stole and exorcise the salt and the water . . . and then sprinkling the salt over the water in the form of a cross. Every time I did it, I thought of myself as being part of a chain that went right back to Elisha. You remember, when he healed the waters and restored the barren land, demonstrating to the people that *he* was now a bona fide link in the chain, anointed by God, through His prophet Elijah, with the power of repairing misfortune.")

What were my father's thoughts about his anointed power of repairing misfortune when, instead of driving his bride along the familiar English road, proudly pointing out to her the sites where he as a priest had first known the experience of grace, he found himself being driven along this same road, which was now the site of his wife's violent death, by the person who had taken her away from him?

After my father returned from his second trip to England, such a lamentable contrast to his first, my initial interest was on the fatal road itself. What had it looked like, the scene of my mother's last conscious moments? Were there any traces left by her on that road by the time he got there? I wasn't after something ghoulish, I just wanted . . . I don't know what I wanted, really . . . more of something out of a melodrama: a note begun desperately in the half second before death and later found lodged miraculously in the high grass after the wreckage had been towed away, a consoling memento he was saving up for me until I was old enough to truly appreciate it: "Tell Margaret that . . ." Then later on, I simply wanted to hear the road itself described. ("A typical English back road, sweetie. Flowers in the ditches . . . it was the height of summer . . . some fairly old plane trees growing along the sides. The driver of the truck slammed into one of those trees, broke it in half, trying to avoid her . . . he was in hospital for multiple fractures . . . I thought of going to see him, but I just wasn't up to it, by the time I had finished with everything else.")

Until my junior year in high school, after Professor LaFarge brought the news of Madelyn Farley's *Pas de Dieux* back to us from one of his New York theater trips, Daddy had never elaborated much on those hours spent in the forced company of my mother's friend as she chauffeured him around on his sad errands. "It was trying for both of us," he would say forbearingly. Though once when I was about fourteen I do remember him indulging in a brief philippic against Madelyn's insensitiveness, against the way she had gone on about those two Cadbury chocolate bars with the orange filling that my mother had been bringing back when she had the accident, and how she and Madelyn had been going to curl up and watch some Pinter play on the telly together and —this was the detail that aggrieved him—how, according to Madelyn, whenever the two of them watched television, Ruth always secretly held back a few squares of her chocolate bar until Madelyn had finished her own, and then insisted that Madelyn take the extra ones as well, making Madelyn a little gift of them. "I did not appreciate her heavyhanded offering of these cozy domestic rituals at such a time," Daddy had said. "It just was not sportsmanlike of her." But then, characteristically, he had gone on to add, "Not that she was trying to be hurtful, I don't think. It was the kind of callousness that comes from a lack of consideration, a virtue she was probably not taught to value very highly by those bohemian parents of hers."

Professor LaFarge's disgrace had fallen on him overnight. He had been arrested in the act of "making overtures" to a young man in the men's room out at the Mall. The youth, who actually had approached *him* first, as they shared the liquid soap dispenser, turned out to be a policeman in leather and denim—and even a gold earring impaling the correct earlobe—hired by the Mall. But nonetheless, the Professor had reached for the bait and the Mall owners swooped to claim him as their example: there had been too many complaints about that men's room, and it was hurting business. Which, as Daddy remarked, was the *really* unforgivable sin that Trevor LaFarge had to pay for.

Shortly after this, Professor LaFarge "did the gracious thing," and took early retirement.

"For the first time in thirty years I am going to have my coffee and croissant in bed in the mornings," the Professor announced to my father in his mock-weary voice. "I am going to reread Homer and Proust in the originals: how many people can still do *that,* anymore? And now, whenever the mood strikes me, I can get in my car and drive to New York and indulge my passion for the theater. This travesty staged by our worthy merchants may turn out to be a blessing in disguise, Walter. If that winsome young gendarme hadn't pranced up to me in his leather leggings, I might well have gone on sleepwalking through my eight sections of Freshman Illiteracy until I dropped."

The Professor also resigned from the vestry, yet continued each Sunday to attend church and take communion. He looked and behaved the same as ever; if you were a stranger to St. Cuthbert's, you would never guess this blasé bald gentleman with his gray-and-white striped beard and rumpled seersuckers, dreamily plodding to the altar rail in his squishy-sounding yellow Wallabees, or thoughtfully munching his donut at coffee hour, oblivious to the steady snowfall of powdered sugar down the length of his necktie, was in disgrace. He was his same old mock-weary self. It was the other members of the congregation who acted different, either going out of their way to be too cordial to the Professor, as if it had just become public knowledge that he had a fatal disease, or else darting him prurient little side glances as he passed. St. Cuthbert's two champion disparagers each held forth in their characteristic styles.

"I remember how LaFarge went around lobbying us all to death several years back for a St. Cuthbert's boys' choir," Ned Block murmured languidly. "I suppose it's a good thing he didn't get it."

Miriam Stacy sidled up to Daddy at the first coffee hour after the disgrace. On that occasion Professor LaFarge had availed himself of the sacrament but forgone the donuts and socializing afterwards in the crypt. "I was frankly surprised to see you-know-who at the communion rail today," Miriam coyly confided to my father.

Daddy gave her a strange look, as if he were surprised to see *her*. "He'd better be there," he told her curtly. "We need him."

"I beg your pardon?" inquired the puzzled spinster.

"I said we *need* him," Daddy repeated rather loudly so that he was sure of being overheard. "I say we're lucky to have him. This church has to have a *few* sinners, Miriam. 'I am not come to call the righteous . . .' You-know-Who said *that*. And He might have added, 'I am not come to call the self-righteous, either.' "

After his resignation from the college, Professor LaFarge made a regular third at our dining table every Friday, unless he was indulging his passion for theater up in New York. Daddy had always been stimulated by the Yale Ph.D.'s conversation and a little in awe of Trevor's patrician background (the LaFarges, he told me, numbered themselves among the FFV's), but now Daddy seemed aggressively determined to make people say, just as the Pharisees said of you-know-Whom: "This man receives sinners and eats with them." "Eats with them every Friday night," our Pharisees could have added.

"Well, it's Friday night again," I recall Harriet remarking as she dropped me off after school in her grandmother's cast-off green Mercedes, which still made its terrible racket but ran perfectly well; Harriet had inherited it on her sixteenth birthday and had repainted it a saucy canary-yellow. "Isn't Friday charity night for your dad's pet pederast?"

"Yes, tonight's his night."

"Does he talk about it, or what?" Harriet wanted to know.

"In some way it hasn't really touched him. He calls himself 'the penitent,' you know the mocking way he talks, but he's not at all contrite. Last week he brought Daddy some scholarly book that's just been published that proves that the early Church was full of people like himself. There were bishops . . . even canonized saints. There's even this one picture of some fourteenth-century German carving of Christ and St. John holding hands. John is laying his head against Christ's shoulder and Christ has his other hand on the apostle's shoulder. It's very sweet. Daddy's reading the book now; he says it's very thought-provoking."

"Hmm. I'll bet," said Harriet.

"Daddy actually enjoys the Professor's company more now than when he was just a vestryman and an FFV," I said. "Daddy finds him more interesting because when a person loses face, Daddy says, and survives it with the aplomb Professor LaFarge has, he gains a sort of power over himself most people never know. It's a power that comes from not having to worry about placating society anymore."

"I'd just as soon do without that sort of power," said Harriet. "Wouldn't you?" From behind the steering wheel, she swiveled to pin me with her yellow predator eyes. On her driver's license their color was listed as "hazel," but they were the beady yellow-amber eyes of a cat or a hawk. When they fastened on you, they wouldn't let you off. Harriet's eyes were major tools of *her* power. She used them, in partnership with her crisp, frankly opinionated way of expressing herself, to make you tell the truth or agree with her, whichever happened to be her aim at the time. She had been my best friend long enough for me to know what was expected of me on this occasion. She wanted my assurance that I had no plans to desert her and the conventional world in which she moved so smoothly for another Romance with the Outsider. Harriet had never quite gotten over my Chloe Niles apostasy, which had begun in first grade and blossomed into a near-total rejection of Harriet during our tenth summer, when I preferred to hang out with Chloe in her aunt's closet, spying on an unsuspecting couple through a hole, rather than sunbathe with Harriet on the dock out at the MacGruders' lake, listening to her portable radio.

But convention itself had vindicated Harriet in the end and returned me with undivided heart to her camp when, at the beginning of our sixth-grade year, Chloe's father and new wife had suddenly showed up in Romulus to collect "their daughter." The new wife was "an heiress," as Chloe's aunt, Mrs. Radford, lost no time in telling everyone, and could not have children of her own. Mr. and the new Mrs. Niles packed up Chloe and whisked her away to West Palm Beach, and when she returned several summers later to visit her aunt, the old Chloe was nowhere to be found. In place of the low-spoken little loner whom I had spent many hours trying to fathom was a jewelry-clanking little mannikin of consumerism with three shades of hair and pink iridescent eye shadow. In a shrill, fakey voice she assailed me with the advantages of her new life. It was like listening to someone recite from a Spiegel catalogue. When she had exhausted the topic of her assets, she did lower her voice in order to speak of her aunt in a coarse, derisive manner. Ashamed of myself because Chloe's aunt had always been kind to me, I joined in by telling Chloe of my mother's old imitation of Mrs. Radford. The new Chloe shrieked wildly at my performance, though it was nowhere near as good as Ruth's had been. But when I was finished, Chloe had cocked her head at me and inquired in her pert, affected voice, and with the condescension of someone totally unfamiliar to outsiderhood, if it had been "hard" for me to grow up knowing everybody said my mother had left my father for a dyke.

No harder than it was for you to grow up knowing everybody said your mother killed herself with another man in your father's garage, I wanted to fling back. But I was my father's daughter. "Why no," I said. "Why should it bother me, when my father and I know it wasn't the case? And besides, 'everyone' *isn't* saying it. Only the people who aren't our friends."

It was worse than if Chloe, *my* Chloe, had died. If she had died, then I could have remembered her as she was. Henceforth, however, I valued my tried-and-true Harriet all the more. Harriet might be conventional, but her conventionalism was in the classic, not the crass mode.

So now when she tilted up her short neck and pinned me with her yellow predator eyes, I made certain that she understood that my fealty lay with her rather than with Professor LaFarge and any powers he might have gained via his sangfroid acceptance of his new outsiderhood.

"It's just that he entertains Daddy," I said.

It was on a Friday night following one of his theater-going binges in New York that Professor LaFarge brought us the program and clippings about Madelyn's *Pas de Dieux,* the first of her "theater-collages without words," which were to make her name and distress and obsess my father so.

The Professor always arrived at the rectory bearing some small gift—a loaf of warm bread he had just baked; a jar of French marrons glacés that we would later have over our ice cream—and an old manila file folder that contained whatever items of interest he had saved up for us during the week. Daddy came to refer to this grimy folder as our tutorial. "Well, Trevor," he would say, greeting the Professor at the door, "what have you got for our tutorial this evening?" And the Professor, handing over his little gift-crock, or warm package, would slyly hug his folder closer to himself.

"Patience, Walter, patience," he would scold in his mock-weary way. "Don't you want to save *anything* for later?"

The "tutorials," which were doled out to us after dessert, when we were having coffee in the living room, consisted mainly of things clipped from the many magazines to which the Professor subscribed or from the Sunday *New York Times,* which he received by mail every Tuesday and went through from beginning to end with his paper scissors poised for the plunge. His two main focuses (or "*foci*" as he would have insisted on saying—I once heard him take Daddy to task for saying "opuses" instead of "opera") were religion and the arts; and since in his opinion both of them were going to Hell in a handbasket, his clippings usually reported the latest damning evidence. As my father to a large extent shared the Professor's low opinion of the contemporary scene, these sessions provided enjoyment for them both. The grubby folder might contain an article from the Professor's favorite right-wing Catholic magazine (" 'Just Say NO' to Altar Girls") or it might harbor a gushing review by a misguided critic of a recent musical or theatrical hoax posing as art up in New York. But however slight the provocation, it would get the two of them going on the overthrow of traditions everywhere, the severing of manners from their meanings, which led of course to the alarming decline of manners themselves, which in turn contributed to the atrophy of the human soul. But however pessimistically the two of them waxed, by the end of these Friday evenings the circulation of my father's mind, especially when he was downcast, would have been stimulated noticeably and he would go to bed in almost cheerful spirits. And the ostracized Professor would go home wrapped in the gratifying cotton-wool of our hospitality, which would get him through another week of his solitary musings and clippings.

On the evening the Professor brought Madelyn back into the rectory, however, he broke precedent by handing over his folder to my father as soon as he had crossed our threshold.

"Well, Walter, I wonder what you are going to make of this. I only got back from New York last night, or I would have called you. Then this morning I thought no, it can wait until I see you. Here, Margaret, oat-bran and carrot bread." He entrusted to my arms a warm, awkwardly shaped bundle. "It's from a new recipe in *Prevention*. Supposed to zap cholesterol, but tasty as well, I hope."

"My cholesterol probably needs zapping. Thank you, Trevor," said Daddy, curiously opening the folder. One of the several newspaper clippings slithered out and floated towards the doormat, but Daddy snatched it up. "Oh," he said, holding it out straight ahead of him to read through his trifocals. "Oh, well my goodness."

"Yes *indeed*, my goodness," drawled Trevor LaFarge. "I thought you would find it interesting."

"What?" I asked.

"It seems your mother's friend Madelyn Farley has put on some sort of sensational play up in New York," Daddy said, continuing to read the clipping.

"Theater-collage," the Professor interjected. "Or, no, wait, 'collage-*theater*.' That's her description, I believe."

"And you saw it, Trevor, did you?" asked Daddy, frowning at the clipping.

"Oh, yes. When I saw the title of the thing in the ad, my curiosity was roused. Pas de *Dieux*? I thought. If it isn't a misprint of Pas de *Deux*, can someone really follow through on such an ambitious pun? Of course, with today's level of illiteracy, I wasn't sure they even knew it *was* a pun. Then when I saw it was being performed at St. Clement's Church, I decided I had to go and see for myself what these 'Steps of God' were all about. Would it be some kind of holy ballet? A morality pageant? I had no great hopes, but one keeps hoping for a happy surprise."

"It certainly doesn't sound like a morality pageant from this report," said Daddy.

"Can I see?" I had been trying to read over his shoulder but not succeeding because, though I was full grown now, his shoulder was still higher than the top of my head.

He handed it over to me abstractedly and plucked another out of the folder for himself. "An Evening with Madelyn Farley's Provocative Theology," the headline of my clipping read.

"Yes, it's her, all right, though you can't see much for that hat," Daddy said. He showed me a small news photo of Madelyn Farley in a wide-brimmed black hat.

"I didn't make the connection until I was sitting in St. Clement's, reading my program," said Professor LaFarge." 'Could that be *Walter's* Madelyn Farley?' I said to myself. But when I read her program note, all doubts were removed."

"Hardly 'my' Madelyn Farley," said Daddy bitterly. "What was in the program note, Trevor?"

"See for yourself." The Professor waved towards the folder. "It's right in there."

Daddy found the program from the folder. There was a pen and ink drawing on the front, of a priest in a chasuble with his arms outstretched; his back was to you and he was standing in a sort of farm cart. The Y-shaped orphreys on the back of his chasuble were filled in with little figures who at first looked as if they were crawling all over one another, but, upon closer inspection, turned out to be in various stages and positions of coitus.

"Oh," said Daddy, after reading inside the program for a minute. "Why, she's written about my goose feathers. And a lot more, too."

"I must admit they created a rather striking effect," the Professor told him, "when, in the last 'Death of God' sequence, those goose feathers began pouring of the priest's mouth. The priest figure, you see, was supposed to *be* God, in all three of the sequences, only his vestments get seedier as history progresses. The first sequence was the Garden of Eden. Only, Adam and Eve were monkeys. The dancers who did the monkeys were rather wonderful. Then God comes in on this chariot, pulled by four angels in black feathers, and He surveys the scene and picks out the monkey He likes best, a female monkey, of course—the dancers wore flesh-colored body stockings and monkey heads—and the angels drag her back to the cart and God has relations with her under His white cope. Then there's a birth scene, but I'll spare you the details. The offspring are twins. Still with monkey faces, but *less* monkeyish. One kills the other and there's some clash-of-opposites music—the score was electronic."

"Cain and Abel, I suppose," murmured Daddy.

"Undoubtedly. Then, Part *Two* was the Annunciation. There was this young girl of about *twelve,* wearing a blue cloak, sitting on a bench in a garden, quietly reading a book. When here comes God again in another chariot, pulled by four angels dressed as praetorian guards this time. He beckons to the girl, but she won't budge. The guards have to go and grab her. They pass her around among themselves and do various choreographic things with her cloak until she changes character completely, throws off the cloak and does this Salome-type dance, and then they carry her over their heads, she's quite willing now, in her body stocking to God."

"Ah," said Daddy, with a grimace.

"Part *Three*, if you want me to go on with this, opens in a ballroom, where half a dozen young couples are waltzing. Then the music grows discordant and they all fall out of step. They dance in opposition to one another, or go off and writhe solo. This one girl, in a fifties strapless net gown, gets bored and wanders off by herself outside. It's all spooky and cobwebby and misty, and she finally stumbles on two hoodlums, or pimps, take your pick, with very small, atrophied wings sticking out of their leather jackets. They're guarding a broken-down old farm cart that has a black curtain suspended from four poles around its wagon part. There's an inhuman grating noise coming from behind the curtain. It sounds as if some machine is dying a horrible death. But she's intrigued, she wants to see what's behind the black curtain. The hoodlums, or pimps, make a halfhearted attempt to stop her, but then each gets sidetracked by his own onanistic pleasure . . ."

"And this all took place in a church?" asked Daddy. "A consecrated church?"

"Oh, yes," said the Professor breezily. "But they often do avant-garde things there."

"Avant-garde is one thing," said Daddy, sighing. "Well, *does* she find out what's behind the black curtain?" He gave me a morose, oblique look. Nobody outside the family knew that Daddy called his depression the Black Curtain.

"Oh, it was God again," the Professor continued, "but rendered into pretty terrible shape by the intervening centuries. And actually all the young woman in the strapless evening gown has to do is just *reach* for the black curtain . . . it springs open to her desire, so to speak. And there *He* was, languishing in a heap in his old cobwebby vestments, a sort of priestly Miss Havisham, uttering the awful mechanical sound. In the *Village Voice* interview, Madelyn Farley tells how she achieved the sound: it's a battery-powered pencil sharpener, amplified. The interview's in there, too. Then they do *their* pas de deux; the young woman in the strapless gown undresses God; she takes off the shabby vestments one by one, and, I must say, Walter, that part was totally authentic. Madelyn Farley certainly did her research, she knows what priests wear, and what goes underneath what: cope, chasuble, cincture, stole, alb—there was quite a little dance with her holding the ends of the cincture, leading Him around . . ."

My father groaned.

"The end is the weakest part of the performance," said Professor LaFarge. "The young woman in the strapless gown strips God down to a loincloth, dancing around Him in a Martha-Graham-y way, and then she leaves Him, crumpled over in His old cart. That's the Death of God scene, when the goose feathers start pouring out of His mouth and some fan device, hidden in the flies, sucks them up and whirls them around. At the end there's just the heap of old vestments in the cart and the snowstorm of feathers, with colored spotlights playing on them—a rather striking effect, but then stage design is her metier, isn't it? Though all the reviews agreed it wasn't really an adequate ending to such a grandiose concept. You never told me some parishioner gave you a sack of goose feathers in England, Walter. How droll. What did you do with them?"

"I gave them to the Rector of St. Margaret's, to make himself a pillow," said Daddy. "And then, as you have read in her program note, I made the mistake of telling Madelyn Farley about it when I went over to England to bring Ruth home."

"The germinal idea for a work can lie dormant for years," began the infamous program note.

Pas de Dieux had its inception on a country road in England in the summer of 1973 when I was doing set designs for the Yvonne Arnaud Theatre in Guildford. My friend, who was in England with me at the time, had just been killed in a car accident, and her clergyman husband had flown over from the States to make the necessary arrangements. I was driving him back from the morgue when he suddenly began telling me a long story about some English parishioner once giving him a sack of goose feathers. I was too upset by my friend's death to really listen, but those feathers came to haunt me afterwards. They seemed such a proof of the inadequacy of words, of the wrongness of any words on some occasions, especially the events in our lives that deal with elemental experiences such as death, love, or transformation.

In *Pas de Dieux,* I am attempting a new form of theater in

which the powerfully charged instinctive levels of human experience are conveyed symbolically through collages of image, movement, sound and dance, but no words or plot or
"meaning" in the linear or literal sense.

"Isn't it amazing," Daddy would say sadly, whenever we were
conducting one of our exegeses of Madelyn Farley's program
note. "Isn't it just amazing how two people can bring such entirely
different readings to the same experience. Madelyn was driving
me along the road where your mother had her accident, and she
was indulging, for the second or third time that day, in a little orgy
of guilt that was becoming pretty hard to take. You know, going
on about how she ought to have driven with your mother to get
the chocolate, but she had wanted to make the most of the remaining daylight to finish some sketches for the Noel Coward play
the theater was doing. Talk about using words inappropriately,
she herself was doing a pretty good job of it that evening. She was
evoking her remorse in a really self-indulgent way. To put it more
unkindly, she was wallowing in the theatricality of the situation
and also managing at the same time to celebrate her own unique,
selfish self. For the second or third time I was hearing how, on the
fatal evening, the light had been fading out of the sky at the same
time life was flowing out of your mother scarcely a mile away, only
she, Madelyn, hadn't been aware of it; all she had cared about at
that moment was finishing those Noel Coward sketches. While her
dearest friend lay *crushed* . . . yes, talk about the wrongness of
words, Margaret . . . she, Madelyn, the driven artist, as selfish and
single-minded as her father when she had a brush in her hand,
could think of nothing but the creation-in-progress. And she was
embarking on that story again, the one she told at the rectory the
evening she stayed with us, about the time her mother was having
that attack of appendicitis on top of a mountain, but old Farley
wouldn't stop painting his view to get her to a hospital.

"And just about then we were driving past a stone cottage with
farm buildings, and I suddenly remembered it was the cottage
where old Mrs. Braithwaite had lived, the lady who had invited
me to tea on my birthday and presented me with a sack of goose
feathers, to make myself a pillow. That's when I decided to cut
short Madelyn Farley's profitless breast-beating session with a
harmless story of my own."

But my father hoarded the *Pas de Dieux* program. It became a permanent resident in the center drawer of his desk where, folded back to the hurtful program note, it greeted him every time he went looking for a stamp or a paper clip, or on an expeditionary browse through his collection of old *Forward Day by Day*s in search of ideas for a sermon. Knowing him, I am sure he couldn't resist glancing over that program note every time he opened the drawer, until he knew it by heart, just as he could repeat to you verbatim every one of Ned Block's criticisms of him all the way back to his beginning days as Rector of St. Cuthbert's.

He also kept the reviews and interviews, adding to them as her subsequent "nonverbal theater-collages" gained her a reputation. Right up until the time Professor LaFarge moved to France, his indefatigable clipping service and frequent theater trips to New York kept us supplied with the latest reports of Madelyn Farley's controversial "enactments," "stagings," "psychodramatic rituals"; no two critics could agree on what to call them, these plotless, "nonlinear" renderings of "elemental human experiences" too hot for mere words to handle. They made good press, she could always be counted on to shock, to repel, to startle: to "stir up your viscera," as one reviewer admiringly put it.

But though her tone was pervasively (and often perversely) sexual, she couldn't keep her hands off sacred themes. All the titles of the works attested to this unholy fascination of hers. After *Pas de Dieux* (which won her an Obie) came *Missa Solemnis,* then *Liturgies* (another Obie for her and one for her composer), then *Holy Desire,* her evening-length extravaganza on the Temptations of St. Anthony.

I think her borrowings of religious lore and objects, the legit-imate tools of my father's trade, disturbed him equally as much as his nervous and increasing certainty that she was somehow feed-ing off *him,* off things she had observed, or interpreted—or misinterpreted—for herself during her overnight stay in the rec-tory, and also putting to use things Ruth may have told her during their time together.

The disrobing of God in Madelyn Farley's first "collage" espe-cially distressed him, because he held himself personally re-sponsible for the accuracy of Madelyn's knowledge of priestly garments, and "what went underneath what." On the evening Trevor LaFarge brought us the *Pas de Dieux* clippings, after the Professor had gone home, Daddy and I stayed up talking into the early hours of the morning and this was when I first learned about

the strange encounter between my father and Madelyn that had
taken place in the sacristy at the same time I was on my way to
school, bumping along complacently beside my friend Harriet on
the school bus, plotting my future intimacy with mysterious little
Chloe Niles.

"It was after Wednesday Mass," said Daddy. "I was putting
things away in the sacristy, when a woman cleared her throat and
I looked around and there was Madelyn in the doorway."

"She said, 'Is this your inner sanctum, Walter?' Can you remember at all that insinuating tone of hers?

"I told her we called it the sacristy.

"'And what do you call that beautiful poncho thing hanging
up there on the cupboard door?' she asked.

"I told her it was a chasuble.

"'When do you wear that?' she wanted to know.

"I told her I had just worn it for eight o'clock Mass.

"'Hmm, sorry I wasn't there,' she said. 'I would have liked to
see you in all your garb, see what you do. I'm beginning to realize
it's a handicap in my profession, not knowing anything about
religion. Like that Christ monogram you found on my shirt last
night. That kind of stuff might be very useful to me.'

"'Well, next time you come, stay longer,' I said. 'Stay over and
go to church. I'll be glad to answer any questions.'

"'Ha,' she said. 'I wouldn't know what questions to ask. And I
probably won't be coming back this way for a long time. That
chas-uble. I don't suppose you would put it on again and let me see
you in it. Or would that be against the rules?'

"'It's not a question of rules,' I said, 'it's just that other things
have to go on first.' By that time, I was in my clericals, and not only
was I anxious to get back and see Ruth—your mother had not
slept well the night before—but the whole idea of vesting for this
woman, costuming myself simply to satisfy her theatrical curiosity,
seemed inappropriate.

"'Like what?' she asked. 'What has to go on first?' She was
really persistent, and I finally decided the easiest thing would be
to *show* her the vestments, describe what went where, without
putting any of them on myself. What could be the harm in that?
I thought. What harm indeed!

"She paid close attention. She wanted to know what each thing
symbolized, as well as where and how it was worn. I explained that
the alb alluded to the robe of mockery in which Herod caused

Christ to be clothed, and that the cincture is also the rope that bound Him during the Flagellation, and I showed her—without actually putting it on—how it has to be tied in order to keep the stole in place, and how we kissed the stole each time we put it on. I explained about the chasuble representing Christ's seamless garment for which the soldiers cast lots. She hung on my every word, she seemed mesmerized, and I began to feel I might have been overscrupulous to the point of having been uncharitable. It even crossed my mind that I could have at least put on the stole and perhaps given her a blessing. I wonder now if things would have turned out differently if I had . . .

"Anyway, the point is, as I was putting the vestments away again, there was a kind of rapport between us—at least *I* felt so—and I told her I was sorry she wouldn't be coming back anytime soon. I confided to her how much Ruth had looked forward to the visit. I told her it had not been easy for Ruth, putting up with me that past winter when I was in the dumps. 'In fact,' I suddenly heard myself suggesting, 'I wish you would take Ruth with you on up to New York for a little holiday. It would do her a world of good to get away for a bit. Especially with someone she thinks so much of.'

" 'She's perfectly welcome to come along,' Madelyn said, 'but I've got to be on the road very soon.'

" 'Well, let's go over to the rectory posthaste,' I told her. 'And you stand beside me and be my ally when I inform my wife she is under orders to pack up and go with you to New York.' "

"It's understandable that they talked about me," Daddy would often muse. "I know Ruth told her about the Black Curtain. That sort of thing lends itself to theater, I admit. It's a vivid image. Like the goose feathers. But what makes me uneasy, Margaret, are certain *assumptions* that seem to run through all the works. Assumptions that make me wonder . . . well, whether your mother didn't complain about me quite a lot."

"What kind of assumptions, Daddy?"

"Well, that men are pretty worthless creatures."

"That's just Madelyn's feminism, Daddy. I wouldn't take *that* personally. She wasn't necessarily thinking of you."

"But then why are so many of her males represented as priests? Or church figures? And even when they're struggling with principalities and powers, even when they are saints, she makes them come off as inept . . . and slightly ridiculous. The St. Anthony piece, for example. All the write-ups of it mention the way he fondled his hairshirt. Did your mother see me as fondling my hairshirt?"

"You're taking it too *personally,* Daddy. Look, she said herself in that interview, after *Holy Desire* caused all the uproar about blasphemy, that she was turned on by religious stuff because it still had 'charge' in it; it attracted her 'Hot Wand.' "

"Oh, yes, that Hot Wand of hers. She was going on about that Wand the night she had dinner with us. And your mother got very upset and started disparaging herself for not being creative. Ruth not creative: imagine! Your mother was one of the most creative people I have ever known. You were probably too young to remember any of that."

"I think I do remember. A little."

"Look, I have nothing against religion or churches," Madelyn Farley told us, relaxing in her 17th St. loft after the opening of her newest controversial piece, which critics are either extolling as "transforming art" or debunking as "trendy blasphemy." (*Holy Desire,* Farley's first evening-length piece, a nonverbal music-theater-dance extravaganza based on the temptations of St. Anthony, achieved the next-to-impossible for hard-boiled New York: on opening night, a whole row of businessmen walked out of the theater, protesting loudly, during the first half hour of Anthony's steamy travails.)

This innovative set designer turned director, who breaks fresh ground—and fresh taboos—with each new work, has turned repeatedly for her inspiration to church liturgy and iconography, though she professes herself to be an adamant nonbeliever. "When it comes to the dictates of my Hot Wand, I simply follow it," explains Farley. "For the past few years, it seems to be going for the hot spots left in religion. And don't kid yourself, some of those old images and ceremonies still pack a charge—only . . ." and she laughs her low, sassy Madelyn Farley laugh, ". . . the charges aren't necessarily where the tired old purveyors of dogma like to *think* they are . . ."

Farley directs our attention to a wall in her loft, which is completely covered with art postcards and reproductions, all of painting or engravings of St. Anthony that, two years ago, during her extended European tour with *Liturgies,* started her Hot Wand "trembling to explode" when she visited a museum in Rome one rainy afternoon.

"Look at his *face* in every one of those artists' works," she instructs us. "Picture after picture of St. Anthony, whether it's Cranach's or Grunewald's or Schongauer's or Jacques Callot's, go for the *face* of the saint, surrounded and plucked at and tormented by all his devils and demons. That's what my Hot Wand did. It went around the whole rest of that summer to the museums of Europe and looked at Anthony's *faces*. And what do you see on those faces? Looks ranging from enthrallment to bliss! Or at the very worst, bemusement—look at the Schongauer Anthony, having his hair and everything else pulled and pummeled by demons: 'I wonder what they will do to me next,' you can practically hear him thinking. He is interested in the *possibilities of his pain in all its variations*. And there are people like that, too, you'd better believe it. These old masters had looked around them and observed human nature; they painted what they had seen. The Parentino St. Anthony at the Galleria Doria in Rome was the one that actually got me—or rather my Hot Wand—started on this new work. I couldn't believe it when I studied that painting closely for the first time. Look, you can see for yourself, even though it's only a postcard: doesn't old Anthony look as though he's in the throes of sexual ecstasy?

"In a way I *am* a believer," concludes Farley reflectively. "I believe in art . . . in the mystery of the artistic impulse. Look at all these old great works. It's not the religion that interests me but the art that came out of it. People made these wonders, people under an inspiration. I am fascinated by the living wallop of that inspiration. Call *it* God, if you like . . . it's okay with me."

"Well, at the risk of having you say I'm taking it too personally," Daddy brooded, "I do feel she might have been thinking of someone like me when she said that about certain people being interested in the possibilities of their pain. I can see how I might come across as a sort of St. Anthony type. I can see how your mother might have portrayed me as a bit of a masochist. However, bypassing the merely personal and speaking in my representative role as a 'tired old purveyor of dogma,' I wish Madelyn Farley's

Hot Wand would go trembling to burst over some other topic besides my poor bailiwick. It's like cannon-balling an edifice that's already in ruins. The church has done a pretty thorough job of wrecking *itself* these last few years, if you ask me. She appears more relaxed in this interview photo, doesn't she? She was so ill at ease the two times I was with her. Though success certainly hasn't improved her looks any. I don't suppose you remember her very well. But she does appear more at ease with herself in this photo."

"She looks exactly like a gloating witch," I said.

VI: THE GOLDEN EGG

On Friday after my midday class, I filled up the gas tank of my Honda Prelude (found for me secondhand at an unbelievably low price by our vestryman Ernie Pasco, who, ever since installing Ruth's hair-dryer outlet all those years ago, had appointed himself equerry of all our appliances and machines) and put myself on automatic pilot for the drive west to Daddy, a trip I had made so many times I could have driven it in my sleep.

I often did travel it in my sleep. Upstairs in Dee Dee's bed in Charlottesville, I would dream that my father was in trouble and needed me. In one dream, someone had locked him up in the house and he couldn't get to the church for a service. In another, a homicidal maniac had slipped into the rectory and was waiting for him with a gleaming ax under Father Traherne's four-poster. I would fling on some clothes (always clothes from my childhood that didn't fit anymore) and float down Mrs. Dunbar's curved staircase, drop through the sunroof of my Honda, which would start up by itself and race me through a traffic-less Charlottesville (surely a dream!) and west along an empty Highway 64 to Staunton, then north along an also empty 81 for two exits, then left onto the winding country road, with daytime-blue Shenandoahs rising over yellow fields, and across the river bridge that rattled, and into Romulus. I never knew what terrible thing I was going to find when I got there, but in all of the dreams except one, I never

arrived at the rectory. In the one exception, I had arrived to find
Daddy sitting in the living room with a bunch of seedy strangers.
There were ashes all over the furniture and on the people my
father sat with, and he was ashamed and not happy to see me.

Professor Stannard had persuaded me I didn't need to come
back for Monday and Tuesday classes before official Easter break
began next Wednesday. "You take the rest of Passiontide off,"
insisted my doting advisor. "You of all people can afford it." Passiontide: practically nobody anymore used that lovely old word
for the two weeks before Easter. I told him this, and it pleased
him. In such a courtly manner the two of us flirted, a sixty-eight-
year-old medievalist and a clergyman's daughter. He loved me in
his way, the old bachelor; he approved of me and looked out for
my interests. Yesterday he had informed me of a new scholarship
just endowed by a rich alumna.

"It's for graduate research by a woman into 'a neglected aspect
of women's history.' Now, normally, I don't go in for that sort of
thing." (A rapid shake of his snowy head set his hound-dog cheeks
trembling.) "*True* scholarship should transcend gender or private
interests. But this would be right up your avenue, Margaret. That
paper you did on Cuthbert and early English monasticism for my
survey course was just superlative. It showed a natural feeling for
the spirit of those times. In my opinion, you would be the ideal
person to resurrect the Abbess Hilda from her centuries of neglect. There's been nothing on her worth mentioning since Lina
Eckenstein's brilliant book on women and the monastic life, and
that was published in the eighteen nineties."

"Hilda of Whitby? But isn't Bede our only real source about
her?"

"Ah, now that's the challenge," he crowed. "Where primary
sources end, empathy must take over. But, mind, I'm not advo-
cating any of that Lytton-Strachey meddling, that 'personal inter-
pretation' sort of thing he inflicted on poor Florence Nightingale
and Queen Victoria. No, you'd build on the base of your Bede—
you'd have to be fluent in Latin and Old English, of course, in
order to cull some of the more interesting secondary sources. And
then after you'd had a good look at what there is, you'd apply the
empathy that I consider to be your gift. You'd use your respectful
imagination, which is, to my way of thinking, another definition of
empathy. After apprising yourself of what is known about her

world and her circumstances, you'd *look into* Hilda, and it's my feeling that the wise Abbess herself would look back at you across thirteen centuries, take an instant liking to you, and reveal herself. Of course," (a flirtatious quiver of the old pink cheeks) "all this would mean putting up with *me* for a considerable number of graduate hours, but I'm trusting that the prospect wouldn't be entirely odious. Does my idea appeal to you?"

"Oh, it appeals to me, but what about the lady who's giving the scholarship?"

"I think you can leave that safely to me. I may be within two years of mandatory retirement, but I still have some say-so around here."

It would certainly please Daddy, my doing graduate work on an important Anglican church figure as well as remaining in commuting distance from Romulus. And it would please Mrs. Dunbar for me to study Latin and Old English in Dee Dee's bedroom and continue to make her evening cocoa. Applying my respectful imagination to Hilda was not something I might have chosen on my own, but perhaps it would get me through the interim until something chose me.

"I guess what I'm hoping," I had told Ben MacGruder over the phone after my talk with Stannard, "is that if I take care of my day-to-day responsibilities in good faith, then my future will take care of itself: I'll get a good ending, like the heroines in the books I like. Not necessarily a *happy* ending but one that I can accept as belonging to me."

"Let me come over," said Ben, who was in his first year here at the university. "I could give you a happy ending right now."

"Ben, it's not in your power to 'give me a happy ending.' " Oh, why did he always manage, with his obsessive *clutching*, to make me say hurtful things?

"Only because you're so stubborn. You know I can put you into a good mood better than anyone else. I think you just enjoy torturing me. First you call and break our date so you can go home to Father Melancholy—"

"Please don't call him that."

"Why not? Grandaddy did. I can remember hearing him say to Nana, 'Well, I expect I'd better run over to Father Melancholy's and check on his blues.' "

"Harriet never had to tell me that. Why do you feel *you* have to, Ben?"

"Because I love you, Margaret. I'm in love with Father Melancholy's daughter. Look, I could plead my case a lot better if you'd let me come over."

"Ben, why does everything always have to be so *urgent?* Here I've just called you to tell you I'm probably going to be right here in Charlottesville for the next two or three years, possibly more if I go on for a doctorate—you'll be gone from here first, even with all your Incompletes. You may even be married by then, to some nice girl your own age while I'm still hanging around here translating old English."

"I *hate* it when you pull your granny act on me, Margaret. You are *three years older* than I am. It was something when you were six and I was three, but not anymore. Now I'm thirteen inches taller than you and can lift you off the ground with one hand and can do a lot of other things to you too, as you well know. What do you want? Someone the age of your father? Someone the age of old *Stannard?* And you *didn't* call me, I called you. You only call me when you want to break a date."

"Look, Ben, I told you why I have to go home this weekend. Daddy's upset because they're trying to take away our corner with the cross. And I want to get his old cardigan off him long enough to wash it, and then he has this talk to give to some group at a priest's house on Monday night . . ."

"Well, you don't have to write his *talk* for him do you? God, Margaret, you sound like Father Melancholy's *mother.*"

"I think we ought to hang up now. This conversation is deteriorating. Which is too bad, because of all the people 'my age,' you are the one I can talk to best about things I really care about. In some ways you know me better than Harriet, though frankly, sometimes I wish you didn't, because you use it to . . . oh, I don't know . . . *devour* me."

"Just answer me this one question, Margaret, and then I'll let you go."

"What?"

"Why is it that you don't seem to *miss* me when I miss you so much?"

"Maybe it's because you never give me a *chance* to miss you anymore . . . you're always breathing down my neck."

"All right," he said, after a hurt silence. "But just remember, we go back a long way. Just remember: I've got your egg."

"As if you'd ever let me forget it. And how many times do I have to remind you that the reason you've got it is because Harriet and I lifted you into the crook of the tree so you could reach it. And *furthermore* . . ."

"Oh, here it comes again about the wet pants . . ."

"Yes, little Ben, when we lifted you up into that tree so you could get the Golden Egg, your pants were sopping wet . . ."

"See how far back you had that effect on me?"

"Oh, don't be disgusting."

"Margaret, you know what I sometimes wish?"

"You've had your one question already, remember?"

"It's not a question then. I was just trying to be rhetorically dainty because you like that. What I sometimes wish is that we hadn't met until we were grown-up."

"Then we still wouldn't have met, would we? Because one of us is still not grown-up."

"Your cruelty gives me hope, Margaret. You know why? That's not a question, because I'm pretty sure I know the answer to it. You couldn't put so much energy into your cruelty if you weren't afraid you cared for me. If you were indifferent, you'd be kinder and politer. I've watched you with others."

"Well," I said wearily, "maybe I am cruel. And that's childish of me. Maybe we'd better call a moratorium on our friendship till we're both good and grown-up. How about another ten years?"

"In another ten years you'll be thirty-two and starting to go dry around the gills. And your father will be retired. Priests have to retire at seventy, I remember hearing Grandaddy tell about some old priest in Newport News they had to carry out of his rectory kicking and screaming. What will you two do, then? Buy a Winnebago and make pilgrimages to religious shrines?"

"Now who's being cruel?" I said, slamming down the phone on him. Then I surprised myself by starting to cry. It had something to do with Ben's bringing up the egg. The Golden Egg Ruth had made for the 1973 Easter egg hunt: her last and most dazzling artistic contribution to our parish life—even if it had been made in absentia and had arrived by United Parcel, as our Christmas gifts had. How I had wanted to keep it, that egg! To preempt it before it ever became part of the hunt. But of course that would be wrong, even if Daddy and I substituted another golden egg.

The Golden Egg was always supposed to be the most beautiful and desirable egg, that's why the rector's wife traditionally made it. Every child wanted to be the one to find it. My mother had made it to be hidden in Elaine Major's backyard on Easter afternoon and claimed by whoever rightfully found it. And it wouldn't be proper for me to claim it even if I had been the rightful finder, because I was the rector's daughter and the egg had been contributed by the rector's wife . . .

Lent of 1973, our first Lent without my mother in the rectory, had come as a relief after the strain of Christmas. During Lent, with its imposition of ashes and penances, it was okay to be sad, it was *comme il faut* to go around looking pensive and downcast when you considered what lay ahead on Good Friday.

Daddy now walked me to my bus every morning. By a vote of the vestry (with only Ned Block abstaining), Wednesday morning Mass had been moved forward a half hour so my father could get me off to school. He always got us to the corner way too early and we would stand there in front of the little outdoor calvary, blowing on our hands and stamping our feet if it was cold. Or if litterbugs had been at work the night before, Daddy would wade at once into the thick ivy and, uttering exclamations of astonishment and disgust, begin weeding out the trash.

It would probably be self-pitying hindsight for me to claim that I suffered on those daily walks to the corner where our Italian-carved savior hung on the oak cross under his shingled roof, his torso with its modest stone drape gracefully twisted in agony. But there seems to have been a dull ache lying in wait for me at the corner where I had said good-bye to my mother on the morning of September 13 and then climbed aboard my bus without looking back at her. The ache became part of the place for me. It was always there, even when I was preoccupied with other things, such as making sure that Daddy was not seen groveling in the ivy when my bus came creeping with its high-pitched wheeze down Macon, carrying all my little schoolmates.

"Wait till I *leave*, Daddy," I'd scold. "Talk to me while I'm still here."

And if the night's leavings were irresistibly abundant and he couldn't restrain himself from plunging in at once to begin his treasure hunt, I had to at least prevent him from kneeling down, or even worse, *lying* down, as he had been caught doing on the afternoon of September 13 when retarded Devonia had bawled out: "THAT MAN . . . HURT!" her half-witted perception turning out to be prophetic. For I was aware that people *did* view my father as "hurt" by my mother's extended absence, and it was more important than ever, I felt, that he should appear upright and dignified at all times in public.

"You can do that after I'm *gone*," I'd mutter fiercely, keeping my ears cocked for the sound of the school bus.

One morning near the end of Lent, I remember, there was no debris, not even a lone flip-top winking defiantly up at us from the ivy. It must have rained the night before, because a mist rose from the daffodil beds on the steep banks of the big houses across from the church. A breeze disarranged my father's dark curly hair like invisible fingers gently playing with it. He was standing in a position I approved of, his feet planted apart, his arms folded in manly self-possession in front of his chest; he looked exactly as the Rector of St. Cuthbert's ought to look.

For some moments he had been scrutinizing the little stone Christ, letting his eyes play up and down the chest and flanks of the crucified figure in a rapt, proprietary way, as if both approving their graceful lines and checking them for traffic grime.

"Well, master," he suddenly surprised me by saying in a tender and confidential tone, rocking back and forth in his black shoes, "it's almost over for you again, isn't it? I wonder when mine will be over."

As the church moved towards its annual triumph over the powers of darkness, the usual preparations were also being made by a bunch of nervous women for the Easter egg hunt, traditionally held at the Major's. This event had taken place in her garden ever since her sons, the present-day bishop and the brain surgeon, had been toddlers, and a great many customs and rules of etiquette had sprung up around the event as customs and rules tended to do whenever the Major was running things.

"It's not St. Cuthbert's Easter egg hunt," my mother would say to Daddy, "it's Elaine Major's ceremony of intimidation for mothers, that's what it is. And it certainly hasn't much to do with *children,* except that she needs them for decoration."

"Now, Ruth," Daddy would say, but his mouth was already twitching with laughter.

"No, I mean it, Walter. The children are just the excuse for her annual display of superiority. So we'll all have to bolt down our Easter roast and rush across town to hide eggs in the foliage of her puh-fectly planted spring borders and in the crotches of her puh-fectly pruned fruit trees. And the way she *assigns* us our eggs! And of course the rector's wife has to make the Golden Egg. And not only does it have to aspire to the impossible puh-fection of Mrs. Hazeltine's famous lace-and-velvet Golden Egg of 1953, but it has to surpass my own production of the year before. I tell you the truth, Walter, no sooner am I putting away the Christmas deco-rations than I start to worry about my Golden Egg. Shall I try chickens or angels this year? Do I do decoupage, or try some needlework, or do I dare sneak, like Clara Jane Buford does, and *buy* my basic egg at the card shop and then rip off the mass-produced frills and add my own personal touches? I'll be pushing my cart through the supermarket, trying to concentrate on my grocery list, when suddenly I'll spot some little yellow scouring pad or a gold label on some imported cheese and I snatch it up like a madwoman—I can use that on my egg! Or I'll be in church on Sunday, waiting my turn in the communion line, aware that I am undergoing my weekly inspection by our ever-watchful flock. Are my heels run-down? Is my skirt too short? Is my hair flying around too much to suit Miriam Stacy? Should I let my arms hang down naturally at my sides, or clasp them demurely over my stomach, or is the tummy-clasp best reserved for after the Sacra-ment? And then suddenly I'll spot the perfect yellow feather in some old lady's hat and all thoughts of sanctity and propriety just fly right out of my head. All I know is that I would kill for that little feather because it would be *puh-fect* for my damned egg."

"What about Ruth's egg?" I asked Daddy during Lent of 1973 when my mother had been gone six months. "She has to come back in time to make the Golden Egg."

"Well now, honey, I don't know. She may *not* be back in time. I'd better speak to the Major and tell her to go ahead and ask somebody else. Just for this Easter, you understand."

"No," I said firmly.

"No?" he repeated quizzically.

"Nobody's supposed to make the Golden Egg except the rec-tor's wife," I said. "*Everybody* knows that. I think we have to call my mother up and remind her."

"Well, I don't know," said Daddy uncertainly.

"I think we *have* to."

His face went through a series of changes. It was like watching him thinking. I remember how powerful I felt when I saw on his face that he was going to do what I said. Or rather, to let me do it.

He and she didn't talk so much over the phone anymore. It was me she called for, but if he answered they exchanged pleasantries for a few moments while I stood by, sighing importantly as I impatiently waited for "my" call. But when I did finally take the receiver, the awful thing usually happened: I clammed up. All the energy went out of me and I could barely utter my yesses and noes. I felt bad about it because she would be trying so hard, going through her routine interrogation. How was school? How was Harriet? Where exactly *was* I right now, in what room? What did I have on? What were we reading these days, Daddy and I?

Sometimes I would hurt her. I couldn't stop myself. Like the time she asked if I had been wearing the red suede gloves she had sent for Christmas.

"They were too small," I told her. "We gave them to Mr. Pasco for his granddaughter."

"Oh . . ." She sounded as though the breath had been knocked out of her. "But I thought your daddy said they fit."

"That was probably to keep from hurting your feelings."

"I see." She sounded peeved. "Well, I wish he had been honest with me. I could have exchanged them for a larger size. They weren't cheap."

"It doesn't matter," I assured her.

"No, I guess not," she had agreed, rather coldly.

The worst thing about these conversations was that when they began I could hear her missing me, but by the time they were over I could feel her almost hating me. What did she want from me? Why couldn't I ask her what I needed to know?

"Well look, Margaret," she had recently taken to saying at the end of these dialogues, "you call *me* when you feel like talking. If nobody answers at Madelyn's apartment, we've gone to her father's place upstate. You're a smart girl. Daddy's got the numbers written down and you know how to dial. I would love it if you called me sometime."

I had taken her up on her offer only once so far and the result was a disaster. I didn't tell Daddy about it. It was like the witch in my closet: you had to keep these things to yourself or they might hurt you even more.

One winter afternoon when the early darkness was making me sad and Daddy was in his study having a counseling session with Miriam Stacy (I could hear her reading her diary to him in an unctuous drone), I crept upstairs to my parents' bedroom and climbed up on Father Traherne's four-poster. Daddy had written both the numbers in his little book he kept by the telephone. I tried Madelyn's place first. The dialing wheel on our upstairs phone was mysteriously sluggish, it didn't go around as easily as when Ruth had been home. (Later when I got old enough to take over the housework I saw that Daddy just hadn't understood the finer points of cleaning.) It took all the power of my small index finger to drag it round and back eleven times, and then, after all that effort, nobody answered. I had to start all over again with the "upstate" number with the different area code. It, too, rang and rang and rang. I was about to hang up when it was snatched up on the other end and a fearsome old man's voice shouted *"YES?"*

I wanted to hang up, but I wanted to speak to my mother more. "This is Margaret," I said, my heart pounding, "is my mother there?"

"Speak *UP!*" cried the angry voice.

"This is *Margaret*," I began, louder.

"There's no Margaret here," the voice shot back.

"No, *I'm* Margaret . . ."

"There is no Margaret at this number and you've interrupted my work."

"No, *I'm*—"

"Listen, numbskull, there is *NO* Margaret here, got that? *NO MARGARET!*"

He cut me off.

When I saw from my father's face that he was going to let us call Ruth in New York about the Golden Egg, I said, "*You* dial the number, and then when she comes on, *I'll* talk." I was not going to risk another collision with any unfriendly voice.

"Yes, *ma'am*," said Daddy. His big fingers spun the numbers and someone answered right away. I knew it was my mother from his expression. Without saying a word, he passed the receiver quickly to me.

"Hello, who *is* this?" Ruth was saying into the phone.

"It's me."

"*Margaret*, baby. Are you all right?"

"I'm just fine, thank you." She sounded really glad that it was me, but I pushed right ahead in a businesslike way. "What I'm calling about is the egg."

"The egg?" she repeated, perplexed.

"You know. The Golden Egg that you have to make for the Easter egg hunt."

There was silence. Then she said, "Oh, my goodness, of course. The Golden Egg." And uttered a strange laugh.

It was on the tip of my tongue to tell her she didn't have to make it if she didn't want to. That laugh had been chilling. I didn't want the egg to make her so resentful that she might decide to stay away from us even longer. Daddy meanwhile had wandered over to the window and stood with his back to the room, giving me my privacy. His shoulders were tensed and hunched, as though he were expecting any minute to have something dropped on him from above.

"When *is* Easter this year?" my mother was asking.

"I think it's . . . I don't know . . . I'll have to ask Daddy."

"Well, go on and ask," she said. "I don't expect he's too far away."

"Not *too* far," I admitted cautiously. "Wait just a minute." Clamping my hand tightly over the mouthpiece, I demanded of my father's stooped and anxious back: "She wants to know when *is* Easter this year?"

"April twenty-second," he said, whirling around. There was a look of naked expectancy on his face. "Don't tell me she . . ."

"Shhh!" I silenced him. "April twenty-second," I repeated into the phone.

"Oh, that late," she said, sounding relieved. "It was much earlier last year. I've never understood why Easter can't stay in the same place, like the other holidays, but this gives me more time. What kind of egg do you think I should make, honey?"

The chronic "I don't know" was almost out of my mouth, but I squelched it in time. This was a crucial moment; everything hung on my answer—at least, I felt it did. "Something real pretty," I said, "like you always do."

"Oh, sweetheart . . ." She broke off in a kind of wail, then regathered herself. "Come on, Margaret, you have to be more specific than that. There's certainly no shortage of *art* materials at Maddy's place. I could probably make something nice. But you

have to tell me what you want. A funny egg or a serious egg? An
understated egg or a show-offy egg? Or what?"

"Serious," I said. "Not too show-offy. And it should have . . ."
I paused, at a loss for the words to express what I wanted to say.
My father was watching me with amazement and something pitifully close to envy. I wished I could ask him for the right words,
but I knew somehow that this was between her and me, and I
might spoil it if I did.

"It should have what, honey?" she was prodding.

It was like in a fairy tale. If I came up with the right password,
the magic kingdom was mine. If I didn't, I would lose everything.
I strained and pushed and some words popped out of my mouth.
"Something with you in it," I said.

"Oh, bless you, honey. Oh, Margaret, I miss you so. I just wish
. . . oh, I don't know. I'll tell you what. I'll start on it right now.
Let's see, serious and not too show-offy and with me in it. That's
quite an order, but it will be a challenge. I guess I'd better speak
with your daddy. Is he there?"

"Just a minute." I handed the receiver to Daddy. "She wants to
speak to you," I whispered elatedly. I could hardly contain myself.
It seemed to me I had heard a turning in her voice that signaled
I had won more than the Golden Egg.

"Oh, Ruth, that would be lovely," Daddy was saying. He cradled the receiver fondly against his cheek. "It will mean a lot to
her . . . it will mean a lot to us all."

I couldn't keep still anymore. I walked in a circle around Daddy's study, on fire with my triumphant new certainty. I had done
it! I had done what no one else could. I had released her from the
magic spell that had kept her away from us all these months.

Daddy's voiced rolled on agreeably. "That's just wonderful,
Ruth. That *is* a first for you, isn't it? And I'll bet you're excellent
at it." This didn't make too much sense, but when he said, "Early
next week will be *fine;* I'll tell everyone," it made perfect sense.
They had come to *their* senses at last and were discussing her
return to Romulus. The two of them over long distance were
acting like parents again, remaking a nest for me in which I could
lie down and fall into a baby's sleep. And yet, they had needed me
to do it for them. *I* had caused it to finally happen.

"I'll tell her," Daddy was saying. "Oh, I'm sure it's going to be
splendid. All right. Yes, I understand. Well. God bless you, Ruth."

He hung up the phone and stood beside his desk, his hand still resting lightly on top of the receiver as though he were blessing it, too. "You were right," he said, opening his arms to me, "it was a good idea, that call."

"I told you," I said, trying to sound nonchalant. I butted my head into his stomach so he couldn't see how ecstatic I was.

"She seemed quite pleased about making the egg," he rumbled above me, smoothing my curly hair down with both his hands.

"I *know* about the egg," I said. "But when is she going to *be* here?"

"Well, not for a while, honey. Maybe not for *a while* yet. She's got a job teaching now. Three days a week, she's teaching life drawing at Madelyn's father's school up in the Catskills. It's the first job she's ever held in her life and she's understandably proud. But she told me she's going to start on the Golden Egg right away and we should have it by United Parcel early next week."

I stayed very still with my head pushed against his stomach, as his jaunty phrases rolled over me, crumbling my brief, wild hope. His voice seemed to come from two places at once, from above my head and inside his stomach, except the one inside his stomach was having to compete with various digestive noises. I believe that was when I not only grasped that we might never be a family again, but knew also that my father himself had suspected it for some time and had even been colluding with her in the knowledge of it.

"Well," he said, releasing me, "I expect I ought to give the Major a quick buzz and pass on the good word about the egg." Then he must have glimpsed the anguish I was feeling, because he added, "I still think we have cause for rejoicing, Margaret, I do. She really *wanted* to make that Golden Egg, and don't you see, that's a kind of covenant."

"What's a covenant?" I asked irritably, fighting down the new hope he was trying to build in me.

"Why, it's a kind of promise," he said. "And it usually has a gift attached, to show that the giver is serious. Like when God made a covenant with Abraham by giving him a son. Or when Jonathan gave his clothes and armor to David because he recognized in him a kindred spirit and loved him as his own soul."

I hung around while he phoned Elaine Major with "the good word" about the egg. As they talked, Daddy's voice got more and more defensively upbeat as he championed my mother's new job at Madelyn's father's art school in the Catskills. Though I couldn't hear the Major's end of the conversation, I could tell she took a grim view of this latest development.

"Yes, I know, Elaine," Daddy was saying, "but you have to remember, Ruth married me straight out of junior college . . . she never got a chance to test her talents out there in the real world . . . and as we *are* living in these interesting times, which are producing so many capable women . . . women like *yourself*, Elaine, don't you agree she has to have her chance?"

From Daddy's face, I could see that the Major did not agree with him, and neither did I.

One late afternoon the following week, the square brown truck pulled up outside the rectory and the UPS man came sprinting up our front walk and rang the bell. He handed me a package weighing practically nothing. It was addressed to me. In those days, you still had to sign, and my father hovered proudly behind me as I printed the letters of my name across the sheet on the clipboard the man in the brown uniform patiently held out for me.

"Well, here it is," Daddy said to me as I carried it into the house. "I can't wait to see what she's made. Shall we open it in the study?"

The tiresome old magic thinking was trying to gain a hold on me again, but I couldn't risk ignoring it. It was telling me where I had to open this package if there was to be any hope of her coming home again.

"Let's open it in the breakfast room. In her window seat."

"Now *that's* a good idea," exclaimed my father with a boyish enthusiasm I found rather annoying. He led the way to the alcove with its yellow cushions trimmed in orange, the bright little corner my mother had made for herself by knocking out a wall in Mrs. Hazeltine's dark old dining room.

We put the package on the breakfast table and Daddy slit the taped ends with a knife. Together we eased out a box. I pulled off its lid, which said "Aquatec Artists Colors," and lifted out a papier mâché egg, about the size of a mango, from a nest of crumpled newspaper. All over its gold leaf surface had been painted little white doves, flying around with strawberries in their beaks. There was a note with the egg: "Dearest Margaret, I hope this is what you wanted. All My Love, Mother." I happened to love strawberries, and the doves were nice but I couldn't deny that the egg was disappointing, even though Daddy was loyally exclaiming, "Oh, how delicate . . . doesn't she have a touch, your mother!" It was my fault, I decided, that the egg was not more stunning. I had said not too show-offy, and it certainly wasn't. But I had expected more than this. Except for its required gold color, there wasn't much to make anyone envious of the lucky child who would find it.

"Wait a minute, there's a hole here," Daddy said. "I wonder . . . now wait just a minute." He held the egg in front of his nose and squinted into it. "Oh my, Margaret! Just wait until you see what's inside!"

"Let me see, let me see," I clamored, snatching.

"Careful now, don't hold it too tight. What you have to do is put your hand over one eye and then look through the hole with the other one." He was guiding my hands and my head. "Do you see it?"

I looked in upon a scene, a little painting, inside the egg. There were two angels in white sitting side by side at the entrance to an open cave and a woman who looked like she was trying to see into the cave. Near to the woman, in profile, was a gardener hoeing a patch of earth. The background was a soft landscape of meadows and blue rolling hills. The woman wore a purple robe and had long, bright hair. The hair was different and shinier than everything else in the little painting. After a moment I said, "I think that's my mother's real hair in there."

"Let me have a quick look," said Daddy. He took the egg back and repositioned it to his eye. "You're right, it is," he said, and went on gazing into the egg until I had to remind him he had said a quick look.

He couldn't wait to start telling people about the Golden Egg. He phoned Mrs. MacGruder first. "Ruth has sent the most amazing egg. I don't recall ever having seen anything like it. It's wondrously made. The outside is quite beautiful, with doves flying around on the gold, which is enough all by *itself*, but then you look into a hole and there is Mary Magdalen facing the angels at the empty tomb. It's a little painting, but what a painting! The landscape reminds me of those early Italian masters. My wife was really hiding her talent under a bushel to an extent I never realized. And the revelations keep dawning on you; first you can't figure out where the light is coming from, the light that enables you to see the little painting through the hole. Then you discover that there are tiny, strategically placed holes in the eyes of certain of the doves. And Margaret was the one to discover that the Magdalen's hair was real, yes, it is actually Ruth's own hair. And then on top of that, there's something beautifully subtle about the whole concept. There's a gardener in the background, but Mary hasn't seen him yet. Ruth has used the Fourth Gospel's story of the Resurrection. You know, that's the one where Mary stays on alone at the empty tomb and the angels ask her, 'Woman, why weepest thou?' And then she looks around and sees the gardener who is none other than Christ. But Ruth has caught that wonderful moment, the moment of impending grace—when Mary's comfort is right behind her, but she doesn't know it yet!"

Then, of course, he had to call the Major and inform her that the egg that was to be the star of her annual hunt was a work of art, worthy of an early Italian master, and from there Daddy launched into an eloquent defense of the egg's absentee maker, his argument to the Major being that Ruth was at last coming into her own, *not* in any self-centered women's libbish way, but—as this egg so wonderfully proved—in a manner that would allow her to use her talents for the glory of God. "Even I, her most uncritical admirer, have to admit that her painting has improved since she's been up there, Elaine. God knows we miss her, but would I be doing right to insist she stop what she's doing—and doing so *well*—and come back to Romulus before she's seen this thing through?"

The Major said something on her end.

"Now, Elaine," chided my father humorously, raising his eyebrows at me in mock exasperation, "you know that wouldn't really solve anything. Besides, do you see me as the caveman type?"

He went around talking up the wondrous egg waiting back at the rectory for its Easter afternoon debut in the Major's garden. He used its existence to justify my mother's extended "vacation" from us. Only it couldn't rightly be called that any longer, because she was working in the place she was supposed to be vacationing. "Ruth has got herself a job for the moment, teaching life drawing at Mr. Farley's school," he would say proudly. Adding confidentially, "It's upstate, she goes up there for three days a week," if it was someone close to us, who didn't need to be impressed or intimidated into accepting the Rector's unconventional family situation. But with others, like Ned Block or Miriam Stacy, who needed to be kept at bay or put in their places, my father would simply inform them coolly, "Yes, my wife is teaching art up in New York."

In the countdown days before Easter, I cherished and pondered the egg. Until the child who was destined to find it dragged it out of its hiding place in the Major's garden with a shriek, it was still mine. I took it out of its box that said "Aquatec Artists Colors" and squinted through the hole and looked at my mother's hair falling down the back of the tiny woman in the landscape. I imagined Ruth standing in front of a mirror, scissors poised, deciding which piece of hair to chop off to put in the Golden Egg; she wouldn't have needed very much. When I had said "something with you in it," I hadn't had anything so literal in mind. As far as I *knew* what I meant, I had just been trying to say that anything she put herself into was all I wanted. The hair, in there like that, was spellbinding, but it was also disconcerting: it seemed to me somehow wrong that another child would own something that had my mother's own hair in it. Had she thought of that when she made it? Maybe not; maybe, having been away so long, she had gotten certain things confused in her mind about how we did things at St. Cuthbert's, and believed she was making the egg for me.

It was actually a relief when Mrs. MacGruder, who was going to help hide the eggs, came and took it away the day before Easter. I think it may have been when I was watching her drive off in the rattly Mercedes with the Aquatec box beside her on the seat that I began to know I was the kind of person who preferred to make a clean sacrifice and have it over with, rather than suffer through ambivalences and false hopes.

Of the Easter egg hunt itself, I have surprisingly few recollections. Ben would have his memory version of it, Harriet would have hers, but all I can truly recall is the sharp, rather nasty green of Elaine Major's svelte lawn in chilly sunshine, and the interesting disaster of the day (Ernie Pasco had mistakenly dyed the uncooked eggs from his wife's refrigerator rather than the hard boiled ones she had left for him before she rushed off to the bedside of an ailing aunt, and there were several messy children as a result), and three-year-old Ben's sopping-wet behind as Harriet and I lifted him into the prong of an apple tree to claim the Golden Egg, cleverly camouflaged in a spray of cut blossoms, which he had somehow, amazingly, spotted from the ground when older, taller children had been walking past it almost at eye level.

"Nana cheated," Harriet would claim later, when we were older. "I'm sure she did. I remember her going on at home about what a shame it was for you to have to give up that egg, Margaret. I'm almost positive I heard her tell Grandaddy that she was going to do something about it. And what I think she did was . . . she knew it would look suspicious if I found it, being your best friend . . . so she primed Ben for it. After all, she was the one who hid it. It would have been so easy to do! Just a word in his ear . . . he and my parents were in Romulus on home leave from Djibouti and he was a new child to everyone, most people there hadn't ever seen him before, so even if he was one of us it would be okay for him to find it. And then Nana could keep it safe at our house. I *know* Nana must have told Ben where it was because it was impossible for *anybody* to see, with all those cut blossoms she had put around it for camouflage."

"Nana did *not* put me up to it," Ben would insist when he got older. "I saw gold shining through the blossoms. The sun must have hit it at an angle where I could see it when no one else could. I found the egg all by myself."

And then later, after he had announced he was in love with me and, with the lover's typical 20-20 hindsight, was discovering portents of this love all over his past, he would tell me, "I felt your anguish, Margaret, and I called on some miraculous powers within myself and they helped me find it."

"Ben, you were three years old."

"Well, what better age to feel miraculous powers? They get educated out of us later. At three we're not all closed in by rationality yet. We're still open to all sorts of communications flying around out there. My powers lasted beyond age three, probably because my parents were stationed in places where I was with black people all the time. They're good at extrasensory stuff. When my father was at the Embassy in Cairo, I had this Nubian servant who looked after me. He slept outside my door at night, and we could communicate without words. I was almost six by then. I remember how it felt. It was sort of like getting into a warm bathtub with all his thoughts. They were very different from my thoughts, there was a lot of running barefoot and seeing animals in the dark . . . things like that . . ."

"That's just wishful thinking, Ben. How do you know they were his thoughts? They sound to me exactly like the kind of thoughts someone would *attribute* to a native . . . 'running barefoot

and seeing animals in the dark.' The real Nubian was probably
thinking about his wages, or worrying about his own children at
home."

"Run it down if you like, Margaret, but I know what I know.
And I *know* I could feel your thoughts that day of the Easter egg
hunt. There was this incredibly sweet sadness coming from you
. . . yes there was. And I chose you that day, even though I happened to be three years old at the time, which you seem determined to hold against me forever. I can still see your straight little
back as you carried your Easter basket down that grassy slope.
Remember how the Major made us all line up with our baskets
and then she blew this awful whistle? For the longest time I used
to think she was a man dressed up in women's clothes and that's
why everybody called her the Major. And then all the other children ran down the slope like wild animals, but you walked. You
had this round, sad little face, and I could see on it you had
already decided not to find anything."

"That's pure fantasy, Ben. Mixed up with wishful thinking, and
things you've heard, and things *I've* told you. You try to fascinate
me with all these old stories about myself, because it makes you the
custodian of all these little pieces of my past I can't remember."

"Well, even if that last part's true, still, I *do* remember things
about you from when I was little and they're going to be part of
me as long as I live. There's not a thing you can do about it, unless
you'd like to kill me."

"Sometimes I think I *would* like to kill you."

"That means you want to kill what I can make you feel."

"Oh, *feel*. There's more to life than what people can make
other people 'feel.' In the sense you mean."

"There may be, but it's unwholesome to think you can do
without it. Unless you're going to go off and be a nun, like that
woman you built the stone wall with."

"It may come to that. I may have to enter a convent just to get
away from you."

"But not yet, hey? What was it you told me St. Augustine said?
'Lord, don't make me chaste . . .' "

"No, 'Lord, make me chaste, but not yet.' "

"That's my girl."

"I was only correcting the quote, Ben. For no other reason
than because it drives me out of my mind the sloppy way you're
always mixing things up to suit yourself."

*   *   *

Around and around we went, Ben and I. The trouble was, I liked him as well as ever in the old way. If only we hadn't messed it up with sex. That had complicated everything. Before the afternoon on the raft out at the MacGruders' lake two summers ago, he had been my little brother almost as much as Harriet's. We shared him between us. He was fun to tease and boss around and he was utterly safe to talk to and unusually perceptive. We had large chunks of the past in common, which I found comforting; and what we didn't have in common, I found intriguing. Spending his early years in countries where the people who took care of him worshiped other gods and lived by different values from our Western ones had made him in many ways piquant and strange. When at age ten he had returned from Brazil with Harriet to make their home permanently with their widowed Nana, his alien orientation was always popping out, either charming or embarrassing us. Some routine activity that we had always taken for granted, he would find hilarious or troubling. He would be bored by our latest fad, then become overexcited by some simple pastime the rest of us had outgrown years ago. He was attracted to people at school who the rest of us never even noticed, and in his early teens began to worry his sister and grandmother considerably by his habit of wandering off into the black part of Romulus and playing pool with the older men and sometimes babysitting for their families in the evenings.

For me, until we had complicated things, Ben had been the perfect interfacing for his sister Harriet. He provided the streak of outsiderhood, which was the thing I missed so in her. Harriet kept us grounded with her common sense, while Ben amused us with his flights of fancy. Harriet was the realist and he was the romantic. She was the loyal defender of the status quo; he the prankish challenger of it. Harriet planned her life, whereas Ben improvised his. When we went places, Harriet drove and Ben sang, and I rode along, happy to have them both.

Then, two summers ago, Harriet's boyfriend Clark from North Carolina had come to stay with them at the lake and upset our cozy threesome. Harriet now went off importantly like a grown-up to do things with her lover, leaving Ben and me behind to amuse ourselves the best we could.

Alone together, we continued to do pretty much what we always had done: swam, talked, sunbathed, and listened to tapes on

Ben's portable radio, which he would sidestroke out to the raft holding aloft, and halfway over always pretend he was about to drop, to make us scream. He was seventeen, but I still thought of him as more like fourteen, and I had just turned twenty; he was a rising senior at Romulus High and I had just completed my second year at U.Va. That summer I was not feeling too good about myself. I was just then starting to question how much of a life of my own I could actually lay claim to. Daddy was in Washington at the College of Preachers, recharging his homiletic skills and socializing with fellow clergymen, and I was staying with the MacGruders, where I always stayed when my father had to be away. Harriet's having a lover had hit me harder than I would have expected. At the beginning of the summer she had naturally confided in me, describing the salient features of this new country she had been to with the same crisp matter-of-factness with which, some years previously, she had described her year in Brazil with her parents.

"It's *not at all* like in the trashy novels," she had assured me. "You have to put *those* expectations out of your head right away or you'll be in for a disappointment. What it is, is more of a negotiation. You give something and you get something. And I can't tell you what a relief it is to have all the *mystery* over and done with. But it's not something you want to rush into, just for the sake of having done it. With all these grungy diseases going around, you've got to pick and choose very carefully. With Clark I know two things: one, he's clean—he's only had one person before me and I know her . . . she's pretty silly but she *definitely* hadn't been sexually active before Clark; and two, we can probably stay monogamous for a while without boring each other too much, because we have a lot of the same goals in common."

Not exactly the kind of travelogue to arouse in the listener a burning desire to rush there, but the fact of Harriet's having gone and my not having been there separated us. It was as if suddenly she had become my big sister as well as Ben's, dashing in and out with the new grown-up luggage of her sex life and her "goals" in the company of a like-minded traveling buddy (both she and Clark had opted for the premed program at Chapel Hill), leaving me and baby brother behind to amuse ourselves until we decided what we were going to be when *we* grew up.

I had been lying beside Ben on the raft one hot July afternoon while Harriet was off somewhere with Clark, morosely contemplating this no-man's-land in which I seemed to be stuck, with Ben's feisty cajun music thumping all around us, when I happened to open my eyes to find Ben staring solemnly into them.

"What's the matter?" I said. "Why are you looking at me like that?"

"Oh, Margaret, there's something I have to tell someone," he said. He looked tragic, but with Ben, you never could tell. He might be in some real trouble, or on the other hand it could be one of his theatricals.

I sighed. "And I suppose you want to tell me, since Harriet's not around."

"Oh, I wouldn't ever tell *Harriet* this," he protested, shocked.

"Okay," I said, "I'm listening. Only please turn the music down."

"But it's 'Sitting in Limbo' . . . it's the best piece on the whole tape."

"Then go on listening to it. But don't expect me to hear you over it. It beats me how you kids can talk and do homework and everything else with that stuff always blasting your eardrums."

The Neville Brothers were cut off in midphrase. There was a wonderful hiatus of pure silence before the natural noises of the lake reasserted themselves.

"You can be mean, Margaret, you know that?"

"Mean? How?"

"Do you really still think of me as a 'kid'? Just Harriet's little pest brother tagging along?"

"Yes and no."

"What's *that* supposed to mean?"

"Yes, I guess I do still think of you as a kid, but no, I don't find you a pest. Not usually, anyway. You can be very good company, when you're not showing off or acting crazy. What is it, Ben? Are you in trouble?"

"That depends," he replied mysteriously.

"On what?"

"Whether the person I am in love with takes me seriously."

"Oh," I said. "I see." The last time Ben had been in love, at fifteen, it had caused much consternation and Nana had been on the point of sending him off to Woodberry Forest, even though it would have left her all by herself at home, a state of affairs she had wanted to postpone as long as possible. The object of Ben's devotion had been Mr. Ritchie, the shy, straw-haired, boyish bandmaster at Romulus High, who, to his credit, had handled the situation with patience and admirable sensitivity. Ben's obsession had eventually decreased as he lost interest in becoming a professional horn player and dropped out of the band; it went on to die a natural death when Mrs. Ritchie gave birth to the couple's first child.

"I know what you're thinking, Margaret, I can read your mind. 'Is it a man or a woman this time?' Well, it's a woman. Are you relieved?"

"I *think* I am." A *woman*? I was thinking. One of his classmates? But in high school, boys didn't refer to girls as women; or maybe they did now. I was also surprisingly depressed by the news; it made me feel more of an anomaly than ever. Harriet had her Clark and now Ben was about to announce *his* new romantic attachment, and here was I, twenty years old, boyfriendless and a virgin, sleeping over with the MacGruders as I had been doing since I was four years old, without even so much as a secret.

"It's an older woman," confessed Ben. "That's why Harriet and Nana would have a fit. That among *other* reasons," he added provocatively, sounding extremely pleased with himself.

An older woman. Where would Ben meet an older woman? At church? There were plenty of older women there, but none of them remotely tempting. Of course, one never could be sure, with Ben, who found attractions in the unlikeliest of people. Was it another faculty member, female this time, at Romulus High? Where else did Ben go, except school and church and hanging out with . . . oh, no! And then I was sure I knew why "Harriet and Nana would have a fit." The older woman was a black woman. Probably the mother of one of the children over in East Romulus that Ben baby-sat with. Now that would be just like Ben. No wonder he was acting so mysterious and pleased with himself! Oh, this would do it, all right: there would be more consultations between Nana and my father, but this time nobody would wait around for him to come to his senses. It would be off to Woodberry Forest for sure, this fall. Unless I could prevail upon him not to do anything foolish. I did have an influence on him. He listened to me with a flattering respect whenever I held forth on some pet subject. In the last year or so, if I mentioned a book I liked, he would go and get it and read it, and want to talk about it with me afterwards. The idea of saving Ben from his incipient, perhaps dangerous folly did not displease me. At least it would give this forlorn sum-

mer a focus. But I would have to be careful. Any overt disapproval, especially about the race question, would be the quickest
way to drive him straight into her arms.

"What is she like?" I asked, laying an arm across my face to
protect my eyes from the sun.

I heard him swallow. I could feel his breath close to my ear and
smell his Juicy Fruit chewing gum. "Perfect," he declared in a
quiet voice, utterly free of clowning or dramatics. "Both outwardly
and inwardly just the perfect person, that's all." A motorboat
droned leisurely past and set our raft rocking upon little slapping
waves.

"Well, that's . . . impressive," I said. "But I still don't get much
of a picture. What is she like *outwardly,* for a start?"

"Oh . . . small. Neat figure. Long-waisted. Not too much hips.
Just the right amount up front. Nice legs with these cute dimples
just above the knees. *Awesome* complexion. Dark curly hair that
looks adorable when it's wet . . ."

When it was wet? Did they take showers together, or did she
wash her hair in front of him or what? Cute dimples just above the
knees . . . just the right amount up front? I was having an attack
of prudishness and was glad I had flung my arm across my eyes
so he could not "read my face," as he was always claiming he
could do.

"She only comes to about my collarbone," he went on, with
audible relish. "But that wasn't always the case. You know, I once
actually thought of her as *big,* before I grew those six inches when
I was fifteen."

Good grief, how long had this been going on? Scenes formed
on the screen of my shielded eyes: some lascivious Cleopatra over
in South Romulus, robbing little Ben of his innocence when he
was scarcely past puberty, hardly old enough to baby-sit! I was so
busy shocking myself with prurient images that it took me a moment to realize Ben had kissed me on the lips.

"Margaret, Margaret," he whispered, nuzzling my wet hair.
"How can you not know I mean you?"

I lay perfectly still for a minute, with my arm still across my
eyes. Then, because it seemed the only course of action, I stood
up shakily and dived from the raft into the water. I swam quickly
away in the direction of the wider lake. If he had dived in after me
then, it might still have come to nothing. We would soon have
been clowning and splashing. Everything would have stayed the

same because Ben would have stayed the same. But instead, he punched the Neville Brothers' catchy song back into existence and composed himself on the raft. Either his luck or his sensitivity had made him do exactly the right thing, because when I had swum far out enough to know it was time to turn around, the first thing I saw in the distance when I *did* turn around was a man, not a boy, lying on his back on that raft. I was far enough away to see him as a stranger might.

I swam slowly back towards the raft, taking pride in my crawl. I admired how my left elbow slashed crisply out of its sunlit spray each time I took a breath, and it thrilled me to know there was nothing underneath me but deep dark water, nothing between me and drowning except this skill my mother had taught me the last summer we were together. I often thought about her when I went swimming in this lake, and sometimes it seemed to me that my body remembered the firm clasp of her hands around my waist. "Go on, Margaret, I'm not going to let go of you. Put your face down into the water and kick. Go on, now, or I'm going to be cross. There is absolutely nothing down there that will hurt you— if you learn to swim, that is. Otherwise, you'll grow up to be one of those people who can never go out in a boat without a life preserver and is always worrying about falling into the water and sinking to the bottom. But when you *do* learn to swim, you'll be surprised how hard it is to do anything but float! The body just naturally wants to float, even when you throw yourself in and *try* to sink to the bottom. Relax and let *go*, Margaret! Trust me."

I climbed back up on the raft beside Ben, who now had *his* eyes closed, and made a self-conscious to-do about shaking the water out of my hair. For now it had become my "dark curly hair that looked adorable when it was wet." I was also extremely aware of my "neat figure" and the dimples above the knees and the "just the right amount up front." Oh, and of course my "awesome complexion." But I couldn't exactly be *sorry* about these things, could I?

Ben reached over and silenced the Neville Brothers once more. "Well, are you horrified?" he asked, his eyes still discreetly closed.

I looked down at the body of this person I had known since he was three. He was built better than Harriet's Clark. He had more hair on his chest and legs than my father did. Once I had helped Harriet heft this tawny, well-built stranger into the prong of an apple tree, his wet behind practically against my face as he scrab-

bled for a hold; now the little boy who had found the Golden Egg
had kissed me on the lips and caused something to flip over in my
stomach.

"I'm not sure what I am," I said.

I suffered from this double vision for the rest of that disconcerting summer. One minute there'd be the golden stranger
whom I'd seen from the distance, spread-eagled on his raft, when
I had turned around in the lake. Just looking at this well-made
male made me light-headed: wasn't it miraculous, the things we
could make each other feel? Harriet's description of it being "a
negotiation" didn't do it justice; it was more like a kind of liquid
dance . . . a sensuous sport. It brought the blood to your face as
well as other places, and made you feel sleek and buoyant afterwards, full of prowess and self-love. And when your partner
brought to it the added element of adoration, there was a lovely
warm afterglow of feeling thoroughly cherished, thoroughly
nested and at peace in someone's unqualified approval.

But then, the next minute, there would be Ben making one of
his clownish faces, or exaggerating to get our attention, or pant-
ing after me like a friendly puppy when I wanted to talk to Harriet, and I'd go clammy with repugnance at my position. What
had I *done*? What extremes of loneliness and insecurity had driven
me to seduce this *boy*, this . . . *baby brother* . . . simply because he
was the only available male in my summer? How scornful Harriet
would be if she knew . . . worse than scornful. And what would
Mrs. MacGruder do if she were to learn that she had harbored a
child molester under her roof? I could imagine her snatching up
her car keys and driving grimly across town in her new Toyota
Corolla—for Harriet now had the old Mercedes—and being
shown by my anxious father into his study. He would close the
door behind them. "Now, Nan, what is it? You sounded really
distressed on the telephone."

"I don't know how to tell you this, Walter, but I must."

I needed a woman to talk to, and the woman who had been
most like a mother to me, Mrs. MacGruder, was now, for obvious
reasons, disqualified. I needed my own mother to tell me whether
I was disgusting, or typical, or what. Ruth would have had stories,
I was sure of it. She would have resurrected something enlight-
ening (maybe funny, too) from her youth. Surely there was some

boy with a tan in her past; perhaps there was even a blanket in the woods by a lake in her past, too. I would have made her tell me, even if we had to keep it a secret from Daddy. "Well, of course, Margaret," she possibly would say. "It's the natural thing. The body just naturally wants to make love, the same way it just naturally wants to float. There's nothing down there that will hurt you—unless you start *fretting* about it."

On the other hand, she had been ashamed of her sister. Maybe, determined to be a virtuous contrast to Connie Roundheels, my mother had remained a virgin until she married Daddy. Before this summer, I had wanted her to be. Now I wanted her not to have been; I wanted her to be like me.

When the summer came to an end, Ben formally asked Harriet if he could borrow her car and take me for an all-day trip to the Peaks of Otter. Both Mrs. MacGruder and Harriet thought I was so good to indulge him in this excursion. "He's developed a little pash on you this summer," Mrs. MacGruder confided to me, "but, frankly, Margaret, I can't think of anyone I'd rather have him admire. You're mature enough to handle it gracefully, and it's kept him from hanging out with . . . well, you know . . . his companions at the pool hall over in South Romulus and at their night club, what is it called?"

"Melody Station," I said, feeling safe enough in my deception to admit he'd taken me there a couple of evenings. "There's this group of musicians he likes to sing with, they imitate the Neville Brothers. Ben's got a good voice, and he's very popular over there."

"Oh, I'm sure he is," Mrs. MacGruder said dryly. "Well, one more year to go. Then if we can just get him into a decent college. Maybe *you* can have a little heart-to-heart with him, Margaret. He esteems you so. I mean, first it was the clarinet and now it's the singing, and who knows what will be next? But try and make him see that he's got to *apply* himself . . . like Harriet does . . . if he's ever going to amount to anything."

"Well, I'll do my best," I said, the virtuous little mother. Hypocrite that I was.

Our day for the Peaks of Otter started off badly and got worse. Ben drove too fast on the Blue Ridge Parkway and flared up whenever I reminded him of the speed limit.

"Do you want to get there or don't you? And we still have the hike to the top of Sharp Top Trail after we get there. If I crawl at the speed *you* want, Margaret, it'll be three o'clock before we even have lunch."

"Well, let's take one of the shorter trails then."

"No, I want us to get to Buzzard's Roost. The view's awesome up there."

It was a weekday and Buzzard's Roost would most likely be deserted; only hikers who were in top shape attempted it anyway. He had it all planned: first Nana's picnic lunch and then . . . "the awesome view." The double role I had played all summer had finally worn me down, and I felt like a cynical middle-aged woman trapped in a rattly old Mercedes with an out-of-temper boy whose lustful designs were ridiculously transparent. Dismayed at myself, because I didn't want to spoil our last time together before I went back to Charlottesville, I kept stealing glances at him, hoping to summon back the golden stranger from the raft. But the stranger did not appear. The double vision had corrected itself, unfortunately for Ben, at the outset of this occasion on which he had set so much store.

We arrived in plenty of time to hike the Sharp Top Trail to Buzzard's Roost. There was no one up there but us. We opened our backpacks and ate Mrs. MacGruder's fried chicken and drank her sweetened iced tea from Ben's thermos. We "enjoyed the view," both the 360-degree one of the Piedmont to the east, the Blue Ridge Mountains, and the Shenandoah Valley with the Allegheny Mountains to the west, and the one for which it had been a euphemism. For the first time, I was not transported, and had the decency to feel sad about it for Ben's sake as well as my own. Of course with his awful sixth sense he knew, although I did my best to fake it. After we were fully dressed again, wearing our sweaters because it had turned chilly, he stood against a rock formation taller than he was and pulled me to him and sobbed into my hair.

But on the way back to Romulus, he won my respect by rallying. He turned on the car radio and sang along with a country music station, and when it faded out he flicked it off and sang by himself. He sang Neville Brothers songs and Bob Dylan songs, and after that he started in on hymns. His own melodic voice, a sweet, high tenor, practically a countertenor, seemed to cheer him up. I joined in with my unexceptional alto and we sang all of

"Amazing Grace" together, then what verses we could remember of other favorites: "Brightest and Best of the Sons of the Morning," "For All Thy Saints," "When Morning Gilds the Skies."

I had not kept my promise to Mrs. MacGruder about having a word with Ben about applying himself, but the irony was, with my double vision gone, I had now become what she had believed me to be all along: that older girl she could trust to handle the situation gracefully. Yes, Mrs. MacGruder or Harriet or Daddy or all of them at once could be spying on us now and see nothing I wouldn't want them to see: just little Ben and Father Melancholy's daughter, blending their voices in a church hymn. And I must admit this thought brought me more relief than pain.

However, we *didn't* revert back to our old brother-and-sister relationship, as I had (rather naively) assumed we would. Nothing stopped; it just became more problematic than ever. I wasn't in love with him, but it seemed pointlessly hard on Ben to shut the barn door once the horse was out anyway. I went back to Charlottesville for my third year of college, and Ben started his senior year at Romulus High. So far, so good. Distance, and all that.

But I went home to see Daddy at least two weekends per month and sometimes more, if he was in the dumps. And there was Ben, on display in the one place I couldn't evade him. Everybody thought he was undergoing a religious conversion. He became my father's most faithful server at Sunday Mass. I had always liked that interlude just before the service began, when I could sit quietly in the pew and review the past week and then let it go and get ready for the next one. If I wanted to express it in religious language, I would have said I was "offering up" the past week, the whole mixed-bag of failures, accomplishments, and incompletes, and inviting the Holy Spirit to contribute its shaping powers to the one ahead. But such language tended to make me squirm. Too many good words and images had been ruined by facile usage and unctuous people. Miriam Stacy "called on the Holy Spirit" before she wrote in her famous diary every night, and would tell you all about it.

Anyway, this restorative interlude of mine was now shadowed by Ben. There he was up there in his cassock and surplice, lighting the candles on the high altar, marking my father's places with ribbons in the Order of Service Book, bowing and bobbing like Baryshnikov every time he passed in front of the tabernacle. It was impossible not to notice that he had a good body and he looked well in the clothes. Liturgical skirts swaying from manly torsos have been titillating women in church for centuries: something to do with the *nolo me tangere* aspect, undoubtedly. The golden stranger seen from the distance on his raft had bitten the dust, but now here was the virile altar server with his swaying skirts. He destroyed my interlude and I hated him for it. My cleansing week-to-week slough-off didn't work anymore—I couldn't "let the past go and get ready for the future" in the same neat way as before, with Ben sticking in the middle of it, leaving a ragged edge. It was like trying to tear off a straight new sheet of plastic wrap from a roll that you had torn crookedly last time. You turn it around and around, squinting for the telltale seam, growing more and more exasperated as you search for the ragged edge so you can rip it out and start straight again. Sometimes you find it, sometimes you pick at it until it gets to be such a mess you have to throw the roll out and buy a new one at the store. But how was I going to rip out what I'd done with Ben? That was there forever, with all its known and yet-to-be-discovered consequences. Yet I couldn't throw our whole history away and start over, either. I started referring to him in my thoughts as my albatross. I had just finished reading *The Rime of the Ancient Mariner,* and it seemed as good a description as any, short of resorting to religious imagery. And I was not about to elevate Ben MacGruder to the status of a cross. Though sometimes during the service when I'd look up and catch him brooding at me from his choir seat while my oblivious father chanted confidently on, I certainly did think of him as exactly that.

Everyone wanted Ben to go to Georgetown University and start studying to be a diplomat, like his father. He dutifully applied, went for an interview, and was turned down. He was an extremely personable young man, the rejection letter said, but his grades were not good enough. So he came to U.Va., which, though rigorous on out-of-staters, turns a complacent eye on its native sons.

"Frankly," Mrs. MacGruder had confided to me, "I can't help believing Charlottesville will turn out to be best, after all. He will have *you* close by, Margaret. Your example will be an inspiration for him . . . let's hope."

VII : PASSIONTIDE

*T*raffic, as I left Charlottesville for the drive home to Daddy, was its usual maddening crawl; it got better once I was off 64 West and headed north on 81. And on the winding country road into Romulus, I was quite alone, just as in my dream drives, only, this Friday afternoon before Palm Sunday, there were cherry, apple, and redbud trees, on the verge of blooming.

On the Romulus side of the river bridge that rattled and shook, I stopped at the Sampson Fish Market and bought some nice-looking lemon sole, and then let Jeff Sampson, whom I had gone to high school with, and whose hands-on salesmanship was so much more pleasant than his father's surly style, talk me into adding some fresh bay scallops and a few shrimps and oysters for a seafood platter. "That way, Margaret, you won't have to fuss with vegetables. You buy a half pound of this tasty cole slaw I just got finished making and you and the Reverend will eat like kings. You'll need batter for the fish. It's our own special mix: yellow cornmeal, herbs, and of course some secret ingredient I'm not going to tell you about, otherwise you could go home and make it for yourself—"

"I've already got some, and it's delicious. You made me buy the large-size bag the last time I was in here, remember?"

"Oh, right. You'll be graduating from U.Va. soon, won't you?"

"Another month to go."

"Found Mr. Right yet?" Jeff was already the father of twin boys and a baby girl. Snapshots of their rapidly changing little faces and bodies, updated with loving frequency, were taped across the glass of the display counter.

"No, not yet," I said.

"Well, don't you worry, Margaret. He'll be coming down the pike directly. Who knows, he might be headed for your house this very afternoon."

"Oh, not this afternoon, *please*, Jeff. I wouldn't have enough fish to go around."

"Want me to throw in another couple of sole, just in case?"

"No thank you," I said, laughing.

On through poor dead downtown Romulus, which like so many American downtowns had had its lifeblood sucked dry by the vampire malls. The flag flew over the post office and the courthouse was still in business, and the Restoration and Rebeautification Society continued to plant seasonal flowers around the Confederate Soldier's monument, but the stores, what few were still open, had become debased versions of themselves. The drugstore was no longer Walgreens where the school bus had dropped little Brian Vesey of the rotting teeth, who ate candy bars and read magazines while his mother worked for the pharmacist, or where Ruth and I once, long ago, shopped for pretty paper napkins for the church coffee hour and then sat on the high stools and had Cokes and crackers and mother-daughter talk; it was now called Cut-Rite, and had torn out its soda fountain and dispensed with a pharmacist. Whenever I drove through downtown now, I got a foretaste of what it would be like to be old: you would go around looking through places and people and seeing them not as they had become, but bathed in the consolingly vivid light of memory.

I swung right, into wide, tree-lined Church Street, our street. When I was little I loved to hear Daddy explain that even though there were now three churches on Church Street, Central Methodist, First Presbyterian, and ours, St. Cuthbert's was the oldest, the only one built before the Civil War, and ours was why the street had been named Church Street. "If the others had been there then, they would have had to name it *Churches* Street, wouldn't they?" I said once, making Daddy laugh.

What on earth was this *traffic?* For I was suddenly aware that I had been creeping along Church Street the way I had grown resigned to creeping through downtown Charlottesville. I stuck my head out the window and saw a solid line of cars ahead of me, all the way to our corner.

Good grief, was this the famous bottleneck that Daddy had been telling me about on the phone? The one that was infuriating the people living up at the top of Macon in Mr. Gaines's Sunset Villas? But how had things gotten so bad *all of a sudden*? It had been nowhere this congested the last time I was home. How had the town let this happen? Weren't they supposed to look at their big maps and see what was encroaching on what was already there, landmarks and corners they were supposed to protect, and call a halt to it *then*? Why hadn't anybody told Georgie Gaines's greedy father he couldn't build any more units of Sunset Villas than the traffic of narrow Macon Street could bear?

This was just impossible! People couldn't be expected to sit in their cars and *inch* down a residential street in a small town. Then I realized with a shock that I was thinking from the point of view of the people stuck in traffic. And I could see how intolerant they would be of a die-hard rector (of a moribund old institution that most people didn't think twice anymore about neglecting for Sunday golf) who thought his corner calvary was more important than their getting back and forth to their villas, the villas on which the city made them pay hefty taxes. Ah, poor Daddy, if they *were* going to slice off his corner, I would have to try and turn his mind to the positive aspects. Thirty thousand dollars: would Greedy George Gaines actually pay St. Cuthbert's that much for a corner and a few acres of swamp? It was unfortunate, though, that the number happened to be *thirty,* because if the deal came about, Daddy would make depressing parallels between his transaction and the one Judas had made.

The traffic inched along until I could see the top half of St. Cuthbert's and the roof of the rectory. Weathered brick and ivy . . . "Grizzled brick," she had called it, the sarcastic woman who had sauntered up our front walk sixteen years ago come next September and taken my mother away forever the following day. "So this is the *rectory*," she had said in her mocking voice: "I had first thought a chilly gray stone, but this grizzled brick creates the same mood. I expected the ivy, of course."

Did I *remember* her saying that, or did Daddy and I devise it later, during one of our many apocryphal rehashes of Ruth's last evening at the rectory? But what I could remember for certain was the profound unease I had felt as I went ahead of the two women down our dark hallway, carrying Madelyn's "power" cereal to be refrigerated. For the first time in my childhood, I had become aware of the presence of darkness in the house where I lived, and I remember connecting this new awareness with the arrival of my mother's friend.

The line of cars crept forward again, snaking to the right for the turnoff into Macon Street, and there was the disputed corner with our little stone Christ hanging in his wayside shelter and . . . oh, no . . . there was my father, in a baggy old sweatshirt, doing, oh, Lord, *what?*

At first sight, he appeared to be embracing the crucified figure's torso, and I underwent a complete déjà vu resurgence of the old shame I had felt that afternoon when Lucy Brush's retarded sister had blurted out "THAT MAN . . . HURT!" and I had looked out of the school bus to see my father groveling in the ivy at the foot of the cross.

As I got closer, I saw that Daddy was washing down the stone figure. He did have his arm slung around Christ's hips, but only for the purpose of maintaining his balance while he scrubbed away at one of the outstretched arms.

At last I could free myself from the line of cars waiting to get up Macon, and pull over to the curb at our corner. As I got out of the car, my father whirled around belligerently, as though expecting trouble.

"Oh, good," he said, his face relaxing when he saw it was me. "Well, it's been some week, but I think we've won for the moment."

"What happened?"

"The Major came through. I knew she would. She got her friend the judge to issue a restraining order on the town until her friend in the legislature has a chance to do *his* job. If he comes through, St. Cuthbert's corner is almost sure to be granted historical status as long as *our* friend remains here"—he patted the gracefully twisted stone savior fondly—"because he is over a hundred years old. Greedy Gaines's nose is out of joint, of course. That's what *this* little vendetta's all about." With an angry wave of his hand, Daddy indicated the traffic creeping up Macon.

"What vendetta? I don't understand." I was not happy with my father's appearance. It was not just the dishevelment of someone who badly needed a haircut, or that his neck looked pitifully naked and scraggly without the crisp white support of his collar.

(Where on earth had he found that baggy U.Va. sweatshirt? It didn't belong to me.) But I also didn't like the glistening pallor of his skin, and I thought he was breathing too fast for someone who had merely been washing a statue. But then I reminded myself my father was not a young man anymore. Actually, I had never known him as a young man. No, my father would soon be sixty and I had to admit he looked his age.

"This manipulated traffic jam. They're repairing a 'pothole,' farther up Macon, that some lady walker from Sunset Villas claims she sprained her ankle in yesterday morning. Mrs. Radford tells me she's threatening to sue the town. Myself, I think they dug the pothole themselves, then cooked up the lady and the lawsuit, just to create this bottleneck so everybody will panic about how bad the traffic's going to be if we don't let them slice away this corner."

In the ivy at my father's feet was a fruit crate containing his cleaning materials. There was the pot we made soup in, filled with dirty water; an assortment of rags, sponges, and scouring pads; and what was obviously an economy-size cylinder of Ajax with a piece of Christmas wrapping paper Scotch-taped around it.

"Why the camouflage?" I asked him, pointing to the Ajax.

"Oh, it just seemed more respectful, I guess, with everybody watching me. More ecclesiastical. Let them think it's some special church stuff. Never hurts to encourage a little awe in people. But you know, Margaret, this Ajax works better than whatever fancy compound the Rebeautification Society used last time. Look how white he is! I thought he ought to look his best in case the newspapers send a photographer out. I thought the editor would have returned my calls by now."

"Is it a good idea to have him so white, if the whole thing hangs on his being old?"

"Well, I thought about that, but I decided it was more important for him to stand out against the foliage. People will look at him afresh. Maybe they'll remember a few things they've forgotten in their frantic chase to get to the top of the mountain."

"Where did you get that sweatshirt?"

"Little Ben. He came over this morning and insisted on washing my sweater. He left this behind as a consolation."

"What was he doing in Romulus on Friday morning? He has classes."

"I expect he had his reasons. Maybe Nan needed him for something. I thought it was right sweet of him to notice about my sweater. He told me Doc had been just as bad about his. When it got unbearable, Nan would sneak it away and wash it while he slept and then dry it on a towel next to the furnace in the basement. It would be ready for him the next evening when he got in from his rounds. He never even missed it, Ben said."

"I could have washed your sweater perfectly well; in fact, I was planning to. Oh, hell, I don't know why I worry if he cuts his classes. I'm not his mother. I'm not even his sister."

"He thinks you hung the moon. That's why he's always coming over and making himself so agreeable to me. He probably thought washing my sweater would please you."

"It's not his place to think what would please me any more than it is for him to wash your sweater."

"You're too hard on that little boy," Daddy commented rather blithely, resuming his scrubbing of the Christ figure with relish.

Little boy, ha . . . if you only knew, I thought sourly. "I'll go on up to the house," I said. "I bought fish at Sampson's, it should go in the refrigerator. And while there's still sun in the garden, maybe I should cut your hair."

"Oh, is it that time again already?" asked my father absently, working up a foamy lather in the folds of the figure's draped torso with the Christmas-papered Ajax.

I drove the rest of the way up the block and parked behind my father's ten-year-old Volvo station wagon—another great find of Ernie Pasco's—in front of the house. The rectory didn't have a garage; it didn't even have its own driveway. In winter when it snowed or iced over, my father had to spend ten or fifteen minutes out on the street with the scraper before driving off on his pastoral rounds. There had been various "surveys" on the part of successive vestry committees to determine whether trees ought to be cut down to make way for a modest driveway, and, should that driveway be granted existence, whether it then ought to culminate in a lean-to built onto the side of the rectory (which some thought would be tacky and ruin the architectural lines) or in a full-fledged garage (which others deemed prohibitively expensive); a fund had been started for the purpose twelve years ago, spearheaded by Dr. MacGruder, who knew what it was like to have an iced-over windshield when you were needed in a hurry at someone's bedside, but as it was never given a name because the vestry members couldn't agree on one ("garage fund" promised a garage, whereas "driveway fund" didn't include any sort of shelter), it was always

being siphoned off for projects that had earned unanimous ac-
cord: the ramps and rails for the handicapped at the front and
side entrances of the church; the renovated social hall in the crypt.

If my mother had stayed around, she could have gotten it
done. She would have shamed them . . . or teased them . . . into it.
If as a bride in her twenties she had been able to persuade them
to let her knock out a wall in Mrs. Hazeltine's venerable dining
room, who knows what she might have accomplished in the fullness of her years?

Entering the rectory, I found my own depression waiting for
me like a faithful friend. Welcome home, it said, I got here ahead
of you, I'm not stopped by traffic jams. You'll find everything
about the same. Need to open some windows, your father doesn't
notice the fustiness.

On his study desk were the photocopied pages of "The Parson's Tale" I had Express-Mailed him on Tuesday, all about the
"horrible synne of accidie" and how to fight it. And he'd been
writing some notes, either for his sermon or that talk, I couldn't
be sure.

"He who hath begun a good work in you will perfect it."

Adrian: ". . . something in us desires our problems, is a
little bit in love with them . . ."
                    (?!)

attributed to Jesus in the Gnostic Gospel of Thomas:
"If you bring forth what is within you,
What you bring forth will save you.
If you do not bring forth what is within you,
What you do not bring forth will destroy you."

"Knock on yourself as upon a door and walk upon yourself as on a straight road . . ." Silvanus? Ask Adrian for
source.

Original sin = repeating our parents' mistakes?

A scary thought, that last. Had it been my father's? And who
was Adrian?

Well, things seemed to be all right enough in here, except for the stale air. I opened a window that looked out on Daddy's garden, backed by the wall Katharine Thrale and I had built. Wild thyme and stonecrop grew out of its crevices, blackberry vines tangled down its sides, and silvery-green lichen patches antiqued its irregular outcroppings: it did not look like a wall built as recently as seven years ago. We had lost track of Katharine. At first we exchanged cards with notes at Christmas. She sent Daddy several tracts, printed by the convent press, that she had written concerning the role of women in the church. Then one of our cards was returned to Daddy with a note from the Reverend Mother. Though Katharine had been productive in the convent, she had decided God was not calling her to take her final vows; she had gone to live in New Mexico, but had left no forwarding address.

On to the kitchen, preparing myself for the usual flare-up of annoyance with what I was going to find there. Daddy didn't qualify as a slob, but he failed to notice things like grease and breadcrumbs. He would empty the garbage pail but forget to put in a new liner.

I squeezed lemon juice over the pieces of fish and put them to marinate in the refrigerator. I found a rotten cucumber in the crisper and disposed of it. Daddy's sweater, washed by Ben, lay on my mother's table in the breakfast nook, competently blocked and stretched, its wrists crossed debonairly upon its chest. It was almost dry from the earlier sun that had poured through the bay window. Though I couldn't have done the job any better myself, I resented Ben's wifely interference. Though he had done it to please me, because I had said it was one of the things I had to do for Daddy this weekend, it had just the opposite effect. It evoked a future that made my spirit revolt. Far worse, but perhaps far more likely, than Ben's spiteful prediction of Daddy and me making spiritual pilgrimages in a Winnebago was the vision of me, with my doctorate, teaching English at some college, while Ben hung around with my retired father, entertaining him and washing the sweaters. Was Ben worming his way into my father's heart in order to earn my gratitude? Forcing his usefulness on me until I capitulated and married him because it would make everybody else happy? I wouldn't put it past him.

Oh, God, what was my life going to be? A commonplace supplication, worn smooth by the eloquence of the ancients. "Thou tellest my wanderings: put thou my tears into thy bottle; are they not in thy book?"

But who and where *was* that God to whom I could address such a question and expect an engaged listener? Where was the bottle collecting my tears, where was the book containing the story of my life, except in the imagination of an inspired psalmist? Though my father was in the religion business and I had grown up surrounded by people who behaved as if the whole question of who God was and where He could be found had been settled for them long ago, I knew it was more difficult than that. I suspected many of them knew it, too, but it was more convenient to keep the knowledge under wraps. The nearest thing to God I could truly call my own anymore was that luminous, focusing consciousness that I sometimes became aware of when I was going about my business, doing the most mundane or disinterested thing, such as making Mrs. Dunbar's cocoa. Then, without any effort or petition on my part, I would find myself contained by an attention that seemed capable of remembering everything I ever did, things I had forgotten myself, and weaving (or having already woven) all of it into the pattern of what I was going to become. But this presence lacked the comforting element I yearned for, because it needed me to get on with its work. I would have liked more of a Parent-God, into whose all-loving embrace I could curl up, into whose perfectly wise care I could give myself over and trust to make the most of me. Yet every day I lived brought me closer to the tired knowledge that belief in, or desire for, any such capitulation was regressive thinking.

I sank down in my mother's old place in the window seat. Without its morning sun, the nook seemed desolate. Some of my sharpest, most visceral memories of her were connected with this spot in morning sunshine where she would drink her coffee and make her lists and paint the watercolors that engrossed her while she was doing them but often made her unhappy afterwards. She had been unhappy the time she had painted me, saying she hadn't caught me. I had felt bad too, as though her failure to catch me was partly my fault.

I ran my fingers over Daddy's washed cardigan, blocked so carefully by Ben on the table. Not quite dry, it already had that clean, fluffed-up feel. It smelled of damp animal and Woolite. It was about the same dun color as a damp old sheep. Considering that it was practically as old as I was, it had held up well. Pringle's

of Scotland, 100% pure cashmere, the faded label read. Had my
mother still loved him on whatever birthday or Christmas she had
given him this sweater? At what point in their marriage had she
acknowledged to herself that the handsome priest who had met
with her in the Green Parlor at her college, the man who, as she
had confessed to him in her first letter, "was too much for her,"
was indeed too much for her, but in the less flattering sense of the
phrase?

It was possible she had been sitting exactly where I sat now, the
sun gone from her corner just as certain illusions were gone,
when she had first called into question the whole life she was
living: the things for which my father lived, having to worry about
pleasing people like the Major and avoiding the censure of the
Ned Stumbling Blocks and the Miriam Stacys ... the Church
itself. What if it all had been a wrong choice, not just her marriage, but the very way of life her husband worshiped? What if the
Christ who had started all this had been after something else
entirely ... as she was now realizing *she* had been after something
else? What did this routine that called itself religion, which could
not cure her husband's sadness, which crimped and cramped her
so, have to do with the brave, proud life she had dreamed of
finding for herself?

Why did I not feel ashamed of putting these thoughts into her
mind now? Maybe because she hadn't been very much older than
I was now when she had sat here. And if I, about to turn twenty-
two, could finally admit to myself that my father, much as I loved
him, was no longer my hero, and sometimes a burden, then it was
not a terribly big leap of the imagination to guess the probable
disappointments that had been festering in her when she left us at
age twenty-eight. After all, we were talking about the same man.
The same charming, beleaguered man with the same debilitating
sorrows and crusades.

And now this latest crusade of his, the corner calvary. I was
glad that he was winning over the forces of greed and bad planning, just as in the past he had won his crusade to stick to Rite One
in the prayer book, just as he had won his crusade to make everyone ... well, almost everyone ... treat Professor LaFarge like
a human being after his public disgrace. But ... oh, what did it
matter, what did it all really add up to, in the long run?

Professor LaFarge had moved to France and was flourishing
without us. He loved the old churches and monasteries, and the

local newspaper with its saint of the day, and fixing up his restored Provencal farmhouse; he had met congenial types, both Frenchmen and exiles like himself, who went antique hunting together and cooked with herbs they had gathered on the hillsides and decorated one another's houses. He admired the local young priest and had written Daddy he was thinking of following in the footsteps of John Henry Newman and going over to Rome.

And though everyone in the congregation flipped automatically to page 323 in the prayer book (those who could not already recite Rite One verbatim in their sleep), and though Daddy's service was said by everyone, even the people who went to the more popular and crowded St. Matthias, to be the most liturgically beautiful and respectful of any in the area, St. Cuthbert's had 88 pledged members and an annual diocesan assessment of $950, whereas swinging Jerry Hope's church had 400 members and an assessment of $10,000. (Religion had become an industry just like everything else, Daddy was fond of declaring: you could tell how "successful" a church was by how much the diocese taxed it.)

And even if Daddy did manage to save the wayside cross at the edge of our property, in ten more years (at the most!) it would no longer be "our" property anyway; after he retired, it would and must no longer be our concern. Such was the custom of our church. He would not even be welcome as a member of the congregation; at least not for the first few years, anyway. If we stayed on in the area, we would have to drive to Trinity over in Staunton to worship on Sunday, because Daddy would give up church altogether before worshiping at St. Matthias. Once a rector retired, if he didn't have the decency to die promptly like Dr. Hazeltine, or move to Florida, he was supposed to remove himself gracefully from the scene that he had helped to shape for decades, in order that his successor would not feel shadowed.

"So! You think I'm old shaggy-baggy again," said my father breathlessly, coming through the back screen door, carrying his crate with the pot of dirty water and the sponges and Ajax. "Shall I fetch the beauty tools from upstairs?"

"No, I'll go. I haven't taken my things up yet." Since when had he gotten this breathless? We would have to have a little talk about his general upkeep. After Dr. MacGruder had died, he had gone to doctors when he was sick, but had made no attempt to find a personal physician. "They're all specialists now, anyway," was his excuse. "I'd have to have one for my nose and another one for my stomach and another for my lungs, and so on. Doc treated the whole man, inner and outer. Besides, except for my Black Curtain, I'm basically a healthy man. I think those Mary Baker Eddy people have a point: there's too much rushing off to the emergency room for heartburn and ingrown toenails. Doc himself used to say that the body itself is the best healer; most things, if you leave them alone overnight, will be better in the morning. And ultimately, when the good Lord wants you, he'll take you anyway."

When I came back down to the kitchen with the scissors, comb, Q-Tips, rubbing alcohol, old toothbrush, and vaseline, Daddy had already seated himself outdoors in his "grooming chair," an old wicker whose seat tipped forward, making it easier for me to get to the back of his neck. He had brought out the necessary brown paper grocery bag, for hair trimmings and used Q-Tips, and had placed it open on the grass by the side of his chair. The glimpse of him through the bay window, sitting there so submissively in Ben's too-large U.Va. sweatshirt, head bowed, hands resting on either arm of the chair, the delicate pink blossoms of the Mt. Fuji cherry tree behind him, just now afire with the setting sun, making his still-handsome, though worn, face the center of its composition, moved me almost to tears. How could I, even secretly, consider him a burden? He was the creature closest to me in the world. Each of us was what the other *had*.

This mood intensified as I took my place behind him and embarked on the most personal of our household rituals. Whereas I might be having trouble these days believing in a God who could be bothered to number all the hairs on my head, I hadn't the least trouble acknowledging that I knew my father's head; I might not know the number of hairs, but I was intimately acquainted with the combinations and configurations of those hairs. I knew the springy way they clumped and fell from a slightly off-center part to either side of his high forehead; I could remember which slabs had turned white first, and was able to please him during each subsequent barbering session by describing to him how richly dark the back of his head still remained. I had learned how to angle and contour with my scissors so that the old-man thinness spreading over his crown was offset and lifted by the still-youthful, almost bushy texture at the sides and back.

He sat with his eyes closed, facing into the late sun. For a while neither of us spoke. Breathing more slowly now, my father gave himself up to the luxury of being tended to. I did the preliminary shaping, then went to work on his ears, first carefully snipping the hairs from the outer rims and lobes, then clearing the growth from the inner whorls. "Yuk! Look at all this hair," I muttered in pretend-disgust. "It's a wonder you've been able to hear a thing."

"Men are hairy beasts," he assented lazily, his eyes still closed. "Especially old ones." This was one of our habitual exchanges.

After that came the Q-Tips dipped in alcohol. Most people don't know that the worst thing you can do is clean the ears with oil. It coagulates and *attracts* the wax. Dr. MacGruder had explained that to us once.

"Isn't it funny that your right ear always has more wax than your left ear?" I held out the two used Q-tips for my father's interested inspection.

"That's probably because my right brain is working harder."

"You're definitely a left brain, Daddy."

"Well, there goes that theory."

I went to work on his nostrils, taking especial care as I snipped around in the inside of his nose; both of us remembered how, at fourteen and new to the art of barbering, I had once drawn blood. Our sessions had begun after his barber had retired and the new man had displayed a callous disregard for the natural flow of my father's hair. Daddy had come home looking hacked at and diminished. "I could do better than that," I had protested, "and I wouldn't charge you twenty dollars, either." "Yes, I believe you could," Daddy had replied thoughtfully.

Next came the eyebrows, first the brushing upwards with an old toothbrush rubbed in vaseline, then the weeding out of strays. There were several unrulies that were always trying to grow straight down into his eyes.

"Now for the finishing touches." This last part was my reward: when I could stand back and survey my cleaned-up father and then, with a few precise and artful adjustments with the scissors—lifting the side hair up and away from the neatened ears; blunt-cutting (thus accentuating) the boyish slab, still dark, which fell over his right temple—remove ten years from his appearance.

My father lifted his shoulders and took in a deep, satisfied breath of garden air, with its mingled smells of freshly turned earth, grape hyacinths, and narcissi, and the first cut grass of the season. "Maybe I'm being precipitate, but I think this thing has lifted," he said.

"You do?" Of course I knew he was referring to the Black Curtain.

"Yes, and . . . perhaps I shouldn't say it, but there's something different about it this time. It feels . . . it feels as though it's lifted for good."

I was blunt-cutting the boyish slab of hair in front, laying it flat against his temple and angling upwards and outwards from the eyebrow with the scissors. "What about it feels different, this time?" I asked a shade nervously, as if the fates might indeed hear, and hasten to correct their oversight.

"Well, I've been trying to define it. It's not that I'm giddy with happiness . . . in fact, I've been rather tired lately. But I feel free of it. I feel something has been completed."

"You still seemed low when we talked on the phone Tuesday night."

"Yes, it was after that. Though I think it may have *started* getting better while we were talking. After we hung up, I did just what you told me, I looked through your mother's letters, to refresh my mind about that old sermon. I read through some of the letters, and, you know, Margaret, for the first time I didn't feel any pain. Oh, I felt regret, and love for her, but it wasn't that old aggrieved sense of having been wronged. It was more as if I were some detached person . . . detached but interested . . . going through the letters, knowing how the story of these two people was going to come out, even though they couldn't know it yet. I felt compassion for them, but it didn't directly affect me anymore. It was just a human story among many others. And given who each of them was, it somehow seemed inevitable. It was bound to turn out the way it did. Yet they had to go through it, anyway, because it was their story."

"That's . . . *very* detached," I said, fluffing out the boyish cowlick I had just rejuvenated and circling around behind him to do the final trimming at the back of the neck. My anger surprised me. It didn't directly *affect* him anymore? How could he say that about the story that had made us as we were today, the story that had made us *us*? I was as unprepared as if he had announced he was abandoning me.

But my anger had the tonic advantage of hardening something in me. It enabled me to ask a question I would have spared him otherwise.

"If you say you felt wronged, Daddy, then there must have been . . . I mean, you must have had some reason to believe she was never coming back even before she was killed in that accident."

"Never coming back? Well, I don't know. Only God knows what was in her heart. Actually I believe there was a good chance she would have come back . . . for you, you know, if nothing else. Perhaps a little for my sake, too. Ruth set great store on honor. She might have come back simply because she felt it was the honorable thing to do. But we weren't getting on too well. I think she was beginning to hate me for not being . . . well, whatever it was she had taken me for in the first place. That was the thing I was finally able to accept the other night, when I was rereading those letters. And then when I was drafting my Palm Sunday sermon . . . you know, about how people can turn against the person they've idolized, if their expectations are thwarted . . . that helped me to see aspects of it, too. Awful as it may sound to say so, Margaret, it might have been more terrible for us all if she *had* come back."

I brushed away the hair clippings from his bare, bowed neck with my fingers and stood behind him, critically eyeing my handiwork. The line at the back was clean and even, but the haircut exposed the old-man wrinkles where the base of his neck met his shoulders. He would do better to wear his collar as much as possible in his declining years, even *under* sweatshirts, I thought cruelly. I already had my next question for him ready: *What did she do, exactly, what sort of things did she do, or not do, to make you think she was beginning to hate you?* Pictures to go with his possible answers, both the ones he would give and the ones he would not, were filling my head.

Perhaps they had been there for years, these pictures. I suspected they had: waiting behind the curtain for their cues, waiting until I was ready to challenge the official story I was raised on— the story my father and I had raised each other on. Waiting until I was provoked into using my own powers of perception and intuition, or—how had old Stannard put it?—my natural empathy, my "respectful imagination." If I could be trusted to "look into" the lore surrounding a seventh-century abbess and come up with something valid and fresh about her, how much better then ought I to be able to read the disposition of a woman whose touch and presence I could remember, whose jokes and views and many of her actual words echoed in me like the oft-quoted phrases from a second Bible, whose blood and genes had given me my life and part of my personality?

Hadn't I just been doing exactly that, back in the kitchen? Sitting in her old place in the breakfast nook and evoking the disappointments she may have been harboring in the weeks and months before she left us?

"How is it doing back there?" asked Daddy. "Are there still one or *two* dark hairs left?" It was the question he always asked at the end of the haircut, but I knew all his tones. Just now behind the humorous vanity of the request I heard his plea for another kind of reassurance, and it wrecked my resolve to have it out with him at last. He had sensed my shock at his last statement. He was afraid he might have gone too far, and he needed to be assured not that his hair was still dark back there but that the person back there still loved him just as much.

"What do you mean, one or two dark hairs," I chided, laying the scissors down on the grass. "It's completely dark back there." I pulled his shoulders back and forth, giving him a little massage. As he moaned softly with pleasure, I was painfully struck by how loose and defenseless his bones and tissues felt under my fingers.

"In fact," I went on, embellishing, "I think the dark is *spreading.* By next haircutting time, it may have reached up to your crown, and before we know it, Miriam Stacy will be going around saying how scandalous it is that Father Gower's started using Grecian Formula on his hair. And then Ned Block will put in his two cents, about the late great Dr. Hazeltine's dignified white sideburns and rosy pink bald scalp having so much more '*presence*' . . ."

"Oh, Margaret, Margaret . . ." My father's shoulders were shaking with laughter, and with relief, and I was so glad I had been merciful. Wasn't it kinder, and better for all concerned, if the two of us went on making this picture together of devoted father and daughter than to call up pictures that would only reproach us with past failures that we couldn't remedy anymore?

At the same time that I was thinking about this picture we made, I also became aware that someone was there to see it. A man had entered the garden from the flagstone path around the side of the rectory. The sun that my father and I faced into was behind him, so I couldn't tell much about him except that he wore the collar of a priest and carried books under one arm. Though he was just now in the act of hanging back, out of an obvious reluctance to intrude upon our intimate scene, there was still an eddy of unrestrained movement about him that suggested him swinging around this corner on previous occasions, confidently sure of his welcome.

"Adrian . . . how nice . . ." said Daddy, springing eagerly to his feet and brushing hairs from Ben's sweatshirt. "Come and meet my Margaret, Romulus's most accomplished barber."

"So I see," said the priest, coming slowly forward across the grass. He was a slim, compact person, light on his feet, dapper in his clericals, somewhere in his early forties I guessed. "It looks great, Father, but then you have something to work with. Not like me." He passed a hand apologetically over his own receding hairline and then extended the hand to me. "How do you do? But I feel I already know you. He talks about you all the time."

"Margaret, this is Father Bonner, from over at St. Matthias. Their new pastoral counselor. You know, I was telling you about him the other night."

"Oh, yes," I said, nodding, as if I remembered a lot more than I did.

"Please, just call me Adrian," he told me, smiling. A chip out of one of his top front teeth struck the one rakish note in his otherwise neat and proper demeanor.

"Stay and have a drink," urged Daddy. He obviously liked this person, whose name I had recently come across when glancing at Daddy's notes.

"I wouldn't want to interrupt. The two of you looked so . . ." He let a pause suffice for whatever the next word might have been. "I'm on my way back from Staunton. I just wanted to bring you these books I promised."

"Oh, bless you for remembering," said Daddy, who seemed to know what they were, since he tucked them under his own arm without examining them.

"What's all that traffic about, down at the corner?" asked the priest.

"Oh, that's the City Fathers' retaliation," said Daddy. "The judge's restraining order came through. So now they've created this 'emergency pothole' that has to be blocked off and slowly repaired, in order to force a 'traffic jam.' Then the Sunset Villas people stuck in traffic will get all worked up and blame it on St. Cuthbert's."

"The order came through, then. I'm glad. You were so worried."

"Oh, well. I can always find something to worry about. Can't I, Margaret?" My father appeared embarrassed to have elicited such a candid profession of concern from the other man. He shuffled the two books back and forth, making himself out to be studying their titles. One was a volume of Gnostic writings, the other was *Insearch: Psychology and Religion*, by James Hillman. "These are great, Father, just exactly what I need," said my father.

"Do stay and have a drink with us," I said to Adrian Bonner. I was curious about him. I couldn't call him "Adrian," especially since Daddy had just reversed himself and called him "Father."

"Well, all right. I'd like to."

"Good for you," said Daddy, clapping the younger priest fondly on the shoulder. "I'm going to excuse myself briefly to shower off these hair trimmings and make myself more presentable. Oh, did you notice how nice our little Christ figure looks down at the corner? I gave him a scrubdown this afternoon. With Ajax. It worked wonderfully."

"I did notice that he sort of shone," commented the other, smiling at my father. "But I thought it was the sun on him."

"What may I fix you to drink?" I asked, as Daddy headed for the house. I was glad he had gone to change. This man was so well groomed, unusually so for a clergyman. Unlike the usual dark, rumply suits of the profession, Adrian Bonner's looked tailor-made. It was of a soft gray-blue lightweight wool that matched his eyes.

"Beer if you have it."

"Oh dear, I'm not sure we do. My father usually drinks Scotch or wine."

"Scotch is fine. It's only that I got in the habit of drinking beer when I was studying in Zurich. It was cheaper, and I could drink more of it without taking the edge off my mind."

"What were you studying in Zurich?"

"Psychology. I was training at the Jung Institute."

"You're a psychologist *and* a priest, then."

"For my sins." He smiled again, showing the chipped tooth. If he had been someone my age, or someone I felt more sure of myself with, I would have bantered back with something like, "Oh really? What *kind* of sins?" But there was a quality about him that put me on my guard against being flip. Yet, if I didn't say anything, he might think I was just stupid or dull.

"People have so many definitions of sin," I said. "Do you have one?"

He looked surprised but not offended. He fitted the tips of his fingers together and gazed briefly upwards into the newly leafed branches of the old sugar maple. "A falling short from your totality," he said. "Choosing to live in ways you know interfere with the harmony of that totality."

He was not a southerner, and spoke in a terse, uninflected way, without any of my father's melodic adornments. It took me a moment to really grasp what he had said.

"But . . . how do you know what your totality is?"

"You learn. You unlearn. You pay attention. You feel where things balance for you and where they don't."

"Oh."

"You look troubled. I didn't mean to be glib or deliberately obscure. I hate abstruseness as much as I distrust easy answers. It's just such a large subject. It's my life's work. But it stands to reason, being Father Gower's daughter, you're at home with such talk. You and he probably discuss things like this every night over the supper table."

"Well, not *every* night," I said, somewhat disingenuously. I was struck by the note of wistfulness in his voice. I had not been prepared for such an easy advantage over this man, and now that I had it, I didn't want to relinquish it just yet. "What is this group of yours that Daddy's going to talk to Monday night? What kind of thing do they expect from him? Is it like group therapy?"

"Not remotely, I hope. I have deep reservations about group therapy. This is a study group that meets at my house two Mondays a month. Mostly St. Matthias people, but some others, too. We focus on human problems, yes, but emphasis on the generic rather than the specific. I don't encourage personal revelations; people in groups aren't always discerning. I try to get good speakers, like your father, who will send everybody home thinking of themselves as less lonely because they are part of something that has been going on for a long time, and not just some freakish late twentieth-century manifestation. For a lot of people, you'd be surprised what a relief it is to know they have company all over the ages. I hope you'll come on Monday."

"Well, I'd like to." To cover my pleasure, I asked, "When have you heard Daddy? I've never seen you at St. Cuthbert's."

He smiled. "When you're serving under another rector, you're supposed to attend his show on Sundays. But since I arrived in January, I've sneaked over here a couple of times. And your father and I meet once a week in his study for some talk. It's a treat for me. After counseling others all day, I get to have someone set *me* straight for a change. Your father's ministry is inspiring to me. He lives it in a way few men do."

"Yes, I think he probably does," I agreed loyally, "but in what sense did you mean it?"

Again, the gesture of the fingertips fitted gracefully together, the eyes lifted upwards while he assembled the words he wanted. He was probably very careful with words. After my attack of disenchantment with my father, it would be a tonic for me to hear why someone as discerning as Adrian Bonner found him an inspiration.

"He's not trendy; he doesn't pose. He's neither a self-transcendent guru nor one of these fund-raising manager types who have become so sought after lately by our Holy Church. He's just himself—himself offered daily. He worries about people, he worries about himself . . . he goes to the hospital carrying the Sacraments in his little black case. He baptizes and marries and buries and listens to people's fears and confessions and isn't above sharing some of his own. He scrubs the corner cross with Ajax. His sermons have real substance; you can tell he wrestled them into shape with his whole mind—and he delivers them with conviction. He makes his services beautiful, he reminds you that the whole purpose of the liturgy is to put you in touch with the great rhythms of life. He's a dedicated man, your father. He's lonely and bedeviled like the rest of us, but he has time for it all and tries to do it right. He lives by the grace of daily obligation. He's what the priests in books used to be like, but today he's a rarity."

Adrian Bonner's words, though spoken in his terse accent, were as mellifluous and soothing to me as if he had been reciting some charming old neglected poem that had once enthralled me before I grew more critical and began to pick holes in it. He restored my father as I wanted him to be; he recalled to me the reasons why it was right to honor him. The very fact that he was a stranger and spoke in the accents of another region contributed to the effect. He wasn't one of us, he had come to Romulus only as recently as January—he had studied in Zurich!—and look how short a time it had taken him to discover that my father was a rarity.

Now I wished I had paid more attention the other night when Daddy was talking about him over the phone. Hadn't he said that Father Bonner had taken him as a mentor? He had said other things about him, too, but I had been more concerned at the time about the nightmare about the dead baby, and about the threat to our corner. And besides, the "Father Bonner" being described on the phone was just a faceless clergyman, an assistant to that feckless liberal Jerry Hope, who was ruining the Church as my father loved it.

Whereas this man was intriguing. He was the sort of person who became more attractive the longer you were in his presence. You stopped noticing that he had so few hairs left on top of his head and were drawn instead to the fine shaping of the head, to his widely spaced gray-blue eyes with their long corners, to the well-kept, smooth hands with the expressive fingers that joined lightly at the tips when he was putting his thoughts together. There was a repose about him that I envied. He seemed to be someone who had found everything I had not found. I wondered if he was married. He had said that the Monday group met at his house; he hadn't said "our" house. If he was a bachelor, he might welcome an invitation to supper, although he seemed exactly the sort of person who would be quite contented to eat alone and read a book.

"What's this? No drinks yet?" Daddy reappeared in fresh clericals, looking every inch the priest that Adrian Bonner had been describing. The haircut was a success. My father was a dignified and handsome man. "Why, nobody's even sitting down."

"We were talking," Adrian Bonner said.

"We were talking about you," I told my father.

"Oh-oh, watch out," said Daddy. "Adrian, I have a six-pack of Beck's, just for you. But guess what? I forgot to refrigerate it."

"That's okay, Father. I often drank it at room temperature when I was abroad."

"You two sit down, I'll get everything," I said, gathering up the grooming implements and the paper bag with Daddy's hair cut-

tings from the grass. As I headed for the house, I heard Adrian
Bonner murmur, "You're a lucky man."

"She's a good girl," replied Daddy. "Though I don't know how
she puts up with me, sometimes."

In the kitchen I hunted out a tallish glass that would be suitable for beer, and put it in the freezer, to get that frosted effect I'd
seen in good restaurants. Sure enough, there was the carton of
Beck's in the pantry. Daddy must have been anticipating a visit
from Adrian Bonner. I put five of the bottles in the refrigerator,
in case he stayed a long time, and the other in the freezer along
with the glass. I shook some cashews into a small cut-glass bowl,
mixed Daddy's Scotch, then decided to inaugurate the Episco-Cat
tray the Ernie Pascos had given us last Christmas. After a moment's deliberation, I covered up the cats with a clean white linen
napkin. Usually I had a Scotch along with Daddy, or, in warm
months, a gin and tonic, but today I would try one of Adrian
Bonner's beers. I wasn't that fond of beer but I felt a desire to
drink what he was drinking. I broke into a pack of the designer
paper napkins that the Major had donated for Palm Sunday coffee hour and arranged three of them in overlapping triangles on
the tray.

They had dragged the wicker chairs into a cozy semicircle over
by the Mt. Fuji cherry tree, facing into the last of the sun, and
were seated, already deep in conversation, when I came out with
the tray. Both sprang up at once, and Adrian Bonner started
forward to help.

"It's okay, I've got it," I said. But my knees cracked loudly
when I knelt to set the tray down in the grass, and to cover my
embarrassment I grumbled, "Now, all we need is a *table* out here,
Daddy, to go with the chairs."

"What an inviting-looking glass," said Adrian Bonner when I
handed him his beer. "But why don't you have a frosted glass?"

Going to the trouble of frosting my own glass hadn't even
occurred to me, but I didn't want him to think I was some goody-
goody, long-suffering angel of the house. "I like it sort of warm,"
I told him.

"You should go to England, then," said Daddy, amused. "You'd
be right at home. Everybody drinks warm beer in England."

"I'd like to go to England," I said, for something to say, as I
handed round the cashews and the Major's expensive paper napkins. "I'd like to go to Whitby."

"Whitby?" repeated my father with surprise, raising his eyebrows at his friend as if to say: What's this daughter of mine up to now? "Why Whitby?"

"Professor Stannard thinks I should do graduate work on Hilda of Whitby. He says he thinks he can get me a scholarship." I sat down in the saggiest wicker chair, warm beer in one hand, tucking my skirt demurely around my legs with the other. The two men sat back down. Adrian Bonner kept his eyes on me.

"But, sweetie," remarked Daddy, "how come you're only telling me this now?"

"It's the first opportunity I've had. He only told me about it this week. And it may not even come through, though he seems to think I have a good chance since he's going to sponsor me. It's a new scholarship. Whoever gets it has to do research on some neglected aspect of women's history. That's the only part of it Professor Stannard doesn't approve of." I gave a shamelessly colorful imitation of my courtly old champion, shaking my cheeks and affecting his old Virginia singsong: " 'True scholarship, Margaret, should *transcend* gender or private interests.' " By the time I got to the " 'mind you, none of that Lytton Strachey meddling,' " I had them both laughing. Adrian Bonner laughed in that taken-by-surprise way people do when they are truly amused and not just being agreeable.

"She gets that art of mimicry from her mother," Daddy told him. "Ruth could do the most wicked takeoffs on people. She would zero right in on a tone or a pet word or gesture and call up a person right before your eyes. She would have you in stitches before long."

"She must have been such an attractive person," said Adrian Bonner quietly.

"Yes, she certainly was," said my father with a rather complacent sigh. He raked his fingers through his flattering new haircut. "But, as I was telling Margaret earlier, just before you came, Adrian, I can finally accept it. God knows why, but I am suddenly at peace. You know, Margaret, there is not a reason in the world why you and I shouldn't go to England after your graduation. We could be there for your birthday. I could show you my favorite old spots, we could spend a few days in London and then head north. The Lake District, then on up to Whitby, maybe even as far as Lindisfarne."

"I've been to Lindisfarne," said Adrian Bonner. "I spent a day

and a night there once. It's a very holy place. It cured my migraines. I haven't had one since I was at Lindisfarne."

"Come go with us again," said Daddy warmly.

"Ah, thanks, I wish I could," said Adrian Bonner, flushing
slightly, probably at Daddy's uninhibited southern hospitality.
"But I'm not sure my boss would like it. I only began work here in
January." Then turning to me, he said: "I think you should see
these places, Margaret. Especially with the project you have in
mind." It was the first time he had used my name.

"Consider it settled," said Daddy happily. "I'll call the travel
agency first thing tomorrow. If we book this far ahead, we can
probably get one of those super-saver jobs. And I'll write to the
British Tourist Board, have them send us some brochures and
maps. You're right, Adrian. She should see these places. Whitby,
Lindisfarne. What a pity poor Colman wasn't a more eloquent
speaker at the Synod of Whitby. Church history might have been
a lot different. I don't just mean the dating of Easter, either. We
would have had more of the spirit of Lindisfarne, more of the
private and less of the public."

"He was probably eloquent enough," said Adrian Bonner, putting his fingertips together again. "He just wasn't as shrewd as his
opponent. Wilfrid was the manager type and Colman was the
mystic. Wilfrid had thought out his argument ahead of time, one
that would impress and frighten the King; whereas Colman just
came down from Lindisfarne fresh from prayer, innocently trusting that his truth would prevail. When managers and mystics
confront each other, the managers almost always win. The world
is their arena; they're practiced in power tactics. Whereas the
mystics have left themselves open and vulnerable by so much
listening for the will of God."

"How true, how true, I never thought of it that way," agreed
Daddy, nodding admiringly at the priest. He cut his eyes over to
me, to make sure I was appreciating his friend as much as he was.
"Why, when you get right down to it, that's the biggest bone I have
to pick with the church today. Too much *managing* and hankering
after the politics of worldly power. Just like old Wilfrid, who was
so impressed with the way they conducted business in Rome.
Though the power politics of the seventh-century church in Rome
seem comparatively harmless, compared to this Madison Avenue
brand of Marxism *our* misguided prelates seem so impressed by. I
shudder to think what they'll come up with when they put their

muddled heads together at Lambeth this summer . . . that is if they have a Lambeth. The Scottish bishops, you know, have threatened to boycott if the Americans ordain a woman bishop in time to send her. Lord, have you seen the pictures of the candidates in the latest *Episcopalian?*" My father chortled derisively.

"How about refills?" I said, rising with what I hoped was just enough spontaneous bustle to distract Daddy from his topic without seeming rude. I could understand his feeling betrayed by many of the recent changes in our church, but when he got on the subject of women's ordination, his doctrinal arguments became wobbly, and then he tried to prop them up with an ungallant, for him, misogyny. I didn't want him to lose face in front of a man whose friendship was obviously important to him.

"I'd love another beer," said Adrian Bonner, drinking up and handing me his glass. In the brief look he gave me, I thought I read understanding.

"Daddy? May I freshen your drink?"

"Mmm . . . why yes, thank you, honey." He handed up his glass of melted Scotch. "I'm not saying that they have to look like Helen of Troy, or even . . . well, Mrs. Thatcher," he disconcertingly pursued, just as if the two of us had been alone and he knew he could count on continuing to be loved no matter what retrograde opinions ventured out of his mouth, "but, my goodness, I don't know when I've seen such a collection of unfortunate physiognomies."

"I wonder if St. Hilda of Whitby had an unfortunate physiognomy," I said from behind my tray, smiling down on my father grimly.

Adrian Bonner laughed. My father looked mildly peeved, as though he suspected me of poking fun at him in front of his friend.

"No, I mean it," I hurried on, holding the bone close and steady before him, hoping it would distract him from his prey. "I mean, she was thirty-three before she decided to enter the monastic life. Her sister married, but she didn't. I'm just saying . . . I only thought about this right now, when you were talking, Daddy . . . I just wonder what she looked like. Bede didn't tell us, I wish he had. He described her teacher, Paulinus, the man who converted her, in great detail. He was tall, with a slight stoop, and he had black hair, a thin hooked nose, and a majestic presence . . ."

"Sounds a little like me," said Daddy playfully. "Well, formerly the black hair. And Ned Block would challenge the majestic presence. Only the departed Dr. Hazeltine is allowed that."

"I'm sure Hilda was a very prepossessing person," said Adrian Bonner. "She would have to have been. Kings came to her for advice. She trained five of the most influential bishops of her time ... she trained Wilfrid himself at her monastery. There must have been a compelling radiance about her"—he darted an amused but respectful side glance at my father—"whatever her ... um, physiognomy."

"That's a point," conceded Daddy sportingly. "So she was old Wilfrid's mentor, was she? I'd forgotten that. If indeed I ever knew it. Margaret, you'd better be nice to Father Bonner. He could be a great deal of help to you when you get into this project of yours."

"Well," I said, turning to leave with my tray of glasses, "I haven't gotten the scholarship yet." I would have liked to toss off something debonair about how it would be nothing but a pleasure to be nice to Father Bonner, but I wasn't certain I could pull it off. Better to say nothing and turn away a little awkwardly, than to risk coming across as flippant, or ... even worse ... archly coy.

The first thing I did in the kitchen, after putting Adrian Bonner's glass back in the freezer (and my glass along with it, this time) was to take out my fish marinade and count the pieces. Barring a loaves and fishes miracle, there was just no way I could stretch this into a filling supper for three people, especially when two of them were men. I considered going back out and asking him anyway—I was sure Daddy would like it—and then, if he accepted, leaving them together in the garden and tearing off to Sampson's for more fish. Did Sampson's close at six or half-past five? I wasn't sure. And even if it was still open, what if I got caught in the traffic jam coming home? "Hmm," Daddy would say, looking repeatedly at his watch, "let's go in and see what Margaret's up to, shall we?" And then they would go inside, and even if they figured out what had happened, the mood would be spoiled. Nothing would have been done, no friendly table laid, and Daddy would probably take him into the living room, which was dreary unless you turned on certain strategic lamps in advance, to light up the right things and throw the wrong ones into flattering shadow. And Daddy might forget, as he often did, and just flip the overhead light switch, and Adrian Bonner would get that oppressed feeling I myself had suffered on many occasions, when Daddy and I had been invited for dinner by parishioners, and upon entering some drearily lit room crowded with too many objects, or with stiff, uncomfortable furniture, or furniture placed uninvitingly, I would have to fight down a revulsion similar to nausea, or even panic, against being forced to remain there for an entire evening.

It was not that our furniture, reupholstered and reslipcovered as it had been, looked or was uncomfortable, and our tables and mantelpiece certainly weren't cluttered with droll little Hummel figures or dust-catching silk flowers. We had bookcases with good books in them and some nice prints of Salisbury Cathedral and the English countryside, and there would be flowers from Daddy's garden in season, when one or the other of us remembered to put some there, but the truth was, we didn't spend much time in this room. I preferred my bedroom for reading, Daddy of course was most comfortable in his study; we did our main talking in the kitchen while I cooked or in each other's bedrooms at the end of the day—unless we watched something on the television down in Daddy's study.

And over the years, the neglected living room had gathered up its resentment and had made its umbrage felt. It had a static, abandoned air about it, like a person who has given up trying to be first in anybody's life. It was the place where the vestry met and for when formal company came. More than any other room in the rectory, it protested the lack of a coordinating presence who would have kept it alive by letting it share fully in the ongoing life of the house and respecting its needs for attention and change. It, too, had suffered the loss of a proud and loving chatelaine who could add just the right grace-note, pull together a cozy corner for threatening times, open up a refreshing vista when things got freer again and everybody wanted more space for themselves. Like the way Mrs. MacGruder faced her sofa and armchairs out towards her garden in summer and turned them back towards her fireplace in winter.

I made my father his fresh Scotch, poured new beers into the two frosted glasses—no need to worry about running out of beer now, there would be plenty, since Adrian Bonner would not be getting invited to supper—and went out again into the pinkish,

rather sad last light of the garden, where in my chair, his long
arms and legs flung out in all directions, sat Ben MacGruder
making himself thoroughly at home with my father and Adrian
Bonner.

"Look who came by," Daddy called out, as if I couldn't see. "My
chief server and champion sweater-washer. Ben says Nana's making her famous spaghetti sauce this evening. Will the fish hold
another day, or not?"

"I thought I was your champion sweater-washer," I said, approaching with the tray. "Or does one interloper's good deed
usurp a lifetime of devotion?" If I didn't have enough fish to
invite this interesting man to supper, I was damned if I was going
to go eat with Ben and his grandmother. I could perfectly imagine
what had happened over at the MacGruders' house. "Hey, Nana,
I've got an idea. Why don't you make your spaghetti sauce and
we'll invite Father Melancholy over. Oh, and I *think* Margaret's
home, too."

"An interloper!" wailed Ben, showing off with his dramatics.
"Oh, my heart is broken."

"May I get you something, Ben?" I asked with utter kindness
and politeness. I hadn't forgotten him telling me, only this week,
that if I were really indifferent to him I would be kinder and
politer.

"That frosted beer looks appealing," he mumbled, unwinding
his legs and getting out of my chair.

I handed him my glass of beer off the tray with a cordial smile.

"But, isn't this . . . somebody else's?"

"Oh, only mine. *Please* take it, I'll get another. Don't worry, it's
a clean glass." It wasn't, but the frost made it look so.

"Well, if you're sure . . ." He giggled. "I didn't mean if you're
sure the glass is clean, I meant . . ."

"I know what you meant," I said. Kindly. Smoothing a little
boy's gaffe.

Chastened, Ben accepted the beer, took a gulp, and, with a
smack of his lips, threw himself down floppily in the grass. "That
sure hits the spot," he declared, grinning up at the two older men
who had indulgently watched his agile display.

I gave Adrian Bonner and my father their drinks and then
graciously addressed the rubber-limbed clown at my feet. "We
would love to come some other time, Ben. You know how we love
Nana's spaghetti, but I *did* buy this fish, just enough for Daddy

and me, and, to be honest, I've been looking forward to a quiet evening alone with him. There are all sorts of things we need to talk about."

"You're not doing this just for my sake, are you, Margaret?" demanded my father gruffly, not quite able to cover his pleasure.

"No, Daddy. I'm doing it because it's what *I* want. But really, Ben" (turning another look of killing kindness upon my guilty secret), "*do* tell Nana to ask us again real soon."

I headed back towards the kitchen to get myself another beer. The mood in the garden was not the same now, Ben had changed it. We would all make a place for him, and there would be small talk about Easter vacation and when Harriet was coming and Daddy would no doubt go over the Palm Sunday processional with his "chief server." As we didn't have a deacon, Ben would have to do the knocking on the door with the processional cross; and he was also going to sing. The best of the afternoon was over.

But as I went swiftly across the grass, I derived a keen consolation in the knowledge that Adrian Bonner watched me go and was probably approving of me: not just my youth and the way I moved (I was glad I had worn a skirt today) and maybe looked (here I reflected that it had been poor Ben himself who had first made me aware of my physical charms, but that was the breaks, wasn't it?), but also the mature way I had behaved. It may even have worked out for the better, that I had not bought enough fish to invite him to stay for supper. This way, he would leave sufficiently intrigued. And I would have the additional consolation of talking about him with my father before we met again on Monday night.

"You found Adrian interesting, didn't you? I thought you might. I don't know when I've enjoyed a person's conversation so much. Besides yours, I mean, honey."

"You don't have to apologize, Daddy. I just wish you'd found someone like him years sooner. You didn't really have anyone to talk things over with on your level. Of course there was Professor LaFarge for a while, but . . ."

"Oh, Bonner's in another *sphere* from poor old Trevor," said Daddy with a dismissive wave of his hand. "This man's background is truly exceptional. He's not only that old American item, the self-made man, but he has really gone into . . . well, the things that interest me most. He makes me wish I were young again and had it to do over. I would study some of the things he's studied. I would take more philosophy and sacred studies courses. Adrian has a doctorate in religion and philosophy from the University of Chicago. He wrote his dissertation on that disturbing figure Valentinus, you know, the Gnostic teacher that the early Christian prelates—the 'manager types,' as he would call them—were so terrified of. Then he trained as an analyst in Zurich. He's even been in the Navy. When he was younger, he was in a Roman Catholic seminary for a while, he was training to be a monk, but he couldn't stand the communal life . . . Adrian's somewhat of a loner. Well, it stands to reason he would be, with *his* background. Then, at age thirty-five, he found us. He gave up his private practice and entered General Theological. Our church is lucky to have him. As for that jackass Jerry Hope, he doesn't have the wherewithal even to *comprehend* the gift Heaven has sent him. The mere thought of Father Bonner as Jerry Hope's *assistant* is enough to make you laugh . . . or weep."

"How did you mean he was a self-made man? Did he grow up poor?"

"Worse than that, honey. He was in an orphanage until he was eleven. A Catholic orphanage in Michigan. Way up on the north lakes, almost in Canada. His parents left him there when he was six, but it was only supposed to be temporary, until they found work. But then the years went by and they never came back for him."

"But that's awful!"

"Yes, wasn't it," agreed Daddy with grim satisfaction. "It was pretty terrible, he's told me some stories that would curl your hair, if it weren't already nice and curly. The life he led there could have destroyed a less determined little soul. There were . . . there were abuses . . . both in the orphanage and after he went to live with a German couple, a farming family who worked him like a mule until he ran away to the seminary." My father frowned and passed a hand down his face. "It's really heroic, the way he managed to survive. Not only survive, but grow up to be the person he is. I wish I could tell you some of the things . . . the only trouble is, they were told me in our sessions, so I guess they're privileged, aren't they?"

"Of course, I understand. How is your fish?"

"Delicious, delicious as always. I like this juicy, lemony taste when you bite in. How do you do that, honey?"

"It's the marinade. You've seen me do it before. Then the batter goes on top and the juice is trapped inside when you fry it."

"You say 'you' but if *I* fried it, it would be an unholy mess."

"That's because you won't ever wait until the oil is hot enough, Daddy."

I was surprisingly willing to abandon the subject of Adrian Bonner for now. There was so much to absorb. There was almost too much. I looked forward to being in my room and going over it all, later tonight. I wanted to try to fill in some blanks for myself and maybe dream on it a little. The feeling wasn't so different from the one I sometimes got during the reading of a really wonderful novel, when I would come across a character or a situation that so thoroughly filled the requirements of my imagination that I would have to stop and lay the book facedown on my chest and take a deep breath before going on.

Accepting our cross doesn't mean taking responsibility for
what we are ... that's arrogance, God made us what we
are, he gave us our circumstances ... it means taking responsibility for what we are *doing* with what we are.

—Walter Gower

VIII: PASSION WEEK

*D*addy went to great trouble for the Palm Sunday service, and
there were some, like Ned Block, who said he took too many
liberties. But as the liberties involved putting things back in rather
than taking them out, he was on safe ground. Someone told him
once that his rival Jerry Hope had remarked sarcastically that
Father Gower over at St. Cuthbert's ought to provide an intermission for his Palm Sunday extravaganza, so that all the ancient
bladders in his congregation could seek relief. But Daddy had
laughed—he must have been in one of his "up" periods at the
time—and instructed his informer, "Tell the Rector of St. Matthias he'd better keep watch over all those infant bladders at his
communion rail every Sunday." For Daddy had been scandalized
when he heard that Jerry Hope gave babes in arms communion
wafers to suck on, "so they would never remember a time when
they hadn't taken the Sacrament."

When I was younger, Palm Sunday, even though you got to
march around waving your palm branch, and go outdoors if it was
warm enough, had been an endurance test for me. "The most
squirm-worthy Sunday in the Church Calendar," my mother
called it. The way Daddy conducted the service, you were there
for almost two hours. But when I got older, I came to understand
and share my father's secret preference for the whole of Passion
Week, with its ever-darkening events, over the big Easter triumph,

which had something anticlimactic about it. Because when you got past Good Friday, the person whose drama it was had said his last lines and breathed his last breath. His earthly performance was over. After that began his friends' visions of him, the remembering of what he had said; the different versions; the contradictions; the guesswork and the interpretations; the setting up of rituals and traditions to console and inspirit the survivors. I'd had experience of *that* phenomenon in my own life.

For the ceremonial of Palm Sunday, or the Sunday of the Passion as the 1979 prayer book called it, Daddy was always looking for new things—or rather old things—to include in his service. He'd read the pilgrim-woman Egeria's fourth-century account of her Palm Sunday in Jerusalem, where the Christians made the services last from morning to night (with a short lunch break). He consulted old missals and priests' manuals, and dug out adaptations of medieval and Latin rites that the Anglicans had brought out of Reformation mothballs during the Oxford Movement. Unlike many of his colleagues, he didn't bless the palms ahead of time and simply hand them out to the congregation; wearing his red cope, he conducted the whole Liturgy of the Palms, a complete little service in its own right, with antiphon, Collect, lesson, chant, and Gospel.

The one thing he sorely missed was a choir. If St. Cuthbert's had had a choir, then half of it could have stayed inside the church during the processional and sung the verses of "All Glory, Laud, and Honor," while the other half stood outside and sang the refrain. That was a very moving thing, he said. Father Traherne had always done it that way, back in Chattanooga. There had been a passable choir at the beginning of Daddy's ministry (the Major herself had been its leading alto), but it disbanded when the choir director, who was also the organist, moved to Richmond. This was shortly after my mother had left us. After that, Daddy felt that he was keeping on top of things just to have someone in the loft who sight-read music and swell-pedaled around the muted, lackluster voices of our congregation. Most people at St. Cuthbert's sang as if they considered the act in slightly bad taste. The few times Daddy had been able to capture a real organist, who actually used the pedals for low notes and knew how to modulate between keys and improvise around the plain tunes, filling up the arched dark space beneath the cross-vaulted ceiling with rich, surging sounds, he had considered himself blessed. But these people, understandably, had a way of moving on to churches with four-manual organs and endowed music programs.

This Palm Sunday, however, my father was able to offer a small musical surprise, just before the Blessing of the Palms. He had talked Ben into singing the story of Jesus' entry into Jerusalem—he had coached him in plain chant—and Ben carried it off with such solemn grace, his pure tenor gliding up and down in the free rhythms as if it had been waiting all its life for just such an exercise, that I relented towards him a little. Several old ladies took white handkerchiefs out of their purses and dabbed at their eyes. It was really stirring. If only Ben could *stay* like that, remote and engaged in something else besides chasing me to death. During his singing, I came close to imagining what wanting him might be like—for some other girl, who saw and heard him just as he was now, with no double vision of earlier and sillier Bens. I even found myself thinking how things might have been different between us if we had lived in another era and he had to go away now—say immediately after this service—to flesh out his manhood in some distant land, or serve his country for three or four years at some inaccessible outpost on the other side of the world. That would give me time to go over the image of this comely, distant young man in his red cassock and white surplice, singing "Blessed is he that *com*-eth . . ." and sustaining that pure, high note. Four, no, better make it five, years would provide me with an opportunity to miss him, to set about re-creating him out of selected memories. I could be "building an emotional investment," as Harriet would put it, and then when he came back, all burnished and mellowed by his experiences, we would see what, if anything, had accrued.

Daddy preached the sermon he'd discussed with me earlier. About the jeering rabble being comprised of the very ones who had most desperately counted on Jesus to save them, to be their conquering hero. Only, he said, they'd had outer conquests in mind and He was promising inner ones. Then Daddy went on to elaborate on how people can turn vicious against their idols when the idols don't live up to their expectations. When he got to this part in the delivered sermon, I thought about what he had said about my mother, while I had been cutting his hair: "I think she was beginning to hate me for not being . . . well, whatever it was she had taken me for in the first place."

Then he went on to speak affectingly about people turning

against *themselves* when they felt they'd fallen short of their own expectations. "But not until we accept our shortcomings can we do God's will in the world. Each person has a specific shortcoming to accept and endure and try to work on. It's that person's task, it is my task. And however painful or shameful or just plain aggravating it is to me, or to you, that very shortcoming is a part of my destiny: it may even be inseparable from why I will have been valuable to the human community. Because, by bearing it, learning it from the roots up, letting it speak its message to me, offering it my mind and my body in which to work itself out, I may be doing my part to heal what is split in the world."

As he leaned forward over his notes, speaking these things with the astonished freshness of someone who had only just finished working them out for himself, Adrian Bonner's praise of my father came back to me and added to the pride and satisfaction I was feeling. "His sermons have real substance," Adrian had said. "You can tell he wrestled them into shape with his whole mind . . . he's lonely and bedeviled like the rest of us, but he has time for it all and tries to do it right."

I was glad we had a bishop today, to add his robust magenta shirtfront and pectoral cross to my father's ceremonies. Bishop Major, home from Arizona to visit his mother, sat forward in his pew, his large, rosy, affable, gray-bearded face trained raptly on my father in the pulpit. His svelte wife, Georgianna, in a dashing green hat with a swooping brim, sat beside him with her wonderful posture, looking more like a Shakespearean actress than a bishop's wife. Her red hair had not lost a shade of its dramatic color through the decades. Daddy and I were invited, along with a few handpicked others in the congregation, to have lunch with the Major and the illustrious couple.

"We cannot receive the Holy Spirit," Daddy went on, "until we accept our own individual life as Christ accepted His." The haircut I had given him Friday was a dashing success; the boyish fringe fell just right over his forehead. He was sweating a little, he had brought out his handkerchief twice during the sermon to mop his brow, but it was warm in the church, the Bishop himself was visibly sweating.

"Each of us is an incarnation. Each of us is a son or daughter of God, fated to experience in ourselves the clash of opposites, represented by the crucifixion. The good news is that nobody has to live out *that* particular crucifixion ever again. He has done it for us. That was *His* redemptive role in the human drama. And He knew it as He rode into Jerusalem on the back of a donkey, followed by the donkey's colt, just as it had been prophesied in Zechariah.

"And now . . ." I saw him turn over to the final half page of the four half pages, single-spaced, back and front, that made up one of his twelve-minute sermons, a format I had been familiar with as far back as I could remember. ("And page four *always* has to be on the back of page two, or it won't work out . . ." "That's right, my smart girl . . .")

". . . and now it's our turn to follow Him by seeking to know our own redemptive roles, seeking to find out what is my part, what is your part, your unique part, in the human drama we find ourselves enmeshed in. Don't let yourself be unduly put down by the jeers, but don't be taken in unduly by the laurels and waving palm branches, either. Just ride your little donkey as best you can, focus daily on those places in your own existence where intensity blazes up . . . and let God do the rest." Out came the handkerchief again, for another brief dab at the forehead and back of the neck.

"You know," he went on, revived, the horse catching sight of the barn door after its workout, "there were originally thirty-nine verses to 'All Glory, Laud, and Honor,' the processional hymn we sang earlier. St. Theodulph, the Bishop of Orleans, wrote that hymn in the ninth century. He was in prison at the time, because Emperor Louis I had suspected him of plotting against him. So Theodulph had plenty of time in prison to write this very long hymn, and legend has it that he was singing it aloud through the window of his cell when the King himself rode past the prison during a Palm Sunday procession. And the King was so moved, the legend tells us, that he repented and ordered the release of the Bishop that very day.

"I want to conclude *this* Palm Sunday by reciting a verse that was removed from the hymn in the seventeenth century. When I recite it, you will immediately understand why it had to go. It just wasn't dignified. It was too much of a red flag for the titterers and jeerers of this world. When I first heard it, back in seminary, I tittered myself, but during the course of my life I have come to have a fondness and a respect for it. It speaks to me, it speaks to me eloquently out of its artlessly simple vulnerability, and I think it will speak to you, too. Here it is, the little banished verse:

Be thou, O Lord, the rider,
And we the little ass,
That to God's holy city
Together we may pass.

"In the name of the Father, and of the Son, and of the Holy Spirit, Amen."

"Was everything okay?" my father asked as he drove us across town to the Major's.

"It was the best Palm Sunday I can remember. Truly, Daddy."

"Ben's singing the Gospel of the Palms went over well, I thought. Maybe I'll prevail on him again, while he's in his church-going phase. Seems a shame to waste that voice."

"Did you see the old ladies take out their handkerchiefs?"

"I did indeed. Even the Major looked moved. It was nice to have Charlie Major and Georgianna there, too. I must say he seemed fairly engaged by my sermon—he said nice things to me afterwards at the door, but then you never know with Charlie. That's part of his style, to appear *engaged* by whatever is directly in front of him. It's certainly served him well enough. *She's* a damn good-looking woman for her age. That hair just goes on and on, doesn't it?"

"I suspect she gives it some help."

"Oh, do you think so?" He seemed genuinely surprised.

"The sermon was one of your best, Daddy."

"You really think so, Margaret?"

"I just finished saying I thought so. You know what I liked best? The part about focusing daily on the places in your own existence where intensity blazes up. And I *loved* ending with the little ass. It was just right. You do that so well. Say something really profound, then balance it out with comic relief. It makes people able to absorb the other better; it takes the pressure off them."

"You say nice things to your old father."

"Only because they're true. I wonder what we'll get for lunch at the Major's. There's one thing I know for sure."

"What is that, honey?"

"It will be cooked puh-fectly, served puh-fectly, and cleared away puh-fectly. And each stage will be accompanied by a little lecture of how puh-fectly simple it all is, if you just organize your time."

"Oh, Ruth—" My father began to chortle, then stopped and looked embarrassed. "It's just that you're so like her," he explained. "It's deeper than physical similarity. I mean, in some ways, you don't look like her at all, you look much more like my mother, but there's an essential likeness . . . something that goes deeper. It's as though she *speaks out of you* at times, only she's mellowed. She's not so judgmental anymore. She's funny, but the funniness isn't because she's threatened. It's because she . . . you . . . the two of you . . . revel in the human comedy. Now there's compassion, as well. Margaret, I think you're your mother *redeemed* somehow. Does that make sense?"

"I *think* it does," I said, disturbed that I could not take more pleasure in his words. On the contrary, I felt stirrings of the same deep anger he had aroused in me during the haircut, with his talk of how everything may have turned out for the best. Where was *I* in all of this, then? If my personality had been built upon her leavings, who might I have been if she hadn't left? If I was simply an improved version of her, was there room inside for me, as well?

Everything always went smoothly (it had better, if it knew what was good for it) at one of the Major's luncheons or dinners, or whatever social event she had decided to bestow on us, but I could never relax at her house. You came in her front door knowing you were expected to show gratitude and admiration. And you showed them, and she duckwalked you around, thoroughly agreeing with you that yes, her table decorations were lovely, weren't they; her collection of Queen Anne and Chippendale tea tables ("If you evah buy one, make *suh*-tain it has ball and claw legs") were just what you would collect yourself, if you'd had the taste and the money; her flower beds and her shrubberies and her trees couldn't have flourished better or been placed more agreeably if they'd been set down by God Himself in the Garden of Eden. She was pure generosity when it came to sharing her bounty with you, but you had to be beholden to her and use what she had given you *her* way. I remembered her once digging up a clump of daylilies from her garden on the spot, because my father had admired their unusual pale greeny-yellow shade. She put them in a bucket of water and sent us right home to plant them, and even told us where in our garden they should go. And we planted them there, too; otherwise, as Daddy had remarked at the time, we'd never have heard the end of it.

Her old mouton coat hung in my closet, and when she had shrunk from a size twelve to a size eight, she had given me all her old Pendleton suits. ("These are too good for the rummage sale, and the young guls are wearing their things looser now, so they ought to be *puh-fect* for you.") I was wearing one of them today because I knew it would gratify her. Ben, who would be at the luncheon with his grandmother, hated me in these suits—he said they made me look like a career girl out of a fifties movie—which was another excellent reason for my choice, I thought.

The other guests today, besides the two MacGruders (Harriet would not be coming home until Wednesday), were a young professional couple who had just joined St. Cuthbert's, Dick and Susan Smith, and Mr. Wirt Winchester, the stuttering lawyer about whom my mother had once said everyone could afford not to hate him, and his wife Milly, who had faithfully played piano for the Sunday school until its demise five years ago. Besides the obvious wish to show off her son the bishop, one of the Major's reasons for this luncheon (her social occasions always had reasons) was to get Milly Winchester together with young, very pregnant Susan Smith, who had expressed her eagerness to assist in restarting the Sunday school.

The Major deplored buffet-style meals, but eleven people was just the wrong number to be seated comfortably around her dining-room table. So she had set up three card tables in the sunroom overlooking her garden. The placecards made it clear what was supposed to get accomplished at this lunch. Daddy and I and Mrs. MacGruder (who could always be counted on to be both amusing and correct) were to admire and entertain the Bishop at our table. Susan Smith and Milly Winchester were to get busy and resurrect the Sunday school under the eagle eye of the Major, who had sacrificed her rightful place at her son's table and banished herself to the company of two women in order to see this task through. And Georgianna Major of the dramatic hair and the swooping green hat was to play dazzling bishop's wife to the appendage-males of this gathering: Dick Smith, Wirt Winchester, and Ben MacGruder.

Bishop Major was already in very good spirits from his mother's sherry by the time we sat down at our table with its puh-fectly appropriate centerpiece of narcissi and blue mertensia and the Major's heavyweight silver pattern ("Federal Cotillion"). Far from seeming to want to be amused or admired by us, he plunged immediately into the subject pressing on my father's mind: the local tempest brewing over our outdoor calvary's interrupting the traffic flow to Greedy Gaines's condominiums at the top of Macon.

"It's going on everywhere, you know, Walter, not just in Virginia. It's happening all over the world. There's just so much space and the space can't get any bigger, but every day there are thousands more people filling it up and all of 'em wanting to do different things with the space. But when it hits close to home, I'm as parochial as the next fellow. It hurts me more when it disturbs my neck of the woods rather than some place up in northern Montana. And it makes me madder than hell when it disturbs my memories and my history. My best friend Merriweather Schaffer and I used to camp out on Sunset Mountain when we were boys; we used to tie our sleeping bags to the backs of our bicycles, and Mother would make us sandwiches, and she and baby brother Billy would stand on the front steps and wave us off as though we were headed into the Himalayas instead of just across town and up Macon Street to the top of Sunset. And now look at our Himalayas! 'Sunset Villas.' I drove Georgianna up there the other day to have a look around. No wilderness or wildlife left, except for a few fat squirrels, gorging themselves upside down from bird feeders shaped like Japanese pagodas. And matching elderly couples in matching exercise costumes marching up and down the little paved lanes, swinging their arms in that long-march way that's all the rage now. I thought we'd driven right into an ad for Metamusil. Except for the hilly terrain, or what's *left* of the hilly terrain after Gaines's bulldozers finished their 'landscaping,' the whole development up there is identical to all these retirement communities we've got out in Arizona. 'Would you believe,' I told Georgianna, 'that Merry and I used to lie up here at night quaking in ecstatic *terror*? From the sheer abundance of wild things! We heard owls and foxes and I don't know what all. Once I woke up, and there in the moonlight was a little circle of what looked like miniature praying Arabs standing around Merry's bag. Poor Merry was killed in Iwo Jima. It was a bunch of raccoons, come to look us over. But my heart almost stopped beating before I figured out what they were, let me tell you. Old Merry never even woke up."

"What I can't understand," said my father, "is how the town has allowed it to get ... well, so out of hand. I mean, Gaines started developing that mountain back in the early seventies. Margaret here used to ride the school bus with little Georgie Gaines, when the Gaineses first moved up there. At the beginning, if you remember, Gaines was only supposed to deforest around the old Wiggins estate."

"Ah, the old Wiggins estate," said Bishop Major, energetically stabbing a heart of artichoke on his crystal salad plate. He swirled it around in the vinaigrette with his fork before popping it into his mouth. A drop of the vinaigrette fell short, onto his broad magenta shirtfront, just below the hammered gold and ruby pectoral cross. "You remember little Eleanor Wiggins, don't you, Nan?" He brushed at the vinaigrette spot briefly with his napkin, then shrugged his big shoulders insouciantly. Catching my eye, he winked broadly across the table.

"Oh, yes, Eleanor Wiggins," said Mrs. MacGruder in her amused smoker's voice, though Harriet had finally succeeded in making her give up smoking.

The Bishop washed down the artichoke heart with a sip of his sherry, which he had carried to the table with him. "Little Eleanor Wiggins," he repeated with a mischievous chuckle. "Now *there's* a story." He sounded as though it was one he would enjoy telling had he not already been committed to the discussion of our local plight. "You're right, Walter, the time to stop it was back then," he went on, anticipating the direction of my father's argument. "*Before* the whole of Sunset Mountain got turned into Metamusil Hill. Then, of course, this whole traffic mess would never have come about."

"That's what I thought planning boards were for," I said, because I thought the time had come for me to say something, and it seemed a reasonable thing to say. If you were the only young person in a group and you spoke up too soon, or too cleverly, you were considered a smartass; but if you waited too long to speak up, you were considered socially inept, or "sullen."

"So they are, indeed, Margaret." The Bishop reached over a large pink hand with an equally large ring and patted the sleeve of his mother's cast-off Pendleton suit. "Planning boards, Environmental Protection Agencies, the whole lot of them. That's what they're *for*, aren't they? The only trouble is, there has to be a hue and cry, there has to be a groundswell of public protest to get their attention. They've got a sheaf of abuses on their clipboards already, and so it's the old story, you know: the wheel that squeaks the loudest gets the grease."

"Well, *we've* begun to squeak, I hope," said Mrs. MacGruder.

"Only, you know Episcopalians: they're so afraid to raise their voices and sound *shrill*. I just hope we haven't left it until too late. But who would have ever thought they'd actually go and try to take away St. Cuthbert's corner? And our precious cross? They can't do that, can they, Charlie? There's just no precedent."

"I'm afraid there is, Nan. I know a case going on right now out in Phoenix, a Baptist church. Big congregation, lots of dough, lots of members with community clout. They're suing up a storm, but the state's going to win, I was talking to a judge I know. The church land is on a major artery, and the state's going to find a way to condemn that land. The church building can still stay there, of course, but the Baptists won't have their pretty front lawn anymore. Oh, but, here's an interesting wrinkle for you . . . this judge was telling me the Baptists would have had a hell of a better case if there'd been a cemetery on that front property. Too bad we can't scare up a few old gravestones in the vicinity of our outdoor calvary."

"I would offer to be buried there myself, if it would help," my father put in. But when Bishop Major shot him a disturbed look, he amended in a more joking manner, "I mean, I would be willing to *book myself in* for later—if it would in any way get these people off our backs. However, your mother's been wonderful, she has certainly pulled a few strings."

The Bishop laughed. "When Mother pulls her strings, watch out—if you're tied to one of 'em. Though, just between us, Walter, I don't know how much Ronnie Atwater can do for her, even if she did help him get through school. The legislature doesn't have a whole hell of a lot to do with preservation. And the Preservation Society he's involved with—I'm talking about the national one—is more into buying up old buildings and getting them restored. Your best bet, *I* would think, is local hue and cry. Mobilize. Raise lots of fuss. Make 'em feel guilty."

"I've telephoned the newspaper several times," said Daddy, "but so far the editor hasn't returned my call."

"Hmm," mused the Bishop, frowning. "Well, now, it's hard to start raising a fuss when the newspaper won't answer your call. I used to know some people down at the *Record*, but since this new lot took over, they probably wouldn't answer *my* call, either." He cast a regretful look into his depleted sherry glass. "Mother tells me Gaines has offered thirty thousand for the corner and that soppy land in back of the church, is that right?"

"Yes, but that's if we don't fight," said Daddy.

"You might want to consider it," said the Bishop.

"Consider . . . ? I'm not sure I understand you, Charlie," said my father, going pale in the face.

"All I mean is, if they're going to win, and my experience in these matters tells me they will win, sooner or later, Walter . . . there are just more taxpayers up there on Metamusil Hill who want that road widened than there are faithful members of St. Cuthbert's who'll go to the wall to keep their corner calvary undisturbed . . . though I would certainly be among the saddest to see it moved, it's part of my history . . . all I'm saying is—I'm playing devil's advocate a little, but at the same time I think it's something you ought to consider—it would be a shame to lose the money *as well as* the corner. It would be giving them a double victory. And the money could be put to good purpose. People are coming back to church, there's a real resurgence of the Spirit, don't you find, Walter? It's my guess St. Cuthbert's could make excellent use of thirty thousand dollars in these challenging new times. You all could relocate the cross closer in . . ."

"But the ivy . . ." falteringly protested my father, "that ivy has taken decades . . ."

"Hell, you could transplant the ivy, Walter . . . you could hire the best landscapers in Virginia to come roll it up like a carpet and roll it down again, like those sod-grass lawns rich people who can't wait put in overnight. You can landscape it like Versailles if you want to, with that kind of windfall in your budget, and *still* have a bunch of money left over for . . . for . . . the new Sunday school"— he nodded towards his mother's table—"and for whatever other programs you'll be wanting when all these new members come flocking in." He waved his large pink hand in the direction of Dick Smith, who, along with Wirt Winchester, but not Ben MacGruder, appeared utterly fascinated by the story Mrs. Major was telling them.

"But, you see, I really feel—" Here my father was interrupted by two teenage girls in matching floral aprons, protégées of the Major, who had begun to clear away our salad plates with much important clatter.

Bishop Major, reprieved by their timely bustle, confidentially beckoned the girl nearest to him. "Listen, my dear," he stage-whispered in her ear, "is my mother serving any wine with lunch, or is this iced tea all we're getting?"

"No wine, sir. Not till Easter. But I'll be taking orders for your coffee or decaf as soon as we get all the chicken vol-au-vents brought in."

"Ah, me, I was afraid of that. Mother always gives up wine for Lent and expects everybody else to keep her company. Look, my dear . . . er, what is your name?"

"Sandra."

"Well, look, Sandra, do you think you could manage to sneak me another glass of sherry? It's in that cut-glass decanter over there. Not the one with the brownish liquid in it, that's the bourbon. The one with the gold-colored liquid. Would anybody else at the table like a dollop of something, if Sandra here can do it discreetly?"

"I feel utterly routed, Margaret."

"There's no need to, Daddy. That's just the way he is. That's his style. You said so yourself, earlier, remember? He just gets *engaged* by whatever's in front of him. He took one side of the argument and then he took the other side. Bishops are political animals by nature."

We were standing in front of my mother's grave. In front of their double headstone, that is: the information on her side all filled in, the final date on my father's side still to come. Our Sunday visit to the cemetery was later than usual today, because the Major's luncheon had gone on until after three o'clock. There was something reproachful and lonely in the fact that the spring afternoon light had already moved off my mother's name, carved in the stone. It was as if she had been waiting for us to come at our usual time, and when we didn't show up, she took the light with her and went on to somewhere else.

"But what was the point of his exercise in forensics? What good did it do our cause, his own mother's cause, the cause of the church he was baptized in? What side of the fence does he really come down on? Admit it, Margaret, he sounded pretty excited about that money."

"Oh, I *admit* it. But that's no cause for *you* to feel routed, Daddy."

The grass had been recently mowed around the graves. Fresh-cut grass always made me sad, though I understood it had the opposite effect on most people. It seemed pretty certain to me that the city *would* send its bulldozers to Macon Street sooner or later, as Bishop Major had predicted, and though the prospect of letting them obliterate our corner where I had last told my mother good-bye filled me with a helpless fury—talk about personal landmarks!—I felt I must save my wits and energy for the preservation of something dearer to me than the corner and its wayside calvary.

Ever since he had turned pale at the Major's luncheon, my father's mood had been sinking. It was as if the morning's triumphs had never been: the stirring Liturgy of the Palms, Ben's singing, the excellent sermon. And what about Daddy's own announcement in the garden on Friday afternoon, while I had been cutting his hair, that he believed his Black Curtain had finally lifted for good? I'd felt skeptical while he was saying it, and a little resentful. All these years of furtive worrying on my part, and plotting rescue missions, and then, pouf, the debonair announcement from the source of all the worry: "I feel something has been completed." Could I really accept that?

But then Adrian Bonner had come swinging around the corner, bringing a new focus to the afternoon, and as the three of us had sat there talking in the lovely pink light, my father luxuriating in this interesting new friend, and suddenly making plans for a trip to England, I had begun to accept it. The whole weekend I had gone around gingerly testing the corners of this happy idea the way you feel around in your mouth with your tongue after a throbbing tooth has been repaired. Could the pain really be over? Had the Black Curtain lifted for good?

Alas, it seemed not.

". . . and that folderol pep talk about the 'resurgence of the Spririt,' people flocking back to church. Whom does he think he's fooling? The Episcopal Church has lost over one million members in the past few years. St. Cuthbert's has lost a third of its congregation. Now I'm supposed to get excited about the *Smiths* gracing a pew, but how long will they last? My liturgy makes Dick Smith nostalgic for his high-church childhood, but *her* passion is for a Sunday school. But how long will it be before she's cursing our mimeograph machine and squirming under Elaine's heavy hand? Young women today are less tolerant of queenly old tyrants like the Major. That child in Susan Smith's womb won't even be crawling around our fusty crypt before she decides to abandon us for Jerry Hope's bank of computers and the visual aids and the nationally famous guest speakers over at St. Matthias. Adrian tells me Jerry's trying to get Mister Roberts to come and talk to their combined Sunday school classes, and he will undoubtedly succeed."

What was it in him, I asked myself, that stopped him from ever believing in himself for very long? I knelt to pick up a small, round stone with little striations of orange in it that lay at the foot of Ruth's grave. When I was little, I always found something to take home—an acorn, a stone, once a single turquoise bead from somebody's necklace. Back at the rectory, I would arrange these things in certain "magical" ways on one of her silk scarves on top of my bureau and hope for a message. Once I planted an acorn and after a few weeks of my faithful watering, it actually sprouted two tiny leaves. But it finally rotted in the soil.

"My ministry has been a stop-gap one. I came along too late, you see. The church I wanted to serve started crumbling a long time ago. Even back in Father Traherne's time, the literal-minded jackals were nibbling away at its foundations, but it's been my fate to preside over its final humiliations. The corner calvary is the final straw. It's much more than a construction of wood and stone surrounded by some ivy at the corner. It's a symbol. Nobody gives a damn about symbols anymore, I know, but they're the language in which we listen and speak to God. I will consider my ministry to have been a failure if I can't even protect the outward and visible sign of this whole endeavor . . ."

"I believe in symbols, too, Daddy, and I think they're important, but your ministry has been more than guarding them. It's had living results in living people and the results are still coming in. Do you know what Adrian Bonner thinks about your ministry?"

"Adrian? Why, no." Deflected out of the seductive rhythms of his song to failure, my father looked briefly dazed.

"He said you are a rarity. That you lived by the grace of daily obligation. He said you lived your ministry in the way few men did, and that it was an inspiration to him."

"Adrian said that, did he?"

"He said a lot more than that, but I don't want it to go to your head. Maybe I'll dole out some more bits and pieces when you're feeling humble again."

"I like that phrase: the grace of daily obligation," said Daddy pensively, running his fingers through his hair.

"Listen, Daddy, how do I go about getting a passport?"

"A passport? Oh, that's right, we're both going to need passports for our trip. Mine's long since expired, I'll have to go and hunt it up. You have to turn your old one in to get a new one. And we'll need your birth certificate. We'll go down to the courthouse tomorrow and make out our applications . . . I remember where to go, unless they've changed *that* around, along with everything else."

When we returned home, there was a little red sports car parked at the corner, and a tall young man down on his knees on the sidewalk, intently shooting pictures of our wayside calvary with a large camera.

"What the hell does he think he's doing?" said Daddy, pulling up sharply to the curb behind the sports car.

"Maybe it's the photographer from the newspaper, Daddy."

"Photographers from the *Romulus Record* don't drive brand-new Italian racing cars." Slamming the car door behind him, my father stalked forth to confront the offender. I got out, too, and followed behind him.

"Reverend Gower!" The young man, puzzlingly familiar, was striding towards us with a delighted smile. "Oh, this is great. I was just up at your house, but nobody answered the bell. Hello, Margaret, you probably don't remember me, do you?"

"You look very familiar," I said, studying his regular, rather pretty features, "but I can't quite—"

"Georgie Gaines. We used to ride the school bus together. I was a year ahead of you at Country Day."

"How can I help you?" Daddy asked with icy politeness, drawing himself up out of his stoop.

"I'm not here on my father's account, Reverend Gower. I work for the *Record* now. They sent me out to do a photo story for tomorrow's edition. I was really disappointed when you weren't home, because I wanted to shoot a roll of you in front of the cross . . . though I believe it's called crucifix, isn't it, when there's a statue on it?"

"That's actually correct," said Daddy, defrosting slightly, though I could see he was perturbed by this odd coincidence of his enemy's son being sent to do the story he had been hoping for. "Though most of us have gotten into the habit of just referring to it as our corner cross, or our wayside calvary."

"And this statue is pretty old. It was carved over in Italy some-where, wasn't it?" The slimmed-down and elongated little rich boy had pulled a small spiral pad and pencil from the pocket of his tweed jacket and was scribbling professionally.

"In Venice," said my father. "Over a century ago. Which qual-ifies it"—he squared his shoulders for emphasis—"for historic landmark status. One of our most loyal and active vestry members has been in touch with a member of the legislature, whom we're counting on to help us attain this status. The figure, by the way, if you want to pursue the ecclesiastical nomenclature, would be called a corpus . . ."

"Oh, right. Latin for body. I had Latin at Exeter. What is his name?"

"His name?" repeated Daddy, raising his eyebrows. "Well, er, I think we can take it for granted everybody knows His name . . . or perhaps we can't anymore?"

"No, sir, I meant the name of the legislator who's helping you get historic status. Sorry."

"Oh," said my father, looking uncertain. "Well, I'm not sure I'm at liberty to say. What do you think, Margaret?"

"I don't see how it can hurt, Daddy. After all, we're on the side of right, aren't we?"

"Very well, the legislator's name is Ronald Atwater," Daddy said, "but perhaps it would be better if you didn't quote us as saying we're on the side of right. Of course, we believe we are, but . . ."

"I get you," said Georgie Gaines. "You don't want to come across sounding like the pharisees. I won't use it, I promise. I don't want to hurt your cause if I can help it, Reverend Gower. *I'm* on your side, though I guess that sounds pretty weird to you. I'm grateful to my dad for all the advantages he's been able to give me, but philosophically and politically, we're at opposite ends of the pole right now."

"I see," said my father, folding his arms and rocking back on his heels.

"Oh, please hold that pose, Reverend Gower," said Georgie, aiming his camera. "But if you would move in closer to the cross."

My father sidestepped into the ivy.

"Great," said Georgie, snapping away. "Where are you now, Margaret, Chapel Hill?"

"No, U.Va. Harriet MacGruder's at Chapel Hill."

"*Scary* girl. I used to be terrified of Harriet MacGruder. She had this way of giving people nicknames that stuck. I guess you remember what mine was."

"No, I can't . . ."

"Oh, come on, you're just being tactful. Reverend Gower, do you think you could maybe rest one hand on the cross? Sort of like you're protecting it? I asked to be assigned this story. It had been lying around on the spindle for most of the week. I told the editor I thought it could be a very important story. You know, a show-down between spiritual and commercial interests. It's been a decade of greed and self-interest, but now people are returning to the real values. They're going back to religion to fill up the existential emptiness. In my last year at Harvard, I took Professor Cox's course on Jesus and the Moral Life . . . you know, Harvey Cox? He's pretty famous. There were one thousand students in the class. We had fifty-two discussion sections. It was the biggest class ever taught at Harvard by a single professor."

"My goodness," said my father, putting his arm around the cross and resting his hand lightly on the shoulder of the savior. "What was your major at Harvard, ah, George?"

"Well, I'm afraid it was Economics," mumbled Georgie Gaines, kneeling to reload his camera. "I was being safe, like everybody else. But since I got back from my trip around the world, I'm beginning to rethink my options. This may surprise you, Reverend Gower, but I'm thinking about going to Divinity School."

"Are you, indeed?" said Daddy. He shot me a glance of wondering amusement over the head of his enemy's son.

I left them talking at the corner and walked on up to the rectory, as I had studying to do. The phone was ringing as I entered.

"Why'd you rush off like that?"

"We had to go to the cemetery."

"Ah, the *cemetery*." A pause, during which I knew Ben was stifling one of his sarcasms about the way my father and I lived.

"Daddy's down at the corner, having his picture taken for the *Romulus Record*. The oddest thing, you know who's doing the story?"

"Blimp Gaines."

"Oh, that's right, *that's* what we used to call him. He's prettied up quite a lot, I didn't recognize him. How did you know he was doing the story?"

"I knew he was working for the *Record.* He's been trying to ingratiate himself with the black population . . . he's got a new social conscience. I heard all about it from my friends at Melody Station. He's trying to do a series on welfare mothers . . . from their side. He's supposed to be smart, the Blimp, practically a genius, but he's naive. He worked on Wall Street for a few months after college, then quit and went around the world. Apparently, he stopped off in India and discovered there were poor people on the planet, and he hasn't been the same since. None of the mothers will talk to him, of course. They figure his 'series' will do them more harm than good."

"Oh, dear, I hope he doesn't do *us* more harm than good."

"I wouldn't worry too much. Father Melancholy can survive more publicity than the welfare mothers. It's almost like small-town melodrama, though, isn't it? Greedy Gaines's son doing the story? The word is that the Blimp *totally disapproves* of his father, and will tell you all about it. But I myself find it a *little* inconsistent that he zips around town trying to save the world and bad-mouthing his father in that Maserati. I mean, who bought it for him, after all? Listen, Margaret, now that you've finished all your daughterly duties, why don't we take a ride up the parkway. I can't offer you a Maserati, but it's a beautiful afternoon and I've hardly seen you."

"I really can't. I've got to study now."

"Just an hour?"

"Please don't beg, Ben. By the way, your plain chant was just beautiful. You made several of the old ladies cry."

"And that's supposed to be my consolation, I suppose? That and the *terrible* lunch, when I had to sit with my back to you and the Major's clunky old silver was so big I could hardly get it under that teeny serving of mystery meat. And that henna-haired hag never shut her mouth. God, Romulus high society is the pits. The Major wouldn't have lasted one week in the Foreign Service, the way she seats her guests. There's supposed to be an equal mix of men and women, in the first place, and, in the second, there's supposed to be at least one interesting person at each table."

"Well, what about yourself?"

"Oh, Margaret, that was cheap of you and you know it."

"Listen, the lunch was an ordeal for me, too. The Bishop really hurt Daddy's feelings. He said Daddy ought to take the money and forget about the corner."

"Yeah, I know. But Nana said he only did that to hurt his mother. Because she had hurt his feelings before lunch."

"What do you mean?"

"Here we go again! Wasting all our time talking about the oldies. Nana just said that the Bishop was standing around swigging sherry before everybody sat down, and he overheard his mother say that if only Billy-the-brain-surgeon-son had been able to come, her day would have been 'puh-fect.' Billy's her favorite. The Bishop's face fell half a mile. Nana said he looked like he was about to cry. So then, later at the table, he had to get back at his mother by putting down her influence with that legislator."

"Oh, Ben, you make *me* want to cry."

"Well, that's a start, anyway. At least it's better than making some old ladies cry."

"No, I meant about the Bishop. Oh, *damn*. Do people *never* get beyond obsessing over their parents not loving them enough? Not even when they're in their sixties and have become bishops? I find that incredibly sad."

"I find something else a lot sadder."

"What?"

"That a certain lovely woman I know would rather cling to the shadows of that dreary rectory and worry about dried-up oldies instead of going for a ride up on the parkway on a beautiful afternoon like this."

Monday morning's *Romulus Record* carried Georgie Gaines's story (CORNER CALVARY: LANDMARK OR BOTTLENECK?) on the bottom of the front page, along with Daddy's picture, one of the ones from Georgie's second roll of film in which he stood beside the cross with his arm draped loosely around the crucified figure.

"I wish they'd used one of the others," said Daddy, studying the picture critically. "There's something a little supercilious about my expression in this one, don't you think? And the way I've got my arm around him . . . I don't know . . . it looks like I'm presuming on a slight acquaintance . . . or trying to claim some of his glory for myself."

"It's fine," I said, though my father, with his unerring knack for spotting unpleasant truths about himself, had once more zeroed in. The camera *had* caught a certain prissy, superior expression that occasionally flitted across his face. It was not his most characteristic expression, and I myself wondered why "they," who-

ever "they" were, hadn't chosen a kindlier or handsomer shot.
And, unfortunately, Daddy was also right about the pose. It did
have about it a slight air of *look who I've got in MY corner.*

"The picture's okay," I loyally assured him, "and the story
reads pretty well. The prose isn't going to win any Pulitzer Prize,
but he got in most of our main arguments."

"Yes," agreed Daddy reluctantly, "though I wish he hadn't
quoted me as saying you couldn't even take for granted anymore
that everybody knows Christ's name. That's *not* what I said. If I
recall rightly, I said: 'I think we can take it for granted everybody
knows His name, or perhaps we can't anymore.' And it was a
confused communication anyway, Georgie was asking the name of
the legislator. Strictly speaking, it shouldn't have been in the piece
at all."

"No, it shouldn't have, but at least the *story* is in, Daddy. Our
side has at least been granted a forum."

"Yes, my love, you're right. And, except for the misquote, I
liked the young man. Odd, isn't it, that Gaines's son is attracted to
the ministry. Tell me, as the daughter of a minister, are you attracted to some secret opposite?"

No, I'm attracted to another minister, I thought. But, yes, it is
secret.

"I'm attracted to the idea of travel," I said. "Let's go down to
the courthouse and apply for our passports. And then go out to
the Mall, to see the travel agent about England."

Ever since Friday evening, I had been waiting for it to be
Monday. Now that it *was* Monday, I was enjoying the rare pleasure
of going slowly and stealthily towards something I wanted. I felt
that by honorably enduring the hours between now and eight
o'clock tonight—bestowing upon every intervening act, however
small or mundane, a steadfast quality of attention—I would only
enhance the anticipated event when its turn came. So even if an
angel had appeared in the breakfast nook, where Daddy and I
now sat with the *Romulus Record* spread in front of us, and offered
to whisk me through eleven hours and drop me at dusk on Adrian
Bonner's doorstep, I would definitely have declined. I guessed it
was just the nature of my personality to want to defer an anticipated pleasure, as, conversely, I preferred to hurry towards re-
nunciation and have it over with, if I knew that something was
probably going to be lost.

*   *   *

Adrian Bonner's house was on Acacia Street, a steep narrow street in walking distance from the old downtown. The houses, mostly two-story, modest frame structures with gingerbread-style trimmings, sat close together on small lots with deep-sloping front banks. A few were still one-family dwellings, but the majority had been broken up into duplexes for older people on fixed incomes, or else had discreet Attorney-at-Law or M.D. shingles hanging from the eaves of their covered porches.

Adrian's house had been recently painted a light gray, with Williamsburg blue shutters. There was a new-looking geranium in a clay pot, on the top step of his porch. It gave the impression of having been set out to provide a welcoming note. Though Daddy had told me Father Bonner used his home as an office for seeing patients, there was no shingle hanging out. In fact, you had to stoop and squint in order to read his name, "The Rev. Adrian Bonner," cut from a printed card and slipped into the slot beneath the doorbell.

We had arrived early, as Adrian had phoned and asked us to come a little before the time, so Daddy could choose which room he'd be most comfortable giving his talk in, and we could set up chairs there.

"I'm wondering if I shouldn't have written out my whole talk, after all," said Daddy as he rang Adrian's bell. "I've got a case of butterflies, Margaret, if you want to know the truth."

"You do great from notes, Daddy, and you know it. Remember what a success you were at Kanuga? Your whole talk was on that one notecard, and you didn't even look at it, once you were up there in front. Besides, it's more intimate to be extemporaneous in a small group like this."

I was frankly grateful to have to be consoling him at this moment, because it distracted me from my own butterflies as I heard footsteps approach the door.

"Well, I hope you're right. I'd hate to let Father Bonner down."

"There's *very* little chance of that."

The door was opened, not by Adrian Bonner, as I had expected, but by a wild-eyed blond woman in her thirties; she wore a striped dishcloth tucked into the waistband of her skirt.

Surely Daddy would have said something about there being a wife. Could it be that he hadn't known, himself? Nevertheless, a strange, resigned calm came into my soul, along with the disappointment. For if he already had a woman in his life, it exempted me from having to plot and ponder how I could best impress him. It left me freer to breathe and just be my usual self again.

"Good evening, I'm Father Gower, and this is my daughter Margaret," Daddy was saying to the woman. "I don't believe we've met."

"Well, I'm *Loretta*," she declared incredulously, as though she would have assumed everyone knew that. "He's up on a *ladder*, looking for more glasses." She offered this information to my father in a mode of arch hilarity, all the while repeatedly scrubbing the palms of her reddened hands down the front of her dishcloth apron. She had not so much as glanced in my direction.

"*I* see," said Daddy pleasantly, edging us slowly into a large, surprisingly bare room, since she didn't appear to be going to invite us in. "Are you, er, from St. Matthias?"

"No, I'm one of his patients. I stay away from the churches, if I can help it."

"Ah, Adrian," said Daddy with relief to our approaching host.

And so, having accepted the loss of him and then gained him back again, all within the space of a minute, without any effort on my part, I stood transfixed in a kind of passive acceptance of whatever would happen, or not happen, next, as he came towards us with that easy, swinging walk I remembered from the garden.

"Hello, Father. Hello, Margaret"—shaking my hand—"it's good to see you again. You've met my helper here? Loretta Pullen. Loretta came over early to help me get things set up." I thought Adrian Bonner himself appeared somewhat nervous.

"A good thing I did, too," Loretta scolded, folding her arms and waggling her head flirtatiously at Adrian. "They were just *filthy* and one of 'em was broken. It's a good thing I saw that old box up there on the top shelf."

"Loretta means my drinking glasses," explained Adrian, with gentle good humor. He passed a hand over the scant hairs on the front of his head. I noticed the dry lines that cut into his forehead and radiated from the corners of his eyes. He seemed older than I'd remembered, but the light blue crewneck sweater he was wearing over his clerical shirt and collar gave him a collegiate air. "Well, it's under control now, Loretta, thanks to you. But now that I got down that other box, I'm afraid there are some more glasses needing to be washed. If you don't mind."

"Why should I mind?" demanded Loretta archly. Since Adrian

had appeared, she no longer saw my father. "That's what I came early for, isn't it?" She marched off.

"Loretta has been through a rough time," Adrian explained to us in a confiding undertone, "but she's blessed with a resilient spirit."

"Resilience *is* a blessing," agreed my father. "Is this where we'll be meeting?" He looked questioningly around the bare room we had just entered. It had only a long table at the far end by the window and several functional chairs placed tentatively in the foreground.

"That's why I wanted you to come early, Father. To decide where you'd be most comfortable. I'm still settling in, which is nakedly apparent. Someday, this room is going to turn into a living room. So far, I've only gotten around to painting the walls. Oh, and I made the table."

"You made that table?" Daddy crossed the room in four giant steps to inspect it. "But, this is beautiful. Walnut, isn't it? I had no idea you were a master carpenter, Adrian."

"I was taught carpentry as a boy."

In the orphanage, I thought.

Daddy was stroking his fingers admiringly along its rich grain.

"Now all it needs is some chairs," said Adrian. "But chairs are harder to make. And finding the time is even harder. I'm afraid the only room that is adequately furnished in this house is my study, which is also my consulting room. That's where I spend most of my time, except for sleeping, although"—he smiled at me, showing the chipped front tooth—"I have been known to sleep there. It's where our study group usually meets, but I was worried you might find it cramped."

"How many people are you expecting?" I asked.

Adrian Bonner looked at me as if I had asked an unusually perceptive question.

"There'll be Adele King, and Captain Ragland, and Margaret Wishart . . . another Margaret"—he tapped me lightly on the elbow and smiled again—"and Tod Dancer, and Art and Nettie Robinson, they're our newlyweds, and Loretta . . . and the three of us. How many is that?"

"Ten," said Daddy, who had been counting along on his fingers.

"Maybe we should look at my study and then decide."

"That sounds like a good plan," said Daddy. As soon as Adrian turned to lead the way, he raised his eyebrows wryly at me behind Adrian's back: *The prototype of the helpless bachelor, wouldn't you say? But we still like him, don't we?*

Though it was definitely going to be a little cramped, the study was quickly decided upon. Daddy could sit at the desk for his talk, like a professor giving a rather crowded tutorial, and if we pushed back the sofa and reangled a Lazy-Boy and another armchair, there would be room to squeeze in the chairs from the room that hadn't turned into a living room yet. I was curious as to what his bedroom would be like.

"This room was a lot wider before I built these shelves," said Adrian Bonner apologetically.

"But the shelves make the room" said my father. "I wish I had shelves this nice. They have such a rich, golden quality. Yellow pine?"

"No, ordinary white. I mixed a Jacobean stain with polyurethane. And sanded between coats."

"And what a collection of old priests' prayer books. Why, look, here's Littledale and Vaux!"

Excitedly, my father took down a little black book and opened it. "Listen to this . . ." he said, reading aloud to us the flyleaf inscription written in an old-fashioned copperplate hand: " 'S. H. Taylor, from T. H. Newby, in memory of his Ordination to the Priesthood, Trinity 1910, and of a year's happy ministry together at S. Martin's Plaistone.' How delightful. I wonder what they were like, S. H. Taylor and T. H. Newby. Where did you get this, Adrian? In such mint condition, too."

"In a used book shop in Chicago, when I was in graduate school. I had no idea of ever being ordained myself when I bought it. I was just attracted to it."

"Well, you showed excellent instinct. Father Traherne had this very same edition. He used to say if there wasn't a prayer for it in Littledale and Vaux, then the situation was probably outside the realm of human events." Flipping to the table of contents, my father proceeded to recite random entries: "For Those at Sea in a Storm . . . For One Insensible or Deranged . . . Before Making a Will . . . After Attempted Suicide . . . With Married Woman After Childbirth . . . With *Unmarried* Woman After Childbirth . . . For One Unlikely to Recover . . . Office for Sending Forth a Missionary . . .' Oh-oh, listen, I'd forgotten about this one: 'Form of Degradation from Holy Orders . . .' Sure want to avoid that one, if we can. Though, these days, a priest would have to go pretty far to warrant being stripped of his surplice and stole."

"*This* is kind of interesting, too." Caught up in my father's enthusiasm, Adrian ran his fingers along a higher shelf and pulled down another book. "Gregory the Thirteenth's Roman Ritual. Not the sixteenth-century edition, of course . . . you'd probably only find one of those in the Vatican Library, but I love browsing through this volume. It's got most of the medieval rituals, as well as an extensive collection of exorcistic material."

"Exorcism, now there's a subject," my father said eagerly, taking the book from Adrian and rather reluctantly handing back the Littledale and Vaux. "Ah, me, but you put me to shame. You say you *browse* in this? My Latin never reached the stage of proficiency that would allow me to browse."

The two of them might have stood there all evening, their backs turned on everything extraneous to their shared engrossment with Adrian's esoteric library, if the members of the study group had not begun to arrive.

They certainly were a mixed bag. Some were definitely saner than others. The one thing they all had in common was their admiration of Adrian Bonner.

The person I liked best, even before I was aware of our curious connection in the past, was Adele King, a willowy old lady with a happy face who arrived with her arms full of cherry blossom branches, which she asked me to help her arrange in a black vase she had brought along.

"Father Bonner has so much, he has been a real gift to us, but I was sure he wouldn't have a vase to his name," she confided to me. "I remember seeing you with your mother, ever so many times, when you were just a little thing."

"You did?" We were in Adrian Bonner's kitchen, along with Loretta, who seemed oblivious to us as she compulsively arranged and rearranged Adrian's drinking glasses.

"Yes, my husband and I would often see the two of you in the old Walgreens. We walked downtown every afternoon from Fern Hill Manor."

"You stayed at Fern Hill Manor?"

"Faithfully. We'd come down every August, from New Jersey, for my husband's vacation. Mrs. Radford always made sure we got the lovely big front room on the second floor, with all the windows. And I remember that pixie niece of hers. You two played together. Harry and I would come upon you in the hall, and the two of you would scamper off like little rabbits. But I do recall your mother well. Such a pretty girl. And you were so wrapped up in each other, sitting up there at the soda fountain. You always seemed to be having real tête-à-têtes. My husband and I missed out on the experience of having children, though our marriage was very happy. Oh, I miss him so. But I'm thankful I wasn't the one to go first. He would have been devastated."

The lovely big front room on the second floor, I was thinking guiltily, as this sweet lady made me such an unexpected gift. Here she was, presenting me with this treasured view-from-behind of my mother and me, wrapped up in each other: a vision that comforted me by confirming something I had wanted to believe had been true. And at the very same time, I was looking through another kind of peephole into the past and seeing a view of Adele King that I could hardly share with her—though it surely would have warmed her lonely widow's heart to have seen it along with me: a vision of two elderly naked people coupling in the afternoon light of their boarding-house room. For it had almost certainly been the Kings whom Chloe Niles and I had watched from the hole she had drilled in the linen closet. That was the room, those were the years. No wonder we had scampered away like shy rabbits upon encountering the objects of our research in the hall, although I didn't remember that part, at all. How selective our memories were.

"We had planned to retire here to the Shenandoahs," Adele King said, deftly arranging the cherry blossoms in the vase. "We were even considering those Sunset Villas that have been giving your father so much concern, but they were out of our reach financially. So we bought a little house right here on Acacia Street. Harry said at least when we got too old to drive, we could walk downtown, only there isn't much 'downtown' to walk to, anymore. But I'm so glad we had eight months together, here in our little retirement house, before he went. Now I want something to put under this vase, so it won't scratch Father Bonner's beautiful table. Loretta, have you seen a trivet around here anyplace?"

"I can't say that I have," replied Loretta archly, not bothering to look around from the sink. "But then how could I, when I don't even know what a 'trivet' *is*?"

"Well, they're little . . . how would you describe a trivet, Margaret?"

"Adele, honey, the last thing in this world you're going to find in this house is a trivet," drawled a stylish lady with frosted hair, who had just swooped into the kitchen with a rustle of silk trousers and a tinkle of bracelets. She disburdened herself of two large bags of groceries in the proprietary manner of someone returning to her own house. "You'll have to settle for one of those cute straw placemats Mindy and Jerry Hope gave him for his housewarming. Oh, haven't you done a sweet job arranging those cherry blossoms." She flashed me a cold smile. "Hello there, I don't believe we've met."

"Margaret Wishart, meet Margaret Gower." The obliging Adele made introductions. "This is our speaker's daughter. I was just telling her I remembered her as a small child."

"Isn't that nice," said Margaret Wishart vacantly, running her eyes up and down my person with the swift expertise of one long-practiced in the art of appraising other females. She seemed to find me satisfactorily harmless, except maybe for my youth.

"Where did you say those placemats were?" Adele King asked her.

"Second drawer from the right," announced a buxom lady just entering the kitchen in a raspberry-colored jogging suit; she was followed by a small, white-haired man in an identical outfit who carried a gallon jug of apple cider hooked in each of his thumbs.

"Hi there, lovebirds," sang out Margaret Wishart. "Don't you all look sweet in your matching suits."

"This is Nettie and Art Robinson, Margaret," said Adele King. "They have just gotten married. Nettie, Art, this is Margaret Gower, the rector's daughter, from over at St. Cuthbert's."

"We saw your father's picture in the paper this morning," said Art Robinson, swinging up on his toes to set down the cider jugs on the counter. "The article was good, too. He got 'em told. I wouldn't go so far as saying most people don't know the *name* of Jesus Christ anymore, but I will say a lot of 'em go around *acting* like they don't remember. But it was a good article. Forceful. I like forceful people."

"Thank you. But, actually my father didn't say—"

"That's why he married me, I'm forceful," boomed Nettie Robinson, rummaging around in Adrian Bonner's kitchen drawer. The combination of her movements with her bulk had the effect of displacing everyone else in the kitchen. "Here, Adele, are these the ones you wanted?" She waved a sheaf of brand-new-looking straw place mats.

"Yes, thank you, Nettie, but I only need one. It's to go under the flowers so I won't ruin Father's beautiful table."

"You couldn't ruin it," spoke out Loretta aggressively, still fussing with Adrian's drinking glasses. "Even if every one of you was to put a lighted cigarette down on it, you couldn't ruin it. On account of all the oil and sanding that went into it. He explained it to me. You couldn't ruin it if you tried. All he'd have to do is just sand it off and put some more oil on it."

"Well, *that's* good to know, isn't it?" said Margaret Wishart, with false sweetness, unpacking an impressive assortment of snacks from her grocery bags and laying them out with obvious approval of her own selections. "Of course, none of us smokes anymore, but you never can tell what other kinds of damage we might get up to." She winked at the rest of us surreptitiously, and I felt compromised because, before I could stop myself, I had smiled "understandingly" back at her, along with Art and Nettie Robinson, to show that I, too, was "in on" Loretta's antisocial behavior. I hoped whatever kind of older Margaret I turned out to be, it would not be someone like Margaret Wishart, though she was undeniably attractive for her age.

Only Adele King came off admirably. Making a final adjustment to her generous spread of pink blossoms, she tucked a straw placemat under one arm and, smiling lovingly at everybody, including the mad Loretta, lifted the black vase and carried it into Adrian Bonner's living room-to-be.

The two other members of the group, Captain Ragland and Tod Dancer, had gone straight to the study on arrival, having neither refreshments to deposit, nor any apparent need to demonstrate intimate knowledge of Adrian Bonner's kitchen. Both were dour men, and both of them doted, in their different styles, on Adrian Bonner. I had hardly been introduced to Captain Ragland, a retired naval officer, before he began lecturing me, as if it were partly my fault, on how his only son had shirked Vietnam. Adrian *Bonner*, in contrast, had enlisted in the Navy and served as a gunnery officer, first on the USS *Wright*, and then aboard the USS *Spiegel Grove*, "named for Rutherford B. Hayes's summer home," the Captain informed me gruffly, "though you couldn't be expected to know that."

Tod Dancer, whom Adrian introduced to me, was an assistant librarian at the community college. Though we were the only two young people here, he shook my hand with undisguised misgiving and kept his eyes averted. He had been born to grow up into a well-built, handsome young man, a little along the lines of a Ben MacGruder, but something had ossified him prematurely. He held himself as stiffly as Captain Ragland, though without the Captain's masculine complacence, and, except when Adrian Bonner was talking to him, he wore a perpetually affronted expression that spoiled his otherwise fine features.

This was the group on whose behalf Daddy had been anguishing. Except for the kindly and likable Adele King, and, of course, Adrian Bonner, they seemed unworthy of my father's preparations. And from what I could observe of him now, the benevolent manner in which he stooped to listen to Art Robinson, the offhand gallantry of his banter with Margaret Wishart as she batted her eyes and flashed her cold smile at him, I was pretty sure he had come to the same conclusion: there was nobody here to be nervous about or—except for Adrian Bonner—to want to impress. Of course there was always the "whatsoever you do unto the least of these, you do unto Me" precept, but, discounting that obligation, it was, I had to admit, a disappointing gathering.

Before we sat down, Adrian Bonner asked us all to join hands for a short prayer. I was beside him and was so sensitive to the pressure of his hand on mine that I retained almost nothing of what he said. That was too bad, because I had been looking forward to hearing how he would pray. It seemed to me that he squeezed my hand twice during the prayer, but then how could I be sure he wasn't also squeezing the hand of Tod Dancer on his other side?

As I had predicted, my father laid down his notes and began speaking extemporaneously to the group fitted snugly into Adrian Bonner's study. His manner was down-to-earth, more personal and direct than his pulpit style, and it struck exactly the right note with these people. He began by telling them he would be celebrating his thirty-third year as a priest next November, and that, for him, Passion Week, or Holy Week if you preferred, was still the most exciting and mysterious time in the entire Church Calendar. If anything, it became *more* thrilling and mysterious every year. Why was that? Because the more he thought about it, the surer he was becoming that the story of Christ's passion and suf-

fering contained the key capable of unlocking the final secret
room at the heart of his own personality and allowing him to step
inside and at last understand the meaning and purpose of his
particular destiny.

You could feel them edge forward in their chairs, observe their
polite attention give way to the more lively human emotion of
curiosity: *Is he going to maybe tell us something really personal?*

Did that strike them as a little grandiose, my father asked
them, for someone to look for the key to his own meaning in the
story of Christ's passion?

Perhaps. But, then again, perhaps not.

Then, he took them briskly through the events of Passion
Week, pointing out the parallels between Christ's drama and the
stages in our own lives: how the Triumphal Entry into Jerusalem
was also ourselves embarking publicly into the fullness of our
powers "with all their attendant snares . . . the misjudgments, the
overreachings, the painful mistakes . . . but we must keep on keeping on, we must live out our own vision of life, just as Christ did.
And as we go along, there are going to be mistakes. If you avoid
mistakes, you've stopped moving . . ."

The Celebration of the Last Supper, he said, in which Christ
ceremonially offered his life in place of the Paschal lamb as a
redeeming sacrifice, is recelebrated every time one of us offers the
"sacred meal of himself" to the rest of the table, in order to continue the process of redemption.

"However, you want to be sure the meat and drink is fit to be
shared, otherwise you may simply be spreading poison, or at the
very least indigestion. Most of us have had our share of indigestible people"—this elicited a round of nods and smiles and a knowing outburst of "Ha!" from Loretta —"and we certainly don't want
to become one of them ourselves. St. Paul wrote about this to the
Corinthians, you remember, when he said, 'Let a man examine
himself, and so let him eat of that bread, and drink of that cup.
For he that eateth and drinketh unworthily, eateth and drinketh
damnation to himself, not discerning the Lord's body.' We have to
prepare ourselves properly, just as a good hostess, or host, properly prepares the banquet, before we can responsibly offer ourselves as a source of nourishment to others."

From there, he went on to the Agony in the Garden of Geth-
semane, which he spoke about with particular feeling.

"Our Gethsemanes are our lowest hours, when it seems all we

are able to do is sleep or pray. The disciples, being only too human, went to sleep; Christ stayed awake, sweated blood, and,
through ceaseless praying and superhuman endurance, resolved
the raging conflict going on inside himself. Through prayer,
through the very nature of prayer, we are able to speak and listen
in new ways. Because in prayer, we are not just talking to ourselves, but admitting another. By entering into a passionate dia-
logue with this other, we are sometimes able to hear our truest
voice speak back to us clearly . . . and tell us what to do next . . ."

Adrian Bonner was sitting on the floor next to my feet. He had
first sat down between me and Tod Dancer on the sofa, because
that had been the nearest place for his body to sink after the
prayer, but then he had stood up again almost at once, claiming
he was "crowding" us, though both of us assured him there was
plenty of room. I didn't think Tod Dancer would mind all that
much if Adrian Bonner's hip and arm grazed his, and I certainly
wouldn't mind if the other side of him grazed me. Nevertheless,
he prevailed and slid to the floor, where he now sat cross-legged,
affording me ample opportunity to study his broad shoulders and
the soft, brownish golden hairs on the back of his neck. I could
have reached out, without stretching, and touched his bald spot.
I was thankful for this imperfection, because an Adrian Bonner
with a head of thick, flowing hair along with everything else would
have been almost too much to bear.

". . . Each of us," Daddy was saying, "has a place of particular
pain. You know what yours is, I know what mine is. And we know
that, when we're in it, all we can do is say, well, I'm sad, I'm
heartbroken, even . . . this is not what I wanted . . . and perhaps
it will never get any better . . . oh, why can't someone remove this
cross from me?

"But then we have to take it a step farther and say, but it's
mine, this particular agony, it's where circumstances met with
myself and made this cross. Very well then, let me be crucified on
this cross . . . this cross of my old expectations versus what is
to be."

Was I in love, then? Never before had anyone brought me to
this state of willing suspension, this mixture of joy and hopeless-
ness. I could have sat there all night simply meditating on the
sight of the back of Adrian Bonner's neck, the pink whorls of his
ears. It made me feel on the verge of a sort of swoon to imagine
myself one day standing behind him familiarly with the scissors,

cutting his hair, or what was left of it. Yet I did not dare to imagine
he might go into similar raptures if I had been sitting on the floor
under his gaze. He would have perhaps admired my curly hair or
my youth. He might have found the slope of my shoulders graceful under my soft gray dress—I had ripped out the shoulder pads
at the last minute, in front of my bathroom mirror, because, even
though they gave the dress its stylish shape, I decided that he, who
probably knew little about women's fashions, might think them
foolish or exaggerated.

If he did admire me, it was probably because he approved of
me as the right daughter for my father. Because I was intelligent
and thoughtful and took good care of Daddy. That was undoubtedly what he had meant when I had overheard him saying to my
father in our garden, "You are a lucky man."

". . . Psychologically understood, the cross of Passion Week can
be seen as Christ's destiny, his unique life story to be fulfilled. To
take up my own cross, then, would mean to accept and *consciously
realize* my own particular pattern of wholeness . . ."

But why should I not aspire? Why should I not hope that,
eventually, I could come to mean more to Adrian Bonner than
just being my father's daughter? "Being Father Gower's daughter,
you're at home with such talk," he had said, after I had asked him
for his definition of sin. "You and he probably discuss things like
this every night over the supper table." We could invite him for
supper once a week, the way we used to have Professor LaFarge
every Friday. The three of us could have good talks. About St.
Hilda, about his Gnostics, about whatever he was interested in.
And then one evening, he would find himself reluctant to leave,
missing me as he drove home . . .

". . . Accepting our cross doesn't mean taking responsibility for
what we are . . . that's arrogance, God made us what we are, He
gave us our circumstances . . . it means taking responsibility for
what we are *doing* with what we are . . ."

I could wait, I was glad I was good at waiting. Because of *my*
particular circumstances, the circumstances I had been given, I
had grown up to be the kind of person who knew how to wait.
And now, if I loved him, I could wait until Adrian Bonner, driving
home one evening . . . perhaps one evening this summer . . .
would suddenly realize how perfectly I suited him . . .

I became aware that there was a suspension in the room. My
father, seated behind Adrian's desk, had stopped talking and was

leaning forward, one hand clasping either side of the desk. His eyes were open, but he looked as if he had gone into a trance. Adele King looked worried. Loretta stopped plucking at a cuticle and stared at Daddy with more interest than she had so far shown, except for his indigestible people remark. Margaret Wishart raised an eyebrow inquiringly at Adrian Bonner, who was in the act of rising to his feet when, in an odd, broken voice, Daddy suddenly resumed.

"Let yourself . . . let yourself . . . be crucified . . . on the cross of your sorrow . . ." my father blurted in this strange, broken voice, as if he were teaching himself each word as it came out of his mouth. "That is what you can offer . . ." He blinked several times and then appeared to come to himself.

"Let your personal sorrows merge with the sorrows of humanity. That is what you can offer, that is what you can give . . ." He hesitated, as though unsure of where he wanted to go next. "That is the meaning of Easter. Easter means that we are constantly granted the right to slough off our old skins and try again . . . to die to our old selves and our old sorrows one more time. And I believe . . . I believe that even our *dying* . . . I mean bodily death . . . in its own way moves humanity forward and brings the human family a chance to try again. Because each time any one of us dies, it will never have to be done quite that way again. And all of our sorrows, the big ones and the little ones, bind us up more closely into the human . . ." He seemed to be searching for an elusive word. ". . . the human fabric, the web of life." He took a deep, ragged breath, and then smiled in an uncharacteristically lopsided way. "Whatever else we may do, or not do, you will have . . . I will have . . . added our sorrows to the dance. Let us pray."

An audible exhalation went through the study. Adele King smiled radiantly at my father with tears in her eyes before she closed them. The newlywed Robinsons in their matching raspberry suits clasped hands and, after exchanging the briefest of complacent glances, which could have signaled either relief that my father's talk had been satisfactorily concluded, or that each was relieved to be here in each other's company and not obliged to go home all alone afterwards, bowed their heads.

"Heavenly Father," my father prayed, in a more or less complete resumption of his old fluent rhythms, "during this week of holy sorrows, let the streams of our personal sorrows merge with the sorrows of humanity. Your most blessed son knew and lived and died with this knowledge of how one flows into the other, and every one of us is here to accomplish the same. That . . . that . . . all those who, beholding the same, shall ponder and adore the mystery and be filled with Thy heavenly benediction unto life eternal. Through the same Christ our Lord, Amen."

Adrian and I reached my father first. "Are you all right?" we both asked.

"I'm fine," insisted Daddy, putting an arm around each of us, as though we were both his children. "I just had the worst attack of absentmindedness I've ever had in my life. I couldn't for the life of me remember what I was supposed to say next. A poor showing, Adrian, I'm sorry. Next time I'll do better . . . if you're foodhardy enough to ask me again."

"But you were magnificent," said Adrian Bonner, sounding as if he meant it. "You've given everybody an enormous amount to think about. That was the best description of prayer I ever heard. You have clarified many things."

"You're kind, and I thank you, but . . . whew! What a monumental blank-out that was!" My father passed his hand over his face, as if to banish the experience.

Others were pressing around him now. I was surprised that some people didn't think Daddy's lapse was a lapse at all, but a sudden spontaneous surge of emotion. "It was so inspiring to me, the way you let yourself be moved by the Spirit," Adele King told him.

"I felt the same way, Adele," chimed in Margaret Wishart, batting her eyes up at my father.

"Well, you're kind," said Daddy, "but I'm afraid towards the end there I just plain blanked. For a moment there I couldn't have told you my own name."

"You're probably suffering from CRS syndrome, Father," said Art Robinson. "It hits us all at a certain age."

"CRS . . . ?" inquired my father with interest, stooping towards the little man. "I don't believe I've heard of it."

Guffawing, Art Robinson beckoned my father even closer. "Can't Remember Shit," he stage-whispered in Daddy's ear.

"An evening just isn't complete for him unless he gets to talk dirty," apologized buxom Nettie Robinson, tugging her bad boy away. "Come have some refreshments, Reverend. You've earned them."

Tod Dancer approached with his stiff walk. Screwing his face up, he asked my father rather accusingly whether he had meant it about some pains never getting any better. "I mean, is that a Christian attitude? I thought Christians believed that if you accept Jesus Christ as your personal savior, you could bear anything."

"Ah, now, you've put your finger on something important, there, haven't you?" said Daddy, becoming animated. "You can bear it, because He's given it significance. That doesn't necessarily have anything to do with its going away, or getting better. It may even get worse. But you *feel* better about it, because you see it in a different context. Am I making sense?"

"But . . ."

"Come and have a glass of cider, Father, and some refreshments," implored Adele King.

With the skeptical Tod Dancer doggedly clinging, Daddy allowed himself to be steered towards Adrian Bonner's beautiful table, decked with the vase of cherry blossoms and platters heaped with fruit and cheeses and bread and crackers and cookies, all resting suitably on the straw placemats that the Hopes had given Adrian for his housewarming. As with all typical church spreads, there was too much of everything, because the provider whose turn it was had felt it necessary to outdo all the others.

Daddy was still deep in conversation with the surly young librarian, and I was standing in the doorway to the kitchen with Adele King, drinking cider and eating a cookie, when Adrian Bonner quietly approached.

"Excuse me, Adele, would you mind if I borrowed Margaret for a moment?"

Utterly taken by surprise, I felt his fingers firmly on my elbow as he led me away. That was the way it went, wasn't it? You had to stop wanting something, or at least forget you wanted it for a minute, before it would come to you on its own. I had hoped I would have a chance to talk with him in a corner before the evening was over, but I hadn't gone so far as to imagine he would actually come and take me off alone.

"I hope Tod Dancer isn't annoying your father," Adrian said as we entered his study.

"Oh, no. He's enjoying it. He takes people seriously when they challenge him." I did not go on to say that it was in Daddy's nature to respect people more when they disapproved of him. Come to think of it, Tod Dancer and Ned Block shared something of the same impacted demeanor.

"I wanted to ask you if you would give your father something for me," said Adrian Bonner. "I wanted to give it to him earlier, but I'm clumsy at giving things to people. It's that priests' prayer book he admired. If you could just put it in your purse, and then when you get home if you would tell him I wanted him to have it in memory of tonight . . ."

"Well, of course," I said, touched by his admission of clumsiness.

"Thanks." He plucked it from the shelf, and, taking up a pen from his desk, wrote something in the flyleaf, directly below the old inscription from T. H. Newby to S. H. Taylor.

"There," he said, putting down the pen. He read over what he had written, then closed the little book and put it into my hand. "Bless you," he said, covering my hand with the book in it with both of his. "You know, Margaret, I hope—"

But I was not to hear what Adrian Bonner hoped.

"Excuse *me*," said Loretta archly from the doorway. She managed to stare at my hand under Adrian's two without acknowledging the rest of me. "I just wanted to know two things."

"Yes, Loretta?" His hands slid back to himself and he was all patient good humor with the "resilient" patient, who must have followed us from the kitchen.

"I wanted to know *first* if it was time to start cleaning up," said Loretta, "and I wanted to know *second* if we've still got our usual date tomorrow afternoon."

"Certainly we've got our date, Loretta," said Adrian with such solicitude that I found myself envying this crazy woman her time alone with him. "But let's not begin the cleaning up yet. Not until people start to leave."

"Just as you say," she mocked, waggling her head at him like a shrewish wife. "But you know *some* people won't start to leave till you give 'em a kick in the pants." Still not looking at me.

"Okay, let's have it," said Daddy, driving us home. "You are my truthteller, Margaret. How bad was it?"

"I know you won't believe me, but it was really good. As Adrian Bonner said, you gave everyone a whole lot to think about."

"But it wasn't as good as Sunday's. Come on, now, the truth."

"Sunday's was more . . . rounded off. But tonight's had more little sparks and sparkles in it."

"Ah, rounded off!" moaned my father, going straight for the one negative crumb I had thrown him. "*This* one was to have been rounded off . . . if only I hadn't had that horrible attack of forgetfulness!"

"What exactly happened, Daddy? You were strange for a couple of minutes there. I was frightened."

"It's hard to describe. Suddenly it was as if my whole consciousness had been erased. And then it came back, but . . . the worst part was that when it did, I could remember how it felt when I didn't know anything. I couldn't think of any *words*, Margaret. I didn't even know what words were! And then, when I *could* speak again, it seemed miraculous that I could do it. You know, put the words together with . . . the intention to speak. But the shape of my talk was gone. I just grabbed things out of the air. I suppose it was all too noticeable. Some of them came to me, from I don't know where. All that stuff about streams of sorrow . . . though I guess that's not surprising, with my predilection for sorrow . . . and then that prayer at the end . . ."

"I liked it."

"So do I, but part of it was the prayer for the blessing of the Christmas crib, not for Passion Week. It was the only one I could think of at that moment."

"Daddy, how long has it been since you've had a checkup?"

"Too long, I suppose. Lord, but I really do miss old Doc Mac-Gruder. He was so practical, he didn't make a fuss. And he understood that the soul was part of the human body. Not like these young technicians. Maybe if I hang on a few more years, there'll be another Doc MacGruder for me. Harriet's going into geriatric medicine, too. *That's* appropriate."

"Meanwhile will you just humor me, Daddy? If you don't like the young technicians around here, I could get you an appointment at the University Medical Center. That might be better, anyway. Before we go to England. I'll ask Professor Stannard the name of his doctor. He's always going to his doctor; he has his blood pressure checked every other Wednesday, in fact, just before my tutorial with him."

"He does, does he? No connection, I hope."

*   *   *

When we got home, I gave him the prayer book from Adrian. He was enormously touched. "I always wondered what happened to Father Traherne's copy of Littledale and Vaux. I guess his widow must have given it away with the rest of his books to the Seminary. But now, Adrian's giving it to me brings something full circle. It's like a chain. Especially considering his inscription."

Under the old inscription "S. H. Taylor, from T. H. Newby, in memory of his Ordination to the Priesthood, Trinity 1910, and of a year's happy ministry together at S. Martin's Plaistone," Adrian Bonner had written, "To Father Walter Gower, a guiding light to others in his profession, in appreciation of his wise words this evening and in fondest hopes that our friendship will continue to grow. Adrian Bonner † , Monday in Passion Week, March 28, 1988."

" 'Wise words'! " scoffed my father. " 'Confused babble' would have been a more honest description. But the fact that a man of Adrian Bonner's caliber should treasure my friendship does make it all seem worthwhile."

I dreamed of my mother profusely. It was a windfall of dreams. Seldom, if ever, had she been with me all night like this. Undoubtedly the dreams had been sparked off by the meeting with Adele King and influenced by other events from the past few days, but nevertheless I kept thinking even as I was dreaming, "This is important. I've got to remember everything."

Of course I didn't. There was just too much. Ruth was accompanying me places, we were going all over together, it was as though she were attempting to make up for all the years we had been apart. At one point, I partly woke. I was sweating and had kicked off my covers. *I have got to get up and write down these dreams,* I thought feverishly. I have got to at least get up and open the window. But I realized the window was already open and a gentle breeze was blowing in, in wisps, like the wisps of the evanescent dreams, and then I went all languid, as if someone had placed a smooth hand on my forehead and whispered, *Don't write down anything . . . just sleep . . . you will remember what you need to remember.*

Then I dreamed again, and these dreams I did remember. My mother was standing in the room and I said to her, "Don't forget to leave the closet door open."

"Do I ever forget, sweetie pooh?"

But, instead of fixing the door exactly right for the witch who lived inside, Ruth took my hand and gently pulled me out of the bed, and off into the closet we went. "I'll bet you didn't know," she said to me, "that this closet leads through an underground tunnel and comes out in Mrs. Radford's linen closet."

We were both looking through a window at two old people making love. Only they were not naked, as Adele King and her husband had been in the old days when Chloe Niles and I had spied on their stringy bodies from our peephole in her aunt's linen closet, they were wearing raspberry jogging suits like the Robinsons. "What you have to realize about Adele King," said my mother, very seriously, "is that she has a strong heart. If you don't have a strong heart, you shouldn't attempt this."

Then we were in Adrian Bonner's living room and, to my consternation, my mother was painting a colorful South Sea mural on his walls. "Never trust a man who has no pictures on his walls," she said, slapping on paint.

"But he might not like this picture," I said, though I was fascinated by the moving, bright shapes. It was like Gauguin's work, only the bodies really were moving. A naked brown man sat up suddenly and drank something from a gourd.

"Now, you'll do his bedroom," said Ruth, handing me a brush. "It's all right. This house is already condemned."

"But that's terrible!" Suddenly I was crying. It seemed so unfair that Adrian would lose the house that he had just moved into.

"We've got to get out of here," my mother said. "They're starting to demolish."

"Let me just see his room first."

"Come *on*, Margaret. Don't you hear the machinery? It's right outside."

"Just let me look at the picture of him in the orphanage," I begged her. Somehow I could see it, a dim, old-fashioned sepia group portrait of several rows of sad-faced children. "I know it's hanging over his bed." If I could get to the room and find him in the picture, I knew he would be mine.

"Sorry, sweetie, but I'm going to have to give you a good kick in the pants," she said. And before I could struggle, some kind of tarpaulin was thrown over my head and I felt myself being sucked out of the house.

There was one more brief dream in which I lay naked on the

table in our breakfast room while Ruth tried to sketch me. She kept fussing at me to be still, but I couldn't, and even when I locked myself in position, my flesh kept dancing and quivering in the sunshine. We both found this so funny we started giggling.

I woke to the sound of my father's agonized breathing. He was standing in the doorway to my room, wearing his bathrobe and pajamas. He was unshaven and in tears.

"Oh, Margaret, I hated to wake you, but the vilest thing has happened. During the night, someone came and sawed down the corner cross. I stepped outside to get the paper and I looked down the street and . . . it wasn't there anymore. And they've done worse than that. I've just been to see. They've mutilated him. Just sliced him up in pieces with their infernal saw. What kind of depraved devils would be capable of such a thing?"

And here we offer and present unto
thee, O Lord, our selves, our souls
and bodies, to be a reasonable, holy,
and living sacrifice unto thee . . .

—Eucharistic Prayer, Rite One,
The Book of Common Prayer

IX: A REASONABLE, HOLY, AND LIVING SACRIfiCE

*T*hey had done a sickeningly thorough job, whoever they were.
From whatever personal motives, or at whoever's instigation, they
had set their infernal saws to work during the dark hours that
shielded them and had accomplished their purpose. Both cross
and stone figure were irreparable. Even the little tiled roof that
had sheltered them had smashed during its fall to the ground.
There had been more than one vandal and more than one tool of
destruction, explained Ernie Pasco, who came over within minutes in answer to my father's anguished phone call, to examine the
devastation.

One person, a strong person, would have had to hold the
wooden cross, he told us, while the other sawed away with an
ordinary chain saw. Once the cross was down, a stonemason's saw
had been used to slice through the figure as it lay more accessible
and prone. The head and both arms had been cut off, the torso
sundered at the waist, the legs severed at the knee, and, as a final
indignity, the fingers and toes thoroughly smashed with a powerful hammer.

"One thing for certain," said Ernie Pasco, shaking his head in
stunned disbelief at the sad remains scattered at our feet, "the
swine who did this wanted to make sure nobody could ever put it
back again. No, no, Father, I wouldn't touch anything if I was you.
Let the police see it the way everything's laying, first. I'm sur-

prised you two didn't hear it up at the rectory. Those buzz saws make some racket."

"I think I did hear it," I said. "But it seemed to go with a dream I was having at the time, about some machinery."

"I guess I must be losing my hearing, along with everything else," said Daddy gloomily. He was unable to tear his eyes away from the chopped-up figure, some dismembered parts still recognizable enough to recall its exceptional grace. "I have an idea who was behind this execrable piece of work."

"I have a feeling you may be right," said Ernie Pasco

By Tuesday afternoon, a number of other people in the community, not just members of St. Cuthbert's, had expressed views similar to my father's about the person who had most to gain from a certain street corner being shorn of its troublesome antiquity. Although when Georgie Gaines had arrived on the scene that morning to express his personal outrage (but also to do a follow-up on his story for *The Romulus Record*), he assured us that, much as he disapproved of Gaines Senior's values, he had to say that the hiring of vandals was just not his dad's style.

"I've had another kind of horrible idea," said Georgie guiltily. He had been sitting on our sofa at the time, his eyes downcast, his long arms dangling between his knees.

"What is that?" asked Daddy.

"Well, sir, it occurred to me that it might have something to do with *my story*. Maybe someone took offense at the way I wrote it. Or maybe it drew attention to the value of the little corpus, and someone thought it would be fun to smash it. If it hadn't been for my story, their attention might not have been drawn to it."

"You mustn't blame yourself," insisted my father. "I wanted the story to appear. I was sure that it would help our cause. Now, oh, I don't know what to think, except that he's gone. But you mustn't blame yourself, George. That won't help anything."

"Well, I still feel terrible," said Georgie Gaines, nevertheless collecting himself sufficiently to begin scribbling notes into his spiral pad. "What will you do now, Reverend Gower?"

"What will I do now," my father repeated morosely, passing his hand slowly down the front of his face. He gazed out at our living room, as if it were some unfamiliar antechamber in which he was merely awaiting details of news he already knew was not good.

"Well, yes," urged Georgie, pencil poised. "I mean, you're still going to fight it, aren't you?"

"I hardly think so," Daddy replied rather caustically. "If he's gone, so is our cause. If a landmark has been destroyed, you can't very well get landmark status, can you?"

"But what about the corner?" persisted Georgie. "You're still going to fight the town, aren't you? And the . . . uh . . . private interests that're trying to take away your corner."

"The vestry will have to meet and decide our next course of action. I don't know how versed you are in the governing processes of our church, but the vestry manages all our temporal affairs. So I really can't speak on their behalf."

"But you spoke the other day, sir. You said—"

"Ah, the other day, that was different," said my father, an obstinate gleam in his eyes. "The other day, I was speaking on behalf of something that *was* my concern. I was speaking on behalf of the symbol that graced our corner. I am in charge of that symbol and what it represents. I remain the guardian and spokesman for *it* even though its outward form now lies hacked into bits. Oh, my business is still with *that*, all right, but not with . . . real estate."

"So you're saying that it's okay with you if they cut away your corner to widen the street?"

"Don't put words in my mouth, son. You did that the other day, you know."

"I *did*?" Georgie protested innocently. "I certainly didn't mean to."

"Well, you did, all the same," said Daddy sternly. "You had me say one couldn't take for granted that everybody knew Christ's name anymore, when you know very well we were referring to the legislator, not Christ."

"I'm sorry, Reverend Gower, it was a misunderstanding, about the legislator. But you *did* actually say that about everybody maybe not knowing Christ's name anymore."

My father waved this away impatiently. "I said it, but it didn't belong in the piece. It presented our exchange in a false context, and I think you should recognize this, Georgie. Whether you end up becoming a minister or an ace reporter, you're going to have to be able to discern exactly where, in certain shady areas, a truth turns into a lie. The line can be almost invisible, but it's always there for the sharp-sighted few."

Whether from genuine contriteness and a desire to become one of the sharp-sighted elite, or because he still needed Daddy for his story, Georgie accepted the criticism with admirable good grace. The two of them continued to talk, and my father's gloom and belligerence diminished a little. It was in response to Georgie's repeated challenge, "But what are you going to *do* now, Reverend Gower? I mean, you must be planning to do something. I mean, if not about the . . . real estate . . . then about the cross," that my father slowly, but with mounting determination, began to formulate the idea of holding a Reconsecration service for the savaged crucifix.

"When would you have it?" Georgie asked, perking up.

"Well, the obvious date that presents itself is Good Friday," said my father. "Probably between noon and three o'clock."

"Would it be in the church?"

"Oh, no. At the corner, at the corner," said Daddy emphatically. "On the site of the desecration. When that cross was fixed into the ground back in the eighteen seventies . . . I'm going to look up the exact date in our archives . . . there must have been a consecration ceremony. You might want to look it up in *your* archives down at the paper, Georgie. There was possibly a story on it. Maybe a picture."

"I'm not sure *The Romulus Record* itself goes back that far, sir. But maybe there was some other newspaper, and we would have clippings from *it* in our archives, only, you know, we call it the morgue."

"Yes, well, look in your morgue," said Daddy. "There might be something. It would give an added dimension to your story, wouldn't it? Consecration . . . desecration . . . *re*consecration." My father's spirits were lifting. "People are always fascinated by historical contrasts."

"Great idea." The young reporter scribbled into his notebook. "Can outsiders come to a Reconsecration?"

"Anyone who wants to come is welcome," said Daddy. A peculiar smile flitted across his face. "The desecrators themselves are welcome to come. After all, what's the harm? We've got nothing else down at that corner for them to destroy."

People flowed in and out of the rectory all day. Some of them brought food, as if there had been a death. Elaine Major, who brought stuffed peppers, was certain George Gaines Senior was the mastermind ("though he wouldn't have done anything *puh-*sonally, of course; a *wuhd* was passed, a simple *wuhd,* to one of his trusted *wuhk*-men, and the wuhk-man passed the wuhd to someone with the tools, and in a few weeks suh-tain puh-sons are going to be re-*wah*-ded . . .").

"I think you're probably right, Elaine," said Nan MacGruder, adding practically, "only I think cash changed hands *before* the event. The kind of people who go in for cross-bashing are going to want their reward beforehand."

"I was so upset when I saw it, I couldn't get out of my car," snuffled Miriam Stacy. "I sat there and cried for at least fifteen minutes. It's a mercy that Mother isn't here to see this, it would have broken her heart."

"It's a s-s-sorry day," Wirt Winchester said helplessly.

"We ought to start a collection right away for a replacement," said Harlan Buford the banker, whom Ruth used to call Harlan Buffoon. "It'll boost morale."

"You can't replace a thing like that," murmured Ned Block languidly. "Venetian stone carving like that is a thing of the past."

"Maybe Venetian stone carving is," said very pregnant Susan Smith, who was determined to start a Sunday school, "but what about something closer to home? Dick and I know a wonderful Appalachian sculptor who works in bronze, maybe St. Cuthbert's could commission him. He's a very devout person and I'm sure he'd be reasonable."

"That swine Gaines," spluttered Ernie Pasco excitedly, doing a nervous little dance on the carpet. "His fingerprints are all over it, he's who I thought of when Father phoned me to come over. I was the first person he called."

"You may be right, Ernie," said Mrs. MacGruder, "but I think we have to be cautious about naming names. We don't want to be sued for slander on top of our other troubles."

"That's a p-p-point, Nan," agreed Wirt Winchester the lawyer.

"Well, *I* am going to go home and get right on the phone to Ronnie Atwater in Richmond," announced the Major. "Puh-haps there is some *clause* . . . there may puh-fectly well be some clause, already written into law, about desecrated land-mahks. Just because a land-mahk has been desecrated shouldn't mean that it is no longer a land-mahk."

"But it isn't a landmark," Ned Block reminded her languidly. "It never was and it never will be now." He peered over his sloping

belly, complacently examined the instep of one of his small, polished loafers, then nonchalantly added, "We might have done
better to have taken the swine's thirty thousand, you know, and
moved the calvary closer to home while it was still in one piece,
and left Richmond out of this."

A white BMW convertible pulled up in front of the rectory late
Tuesday afternoon, and the swine himself, with a humble solem-
nity that contrasted uneasily with his expensive haberdashery and
glowing suntan, inquired respectfully whether he might have a
few private words with the Reverend Gower. After about fifteen
minutes, they emerged from Daddy's study, exchanged pleasantries about the spring weather and my imminent graduation—Mr.
Gaines seeming especially intent on reminding us that his Georgie
had ridden the school bus with me when we had gone to Romulus
Country Day—and then the BMW convertible drove off.

"What was that all about?" I asked.

"Oh," said my father, "declaring his deep sympathies for our
loss. Offering his help in finding the villains. He even offered to
contribute a bounty for their apprehension and arrest. Of course
he's aware that people are talking about his being involved. He
isn't a regular churchgoing man, but he takes his Bible very seriously. He offered to swear on it that he had nothing to do with this
vicious act."

"Did you *let* him?"

"You know I've never gone in for that sort of thing. He was
disappointed. The ceremony would have been a kind of business-
man's handshake for him. Whereas, this way, he'll have to endure
the uncertainty of whether I believe him or not."

"Well, do you?"

"I'm not sure. It's entirely possible that he had nothing to do
with it. Who knows, maybe young Georgie was right: maybe it *was*
something in the newspaper story that attracted the destructive
elements. I've also been wondering whether it was something
about me in particular that brought it about . . ."

"In *you?* Oh, come *on,* Daddy!"

"No, it's conceivable. That supercilious, self-righteous picture
of me. You and I were discussing it yesterday morning. The *exclusive* way I stood there, with my arm around the savior, challenging anyone to mess with us. I may well have been the red flag
to some desperately unhappy types. Sitting around, out of work in

some tavern, with the newspaper. Then they glimpse *my* pompous face and one of them says to the other, 'I'd like to bash him.' And the other, who's more practical, says, 'Well you know what we *can* bash . . . and it'll serve the same purpose . . .' "

"Oh, please, Daddy. Even the police said it was organized work. Desperately unhappy types would just have driven by and bashed it and raced off again. I put my money on Mr. Gaines, whether he wanted to swear on the Bible or not. Though I agree with the Major and Mrs. MacGruder, he kept his hands clean. Except for the money that got passed. Or will get passed."

"Speaking of money, you know, he came right out and mentioned the thirty thousand. He said the offer still stands. Though he wouldn't have had it happen that way for the world, he said, the land is still worth the same value and he's willing to talk to the vestry at their convenience. Ned Block will be glad to hear that. Perhaps I should call him and brighten his day, tell him all we've lost, after all, is a mere savior. Well, they can do what they like about the corner. It's not my concern. And in a way it doesn't matter whether Gaines was behind it, or my supercilious face, or whether it was just random violence . . . two or three people high on something and wanting a little action. It's not my concern anymore."

"But . . . I don't understand . . . what *is* your concern, then?"

"I simply want to right what has been wronged under my care. I have no more grand ambitions than that."

I was frankly puzzled by a new quality in my father's dejection as he continued to receive friends and shocked sympathizers— and the requisite handful of busybodies who always show up on such occasions. I had lived with, and learned to identify, the whole range of his moods, but there was something different about the present one, and I kept changing my mind about whether I should be alarmed by it.

Since this morning, when, unshaven and in tears, he had wakened me with the news, something had been shifting in him. Now the depraved devils had been demoted on the scale of viciousness to the merely desperately unhappy, and it didn't matter who had sent them, or whether anybody sent them at all, or whether or not the vestry decided to take Mr. Gaines up on his offer to buy the land; the corner of St. Cuthbert's had become simply "real estate." My father seemed to have relinquished all extraneous territory in order to focus his attention solely on the ravaged cross. Even his brief foray into blaming himself had a certain perfunctoriness about it. There was very little emotion involved in the exercise: he seemed to take just as much interest in going on to conjure up the motivations of the bashers in the tavern who might have taken offense at his photo in the newspaper. It was as if he were . . . what? Ridding himself of personal feelings, or ridding himself of *himself*? Sharpening his focus, or narrowing down his hopes? Honing down to the essential meaning of his ministry, or . . . giving up on it? The thing that puzzled me about this new melancholy was its different tone. It was not his old self-reproachful melancholy, or his bitter melancholy, or his resigned melancholy. If anything, it was more of a resolved melancholy. It was almost like a *fulfilled* melancholy.

Toward evening on Tuesday came the Rector of St. Matthias, in the company of his new pastoral counselor, Father Bonner.

Jerry Hope threw his arms around my father. "This is a terrible thing, Walter. What can we do? Just tell us and we'll do it. Won't we, Adrian?" Then he threw his arms around me. "Always a joy to see you, Margaret, even on such a despicable occasion."

Over the years my father's despised rival had become less offbeat and more patriarchal in appearance, at least, if not in his church practices. To observe him now, in the full dignity of his clerical black, with his snowy hair and eyebrows, and rather patrician features, you might never guess that this man regularly encouraged his congregation to interrupt him during sermons and had been known to bait them if they didn't; that he kissed anyone and everyone on the mouth who would let him during the Exchange of the Peace; or that he made a point of serving communion wafers like cookies to babies at the rail, frequently pausing in the middle of a "Body of Christ . . . Bread of Heaven . . ." to converse with a tot in its father's backpack, or to adjure a reluctant babe to "Eat up now, little Tommy, I'm telling you, this is good stuff!"

Adrian Bonner did not hug my father, but he took his hand and gave him a look of tender concern. "I wanted to come sooner," he said, "but I've had back-to-back sessions straight through the day."

"Everyone wants an hour with my pastoral counselor," said Jerry Hope, massaging Adrian vigorously between the shoulder blades. "I believe if Paul Newman came to town and set up shop as a counselor, Adrian here would still be the more popular. Now tell us what we can do for you, Walter, besides drawing and quartering the infidels . . . if we could find them. Adrian and I stopped off at the corner and saw their handiwork. It's enough to make you weep."

"I did just that, early this morning," said Daddy. "It's very kind of you to come by, Jerry. I'm going to hold a Reconsecration service for the . . . well, what was formerly the calvary . . . on Good Friday. That's the thing uppermost on my agenda at the moment."

"A Reconsecration service, now that's a nifty idea. And on Good Friday's certainly appropriate. If you'd like me to participate in any way . . ."

There was a flicker of hesitation, during which anyone who knew the history of these two could read plain on his face my father's misgivings about the manner in which the other priest conducted his own services, and could also read Jerry Hope's perception of my father's misgivings. "Though you'd probably rather keep it a family thing . . ." the Rector of St. Matthias quickly amended.

But Daddy did himself proud. "You are family, Jerry. I'd appreciate it very much if you would take part. You, and Father Bonner, too, I hope. Adrian, here's undoubtedly an opportunity for us to consult the Littledale and Vaux. I was going to phone you this morning and tell you how deeply touched I was, but"—he gestured in the direction of the corner—"things fell apart."

"Adrian tells me that you gave a splendid talk to the study group last night," said Jerry Hope. "I was hoping to go, but we had an AIDS seminar for the young people, and I had to introduce the doctor."

"It was kind of Adrian to say so," said Daddy, "but I blew a fuse halfway through.I couldn't even remember what I was there to talk about for a minute."

Jerry Hope laughed joyously. "That's happened to me, too, on any number of occasions! Why, only last week, I was meeting with our Overeaters Anonymous group, only I got it mixed up on my schedule, or my secretary did. I thought I was addressing our Debtors Anonymous group. But, thank the Lord, one gal spoke right out, I encourage them to speak out, and I'm glad she did. 'Whoa there, Jerry,' she says, 'we're your big eaters tonight, not your big spenders. Give us a break!' "

*   *   *

After Adrian Bonner drove away with his rector, and Daddy and I were left alone for the first time since early morning, a dismal mood overcame us both.

"Do you feel like eating anything?" I asked. "There's all this *stuff* people brought. There's the Major's stuffed peppers."

Daddy groaned and sank lower in his chair.

If Adrian Bonner had come by himself, I thought, I would have asked him to stay for supper. As it was, I'd had a strong urge to grab his sleeve as he followed Jerry Hope out the door and whisper urgently, "Please come back later, Daddy would really like it if you did." But I couldn't bring myself to do it because it felt falsely dramatic and somewhat cheap: playing on my father's need to win something I desired for myself.

"I'm not hungry, either," I said. "Would you like a drink?"

"I don't believe so, honey. How about you, though?"

"No, I don't want one, either."

We continued to sit, enfeebled by our separate stupors, in the living room, where we almost never spent time alone. It was not yet dark enough to turn on lamps, and even if it had been, I wouldn't have had the energy to turn them on.

"I think I'll walk down to the corner," Daddy said presently, dragging himself up out of his chair. "Want to come?"

We had walked down to the corner at least ten times during the course of the day, together and along with other people who had come to commiserate and survey the destruction. Daddy had walked down there by himself at least a dozen more times. "Maybe not this time," I said listlessly.

Yet, as I heard his footsteps fade off down the pavement, I was overpowered by remorse. I was suddenly struck by the ominous notion that if I did not at least *watch* him walk to the corner through the window that I would lose him.

I sprang up off the sofa and craned at his retreating figure through the gaps in the shaggy old rhododendrons that partially obscured the windows alongside our front walk. Then a further superstitious imperative told me that, in order for it to count, I must have a *full view* of him, all the way down to the corner, and so I raced upstairs to his bedroom, the only room that afforded the required view.

I was surprised to find the room dark and the bed unmade, until I remembered that it was when he had gone down to get the paper early this morning that he had discovered the fallen cross. On mornings when he didn't have an early service, he was in the habit of taking the paper back to bed with him, often before daylight, and reading it while slowly sipping a glass of warm water until his recalcitrant digestion could be coaxed into performing its morning regimen, a routine devised for him years ago by the accommodating Dr. MacGruder.

I slid back the curtains and looked down on my father, sauntering to the corner. Oddly enough, he did not walk like a dejected man, or even a tired man. He headed for his destination slowly but with intention, like someone with a task ahead of him that he looked forward to doing.

After reaching the corner, he paced back and forth with his hands clasped behind his back. In the act of pacing, he would glance sidewise at the ruins, then quickly look away. Then glance at them again, and look away, and pace some more. I thought I understood what he was doing, it was the kind of thing I might do: force myself to look at something painful in small doses until I got to the place where I could look at it steadily without it breaking my heart.

All I could see of the damage from here was the peak of the little smashed roof, the roof I had once questioned my parents about when I was little, asking why the church had bothered to build it over the suffering Jesus, since he was going to die so soon anyway. After the police had come this morning and looked at the way everything lay, as Ernie Pasco had told Daddy they ought to do, and had asked their questions and written their report and gone away, Daddy had knelt in the ivy and carefully laid out the hacked and smashed up pieces of the stone Christ into some semblance of his former shape and then placed what was left of the roof over the little figure for protection.

Suddenly Daddy dropped to his knees. His head disappeared behind the peak of the fallen roof. What was he doing under there? I felt the rise of the old childhood alarm in myself: what would people think, what would the passing traffic think, of my father crawling around on his hands and knees in the ivy? There wasn't much traffic this evening, I cynically noted. Now that the landmark no longer stood in the way of a widened Macon Street, where was the bottleneck that had caused all the ruckus?

My father's head reappeared. He cradled something in his arms, then staggered to his feet with it. It appeared to be a piece of the broken figure, a large piece from the way he was shifting about, trying to get his balance.

Oh, no, he wasn't!

Oh, yes, he *was*. He was carrying it, under apparent strain, up the street. Where to? The church? Was he bringing it back to the *house*? Wherever, he would surely kill himself. Was that what he wanted?

In another half second, I would have rushed down to stop him. But at that providential moment an old vintage Mercedes painted a zippy yellow pulled up alongside my father, and out jumped Ben MacGruder. Waving his long arms and calling out something, he strode over and wrested the burden from Daddy. Even he, young and strong as he was, shimmied under its weight until he got it hefted just right. I watched the two of them, my father gesturing expansively to the laden Ben, transport what appeared to be the chest and shoulders of the Christ figure up the sidewalk past the boxwood hedge, and then, stopping briefly to consult with each other, turn right and go up the two steps and into the church.

I did go down then, to see what they were up to. They had laid the piece of broken statuary in a corner of the little chapel at the rear of the church, under the organ loft, and were standing there together in the gloom, hands on hips, as if considering what to do next. Ben's T-shirt was soaking with sweat.

"I just got in from Charlottesville and Nana told me the news," said Ben, still breathing hard from exertion. "What low, mean rats! And what a stupid waste, having to go back to Charlottesville for four measly classes before Easter break! That's what I get for trying to please everybody! And it wasn't even worth it. One of the instructors himself canceled a class. If I had only stayed here, I could have been with you all this morning when it happened!" I could detect behind his outrage the same kind of spurious pleasure that had kept me from appealing to Adrian Bonner to come back to us this evening. Ben was relishing the event, even as he deplored it, because it gave him a legitimate opportunity to be here with me.

"But you were here when I needed you most," Daddy assured him. "Margaret, I decided it just wasn't safe to leave the poor corpus down there overnight. I know they've broken him up pretty badly, but they . . . or somebody else . . . might take it into their heads to smash up what's left of him. So Ben and I are going to carry the pieces up to the church and they'll repose here in the chapel until Friday morning. They'll keep company with the Reserved Sacrament Thursday night, which is fitting. And then, on Friday morning, Ben's agreed to help me carry them back down to the corner again, for the Reconsecration service."

"Couldn't we *drive* the rest of them up tonight in my car?" Ben asked.

"That's an idea," said Daddy, who obviously hadn't considered the possibility. "For that matter, I guess we could drive them down to the corner again on Friday morning. But then, *after* the Reconsecration, I had in mind that some of us would carry the pieces home to the church . . . we'll have to work out exactly who'll carry what when we have a better idea who's coming. I would suppose Jerry Hope, being clergy, will have to carry something. And Adrian, of course. And the warden and members of the vestry. I'm going to have to plan this thing out very carefully. And we will need pillows, or containers, or something, for all those poor fingers and toes . . . some of them are practically reduced to powder. Now, the heaviest piece is this big one we've just brought up . . ."

"I guess you'd better let that be my piece on Friday," said Ben, lacing his fingers together and popping the knuckles. He glanced at me slyly, waiting for his reward.

Well, he had earned it. How could I be ungrateful for his timely arrival, and for his strong, young body that had relieved my father of his self-imposed millstone? Ben was a part of our lives, and it was not his fault if he happened to be hopelessly in love with me. Now I had more understanding of what he was going through: wasn't it possible that I was embarking on a similarly hopeless course myself?

So I invited him to supper, saying easily to him the words I hadn't been able to bring myself to say to Adrian Bonner. The expression of straightforward charity is so much easier on one's nerves and pride than covert desire. Of course he stayed, and, I had to admit, turned out to be a lively and comforting third at our table at the end of that awful Tuesday in Passion Week.

CALVARY CORNER SMASHED: RECTOR INVITES VANDALS TO RECONSECRATION SERVICE ON GOOD FRIDAY was the headline in Wednesday morning's *Romulus Record*.

More phone calls and visitors. The ministers of the other

churchẹs on Church Street, Central Methodist and First Presbyterian, asked if they could take part in the service.

Adrian Bonner phoned, between counseling sessions, to tell
Daddy that the Rabbi who had come to talk to the study group on
the universality of the Joseph story had just called him from
Roanoke after reading about the vandalism in *that* city's paper and
had asked Adrian to convey his deep indignation to Father Gower,
and to suggest to him that the Reconsecration service he was in the
act of planning was somewhat analogous to the situation of the
Jews rededicating the sanctuary profaned by aliens in the time of
the Maccabees. Though the cross was not his symbol of faith (and
indeed had not always been a friendly symbol to his people), the
Rabbi wished Father Gower every good wish in restoring its sanctity during this holy time for Jews and Christians alike, and if he
himself could be of any use, he would be glad to oblige.

"Tell him," Daddy said to Adrian, "that I would be extremely
honored if he would be part of the service. That is, if he's willing
to drive all the way up here from Roanoke."

Then off Daddy went to his study for his *Apocrypha,* and came
back excitedly reading aloud to me from Maccabees. "The Rabbi's
right, it *is* analogous. Why, when you think of it, Margaret, if these
Maccabee brothers hadn't rededicated the temple in 165 B.C.,
there might have been no soil for Christianity to grow out of later.
This is so suitable . . . so suitable. I hope the Rabbi will be able to
come."

Harriet MacGruder, just arrived from Chapel Hill, showed up
on our doorstep at the same time Adrian Bonner did, in the early
afternoon. I hugged Harriet passionately while Adrian stood to
one side, smiling quietly.

"My goodness," grumbled Harriet, as we didn't usually go in
for embraces, "you must *really* have been having a rough time
over here. How's your father? Nana said heartbroken, Ben said
frenetic."

"Both, probably," I said, releasing her. "Have you met Father
Bonner? He's the new pastoral counselor over at St. Matthias.
Adrian, this is Harriet MacGruder, my best and oldest friend."

"So I gathered, from the warm welcome," said Adrian. The
two of them shook hands with a show of cordiality, though I could
tell from the way they looked right through each other that neither of them had really registered the other's true essence.

"I was going to ask the same question," said Adrian. "How is your father?"

"He's shut up in his study with stacks of books all around him. He's gotten really involved in planning the Reconsecration service. I do hope your rabbi will be able to come on Friday."

"Rabbi Eisenstein will definitely be coming. He's driving up late Thursday and spending the night at my house. I just spoke to him on the phone and wanted to come right over and tell your father."

"Daddy will be so pleased to hear that." Harriet had got the hug meant for him, but now I allowed myself to give his sleeve a grateful squeeze. "Just go on into the study. And, listen, if you're free, please have supper with us this evening. Daddy would like it so much." Harriet's presence, the fact that she obviously regarded him as just another priest, had made me brave.

"Thank you, I'd like that. I have the rest of the afternoon and evening free, which is a rare thing for me."

Harriet and I went up to my room to talk, as we had done about a thousand times over the course of our lives. But today my room was inconvenient because the doorbell kept ringing and I would have to run downstairs and talk to whoever had rung it and then run back up. So, after Miriam Stacy had dropped by for no apparent reason I could see, except to keep herself abreast of the excitement, and Susan Smith had delivered a brochure featuring the work of the Appalachian sculptor who worked in bronze and who had told her it would be a sacred challenge for him to make St. Cuthbert's a new Christ—and just let the vandals try to saw through bronze!— Harriet and I relocated ourselves downstairs in the living room.

"Well," said Harriet from her end of the sofa, pinning me with her yellow eyes, "have you decided yet what you want to do with your life?"

"I may go on to grad school. Professor Stannard thinks he can get me a grant for Medieval Studies. It has to be about a woman, that's the only stipulation. We decided on St. Hilda of Whitby."

"Oh, St. Hilda," said Harriet, not very enthusiastically, "She's that one they're always naming altar guilds after."

"But that doesn't really do her justice. She was a lot more than *needlework*. I'm not sure she even did needlework. She was a very influential person. She trained bishops and mediated arguments between rulers, and was very advanced in her notions of education. Her monastery was for both sexes. And except for Bede's history of the early English church, there isn't a whole lot known about her, so Professor Stannard says it will need somebody with a natural empathy for those times."

"Well, we all know you've got *empathy*," said Harriet. But she sat there looking as if she had reservations.

"Oh, and Daddy and I are planning a trip to England in June. In fact, we booked our tickets Monday."

This news appeared to mitigate her reservations somewhat, but before she could say anything the doorbell rang again.

It was Georgie Gaines, accompanied by his notepad. "Hello, Margaret, is your dad free?"

"I'll go and check. Come and wait in the living room. Harriet's here."

"Harriet *MacGruder*?"

"That's the only Harriet I know."

"Well, okay." With a nervous little titter he followed me into the living room.

When she saw I was bringing back a tall, handsome, well-dressed young male, Harriet, who in my absence had drooped into a morose slump, shot up her spine with alacrity and lifted her neck to its maximal tilt.

"Hello, Harriet," said Georgie, edging forward with his right hand held out warily, as though appeasing a ferocious dog. "It's great to see you again. You're looking just . . . great."

Harriet extended her hand to the handsome stranger stooping obsequiously above her. She squinted up at him, puzzled. Then a cruel gleam of recognition lit up her yellow eyes. "Well, my goodness," she drawled slowly. "If it isn't the Blimp."

As they went on to exchange information about themselves, Georgie Gaines seemed to shrink in height and resume his unfortunate childhood proportions, while Harriet, second by second, became more the condescending queen.

"*Well*," she said at last, patting a place on the sofa beside her and drawing herself up high and straight in a corner so that the fat boy of yore might have plenty of room to spread his self out, "sit down and tell me about yourself. How was Harvard? Are you going to go for a career in the news media, or is this just an interim thing?"

I left them and went down the hall to Daddy's study. The door was closed, so I drummed my fingernails on the panel—our signal that it was me.

"Come in," called Daddy. I was surprised at how strong and happy his voice sounded through the door.

Adrian Bonner had pulled up the chair we called "the Miriam Stacy Chair," because she always sat in it when she came for her sessions and we always found a Kleenex or two stuffed beneath its cushion each week. He and my father sat side by side behind Daddy's desk, which was cluttered with various prayer books and missals, and Adrian was bent over an open volume in his lap, frowning intently as he searched through its pages. Only my father looked up at me, his hand still in the motion of scribbling words on a yellow pad. "Yes, my love?"

When he said "my love," Adrian Bonner raised his eyes from his book and looked at me the way people do when an interruption turns out to be a pleasant one, and I had an intimation of what it would feel like to one day knock upon and then open the door of another study and be welcomed by those same gray-blue eyes, lifted unbegrudgingly out of some esoteric book.

"Georgie Gaines is here with his reporter's notebook again. He wants to know if you're free."

"Sure. Send him in," said Daddy with a wink. To Adrian he said, "I have to be careful what I say to him, because he's likely to put it in a headline like this morning's, but he's on our side. I like the boy, even though he is that man's offspring. He's actually considering the ministry, he told me."

"Is he?" murmured Adrian Bonner. He did not sound at all interested in Daddy's new protégé, but he gave me an approving smile before returning his attention to the book in his lap.

Harriet and I drove to the supermarket in her new car, a saucy silver Toyota hatchback, a combined graduation gift from her parents and her grandmother. It drove with a spritely pickup and had that irresistible new smell, and I couldn't understand what it was about it that put me suddenly in a mean mood, especially since I knew I had Adrian Bonner to look forward to all evening. Was I *jealous* that Harriet had a new car and I didn't?

It wasn't until I was standing in front of the fresh produce, trying to decide between spinach or broccoli to go with the chicken, that I realized I had always had bad feelings about silver cars since Madelyn Farley had driven my mother away in that silver Mustang.

"Any special boyfriend yet?" Harriet asked, helpfully holding open a plastic bag for the vegetable I could not seem to decide on. Some people hated spinach. Others hated broccoli. Which would they have been likely to overdo in the Catholic orphanage in Michigan where Adrian Bonner had spent the years from six to eleven, waiting for his parents to come back and pick him up? It would be gratifying to tell Harriet about my attraction to him, but it would make me angry with her if she didn't approve. I was already a little miffed with her for her unenthusiastic reaction to my graduate plans. What if I told her I was falling in love with Adrian Bonner, perhaps had already fallen in love with him, and she slighted him the way she had slighted Hilda of Whitby?

"No, there's nobody special yet," I said, finally choosing the broccoli because it would look nicer on the plate. I would steam it first, then sauté it in a little butter and garnish it with slivered almonds. Even if they had overdosed him on broccoli at the orphanage, it would have been cooked gray and would certainly not have been garnished with slivered almonds. "How are things between you and Clark?"

"Oh, the same," shrugged Harriet. "Clark is as clean and dependable as ever, and we still have the same goals. But I think he's only going into geriatric medicine because I am. He's much more suited for anesthesiology." She said it contemptuously. We drifted on to the next aisle. I must remember to get another six-pack of Beck's, I was thinking happily, when she snorted with her dry little laugh and said, "Isn't it amazing what time and a little *polish* have done for the Blimp. Who would have thought it?"

"He's still scared to death of you," I said.

"That's not a bad thing in itself, you know," she replied, rather pleased.

I was feeling close to her again, until, as we drove back to the rectory, she remarked, "It's too bad you were in such a hurry to invite that prim and proper priest to supper to please your father. I was hoping you and I could have the evening all to ourselves."

"What makes you call Father Bonner prim and proper?"

"I don't know. He just seems to take himself awfully seriously, that's all."

"Well, so do I. Am I 'prim and proper'?"

"Not in the way he is."

"What way is that?"

She shrugged, obviously not very interested in formulating it further. "Oh, *I* don't know. He holds himself so . . . Like he's afraid somebody will intrude on his space. And you *don't* take yourself seriously. You take some other people seriously, but not yourself."

"I don't see how you can say that, Harriet."

"When is the last time you have done something completely for yourself? Because it was something you wanted?"

When I asked Father Bonner to supper in your presence, I thought.

"When I chose the broccoli over the spinach back in the supermarket," I said.

She didn't deserve a serious answer. And as I had done many times before, I closed myself off from her, without her even knowing it, because I despaired of her being capable of seeing me whole, even if she was my oldest friend. Her little brother Ben, in these last few years, had grown better able to perceive me than Harriet. The movements of Ben's mind more closely resembled the movements of mine. He picked up on people's silences, set great store on interpreting those silences. He seemed more interested in knowing the undersides of people. If I had pulled the broccoli over spinach answer on Ben, he would have said, "Oh, Margaret, that was cheap of you and you know it." Whereas Harriet laughed approvingly, as if she wished I would go in more for these flip retorts. Of course, Ben was in love with me, and Harriet wasn't.

Could anyone—even a lover—see anyone else whole? Perhaps not. Perhaps there was no set and solid whole of anything, wasn't that what the scientists were telling us now: that a tiny molecule (or a whole bunch of molecules that made up a person) responded according to how it was being observed?

I had never, not once, thought of Adrian Bonner as holding himself back, as if he were afraid someone would intrude on his space. People behaved differently to different people. Maybe he just hadn't warmed to Harriet. Would she have preferred him to throw his arms around her the first time he ever met her, as Jerry Hope probably would have done? Maybe Adrian did hold himself aloof occasionally, turned himself off. Would it be any wonder, when you considered that he spent most of his day listening to people, one after another, letting the Lorettas of the world cling to him like a life raft until they were capable of swimming off on their own? And wouldn't it be understandable if he kept a lot of himself in reserve? He must have had to teach himself reserve, all those years in the orphanage, when he kept waiting and hoping for the parents who had promised to come back for him and never did. And then, according to Daddy, there had been "abuses." Wouldn't it be understandable that an abused child would grow up to be a reserved person?

If nobody was capable of seeing anyone else whole, how did God see us? But our concept of "whole" probably seemed a touchingly jejune notion to God. I tried to think about this alone in the kitchen while I peeled away the tough, outer stems of the broccoli (they had never done *that* in the orphanage, you could be sure). Perhaps in God's realm, wholeness encompassed infinite other layers my brain couldn't even imagine. Layers including not only space, but time. And other dimensions beyond space and time. Levels of spirit, too. I pricked the boneless chicken breasts with a fork and poured Tamari sauce over them, grated some fresh ginger and sprinkled it on, then squeezed lemon juice on top of that. Levels stretching into infinitude. Levels beyond *levels*. As I sloshed the marinade around in the Pyrex dish so it would sink in faster, I had a fantasy of Adrian Bonner wandering down the hall (after all, he was only as far away as Daddy's study this very minute) and into the kitchen, and inquiring of me as Daddy often did: "What were you thinking, Margaret? You had such a serious expression on your face." (Yes, Harriet, *serious*!) And, in my apron, I would turn to Adrian and say, "Well, I was just trying to imagine the kind of wholeness God can see when He sees us whole, only I can't, of course, my mind won't take it in. But still, I like to try."

And he would take me in—perhaps not wholly, but more fully than anyone else had yet, because he was capable of it; he would see and slightly envy my youth, he would appreciate, I hoped, the attractiveness Ben kept assuring me he saw in me; he would discover, via the symbol of my apron and the evidence of foods being carefully prepared on the counter, my willingness to serve; and, topping it all off, would be my mind, grappling bravely with the ineffable dimensions of the spirit—and Adrian Bonner would think to himself: This is the woman I have been hoping for all my life and now I have found her in my friend and mentor's own kitchen.

What an inconvenience, that he told his life story to Daddy in privileged sessions. Daddy probably knew all the things I needed to know.

But didn't I have the whole evening ahead to find out more about him? I was good at that. I knew how to ask people seemingly casual questions and then let them talk until they revealed things about themselves. What to have with the chicken and broccoli? Sliced tomatoes for color contrast, and brown rice for a carbohydrate. I would have to remember to fill the salt shaker and put it on the table for Adrian. Daddy had stopped using salt back in the Trevor LaFarge days, when the Professor's doctor had convinced him it was bad for one's blood pressure. Dr. MacGruder had been dead for several years by then, and Daddy, loath to look for another doctor, had jokingly declared he would just take all the advice his friends' doctors gave to *them*. That was another thing I had to do: make Daddy get a checkup before we went to England. Maybe I would take Adrian aside tonight and ask for his cooperation. ("Daddy's so stubborn about modern doctors, but perhaps *you* could convince him . . .") It would be one more means of drawing him closer into our lives.

But of course how you imagine something ahead of time and the way it turns out are always two different stories. Whether it's a looked-forward-to evening, or a trip, or even just what you will say to someone the next time you see him, the real thing is invariably different. Sometimes just a little bit different, often unbelievably different. Why, then, did people spend such large portions of their days and nights plotting scenarios that they knew from experience would never go off exactly as planned? Why didn't they learn? Some got the big lessons sooner than others, but they still didn't learn. A child rides the school bus home, imagining the afternoon ahead with her mother. The reality of that afternoon, when it comes, proves to have been completely beyond her imaginative powers. Why, then, didn't people get wise and stop wasting time living out their future hours before they got to them? Why didn't they just live in the moment, let the present carry them along, like the animals and all the rest of known creation?

Because they couldn't, even if they wanted to. They couldn't, because they'd been made differently. Their brains had been built to plan, even if those plans would never be exactly mirrored in reality. And why wouldn't they be? Why not? Why never? Why always the discrepancy, sometimes small, sometimes mindboggling? Was it some cosmic jest, some cosmic carelessness?

Or was it a lesson, a stepping-stone our minds were simply not agile enough to bridge yet? Was the unpredictable aspect of life one of the corners of existence where Ultimate Reality hides? Could it be that the unpredictable was one of the methods God used, again and again, eon after eon, to stretch our minds towards His? ("Where wast thou when I laid the foundations of the earth?")

And so, because I was made that way, because I could not resist doing it, I lived in advance the scene of Adrian Bonner having supper with us. I laid a white cloth on the dining-room table, set it with Ruth's silver and china, floated a low spray of the Mt. Fuji cherry blossoms in a glass bowl for a centerpiece, and saw and heard the three of us sitting in this room and eating the meal I was preparing. I put words in each of our mouths, and kept the other two quiet while my speaker-of-the-moment was holding forth. I chose our topics of conversation as well as their sequence, I elicited valuable personal information from Adrian without his ever once feeling probed or "intruded upon." I arranged for several silent exchanges, during which Adrian and I, seated facing each other at the table, with Daddy at the head, would read the growing mutual attraction in each other's eyes. The tempo of the meal I set somewhere between a graceful adagio, with a few intermittent passages of brisk andante—not just because the destruction of the corner cross set a somber note, but because this would be only the first of many such suppers. The long summer stretched ahead of us, didn't it, replete with promises of as many other topics and menus and tempos as I could imagine? If all went as I was planning for it to go, we would strike a variety of notes together, the three of us, in the ampleness of time. Nothing had to be rushed. In between each meeting, there would be silences as important as the meetings themselves, silences during which the most reserved of persons would be able to relax his boundaries as he became more and more aware of the growing harmonics between himself and another.

The tempo of the real supper that transpired that Wednesday night was a vivace that kept breaking into a presto. My father and Adrian had excited each other's minds. Daddy's "fulfilled melancholy" of earlier in the day had been replaced by a confident, almost manic exuberance. Adrian Bonner was flushed and hearty and light-years away from Harriet's image of a prim man guarding his "space." As they congratulated themselves on the service

they had put together out of old prayer books for Friday's Reconsecration service, they kept interrupting each other. Both men ate
with gusto, but didn't really pay attention to their food. Once I
had adjusted my expectations, I didn't mind their paying so little
attention to me. There would be more of these suppers, many,
many more, if they were enjoying themselves so much at this one.
Also, it was a rather novel experience for me, to be so completely
the Martha. I had grown up being my father's Mary, who happened to be able to cook as well as Martha.

The two men ignored me blissfully, then would catch themselves doing it and ask my opinion on something, or toss me
outrageous compliments. Adrian said he had never known
chicken could taste like this; and the broccoli! this was a different
vegetable from his former idea of broccoli. My father told him I
got it from my mother, being able to make ordinary foods, things
you had been eating without noticing all your life, into something
special. Then back they went to their own talk.

"The thing about a ritual," Daddy said, "is that it brings con-
tainment and acceptance to people. The sacramental life is a sort
of sanity filter against the onslaughts of existence . . ."

". . . a way to control its intensity and dosage," finished Adrian,
drinking up his beer.

I got up quietly and went to the kitchen and got another Beck's
from the refrigerator, and, equally as unobtrusively, refilled Adrian's glass. He gave my elbow a passing squeeze of thanks. "There
was a Jesuit studying with me in Zurich, at the Institute. I once
asked him, 'What if you as a priest stopped believing? What would
you do then?' 'Make a fist in my pocket,' he said, 'and go on with
the ritual.' "

"Exactly!" agreed Daddy. "Although my problem as a priest
these last decades has been keeping my fist in my pocket when
they keep diminishing and degrading rituals *I* still believe in as
much as ever."

I removed the dinner plates and brought in fruit plates, a
platter of seedless red grapes, a selection of cheeses, and a basket
of bread.

"I liked what you said about the meaning of Easter in your talk
Monday night," Adrian Bonner told Daddy. "I used it to advantage with someone in a counseling session this morning."

"What exactly did I say about Easter? That was after my lapse,
you know, when I was babbling. These are beautiful grapes, Mar-

garet, and just look at the way she's arranged grape leaves from our old grapevine that hasn't produced anything in years. Pretty."

"It is," agreed Adrian. "You said Easter means that we are constantly granted the right to slough off our old skins, to die to our old selves and move humanity—or did you say the human family—forward."

"Oh, yes, yes, now I remember. Pity, I had such a good conclusion prepared, but it went completely out the window with my lapse. Actually, I had gotten some of it from you, Adrian, from one of *our* sessions."

"From me?" Adrian Bonner took several grapes from the big bunch on the platter in the way I had been explicitly taught not to: just pulling them off from their stems and putting them straight into his mouth instead of breaking off a bunch and eating them from his plate. But this unwitting social blunder oddly cheered me, it lessened the gulf I was feeling between us tonight. He may have had interesting talks with Jesuits in Zurich, but there were still a few things I could teach him.

"Yes," said Daddy, taking his grapes to his plate in the proper way. "One afternoon you were thinking aloud about . . . oh, aspects of your development, that kind of thing, and you suddenly said you wondered if original sin might not have something to do with repeating our parents' mistakes. That struck me. I wrote it down later."

Just above Adrian Bonner's balding head were my mother's two watercolors, of St. Michael's and St. Philip's churches, done on her honeymoon with my father in Charleston. At what age had I first realized with a sinking heart that the tiered steeple of her St. Philip's tilted precariously to the right and that all the columns on St. Michael's portico were the same size, even the ones in the background? After that, I was nervous when Daddy proudly pointed out Ruth's artwork to visitors, though they always said flattering things. Nobody else ever responded the way Madelyn Farley had, on Ruth's last evening with us, when Daddy had said of the honeymoon watercolors to our visitor, "I think they're lovely, don't you?" and Madelyn had retorted rudely, "Well of course they're *lovely*. Everything she does is lovely, but I hardly think that's the point. *Lovely* is the art of pleasing others. Art is about pleasing yourself."

And yet Ruth had taught life drawing at an art class after she had left us, hadn't she? And in that exquisite little painting inside the Golden Egg that now belonged to Ben, there was evidence that my mother's art had developed far beyond what it had been on her honeymoon. Another aspect of these Charleston watercolors that made me slightly nervous, as I had grown older, was the fact that my mother had had the time to do them on her honeymoon. Where had Daddy been all those hours? Inspecting tombstones, or the architecture of the churches?

"I am finally understanding just the tip of the iceberg about what the Resurrection means," Daddy was saying to Adrian. "I'm talking about the Resurrection as it applies to each of us. It means coming up through what you were born into, then understanding objectively the people your parents were and how they influenced you. Then finding out who you yourself are, in terms of how you carry forward what they put in you, and how your circumstances have shaped you. And then . . . and *then* . . . now here's the hard part! And then you have to slough *off* your 'original sin,' in the sense you defined it, Adrian. You have to go on to find out *what* you are in the human drama, or body of God. The what *beyond* the who, so to speak."

I was imagining myself and Adrian Bonner on our honeymoon.

"Some people never make this transition beyond our parents and what they did to us, of course," Daddy went on, helping himself to a wedge of brie. "They never even come close to shedding their *who* for their *what*. On the other hand, a few brilliant souls get there fast. Look at Jesus. He took responsibility for the greater mission right from the first; he didn't have time to spend years analyzing why he was the way he was. I mean, where in the Gospels do you ever hear Jesus saying, 'My mother said this, my father did this . . . the reason I'm this way is because they . . .' "

"Oh, Father, that's marvelous," said Adrian, laughing. He took some more grapes. This time, he broke them off the correct way. Either his former mistake had been an unconscious regression, or he had observed Daddy and was a fast learner.

Perhaps we would end up inviting Daddy to come along on our honeymoon. Objectively, it might seem a little unnatural, but weren't we three unique individuals? And they enjoyed each other so much. We would have to make our own rules, and let the Ned Blocks and the Miriam Stacys, who were still stuck low down in their *who*-ness, say what they would about the way we behaved.

"Couldn't even death, our physical death, be merely the

sloughing off of another old skin?" Daddy was saying. "Couldn't
it be just one more transformation? I think I am going to go into
that some, in my Easter sermon. Margaret, you're rather quiet this
evening, honey."

"I've been listening."

"There's a lot to listen to, isn't there?" Adrian Bonner said. He
gave me, if not exactly a look of growing attraction, at least one of
sincere appreciation. He had approved of my reticence, then,
which allowed him to give his full attention to all the good things
my father had been saying.

After he had gone home to his little house on Acacia Street,
and Daddy was back in his study writing a short homily for the
Maundy Thursday service, I stood at the sink, washing Ruth's
good china by hand and looking out at the beautiful night. The
moon, almost full, was so bright it made tree shadows and chair
shadows on the grass in our backyard. I was looking out on Daddy's haircutting chair, the old wicker that slanted forward, that I
had been standing behind when Adrian Bonner had wheeled
around the corner of the rectory and into my desires. Only last
Friday. Less than a week ago. What had I *expected* to happen
tonight? It was just that the imagination went tearing off so, when
you gave it the least little bit of a push.

Was I contented or disappointed? What did it really matter,
especially in the light of the things we had been talking about
tonight? (Or they had.) The earthbound *who* in me was definitely
disappointed, but maybe this tension, this lesson in forbearance,
whatever it had been, was a necessary condition in the growth
towards my *what*-ness. But still, it seemed a shame, almost an
insult to the beauty of the night, that Adrian Bonner had simply
shaken my hand at the front door and gone home, probably to
read a book.

Daddy just couldn't turn off his engine. I was already in bed,
perfunctorily skimming my Chaucer, when my father came
breathlessly upstairs and stretched out beside me on top of the
covers.

"Well, Margaret, what a day, huh? What a *week*. Adrian was an
enormous help to me today in preparing for Friday. I'm still sick
over the cross, but I'll tell you one thing: This will be a service
people remember. It will draw the community together. The community of *believers*, at least. Adrian's stimulating, isn't he? I believe
he really enjoyed himself. He's a lonely man, but I hope he will

adopt us as his family. Well, you're not going to believe this, but I have Friday's Reconsecration service all typed up—Adrian and I found a model office for what we wanted in the Littledale and Vaux; it's a form of reconciliation for a profaned font, but the prayers, the psalms, the lessons suit almost perfectly, with some individual adjustments for our situation. *And* I also sketched out a sermon for Friday evening's Mass of the Presanctified and the Adoration of the Cross. Let's hope we have decent good weather for the outdoor service Friday noon, but not *too* good. I've always felt blue sky and plump little sailing clouds are somewhat of a mockery on Good Friday, though it's all God's weather, isn't it, so we'll take what we get, right? *And* I also have tomorrow's Maundy Thursday homily ready. I decided to tackle some salient parts of our Lord's Great High-Priestly Prayer after the Last Supper in John 17, something I haven't felt up to in years, but I'm somehow rearing to go all of a sudden."

"That's great," I said sleepily.

"*And,* don't faint now, I have my outline for Easter Sunday, the essential points—I *am* going to follow through on that conversation we were having at supper, you know, the many transformations of the human spirit, even after the death of the body; I scribbled it all down cogently and if I can grab a moment between now and Sunday I'll type it up . . ."

"I can do that for you, Daddy, you've got so much . . ."

"No, no, no, I wouldn't dream of it. You've got your exams to study for. I may just try to construct it from my notes Sunday morning. Unless I have another of those . . . what was it that little fellow in the pink jogging suit over at Adrian's called them? . . . 'CRS' spells . . . I should be able to wing it right through. I haven't been prepared so well and so *ahead of time* for all my Passion Week sermons in years, Margaret. I can't say where this surge of energy has come from, but it has certainly come when I needed it."

Maybe it has come, I thought, lying there trying to keep my eyes from closing, *because* you need it. Perhaps if my father had been in charge of a busier, more demanding parish, he would have been less depressed. Perhaps he wouldn't have been depressed at all, there wouldn't have been time.

I dozed off, but he obviously wasn't aware of it. When I jolted awake, he was chattering animatedly about his boyhood in Chattanooga, after he and his mother went to live in the carriage house on the Dudleys' estate.

"He bullied me, Stewart Hampton did, but looking at it from his side, after he's been dead all these years, I can see I was a threat to him. I was an interloper; moreover, I was competition. Mrs. Dudley was always holding it up to him about my good grades and my thoughtfulness. So of course he devised little tortures and torments. The worst of them were the ones I couldn't say anything about, like the time he convinced Jonas, the Dudleys' chauffeur who doubled as butler at mealtimes, to keep lowering the platter when he stood to my left and I was serving myself. Well, I made a mess more than once, because that platter kept sinking as I was trying to get the serving spoon and fork under the meat. And when it came to *peas,* and it seemed the Dudleys were always having peas—forget it! I stopped eating peas. I had finally caught on to what was happening, but I knew if I said anything to Mother it would hurt her, because then she would be obliged to say something to Mrs. Dudley and it might spoil their rapport, and I also knew that if I confronted Stewart Hampton with it, he would either deny it or think me a whiner. So I toughed it out, just managed with the meat the best I could, and stopped eating peas. Then, after that, came a few trials and tribulations outdoors—he gave me what he told me was his best bicycle to ride, but neglected to tell me it had no brakes until I had started down the hill. I got pretty badly banged up, but I blamed it on myself: I said it was silly of me not to *test* the brakes before setting off down a big hill. And, oh, there were some other pretty imaginative 'tests' on his part, a couple of them rather smutty . . ."

". . . what he put into your peanut butter sandwich that time was a lot worse than smutty," I reminded him sleepily.

"Ah, yes," said Daddy ruefully. "But we were only nine, remember. Nine-year-old boys are scarcely human."

"*You* sounded pretty human to me."

"That was because I had the loving influence of my mother. And I had a spiritual father in Father Traherne, although I never told him about Stewart Hampton's antics, either. Father Traherne was very fond of the Dudleys, it would have been awkward for him. Besides, I was never sure Stewart Hampton really mixed what he said into that peanut butter. Why should he go to the trouble? Not to mention the disgust to *himself.* It was enough for him to see the look on my face and watch me upchuck. Besides, here I am, still alive and kicking . . . happier with myself than I've been in years . . . keeping you from getting your sleep. And poor

Stewart Hampton's bones, or what they could gather up of them in Korea, are resting in the family vault in Chattanooga. He never even got to be a man, so to speak. He never had a wife or a child, or knew the pleasure of finding the work that suited his nature. Maybe this summer, after we get back from England, you and I will take a little trip down there and pay a visit to your grandmother's grave . . . you are so like her . . . and I can show you the Dudleys' estate . . . there are none of them left now, but I'm sure we could talk our way in . . ."

I must have dozed again.

". . . but I am sure I got as far as I did—not that I am saying I got all that *far*," Daddy was saying, "because I had my mother's love and the belief of a few other good people I admired. Whereas *he* had nothing and nobody. He grew up all alone with neither parent to protect and guide him, and moreover prey to institutional viciousness, forms of degradation to the human spirit of the sort I am ashamed to say I didn't even know existed until I did some prison work in Nashville for Field Education during my last year of seminary . . ."

What was he *talking* about? Stewart Hampton, who had had both his parents and millions of dollars, growing up with "nothing and nobody"? *What* "institutional viciousness" could my father's spoiled little tormentor have known?

"And if that wasn't enough, then those foster parents . . . those sadistic German Catholic farmers . . . yet he survived all of it. Why, it's made him largely into what he is. It could have gone the other way and made him vicious, or eccentric and uncaring. It just goes to show the power of the Holy Spirit when a person lets it work in him. It's beyond our comprehension, but I'm convinced it keeps the world going . . ."

Oh, damn my sleepiness, he had been talking about Adrian Bonner! What had I missed? How could I get it back without admitting I had dozed off?

"Well, *he* certainly seems to have found the work that suits his nature," I said. "And he's such a nice man. It's a wonder he doesn't have a wife or children."

"Oh yes, Adrian's a fine man. The world could do with more like him. Adrian will mean a lot to a great many people. But I doubt if he'll marry. I think it's likely he won't."

It was an indication of how drowsy I was that I couldn't feel the distress I would have felt if I'd been totally awake. "How come? He's not gay, is he?"

"Oh no, certainly not," said Daddy. "Though it might have gone that way with somebody else. No, Adrian—well, I hope I'm not betraying his confidence when I say that he's chosen a way of life that appears to be agreeable to his needs. I admire him for his strength of purpose."

" 'Choosing to live in a way that won't interfere with the harmony of his totality,' " I quoted Adrian Bonner with a sigh. Had he taken a vow of chastity? Was that what my father was implying? I had heard that some Anglican and Episcopal priests did that, but I didn't want to hear Daddy say it, if he knew it to be the case. As long as he didn't say it, there might be a loophole. But tonight I was too tired to think what that loophole might be, or how I might squeeze through it.

"That's profound, Margaret. You never cease to amaze me. I am a lucky man."

Adrian Bonner had said that, too. "You are a lucky man." How happy I had been, when I overheard him telling Daddy that. And perhaps I had foolishly leapt to the conclusion that Adrian Bonner might wish to share in such luck himself.

Shortly before, that Friday afternoon, I had also heard from him the "profundity" that Daddy was now giving me credit for expressing. When I had asked him for his definition of sin, Adrian Bonner had fitted his fingers together and looked up into the branches of our old sugar maple and replied: "A falling short from your totality. Choosing to live in ways you know interfere with the harmony of that totality."

What if the harmonious life, as he defined it for himself, excluded me from its totality?

"Well, people have to do what they have to do," I said resignedly. I closed my eyes and folded my hands like an effigy on top of the covers and hoped Daddy would take the hint and say good night.

"I hope I haven't been indiscreet," he went on, "but, after all, you and I are old cronies. I know I've let slip a lot of things to you over the years about our wayward flock; I used to do the same with Ruth. It's human nature, to let things slip. But I wouldn't want to betray Adrian's trust. God knows, enough people did in his young life. Oh, oh, I'm putting my little girl to sleep. I'm better than a sleeping pill, or a boring book. Well, I'm off to bed myself. Tomorrow is Low Moor Nursing Home, and Maundy Thursday. I'm glad we don't go in for foot-washing here at St. Cuthbert's. What if I had to wash Ned Block's feet. Can't you see me, removing those dainty loafers and pulling off his red socks? And he'd be looking down at me over that Humpty-Dumpty belly, watching my every move, and he'd probably say something like, 'Oh. Pity you are using a *white* towel. Dr. Hazeltine always used a purple towel.' Okay, enough, honey, I'm gone."

"No, wait." Now that he was finally going, I felt guilty about rushing him off. "There's something else I wanted to ask you."

"What is that, honey?" He sounded a little apprehensive; was he afraid it was something else to do with Adrian Bonner?

"You know when you were talking about some people never getting beyond their *who*-ness to their *what*-ness? Have *you*? I mean, do you know what you are, where you fit into the human drama or the body of God?"

"Oh, I see myself maybe as a purveyor of heirlooms," said Daddy, after a minute. "Or maybe just a bridge. Some people have to be bridges, you know. Even old Moses didn't get to enter the Promised Land. Not that I'm comparing myself with Moses. I'm pretty small potatoes in the long parade of human development, but I do think I've filled a gap. And, of course, in terms of the liturgy—the *old* rite that I love—I've tried to offer my self, soul, and body as a reasonable, holy, and living sacrifice."

"You've done a lot more than fill a *gap*," I said, feeling protective on his behalf. "You've been a loving, caring, charming father. You've taught me what's important and what isn't."

"Ah," he said teasingly, "now we're back into the *who*-ness, aren't we? But I thank you. I wish it could have been the three of us, you know, with your mother here, too, but since that wasn't to be, I'm glad you feel we've done all right." He laid his hand across my forehead as he had done on thousands of previous nights before ending our day with one of his personalized prayers, no two of which were ever alike. "I've had my lows . . . God knows I've had my lows, but together we have held the fort."

On Maundy Thursday, he left the house before I awakened. It was his Thursday to go to Low Moor, an Episcopal nursing home fifty miles southwest of us, almost to Clifton Forge. He and Jerry

Hope and the Rector over in Staunton took turns with the Mass and healing service there.

The Romulus Record was open on the table in the breakfast nook, beside Daddy's empty coffee mug and a plate with toast crumbs. Not much of a breakfast, for someone who had to drive a hundred miles. This morning our story had been downplayed to a brief item on page three ("Ecumenical Service Slated for Vandalized Cross"). No byline for the Blimp today. Also it said that Father "Walton" Gower would officiate at the noon service tomorrow. Sic transit gloria. I hoped the misprint, or mistake, would not have lowered Daddy's spirits. He had a long day ahead of him.

And so did I. It was a beautiful morning, reproachfully so, the kind of morning on which lovers packed picnic lunches and took a blanket and went off into the mountains. Yet there were millions of other people who had to get through this day the best they could, if not ecstatically, then honorably.

I decided to honor Maundy Thursday by cleaning the kitchen. This was the day for getting clean and starting over. In ancient times, penitents prostrated themselves before the congregation, and after prayers were read over them and hands laid on them, they were readmitted to communion. If you were high and mighty, it was your especial duty to humble yourself on this day, in keeping with the *mandatum* of Christ, "that you love one another even as I have loved you." Queen Elizabeth the First "kept her Maundy" in the great hall at Westminster by washing the feet of twenty poor women. In monasteries all over Christendom today, abbots and superiors knelt down on bare floors, washing and patting dry the feet of the lowliest kitchen monks.

I had an unbidden and too-graphic fantasy of Adrian Bonner, clad in his beautiful tailored blue-gray suit and clerical collar, down on his knees washing Loretta's bare feet while she folded her arms and smirked in manic hilarity upon his balding head. Her toenails were long and prehensile and painted a come-on shade of purplish red. There was dirt and a sour smell between the toes. But Adrian respectfully washed and wiped dry each toe, not in the least put off. He rejoiced in his homage to this needy patient, because it fitted—as a lovers' picnic and whatever else might transpire on such a picnic would not fit—into the harmony of his totality.

I threw out his empty beer bottles, disgusted with the modest

Martha I had played last night. If you weren't something, you shouldn't playact at it. If you did, you'd have nobody to blame but yourself if, one day, the people for whom you'd been playacting saw you as what you had only been pretending to be. I did not want to be Adrian Bonner's Martha *or* his Mary. Adrian Bonner was not Jesus Christ. He may have sworn off women, but that still didn't make him Jesus Christ. Besides, who knew about Jesus Christ? Who really knew for sure?

I attacked the spice shelf, unscrewing each bottle and sniffing; if there wasn't a definite smell of an herb or a spice, it went sailing into the trash bag. Better to have a clean space filled with nothing, than a cluttered space filled with things that were of no use to you anymore. My rubric for getting through this day.

I did a ruthless number on the refrigerator. Out went the rest of Miriam Stacy's tuna and noodle casserole, plastic container and all, from Tuesday's influx of covered dishes after the destruction of the cross. We had far too many plastic and metal-foil containers that jammed drawers when we tried to open them or clattered down on our heads from top cabinets, when we were looking for something else. Out went the Major's latest offering of stuffed peppers. Daddy hated stuffed peppers with a passion, but who was going to tell the Major you didn't love her stuffed peppers? So, every time there was a crisis, here came more stuffed peppers. I believe she froze them, a half dozen at a time, for us. Since these were in a handsome smoked Pyrex dish with "E. M." printed magisterially in black ballpoint on a piece of tape on the bottom (as though there weren't the remotest chance that we might dare to know any *other* E. M.), I would have to wash it and return it, though, in my present mood, it would have been sheer joy to dash it to bits on top of Adrian's empty beer bottles.

The big black plastic garbage bag was filling fast. One must purify one's refrigerator with the same rigor as one purified one's heart.

Inspired by my own flurry of divestiture, I filled an entire new garbage bag full of *all* those horrid, clattering, metal-foil containers that had been multiplying on us for years. There were probably some here that went back to my mother's funeral. What had we been saving them for? Memorials to people's kindnesses to us? And was it always kindness?

"Do-Gooder Dishes . . ." I muttered aloud, ". . . Sanctimonious Cuisine . . ." I was dragging the two bulging trash bags awkwardly down our back steps when Ben MacGruder loped around the side of the rectory, his bright hair bounding and gleaming in the sunshine.

"You were talking to yourself," he accused cheerfully as he relieved me of the bags, and swung them, one on top of the other, into the garbage pail. They wouldn't fit in. "Looks like it's time to go to the dump."

"Well, too bad. The dump permit sticker is on Daddy's car and he's gone to Low Moor."

"Somebody is in a bad mood. Did I do something wrong?"

"Oh, always *you*!" I snapped, then reminded myself it was Maundy Thursday . . . "love one another even as I," etc. Besides, what had Ben done wrong, except love me? It wasn't his fault that I wanted someone else to love me.

"I'm just tired," I said, sinking down on the back step. He immediately sank down next to me. The sun felt good. It occurred to me that this was probably the first time this spring that I had sat down and stuck my face up to the sun. Simply that. With no plans or worrying about rushing off to my next task, not even any philosophical observations about sitting in the sunshine.

We sat there without speaking. He didn't try to sidle over, hip to hip, or kiss me or hold my hand. He just sat decorously on his side of the step, and I appreciated it.

"Harriet is unbearable," he finally said. "Since she's been home, she's been just unbearable. She knows everything, and she thinks she has the right to tell everybody how to live their life."

"Why? What's she said to you?" My interest perked up, because I was annoyed with Harriet myself.

"Not just me, though I came under fire last night, until I escaped over to Melody Station and sang some Cajun with the boys. And then I got flak about *that*, this morning. My undesirable friends. All on dope. All black people are either on welfare or dope. The way she *generalizes, my sister*! She thinks life ideally should be a series of *goal*posts, and you have to march, march, march, in a straight line from one to the other. No deviations. And no deviants, *please*! She's worried about me because I haven't brought home some debutante from U.Va. who will help Nana set the table and knows the correct house gift to bring and how to write a proper thank-you note. That could mean *I'm* deviant. I mean, never let us forget the time I made a fool of myself over Mr. Ritchie at Romulus High. And if anyone starts to forget it, depend on old Harriet to bring it up again! And now I spend all my spare time making music with darkies at their night club. I may turn out to be one of those twisted young southern gentlemen who are partial to black boys. It was on the tip of my tongue to tell her, 'It's only because the woman I love won't have me,' but I spared you, I've been faithful to our secret, I swear, though it wasn't easy last night when she started in on me. Now she's worried about Nana, because Nana doesn't 'do' anything with her life, except cook wonderful meals, and keep a house for my parents and us to come home to whenever we like, and do church work and volunteer work."

"What else *should* she do?"

"My sister thinks Nana ought to *train* for something. Computer science . . . or get her real-estate license! Can't you just see Nana driving prospective buyers around Sunset Villas, telling them, 'Now this is where my little friend Eleanor Wiggins lived, when all this land was still the Wiggins Estate . . .' "

"How about me?" I asked. "Did I come under Harriet's fire?"

"She didn't say too much about you. No, wait, she did. She said you'd do better to think about going into the ministry, like Georgie Gaines, rather than hole yourself up in an ivory tower with some seventh-century nun. I defended you, but for my own selfish reasons. Listen, Margaret, I promised myself I wasn't going to bring this up, but we could get an apartment together next fall in Charlottesville. Wait, don't say anything, I'm not talking about sleeping together, we could each have our own bedroom and bath. You'd be so good for me, you'd make me study, and I could do the chores. I can even do stir-fry, and hamburgers, and a pretty good imitation of Nana's spaghetti sauce, her secret is clove powder, you know. We'd just be roommates, it's done all the time. I know two guys who share a house with a girl. They take turns cooking and cleaning, and then she has her own boyfriend with his own place. Don't say out-and-out no, Margaret, please, not on this beautiful day. Give me some hope."

"Oh, Ben, what would Nana say? And if I do go back in the fall, which is not at all certain—I might not get that grant—Mrs. Dunbar would be crushed if I didn't stay on with her."

"She'd find somebody else to move in. You can't live your life for Mrs. Dunbar. And I think Nana would go for it. She trusts you *utterly*, Margaret. As far as she's concerned, it would be like I was sharing an apartment with Harriet . . ."

"Ben, you're pushing."

"I'm sorry. You do this to me, Margaret. I can make the most rigid resolutions to be *cool,* and before I'm with you five minutes I'm down on my knees begging."

"You're not down on your knees, stop exaggerating. Oh, I wish we could go to the dump and get rid of all this garbage!"

"We can, if you want."

"You don't have a sticker, either. They've gotten really strict since they found out all these out-of-state trucks were driving across the mountain to dump their toxic stuff on us."

"Yes, but my friend Bobby from Melody Station is on the gate weekday mornings. I was singing with him last night. He knows we don't have any poisons. That big *pail* won't fit in the trunk of the Mercedes, but the bags will, if we sort of smush them around. They aren't going to leak, are they? Go and get another one of those Glad bags, will you? We can lay it on the bottom in case something does."

"Yes, sir."

"That's a good girl. If your heart's desire is to go to the dump on this beautiful morning, at least it is in my power to satisfy that."

At the dump, sitting in Ben's old hand-me-down Mercedes while he slung my morning's work with perfect aim into the most recent pit dug by the ever-employed bulldozer, I surprised myself by starting to cry. The tears rolled out of my eyes and down my face; I didn't know why. It was everything and nothing. It was the delighted smile the big black man on the gate had given Ben as he waved him into the landfill as if it had been his own vast private estate, it was the realization that I could just sit there with my head bowed and my shoulders slumped and let somebody else take over for a while.

And it was such a wrenching mixture of beauty and sordidness, sunshine and mud, here at the dump. All these prime acres of degraded landscape, contrasted against the breathtaking beauty that surrounded it. Spread out on three sides of this hell-hole, crammed with our mounting clutter and stinking with our garbage, were the Shenandoahs, and beyond them the Alleghenies, and beyond them West Virginia—the Romulus Landfill had the best view in town. It was also, maybe, the sight of the valiant young willow, toppled sideways by a recent brush with the bulldozer, but still clinging with its unfortunately placed roots to the shattered earth beneath; it had put forth a delicate green foliage on every one of its doomed and graceful branches.

But perhaps, most of all, it was the gulls that made me sad: hundreds of them, hovering and circling eagerly over the smelly pit into which Ben had just slung our garbage, or perched on other garbage bags that had not quite made it into the pit, and which they had ripped open with their beaks; and more gulls marching around in the deep, wide tire tracks left by heavier vehicles, their white breasts spattered with red mud. One of them was tugging at a dirty diaper that had been run over by a tire and was stuck fast in the mud.

"Phew!" exclaimed Ben, sliding behind the wheel and slamming his door. "Let's get out of here. Hey, honey, you're crying!"

"I think it's just . . . all those *gulls*. They're supposed to be seabirds. Why are they here in this ugly place? How did they even get here?"

"How did they get here? Well, they follow the barges from the Chesapeake Bay up the James River . . ." He angled the old Mercedes around a treacherous-looking hole and then swung sharply left to keep from disturbing the gull with the diaper. ". . . and then they stop off to see friends at the Presquile Wildlife Refuge, where some of them decide to play it safe and go on back to the bay again, while others, the ones who will never be satisfied with where they are, head on up the James River some *more* until it dwindles and dwindles, and they start to despair, but then one of them, the optimist in the bunch, or maybe just the one with the sharpest sense of smell, gets wind of the Montebello fish hatchery, and he says, 'Come on, guys, just a little farther . . .' and while they're putting up *there* for a few weeks, gobbling the little trapped fishes, they meet some gulls returning *east* who tell them about this *awesome* landfill, just a *little* farther on, in a place called Romulus . . . Listen, Margaret, I'm taking you for a drive up on the Parkway. You need some altitude, honey. Your father eats with the old folks at Low Moor after his service there, so you don't even have the excuse of having to be home in time to fix his lunch. And Nana's inviting you two for fish chowder after the six o'clock Mass. She knows how Father Melancholy always puts himself through that liquid fast of his on Good Friday, so she's filling the chowder full of nourishing stuff, to get him through his busy day tomorrow."

"How do you know all that? About the gulls? I don't mean all that anthropomorphic *fantasy* stuff, but how they get here?"

Ben waved at his friend on the gate and passed out into the road. "Because I pay attention to the world around me. And because when I don't know something, I make it up. Listen, Margaret, those gulls are perfectly happy. Did you see how fat they were?"

He took us north up the Skyline Drive, which I thought showed delicacy. I had been afraid that as soon as I had agreed to the ride, he would race stubbornly south towards Peaks of Otter, hoping for a different outcome from the one two summers ago, when we had failed to reach the heights of passion at the top of Buzzard's Roost.

This time we motored leisurely as an old retired couple, staying well under the parkway speed limit, both of us rolling down our windows and absorbing the spring. We took deep breaths and each of us would sigh dramatically from time to time. Ben was right about "altitude." As Harriet's hand-me-down Mercedes took each ascending curve, I felt the lifting of a weight. If Ben hadn't showed up, I would have gone on cleaning the house, room by room, immuring myself in the dust and shadows while the sun crossed the sky of a day that would never repeat itself. We could both use this respite into nature from our respective people throes. I'd had the shock and frantic aftermath of the vandalized cross, plus my emotional thrashings over Adrian Bonner, whereas poor Ben was suffering a continuation of his old thrashings over *me*, plus the fresh attacks on his life-style from his conventional sister, who certainly did seem formidably full of herself these days.

Up, up, up labored the Mercedes, whose rattly diesel purr had been one of the familiar sounds of my childhood. Ruth used to imitate Nan MacGruder complaining that Dr. MacGruder never had time to have the engine tuned. We drove through sun and shadow, through dense forest and out again into fresh vistas. When the road wound through forest, you were enveloped in the strong, mulchy odor of the earth as it grew warmer. New growths of ivy mingled with periwinkle, and graceful, feathery clumps of young fern poked up through the blanket of last fall's leaves and the leaves of the year before. Then out again once more into the bright sunshine and there below us would be some dazzling sight:

another sweeping view, or ravishing acres of redbud trees in full bloom, staggered down a steep slope, mingled with cherry and apple. The delicate scent of their combined blossoms would waft through the open windows of the car.

Ben pulled off at an overlook, and we got out of the car and walked around. There was a plaque describing how the Shenandoah Valley that lay below us had come into existence through the gradual withdrawal of a shallow sea, leaving behind it a nearly flat valley floor, honeycombed beneath the surface, in some places, with limestone caverns.

"Did you ever go to the Luray Caverns?" I asked him.

"God, yes. Once when we were on home leave from Egypt. Mother and Daddy had a horrible fight *right down in the caverns*. With all these other tourists around. Harriet was embarrassed and I cried. But I was really crying because I had wanted this little box of maple sugar bears in the gift shop and now I knew I wouldn't get them, because we'd be dragged straight back to Nana's so they could go off somewhere and finish their fight. I don't remember a single *thing* about those caverns, though we studied them later, in science class at Romulus High. Did you ever go?"

"Yes, when I was six. It was the summer before my mother left us. Daddy had just come out of a depression and wanted us to go on a family outing. I remember the caverns very well, and I remember the backside of our guide. She had on this wraparound denim skirt that didn't quite make it all the way around her tummy. She and Ruth were talking about losing weight, and my mother pretended to have a weight problem to make the other woman feel better. But you know what was bothering me just now, Ben? I can still see the backside of that lady tour guide just as clearly as anything, the way her hips wiggled, the little round collar of her flowered blouse, even her *shoes*. They were navy-blue canvas, with crepe soles. But I can't see my mother at all. I have absolutely no picture of her. The way she walked, or even what she was wearing that day."

"Well, maybe you had other things on your mind. Just like I did. I didn't give two hoots about 'stalactites' and 'stalagmites.' Did *you* really pay attention to them?

"Yes, because Daddy and I were trying to outdo each other in seeing apocalyptic formations."

" 'Apocalyptic formations'? At six years old?"

"Oh yes, we saw a snake with two heads and an angry old man, sort of like God, with an eagle on his eyelid . . . I remember I was really pleased with myself for seeing so many scary things. I was pleased to be impressing Daddy."

"There you are, then. You were more interested in your father that day. Just like I was interested in those maple sugar bears I knew I wasn't going to get. That's why you can't remember what your mother had on."

"Yes, but why should I remember that ridiculous lady tour guide?"

"I don't know, maybe ridiculous people just stick in the mind better because we don't take them seriously. We see them in parts. That's the trick of caricaturing somebody, isn't it? You select a few parts, the more ridiculous the better, and emphasize those. You know. Nixon's ski-jump nose, Jimmy Carter's garden-fence teeth . . . Your mother wasn't pieces or parts to you, she was this whole serious flowing *phenomenon* to you, without boundaries. She had her particle aspect and her wave aspect, and you can't separate the two, any more than you can concentrate on them both at the same time. It just can't be done."

"What on earth are you talking about, Ben?"

"It's from quantum physics. It's a concept I've been working on, this past week, to help me understand why I'm in love with you. I got inspired, for a change, in physics class last week when the graduate instructor was explaining to us about the wave/particle duality. She said this one interesting thing that really grabbed me. She said, 'Of course we can never fully know an elementary particle, we can never pin it down to its essence.' Because, she said, when you're focusing on the *particle* aspect, you are observing the individual particle, like one separate marble or something, and when you are observing the *wave* aspect, you have to forfeit your close attention on the one marble in order the see the movement and the pattern it is making with all the other marbles that are overlapping and interwoven with that particle. And that's when I thought of you, Margaret. You're just my quantum person, that's all. I will never fully grasp you, or fully understand you, but what gives me *hope* is that, the longer we know each other—and we go all the way back to the Easter egg hunt of 1973, our fifteenth anniversary is day after tomorrow—and the longer our particles keep knocking together and interacting, the more we'll be bound up in the same wave."

A car door slammed, then another. We were no longer alone

on the overlook. I was not sorry, though the particle theory as metaphor for human relationships certainly had its prospects. Strolling away from a black Cadillac with a Pennsylvania license plate was a handsome couple, somewhere in their mid-to-late forties. Both of them were tall and slim and wore walking shoes and khaki trousers and lightweight windbreakers. They had similar short, gray, feathery haircuts. The woman nodded pleasantly; the man said "hi," with a brisk, masculine upraising of his palm. Then they turned their backs on us and surveyed the view, even turning their heads the same way at the same time, before setting off in opposite directions down the steepish slope. The man tramped scoutlike into the underbrush, probably in search of an outdoor bathroom, but the woman, arms folded across her chest, as if she were loosely embracing herself, strolled down the embankment in her surefooted white walkers, stopping to examine the new growth on various shrubs and trees.

"What were you thinking back there, when you were watching that couple?" Ben demanded as we were driving home. "If I know you, you had worked out their whole life story."

"No, I wasn't so much thinking about who they were as who they *might* have been. That woman seemed so at home with herself and her marriage. My mother might have been like that, if things had worked out differently. She and my father might have ordered casual clothes out of catalogues and gone on trips, through not in a new Cadillac, with my father's salary. She would be about that woman's age now."

"You know what *I* was thinking, while I was watching you watching them?"

"No."

"I was thinking we might look like that, in twenty or thirty years."

"*You* might look like the man, Ben dear, but she was at least a whole foot taller than I am. And as people age, they get even shorter. When I am her age, I will probably be rather dumpy."

"Well, even if you were an outright *butterball,* I would love you all the same."

"Just your old quantum butterball."

"You can really stick the knife in, can't you?"

"I'm sorry, I didn't mean to stick any knife in. Oh, *Ben.* Please don't *glower.* This has been such a nice outing, and I really needed it and I thank you for kidnaping me and whisking me up here to all this loveliness. Please, Ben, let's be friends."

" 'Let's be friends,' " he mimicked bitterly. "I hope one day someone you're obsessed with says that to you."

Daddy was pacing up and down in front of the church. "I was beginning to get worried," he said, striding out to Ben's car and opening my door.

"But you couldn't have been home long, Daddy. It's only a little after three . . ."

"I didn't stay for lunch at Low Moor. Too much on my mind, too much to do here. They understood. Dear old ladies, I get very attached to some of them. And then"—he snapped his fingers—"off they go, between one visit and the next. It takes some getting used to, no matter how long you've been in this business. This *one* favorite of mine, she'll be ninety-eight in May, told me a wonderful story today. One of the young nurses, probably just trying to make conversation, asked her if she'd made plans for her funeral yet. 'I mean, you are getting up there, Miss Anderson,' this young nurse said. 'It might be a good idea to . . . you know, kind of decide what you *want* . . . pick your hymns and all.' Well, without batting an eye, Miss Anderson said to that young nurse, 'Thank you so much for reminding me! If you'll just bring me my *appointment book,* perhaps you and I can pick out a day suitable to us both.' "

"That's funny," laughed Ben. "We went to the dump, and then it was so beautiful I talked Margaret into driving up the parkway. We only went as far as Flat Top. It was very refreshing."

"Good, good, I'm glad you two had a nice time. Before you rush off home, Ben, I need you to change the lamp over the Altar of Repose. It has to be clear glass for the Sacrament."

"Sure. What time to you want me back at the sacristy? Five-thirty?"

"Quarter to six will be okay. We'll have *two* servers this evening."

"Oh, is Colin Winchester home? I thought he was going to St. Croix."

"No, I have another server," said Daddy. "An old-timer. Ned Block has agreed to help out."

"Oh. Shall I put the humeral veil around you, or do you

want . . . Mr. Block to?" Ben looked confused. He and I had often discussed Ned Block's animosity towards Daddy.

"Let's let Ned. It would mean a lot to him."

"Ned *Block*?" I said as soon as Ben had gone inside the church to change the lamp, in the chapel under the choir loft where the consecrated wafers would spend the night. "What's been going on around here, Daddy? Have you had any lunch at *all*?"

"I fixed myself a cheese sandwich. And I had some ice cream I found in the freezer . . ."

"Great. A real cholesterol orgy."

He cheerfully waved away my scolding. He was in a wonderful mood, although a bit "hyper."

"Walk down to the corner with me, Margaret, and keep me company while I tidy up the ivy—Georgie Gaines phoned to say a local television crew will also be covering our Reconsecration service tomorrow—and I will tell you about a small miracle—I mean, there's no other word for it—that occurred inside the church a little while ago."

Obediently I followed him. I felt guilty for being away so long without leaving a note. And guilty about his lunch of cheese and ice cream. But how could I have known that he'd decided to return early from the nursing home?

"What's the miracle?" I asked.

"Well, I got back, and you weren't around. But since your car was parked in front, I figured you were off with one of the Mac-Gruders . . . I phoned Nan, and sure enough, she said Ben had headed over here late this morning . . . we're invited for fish chowder after the service tonight . . . Nan is so transparent, she's afraid I'll collapse from my Friday fast, but I won't, I always drink plenty of liquids. Besides, it does a person's system good to clean itself out. So, anyway, I made myself a cheese sandwich . . ."

"Did you notice anything about the kitchen?"

"The kitchen? No, should I have?"

"Honestly. *Men.* Just that I spent the entire morning cleaning it . . . I threw out *bags* full of old junk!"

"Bless your heart. Come to think of it, I did get a kind of sparkly feeling sitting in your mother's window seat eating my sandwich."

"Go on about the miracle."

"Well, I wandered over to the church, and I saw Ned Block's

car and almost turned around and slunk back to the rectory. Then I said to myself, 'This is silly, you are the rector here, you have *been* the rector here for nineteen years, isn't it time you stopped letting this poor slob make you feel like you're trespassing?'

"So, anyway, I proceeded. Ned was standing in the narthex, with his hands in his pockets, looking over the Vigil list I'd posted for tonight.

" 'Well, Ned, what watch have you signed up for tonight?' I asked, and he replied, as I knew he would, that he 'always' took the nine to ten.

" 'That's an important one,' I said. 'It's late enough in the evening for a person to be tired, but not so *dramatically* late as the ten-to-midnight watches.'

"He nodded sanctimoniously, swaying back and forth on those little feet, and not looking at me directly in the eye, as he usually doesn't, and I thought, I walked right into that one, didn't I? Here it comes, as soon as he can rev himself up out of his languor, here comes his next predictable line, about the good old days of Dr. Hazeltine, when the church had more members and the Vigil at the Altar of Repose was an all-night affair. And then I don't know what came over me, Margaret, but I suddenly heard myself saying, 'Listen, Ned, I'd like to ask a favor of you. I only have one server this evening, and I'd like to have incense *and* a crucifer when we carry the Sacrament down to the Altar of Repose. I know it's late but I wonder if you'd be willing to help me out?'

"And, Margaret, he kept swaying and looking down at his shoes, and I thought, he's going to refuse, it was a preposterous idea of mine, it's been umteen years since this man was an altar boy, he probably doesn't know the ropes anymore and he'll only be more resentful than ever towards me for having embarrassed him. But then he looked up and said in this strange, low voice, almost a whisper, 'I'd be honored, Father, if you think we can find a cassock that will still fit me.' He said it so *humbly,* for Ned Block, and then I saw he was looking directly at me and that there were tears in his eyes. For a moment I thought he must be on the verge of some kind of breakdown.

"I said, 'Oh, *that* won't be a problem, I'm sure, Ned,' though I was far from sure it *wouldn't* be. 'Let's go into the sacristy and see what we can find,' I said. So he came back to the sacristy with me, and thank God we found one that did fit him, and as he was buttoning it over his belly rather pridefully, well . . . ! Out came this sudden *torrent*. About how the happiest years of his life were when he was Dr. Hazeltine's chief server as a teenager, and how he had considered entering the priesthood, but his rich uncle had talked him out of it, and then, some years after his marriage, he had gotten his wife to agree to their going out west for her asthma and he had found this program out there where he could study for the diaconate, but then he wasn't accepted into the program and her asthma got better from some new drug that had just come on the market, and then . . . listen to this, baby . . . *at the exact moment I had showed up in the narthex,* he had been recalling the pride with which he used to drape the humeral veil around Dr. Hazeltine's shoulders on Maundy Thursday . . ."

"Oh, Daddy. Now I see why you . . ."

"Yes, yes, you see what I mean, Margaret, the coincidence of it, if anything *is* a coincidence . . . the congruence of his thinking what he was thinking and my meeting him there exactly *when* he was thinking it, and then my asking him. I mean, what if I had turned back and not gone into the church, out of my pride, be-cause I was afraid he would criticize me yet another time? I would have failed him, perhaps at the very moment when he most needed assurance. And what kind of priest would I have been then?"

Burne off my rusts, and my deformity,
Restore thine Image, so much, by thy grace,
That thou may'st know mee, and I'll turne my face.

—John Donne, "Goodfriday, 1613. Riding Westward."

X : GOOD FRIDAY

"This is good orange juice, Margaret, but isn't it mighty thick?"

"Oh, do you think so?"

"Come on, now, Miss Innocence, what all did you grind up in that rackety old blender?"

"Just some banana and a little yogurt."

"Oh me. A poor sinner can't even have himself a liquid fast one day out of the year."

"It still qualifies as liquid, Daddy. You could run it through a sieve. If you'd seen this in a bottle at the supermarket, with a label that said Orange-Banana-Yogurt Juice, you would have bought it as a juice, wouldn't you?"

"Just teasing, honey, I know you have my best interests at heart. Okay, it's a liquid, and this is going to be a long day. I'm off to the hospital now."

"The hospital?"

"The Smiths had their baby a little after three this morning. A Good Friday baby boy. Dick called me early this morning. Susan's a little crestfallen because she had done all that Lamaze training and then at the last minute the baby turned himself around and the doctor opted for a Caesarean. However, with a Cesarean, Dick says, the baby comes out looking beautiful. He's the most beautiful baby in the nursery, of course. We'll be having a baptism in a few weeks. I like it best when they're infants. The older ones can sometimes be a problem. Do you remember that four-year-old girl?"

"The one who tried to scratch your face and finally had to be held out flat like an ironing board by three adults. And they weren't even members. They never came back after that Sunday."

Daddy laughed and drained his doctored juice. (I had also sneaked a little blackstrap molasses in it.) "I thought I was dealing with an exorcism that Sunday," he said. "I should take some sort of bouquet to Susan. We've still got red tulips, but are they enough for someone who is going to revive our Sunday school? Oh, when Dick called and woke me, I was having the sweetest dream about your mother. I wish I could remember more of it."

"What do you remember?"

"We were lying next to each other in the middle of a green field. Only we weren't on the grass, we were on this big square slab of stone, kind of like a shuffleboard court. But it wasn't uncomfortable; on the contrary, I felt very happy. We were propped up on our elbows and she was reading John Donne's 'Goodfriday, Riding Westward,' aloud to me from that little book of metaphysical poets she sent me. I couldn't see her face, because her hair had fallen forward, but it was her voice exactly. The words weren't the words of the real poem . . . you know the way with dreams . . . but as she was reading I felt I suddenly understood the whole thing, the mystery of God, everything. It just wasn't a problem anymore."

"And then Dick Smith woke you up."

"Yes. I tried to hold on to some of the words and ideas but by the time I got through congratulating Dick they had evaporated. But, still, it was nice, hearing Ruth's voice so clearly. It was exactly her voice."

"That's great," I said, feeling somewhat bereft, probably because I wasn't in it. But that was unreasonable, wasn't it? Daddy hadn't been in my dream about her, earlier this week, when she and I had been painting erotic murals on Adrian Bonner's walls. And I hadn't shared my dream with my father.

"I think I'll step over to the church with my clippers and purloin a few of the saucer magnolias for the Smiths. That way I could tell them they came right from the churchyard. Should I mix in some red tulips, too? No, I'll just take the saucer magnolias. More elegant by themselves."

"Well, why ask me, if it's just a rhetorical question?" I said irritably.

"Oh, you think I *should* mix in some red tulips?"

"*NO!* I don't know. Does it make all that much difference? I mean, you said yourself they'll probably transfer to St. Matthias before the child is crawling."

"I did say that, didn't I? But I feel more positive this morning. My poor girl. I should keep these tiresome old gloomy spells to myself. I hope I haven't transferred them onto you. I *haven't*, have I?"

"No, Daddy, of course you haven't." I was in a vile mood this morning, but it was not his fault. I reached across the table and touched his hand, to make amends. We sat facing each other in Ruth's kitchen window seat. It was eight-thirty in the morning. The sky was in keeping with Daddy's idea of proper Good Friday weather, overcast, but with a slight silvery glow. A number of long, lean, painterly looking purplish clouds stretched somberly across the low horizon. I could see the disputed red tulips from where I sat, swaying in their slight breeze in front of the dry wall Katharine Thrale and I had built. I picked squeamishly at the instant oatmeal I had prepared for myself, with milk and brown sugar and the tail end of the banana that had gone into Daddy's "energy drink" sliced on top. Yet who was the one in need of energy here? I wanted to crawl back in bed, and the day had hardly begun.

"I'll be on my way, then, honey." He slid his long black-suited figure out of the window seat and carried his juice glass conspicuously to the sink, washing it out with lots of detergent suds and rinsing it for at least a whole minute before placing it upside down on a dishtowel. Ordinarily he would have just left the glass on the table. He was making amends for being gloomy and tiresome. In so many ways, we were like an old married couple. As he bent his neck over the sink, I saw that he was wearing the gold collar stud Father Traherne had given him for his ordination.

"Aren't the other ministers coming early for some sort of briefing, Daddy?" I regretted my bitchy remark about the Smiths transferring to St. Matthias, and didn't want him to rush off before I had smoothed things over.

"We're gathering in the sacristy at eleven forty-five. I've typed out a little order of service and what each one's supposed to read.

The parishioners will assemble at the corner with their prayer books so they can read the responses to the psalm. Oh, and Adrian called last night, while you were still over at the MacGruders watching your movie. The Rabbi arrived from Roanoke, and they were talking about Jung and the Book of Job. He's in one of the Reform branches and has a searching mind, Adrian said. We've made a last-minute change in the service that I think is going to be very effective. I'll do the 'Then will I sprinkle clean water' passage from Ezekiel, while Jerry Hope asperges the pieces of the crucifix, and then the Rabbi will repeat the Ezekiel passage in Hebrew."

"That sounds good. Only how will everybody know the Rabbi's saying the same thing in Hebrew?"

"I hadn't thought of that! Whatever would I do without my smart girl? I'll explain beforehand."

"Yes, do. Then it would mean more to everyone. Daddy, I doubt if there's ever *been* a service like this in Romulus."

"I was thinking the same thing myself. I deplore the circumstances that brought it about, but, who knows? Maybe with God's help, we can turn a nasty act of violence into a rare occasion for reconciliation. All kinds of reconciliations. I mean, look at me and Ned Block! Maybe that poor smashed savior has already begun to do his work. Ned's going to be my thurifer for the service; he asked if he could. And Ben is supposed to be here by eleven, to drive all the pieces down to the corner and lay them out."

I gave up on my oatmeal, by now a cold, pasty mess. "Well," I said, sliding out of the window seat, "I'm sure he will be, then. If not before."

"Poor young Ben," chuckled Daddy, hovering beside me at the sink to brush my cheek with a kiss. "You are certainly his Belle Dame Sans Merci, I'm afraid."

I did not reply. I was already busy scouring out my oatmeal bowl and engaged in an intense bout of self-disgust as I reviewed my behavior of the evening before. Ben and Harriet and I had been watching *St. Elmo's Fire* on the VCR in the MacGruders' basement den, then Harriet had received a mysterious phone call and left the house, saying she might not be back for a few hours, and so, while Mrs. MacGruder was on her knees before the Altar of Repose, doing her ten to eleven vigil at St. Cuthbert's (and while Adrian Bonner had been discussing Jung and Job with the Rabbi from Roanoke), Ben and I drank too many rum and Cokes and toppled back into our old fallen ways. Only, it had been worse than ever, because I longed to be with someone else. I had simply been drunk and, also, it had been an act of pique against my circumstances. The movie, about twenty-two-year-olds, none of whom seemed to have any relationships with their parents, much less ever to think about them, had made me feel I was not living the normal life of a person my age in contemporary America. And so I had taken it out on Ben.

I absently returned my father's kiss, not bothering to look up at him.

"I'm off to snip a few saucer magnolias," he said cheerfully. "Hold the fort till I get back."

I heard him take the clippers from the hardware drawer, but I was so absorbed in my own hungover remorse that I wasn't even aware when he left the house.

By eleven, I had straightened my room and changed the sheets on both our beds and was in the process of making Daddy's bathroom presentable. As a long-time resident of a rectory, I'd had ample experience of the "wandering" propensities of curious parishioners, who, it seemed, could not resist furtive trips upstairs to check out the bedside reading on the rector's night-table or the names on the pill bottles in his medicine cabinet. Once when I was about fifteen, I had slipped out one Sunday during coffee hour so I could go back to my room and continue reading *Lord of the Rings,* and there, standing casually in the doorway of my closet, was a woman who'd only been to St. Cuthbert's a couple of times, going through the pockets of my clothes. Caught in the act, she stared me down and brazenly drawled that she had just quit smoking and, overcome by a sudden nicotine fit, had simply been hoping to find a cigarette. But she didn't come back to St. Cuthbert's again.

The Romulus Record was folded on top of Daddy's toilet tank. We were front page again, lower right; no picture, just a short piece recapitulating the smashing of St. Cuthbert's corner calvary, and announcing the outdoor Reconsecration service at noon today. Georgie had his byline back and the Rev. "Walton" Gower's correct Christian name had been restored to him.

Daddy's bedside table passed inspection. Wayside Gardens and Burpee catalogues, and a stack of brochures concerning our upcoming English trip that the travel agent had sent. I examined a couple of these. The places looked interesting, like places out of books should look; then why was I filled with a sense of unreality, and of something akin to repugnance? Did it have something to do with the prospect of visiting the place where my mother was killed? Or was it just more reaction from that dumb movie last night that had made me feel like a freak? How many girls today went to England with their daddies after college graduation? The modern girl would be bicycling through Europe, or backpacking through Nepal with her lover. Stashed away in the pockets of their cutoff jeans would be the requisite dope and lubricated colored condoms, or birth control pills (or more likely both, given the health concerns these days).

But actually, those scenes appealed to me not at all, though I thought they probably should, if I were "normal," whatever that word meant. I *would* rather go to England with my father and see where Ruth's car hit the truck and get it over with at last, and then, after we had hugged each other and cried some, Daddy would show me his old haunts and grow young again as he told his clerical anecdotes. He'd guide me through the architecture of the great cathedrals, as well as the obscurer Saxon and Norman churches, and we'd go up north to the holy shrines, to St. Cuthbert's and St. Hilda's old haunts. Only . . . it would have been nice to go with someone else, as well.

After last night's backsliding with Ben, I felt I might be able to forgo sex for a long while, maybe for several years . . . even longer. I mean, what was the point, when it was just some nuzzling and an insincere spasm, and then the shame and letdown afterwards when you were alone and had to admit to yourself that you really yearned for the body of someone else: some maybe-impossible someone else? This morning I felt capable of taking a vow, myself: Never again will I share my body with someone unless I am in love with that person.

Was this a "normal" impulse for a nearly twenty-two-year-old woman in late twentieth-century America to be having?

Well, what if it weren't? Perhaps it was too late for me to be what other people considered normal. And was what the people who had made that movie considered normal, "representative of the era," a status which I aspired to, or a condition I despised? I wanted to behave according to the beliefs that were really mine.

As I had predicted, Ben's old Mercedes pulled up promptly in front of St. Cuthbert's, and, from behind Daddy's curtain upstairs, I watched him carry out the broken pieces of statuary and cross, including the shattered bits that had been laid out on kneeling cushions and secured with plastic wrap until they could be set in place. Ben respectfully laid the pieces into the backseat of the car for their short ride to the corner, where he parked and just as respectfully unloaded them and laid them out in the ivy bed according to Daddy's instructions: in a semblance of the old form, only fallen. I was sure Ben knew I was somewhere in the background, but was grateful that he kept his attention on his work and did not dart possessive glances at our windows, had not "dropped by" for a minute, or exercised any of those rites of familiarity most men in his position would feel they were entitled to on "the morning after."

Already by eleven-forty, a crowd had gathered at the corner. Cars were parked all the way up one side of the street in front of the church, and down the other—a dispensation allowed us by the police department for Sundays and special services. The traffic flow along Macon Street was sluggish, but mainly because the passing cars slowed to see what was going on.

All our faithful parishioners were there, with prayer books borrowed from the church or their personal ones. There were other faces I recognized. The friendly Mrs. Adele King from Adrian's Monday study group had discovered her former innkeeper from the old Fern Hill Manor days. Mrs. Radford, a wizened effigy of her former self, had been in and out of the hospital this past year, "riddled with C," as she had confided to Daddy, who had visited her there. But she had put on rouge and done her hair and dressed, and had apparently walked all the way down Macon on her aluminum cane, and was chatting happily with her old star boarder, for whom she had always saved the big front room with all the afternoon sunshine. I recognized some Presbyterians and Methodists, and there was an impressive turnout of Jerry Hope's flock. Elaine Major had already corraled a smartly dressed St. Matthias couple and was pointing out something to them in her personal prayer book: the expensive blue leatherbound chancel edition with a gold cross embossed on the front. There was a pale young man in a wheelchair, with a tanned, muscular man pushing him, and other people I had never seen before, who seemed unsure of themselves or out of place, but were trying to strike suitably cautious or devout attitudes, and then there was a smattering of the sort of people who always show up when there has been any public notice of a free show, or some free trouble.

Two men in jeans and T-shirts, one with a dragon tattoo winding all the way up his bare arm, were intently examining the remains laid out in the ivy. The one with the tattoo dropped down on his haunches and pointed out the places where the Christ figure had been sliced cleanly through. He mumbled something to his companion. "Sure looks like it," the other said professionally. They were obviously discussing tools and methods. A couple of curious workmen on their lunch hour, or the vandals themselves? After all, Daddy's invitation for them to be here had appeared in Wednesday's headline. But would they be so open about it, walking right up in front of everybody like that? And there had been something respectful about the way the tattooed one had hung back from actually touching the Christ figure. Maybe I was naive, but I exonerated them then and there.

The red Maserati of the star reporter himself rumbled slowly past. Where were all the parking places? The low-slung sports car gathered speed and whipped around the park in a burst of impatience, repeated the vain search for a space, and then roared off out of sight. Within moments, however, here came Georgie Gaines sprinting across the park, flash camera in hand. He wore an impeccably pressed lightweight khaki suit, pink shirt, and red bow tie.

Harriet beside me uttered a derisive snort. "How *dapper* the Blimp looks. And see how he can run now!"

At seven minutes before noon, the white van from WROM-TV cruised purposefully up towards the church. Undaunted by the lack of parking, it drove straight through the middle of the empty space reserved for the fire hydrant across the street, hopping the curb and bumping onto the grass of the public park. It made a complete U-turn so that it faced the street and stopped. A young woman in a very short black leather skirt and safari jacket got out of the passenger side. She was wearing a microphone around her neck and carried a black canvas bag that seemed full of things. The driver, an overweight man in low-hung trousers and a crumpled white shirt with the sleeves rolled up, went around to the back of the van, and emerged again with a video camera, which he hefted onto his right shoulder and held on top with his right hand, the way someone might carry a clinging but ungainly pet.

The two consulted briefly, the young woman doing most of the talking, pointing rapidly here and there, tossing her hair a lot, and stopping several times to feel her backside as though checking that the leather skirt was still in place. Then the two of them headed towards us, the young woman quick-stepping importantly, the cameraman shambling along in tow, stopping once to pull out a handkerchief and mop his sweating face. At their approach, a self-consciousness went through the crowd: *We are going to be on TV.* Certain people stood up straighter and adjusted their profiles; others went suddenly nonchalant.

The young woman went straight for Georgie Gaines, who had joined Harriet and me. "Listen, George, is this thing going to start on time?"

Georgie introduced her as Sharon Lake, the producer of this segment about to be taped for the local evening news. Sharon endured the introduction, tossing her hair impatiently, and obviously making no effort to retain our names. She then promptly got back to business.

"What exactly's supposed to happen here, George? When is the part where the priests detoxify it, or whatever they do? I need to know the order of events." She spoke to him as though he worked for her, not *The Romulus Record.*

"As I understand it, Sharon, the clergy will march down here in procession," Georgie told her. "Any minute now, they ought to be coming out of the sacristy door."

"Better get your bars and tones, Franko," Sharon ordered the cameraman. She did a deep knee-bend, showing lots of thigh in the process, and withdrew from the canvas bag a small piece of equipment that she handed briskly to "Franko," who plugged it into his camera.

"And then there'll be an order of service . . ." the obliging Georgie went on to his comrade in the media.

The cameraman was making little beeps with the piece of equipment.

"Sort of exactly what *is* the order of service?" demanded Sharon Lake.

"There'll be some readings from the Bible by the different ministers, some prayers, then they'll sprinkle the holy water . . . you know, to reconsecrate the vandalized crucifix. That's the part I believe you were referring to, Sharon. It's the *cleansing* part of the ceremony, Reverend Gower told me, and then after that comes the incense, which is the *dedicatory* part. And then church members will carry the pieces of the cross back up to the church."

"There's not going to be a lengthy *sermon,* or anything, is there? Because we've got something scheduled in Varnerstown for one o'clock."

"Oh, I wouldn't worry . . . *Sharon,*" Harriet suddenly drawled out with deadly sweetness. From the way she emphasized the producer's first name, I could tell she was up to her worst. "In our church, we don't have lengthy sermons. Ours are real short, and if you don't go in for thinking, they're over before you know what hit you. That's 'sort of exactly' what we have at St. Cuthbert's."

Sharon looked at Harriet as though she had just made a speech in a foreign language. Then she tossed her hair and glared towards the church, consulting her wristwatch. Georgie Gaines blushed the color of his bow tie. As a former victim of Harriet's cruel tongue, her present mischief had not been lost on him.

I was about to explain that Daddy wouldn't be giving a sermon at this particular service, but at that moment the Major's voice silenced the waiting crowd: "Heah come ouah *cluh*-gymen. So now we shall *all* want to obsuhve silence."

The sacristy door had swung open, and Ned Block, in black cassock and white surplice, carrying the thurible, advanced solemnly towards us with his dainty, performing-bear walk.

"Are we rolling, Franko?" asked Sharon Lake. "Are we at speed?"

"Yo," snapped the cameraman, who had suddenly galvanized into a figure of authority. The beast on his shoulder made soft, satisfied clicking sounds. At last it was getting its meal. Sharon, whose microphone cord was now attached to the camera, stumbled sideways and almost tripped over the curb when Franko tugged them suddenly into the street to get a better angle on the oncoming procession.

Ned Block was followed by Ben, carrying the processional cross. His black skirts swayed sideways with the vigor of his walk. He looked perfect for the occasion: knightly and remote.

Next came Reverend Holt from Central Methodist, in his rumpled black robe, and First Presbyterian's Reverend Dendy, who was a Doctor of Divinity and sported bands of rich purple velvet on the flowing sleeves of his well-pressed black gown. Daddy had agonized over this and finally put them side by side instead of one going ahead of the other, because clergy, he said, outdid royalty, they even outdid *academics,* when it came to jealousy over who was put where in processions. Next came the Rabbi from Roanoke in a business suit and dark tie, a slight, elegantly made man with a thick head of curly gray hair, who frowned when he saw the cameras. (Georgie Gaines had joined his TV compatriots in the street and was busily clicking away.)

Next came Adrian, carrying the aspersorium. He wore a plain white linen alb, with cincture and stole, and, compared to fresh-cheeked Ben, really showed his age this morning. There were dark smudges under his eyes, and his wisps of thinning hair strayed untidily onto his forehead. But it was the first time I had ever seen him in liturgical vestments and it made my stomach do a small lurch, despite his worn appearance under this harsh, me-tallic sky. He walked with his head slightly forward, like a low-ranking monk, as if he did not expect, or particularly wish, to be noticed. After Adrian came the extroverted Jerry Hope in his alb and stole, supremely conscious of the cameras, and approving of them as much as the Rabbi disapproved. Over at St. Matthias, they'd had a sound system for years, and, unlike Daddy, Jerry allowed camcorders at baptisms and weddings.

Daddy came last, as celebrant. In the magnificent red, embroi-dered cope, clasped at the neck by the intricately worked morse, he was undisputedly the king of this parade. Initially, he had told Georgie he couldn't use the camera *at all* during the service, there were to have been just a few shots of the procession at the end, when people were carrying the pieces of the broken Christ back to the church, but then the television people had elbowed in, and everything changed. After all, said Daddy, this had become a community event.

"We'll just have to try to proceed without taking any notice of them," he had resolved. "They'll do what they came to do and we'll do what we came to do. And, after all, we must remember: The people looking at us in the newspaper, or watching us on the local news this evening, *won't see* the cameras and the journalists rushing around. They'll only see what we were doing. And we will be doing it with the proper respect and dignity."

The crowd had moved back to make room for the influx of clergy, and after a prayer, Daddy explained the purpose of this service. To set right a wrong; to reconsecrate a sacred object that had been vilified. For the benefit of anyone who didn't know, though it was doubtful such a person was present, he briefly recounted the desecration (". . . by whom, and for what motives we shall perhaps never know") that had occurred at this corner sometime during the predawn hours of Tuesday morning.

"We can't restore what has been lost, we can't make this beloved and beautiful object whole again," he said, "but we can renew our faith in what it stands for. Think of this service as a burial service, if you will; we can't bring the body back as it was, but we can bless its broken pieces and respectfully lay it to rest here on Good Friday, with Easter just around the corner, and, in doing so, affirm our belief in the spirit that it housed, the spirit that continues to live."

The Rev. Dr. Dendy then stepped forward, pulled a notecard from the recesses of his purple-banded sleeves, and intoned his assigned passage from Isaiah in his impressive orator's voice: " 'Behold, I lay in Zion for a foundation a stone, a tried stone, a precious corner stone, a sure foundation: he that believeth shall not make haste. Judgment also will I lay to the line, and righteousness to the plummet: and the hail shall sweep away the refuge of lies, and the waters shall overflow the hiding place.' " Looking well satisfied with his performance, the Rev. Dr. Dendy stepped back, and the notecard disappeared up the voluminous sleeve again.

The Rev. Holt edged modestly to the forefront in his rumpled black robe. He consulted his notecard, which he had not tried to conceal, even during the procession. "A reading from Ephesians," he announced soberly. "Chapter two: verses fourteen through twenty-two." Holding the card some distance away from his eyes, he proceeded to read, in a sincere but lackluster voice, a passage that continued to speak in metaphors about stones and buildings. I began to discern a context in what Daddy and Adrian had spent so much time putting together. However, when the Rev. Holt got to the part about Jesus Christ being the chief cornerstone, I did sneak a nervous glance at the Rabbi from Roanoke. But I needn't have worried. His keen features expressed polite attention to the passage being read, and that was all.

It was Adrian's turn. He stepped forward in his white alb, clearing his throat several times. He sounded as though he were coming down with a cold.

"Please turn to page 761 in your prayer books," he said

hoarsely. "Psalm 118. We'll read verses five through twenty-nine. I'll begin, and we'll alternate. But first, take a moment to look around you, and if you see someone near you who doesn't have a prayer book, please share yours with that person." He paused to allow time for the necessary leafing of pages and shifting about of bodies. Nan MacGruder stepped quietly over to the young man in the wheelchair and offered her open prayer book, indicating to him that she and Milly Winchester could share Milly's book. The Major already had in tow the well-dressed couple from St. Matthias. Dick Smith, fresh from the hospital and glowing with his new fatherhood, practically collided with Ernie Pasco as both rushed forward to press their prayer books on the two workmen in jeans. Dick Smith won.

" 'I called to the Lord in my distress,' " began Adrian Bonner, in a quiet, personal voice, as though he were confiding something private and rather amazing; " 'the Lord answered by setting me free.' "

" 'The Lord is at my side, therefore I will not fear; what can anyone do to me?' " came the murmured response from the gathered group. Some voices sounded more convinced than others. During the beat of silence between the verses, Miriam Stacy's sinuses began to drain.

Adrian withdrew modestly and his rector, Jerry Hope, bustled forth, beaming as though he were about to announce wonderful news. "The Holy Gospel of our Lord Jesus Christ, according to Luke," he proclaimed, his delighted eyes professionally working the crowd, snapping up individuals for acknowledgment, then pausing for a doting freeze-frame of the media people, who suddenly came to life and began scuffling for closer positions. The Reverend Jerry Hope was one of them.

He then read the Crucifixion passage, pausing for a dramatic moment after he had spoken the line "Then said Jesus, 'Father, forgive them; for they know not what they do.' " His eyes worked the crowd again.

A few people crossed themselves. Like a plainclothesman on duty, Ernie Pasco's suspicious brown eyes were darting here and there, hoping to light on The Guilty Face, or Faces that would reveal the telltale remorse over this passage. The two workmen in jeans stood awkwardly sharing Dick Smith's prayer book. Their faces revealed only that they were bogged down somewhere back in the text of Adrian's psalm.

Daddy and Jerry Hope came forward together. Daddy announced that he would now reconsecrate the broken cross and figure; his colleague, the Rector of St. Matthias, would asperse while he himself read from Ezekiel. Following the aspersion, Rabbi Amos Eisenstein, who had kindly driven all the way up from Roanoke to take part in this service, would repeat the same passage from Ezekiel in the language in which it had originally been written in the sixth century before Christ. Then there would be the censing and the closing prayer, after which he himself and a server and members of the vestry of St. Cuthbert's would come forward and carry the pieces of the crucifix back to their church where, in near future, a suitable repository would be built for them in the crypt.

Officious hissings to Franko from Sharon Lake, accompanied by more footwork, were disagreeably audible as Adrian passed the aspersorium to Jerry Hope.

" 'Then will I sprinkle clean water upon you,' " Daddy began reading in his mellow voice, the voice that the late Dr. MacGruder had called "our pulpit treasure," " 'and ye shall be clean . . .' "

Georgie's newspaper camera snapped away. It sounded clumsily staccato and loud, next to the smooth, insidious clicking of Franko's video equipment.

Jerry Hope moved into the ivy and, stooping, began sprinkling water with a silver-handled sponge upon the head and shoulders of the little broken Christ.

". . . 'A new heart also will I give you, and a new spirit will I put within you . . .' " Daddy continued.

Jerry Hope moved slowly, with showmanlike thoroughness, around the ruined crucifix.

"Get closer!" hissed Sharon Lake, forcing an opening for herself, her microphone, and her cameraman-on-a-leash, between the Major and the well-dressed couple. I was trying to honor Daddy's intention of taking no notice of them, but they were making too much noise. I was so busy resenting them that I was distracted from the blessing, which had been the purpose of the whole occasion.

" '*Vezarakti aleichem mayim tehorim* . . .' " The Rabbi was now speaking in a harsh and deeply foreign tongue. He held no book or notecard. He knew his passage by heart. He was impressive and different. He was news in Romulus. The journalists liked him as much as he disliked them. He aimed his face at the sky to avoid looking into their cameras or at the microphone being thrust longingly towards him by Sharon Lake.

Then Ned Block opened the thurible and approached Daddy, who put the incense on the coals, blessed it, and stepped into the ivy himself. As he circled the fallen figure, censing and silently praying the Lord's Prayer, I recalled the many times I had watched him censing the remains of our parishioners in their coffins at the end of the burial service.

"Let us pray," said my father. "Oh, Lord, who on Maundy Thursday didst say to Thy disciples, 'This is my body, broken for you,' permit us to use this occasion to offer Thee all *our* broken parts. We ask Thee to take our broken friendships, our broken dreams, our broken promises, promises we made both to others and to ourselves; take the broken bodies of some of us, and the broken hearts of all of us. And take unto Thee everything about us that we may not know is broken, or is going to be broken, and make all things whole again in Thyself. Amen."

"Amen."

Ned Block reclaimed the thurible. Jerry Hope had held on to the aspersorium, and Adrian took Ben's processional cross. The other clergymen formed a line behind him, and the procession began parting the crowd for the homeward journey. Ben Mac-Gruder stepped into the ivy to give pieces of the reconsecrated figure and cross to the assigned persons. Ernie Pasco got the legs and the vertical to which they were still attached. He proudly staggered into the procession with his burden, which was a double one, since the legs had been severed at the knee. Wirt Winchester and Harlan Buford received an arm each, along with the attached parts of the crossbar. Elaine Major, sturdy purse dangling from a forearm, accepted a kneeling cushion on which had been placed a portion of the smashed extremities. Nan MacGruder, who had taken her late husband's place on the vestry, handed her purse to Harriet and claimed the other kneeling cushion with the rest of the commingled shards of fingers and toes. The two women joined the processional.

Daddy stepped forward and held out his arms for the head of the savior, along with the top piece of the upright. Ben then readjusted the folds of my father's cope. Because of its capelike restrictions, Daddy would have to walk with his hands stretched forward, bearing the head and attached piece of cross upon his inner arms. Ben at last stooped and wrestled the heavy torso piece into his own embrace and slipped into line ahead of Daddy.

Off they went, in silent procession, bearing their blessed figure home.

There was a sudden relapse into formlessness. Though the rest of us belonging to St. Cuthbert's were trying to join the procession, a blockage had arisen, caused by the uncertainty of some people over what to do next, and by the decision of others to depart quickly.

Harriet had gone on ahead of me in the procession, because Miriam Stacy had clutched my arm to tell me how devastated her dear mother would have been if she had lived to see this bare corner, without its precious landmark. I endured her emoting, meanwhile trying to keep us moving along.

Then I noticed two things: one, that the sun was coming out behind the edge of a long purplish cloud. And two, that the TV people and Georgie had all three started running up the middle of the street. They looked as though they intended to run right into the middle of the procession. The TV cameraman, dragging Sharon Lake behind him by her cord, was still shooting, whereas Georgie had stopped taking pictures and was just running.

"It's your father, he's fallen," Harriet called back to me. She broke out of the procession and started running along the grassy embankment by the boxwood hedge.

"Excuse me," I said, jerking my arm from Miriam Stacy's confiding clutch. I shoved past people into the street and started running up the middle of it. Already I could see that the procession had completely broken down by the saucer magnolia, just after the boxwood ends and the walkway up to the church begins.

"Is this part of the service, *too*?" Sharon Lake was demanding.

"No, you ass," Harriet's clear voice sailed back. "The man is *hurt!*"

By the time I managed to push through the circle of people around my father, Harriet was already kneeling on the ground beside him, unbuckling the brooch of his cope. He lay on his back in a curiously flaccid way, under the magnolia.

"Don't try to move him," Harriet was ordering someone. Adrian Bonner, down on his hands and knees close to Daddy's face, his stole falling forward, was repeating, "Father? Father Gower?" in a forlorn voice.

Ben, holding up his skirts, raced towards the rectory as fast as his long legs could carry him.

"He's had a heart attack," said someone.

"He's dead!" cried someone else.

"No, he isn't! See? He just moved that arm."

"His eyes are open. He's looking at something over there on the ground."

"It's the head of the little Christ. He dropped it. Someone pick it up and take it into the church. He doesn't like it lying there on the sidewalk."

"Is anybody calling an *ambulance*?"

"My brother is," said Harriet, freeing my father's shoulders from the heavy cope.

I knelt on the ground between Harriet and Adrian, trying to center myself in my father's gaze. He kept looking urgently to his left. "Daddy? Can you speak to me?"

"I think he's had a stroke," said someone. "See how his mouth and cheek are drooping?"

"Margaret, can you get his collar off, without turning his neck?" Harriet asked.

I slipped my hands carefully beneath his neck, which was slick with sweat, and felt for the gold stud that Father Traherne had given him for his ordination. With difficulty, I began to work it out of the buttonhole in the back of the stiff collar.

"Move *in*, Franko," Sharon Lake ordered her cameraman. "I want to get this. Scrap Varnerstown if we have to."

At what point did he stop recognizing me? At what point did he no longer know I was his daughter anymore? I mean, I know now that as he lay there under the saucer magnolia, he had lost the power to speak, or to understand human speech. If I had known it then, what would I have done? Would I have been able to bear it?

But what did *he* know, as he lay there? What kinds of things could he still know? He couldn't think the word "Margaret," they tell me. He had lost the word for daughter. For female. For person. For body. He could no longer translate his own thoughts into words, or interpret other people's words. But did he still have ways of knowing, from the other parts of his brain, before "all his software" got flooded, as one of the technicians at the hospital was trying (kindly) to explain to me later—did he still have ways of singling me out among the many blobs hovering and pulsing around him, making their unintelligible sounds? (The Major's brain surgeon son Billy told me, after examining the CAT scan pictures, my father was probably still able to hear us. Probably, but not certainly: the hearing center lay awfully close to the speech center. But he could still *see:* the occipital lobe was farther away, herniation had not yet seeped down to destroy it, though he could no longer control the movement of his eyes.)

Could he still recognize, then, that one of those animated blobs above him, coming between him and the sky (only no word for sky anymore) was a *special* blob, connected to him in a way none of the others were, connected from way, way back? The particular one who was removing some choking object from his neck—although he wouldn't have known it was his neck, as such, only that it somehow *belonged* to him and was causing him pain by going *against* him. Would he have been able to feel the powerful waves of concern, of sadness, of love—even if he could never again call them by their name in human language—flowing towards him from that particular figure in the landscape?

Believe it, if it gives you comfort, some say.

But I don't want comfort. I want to know all I can know about what *he* knew and felt.

It seemed forever, but Ben tells me the ambulance was there within seven minutes from the time he called.

And then came the next forever, which Harriet later said had been only about twelve minutes, during which two clean-cut, efficient paramedics (one introduced himself as Paul and asked me about my father's medical history, while his partner went straight to Daddy and began examining him) performed a number of procedures on him.

They put an IV in his arm. The other one, called Steve, had a polite but firm exchange with Harriet, who was being uppity about her premed status. Steve then reached in his pants pocket and handed her a card, which made her blush and go silent when she had read it. But after that, Paul asked her to hold the IV bag. They covered my father's face with a green plastic mask and gave him oxygen. Taking shears from a holster in his belt, Steve cut away my father's alb and clerical shirt; they pasted electrodes on his bare chest and hooked him up via colored cables to a heart monitor. All the time they worked on him, they communicated in a cryptic language that conveyed alternately hopeful and terrible messages. "Airway intact" sounded good, but "aphasic" didn't. Neither did a "blown pupil." What were "occasional PVC's"? What was "Cushing's Reflex"?

While this was happening, many of our parishioners had gone inside the church to pray. I made a mental honor roll, later, of the ones I noticed slipping away to the church. To remind myself how attractive it was, that style of caring. When you realized there was nothing you could do to help, you removed yourself to a middle distance and showed your concern by waiting. And praying. Rather than giving in to that lower part of human nature that relishes sensation, and wants to stick around and "watch what happens," leering and craning and making unhelpful comments, even when you're taking up precious space and oxygen.

Then the one called Steve said, "It's a definite CVA," and, though they didn't alter their efficient demeanor, they became more concerned. Paul looked quickly around at the people gathered in discreet, and not-so-discreet, clusters, and at the television crew. "Let's get him inside the ambulance,"

They went off at a brisk pace to fetch the stretcher. While they were dropping its wheels, I asked Harriet, who was still holding the IV bag, if she knew what they were saying.

"I can't be sure of *all* the words," she admitted humbly. All her arrogance had gone out of her. "But it's a stroke, and it sounds pretty serious."

Paul removed the green mask from Daddy's face and replaced it with a clear mask and Steve rhythmically squeezed an attached bag. Then Paul went around behind my father's head and slipped his hands under his armpits, and Steve lifted his knees, and together they carried him to the stretcher. His body looked loose and floppy between them. The skirt of his alb was hiked up around the knees of his trousers. His chest, white and sunken, was still bared, with the electrodes stuck on it. Where was his stole? I couldn't remember anyone removing it. His long feet in their black shoes dangled. How thin and breakable his ankles looked in their black socks.

They belted him in on the stretcher and wheeled him to the back of the ambulance. Harriet moved obediently along beside, holding aloft the IV bag, until they lifted him into the ambulance and Steve relieved her of her duties.

"You can ride with us," said Paul to me. "Go ahead and sit up front. We have one more thing to do back here." Then he jumped into the rear of the ambulance with Steve and my father and slammed the doors.

Harriet followed me around to the passenger side and gave my shoulder a firm squeeze. "We'll be right behind you," she said.

"You mean at the hospital?" I asked, climbing up into the ambulance.

"At the hospital and . . . whatever. We're your family, too."

"What was that card he gave you?" I asked.

"Oh, just a little something to keep me in my place." She fished in her jacket pocket and handed it over. "I'll go get Nana out of church and we'll follow you to the hospital."

I sat in the cab of the ambulance, with the windows closed, and watched the people milling about or leaving. The air-conditioning was running, so I couldn't hear anything from outside, but I could hear, all too well, the paramedics in back, doing something to my father. I heard Daddy choke, as if he were going to throw up. One of them said: "His gag reflex is normal."

"Is it going in?" the other one asked.

More awful gagging. I wanted desperately to look back through the narrow, open walkway that connected the cab of the ambulance with the back part, but was afraid if I did, they might say I couldn't ride with them. By this time I had read Harriet's card: "WE OPERATE UNDER SPECIFIC PROTOCOL DESIGNED BY THE EMERGENCY PHYSICIANS ADVISORY BOARD IN THIS EMS REGION. IF YOU WISH TO PARTICIPATE IN THIS PATIENT'S CARE, YOU MUST CO-OPERATE WITH THESE PROTOCOLS." Poor Harriet.

Through the opposite window, I saw the WROM-TV van bumping out past the fire hydrant. It turned right and drove off. The show was over. At this location, anyway.

Daddy gagged again. "Got it," said one of them.

"Let me get one more set of vitals," said the other.

Adrian Bonner moved into sight. He was walking slowly along to the sacristy, accompanied by the Rabbi from Roanoke, who was talking. Adrian's head was bent. He nodded, once or twice. He still had the modest look of the low-ranking monk in his white alb. There was something bewildered and lost about him, too. He was holding something between his hands that resembled a small, flat silk pillow. From the protective way he cupped it, I deduced that it was Daddy's folded stole.

Some pump thing was being rhythmically squeezed, in the back of the ambulance, every few seconds.

"He's sky high," said one of the paramedics. "He's gonna blow soon."

It was a fifteen-minute ride from St.Cuthbert's to the hospital. I knew, because I had often driven it with Daddy, when he went to see people there. Old Mrs. Stacy when she was slowly dying. Miriam when she had her hysterectomy, then her gall bladder, then her thyroid operations. The Major after her famous Kidney Stone. So many others. They liked to see a young person's fresh face, Daddy would say. I went to the hospital with him the night Dr. Mac-Gruder, burnt to a crisp from rescuing the horse in the fire, had hung on to life for several hours in the emergency room, but I didn't go in with Daddy to see the patient that time. Daddy went off somewhere alone, with his Oil Stock and purple stole, and I had sat outside in the waiting room with Nan MacGruder, who kept shaking her head and repeating angrily in her smoker's voice, "It wasn't even his horse. That's just so typical of him. It wasn't even worth saving, it had spavin's disease. But that's just so typical of him, too." And then she had said, "He had time for everyone except his own family," and took a handkerchief out of her purse and blew her nose. "*Has* time," she had corrected herself. "He's not gone yet."

The one called Paul drove. He made me put my seat belt on. He asked me how I was doing. How is my *father* doing? I wanted to ask, but was afraid it would violate protocol. Also I wasn't sure I wanted to hear. If I didn't ask, maybe there was still hope.

We wove in and out of traffic, Paul bleeping the siren to clear the way. He parted resistant bottlenecks with a fiercer, high-pitched ululation. "This is Romulus Unit One," he said over his radio.

"Go ahead, Unit One," a woman's voice said.

"We're bringing in a sixty-year-old male, b.p. two-fifty over one-forty, heart rate of forty, with occasional ectopy, right-sided hemoplegia, a blown pupil, and aphasia. Remainder of physical exam unremarkable. We have him monitored and a line of Ringer's Lactate going. He's nasally intubated, and we're hyperventilating him at this time. There is no significant past medical history, and no suspicion of diabetic incident. We have an ETA of fifteen minutes. Any further orders for us?"

"None. Bring him in. We'll be waiting."

* * *

Sixty-year-old male. In the old, unenlightened days of Romulus, days I could still remember, it would have been sixty-year-old *white* male. But we didn't say it like that anymore, even in Romulus.

Nameless to himself by then, he was also nameless to them. He was not the Rev. Walter Gower to them, or even the Rev. "Walton" Gower. That didn't mean they wouldn't do their best for him, but it was his body they were interested in, what was going wrong with that body, what they could do, with all their training and acronymic vocabulary, to fix it. He was a case. A statistic. Sixty-year-old men are statistically slated to fill a certain quota of strokes and heart attacks, and on today's date, Good Friday, 1988, he had contributed his body to the statistical quota.

When did he last truly register me, take me in, think to himself consciously, even if only as a sidebar to his main preoccupation, "Yes, there's my daughter Margaret."

It must have been at the corner. It had to be at the corner, because, after he had fallen, so they tell me, he never knew me as his Margaret again.

He must have looked at me at least once or twice during the service. When, when? And why couldn't I have been looking back? Then I could at least cling to the (small) consolation of a last, remembered, mutual glance between us. So often we had exchanged such glances. *Isn't this awful,* we would communicate wordlessly. Or, *Isn't this grand?* Or, *This isn't as bad as we expected.* Or, *Well, well, this is different from what we expected,* or, *This is a pleasant surprise.*

But, since I can't have that, I'll settle for a last, loving, fully conscious glance from him to me. Maybe it happened while the Rabbi was intoning those harsh, exotic words, to which I was paying attention. Mmm, *very* effective, Daddy may well have been thinking proudly, casting a quick look my way to see that I was feeling the same: *My Margaret looks impressed. Yes, people will remember this service for a long time to come.*

Or perhaps he had looked my way previously, during his own reading of the passage from Ezekiel, when Jerry Hope was aspersing the broken figure. (*She loves and respects her old father, my girl. We haven't done so badly together. We have held the fort.*)

But, oh, God, immediately after my father had begun the

Ezekiel, that was when I had gotten so furious with Sharon Lake and Franko for making their noise, and had been resenting them rather than paying attention to the blessing.

Yes, it was possibly just *then* that Daddy had tried in vain to catch my eye, as a way of sharing with me this moment when he was setting right what had been wronged, performing his job as purveyor—and protector—of heirlooms, as he had described his mission during our last "good night" talk. (During which I had kept falling asleep! What had I missed? At the time I had been furious with myself for missing things about Adrian; now I regretted those little pieces of Daddy's history, which only he could convey to me, and which now were lost forever. And why, why, hadn't I returned his kiss at the sink early on Good Friday morning, before he went out to cut the magnolias for Susan Smith? And just before *that,* I had practically picked a fight with him over the red tulips! I hadn't even looked at him when he left the kitchen. When my father walked out of our kitchen for the last time, I had been rinsing out my oatmeal bowl and completely engulfed in profitless remorse over my backsliding with Ben.)

I hope, if my father *did* happen to look at me at just that moment when I was being so annoyed with the TV people, that he didn't mistake the look on my face for boredom—or annoyance with the service, or—please God, not—with *him.*

I could write a handbook on mourning: how it weaves in and out of the ordinary traffic of your days, for weeks and months (and maybe years), sometimes diverting you with just a sharp little *blip* of reminder, like the warning blips from Paul's siren ("Pull over to the side of whatever you are doing, and remember!"); other times bringing you to a full stop with a piercing, extended wail, requiring you to leave traffic altogether, turn your ignition off, put your head down on the steering wheel, let yourself be overwhelmed by the incredible words "Never Again," and wait for your breath to come back.

And the ache that you treasure, that unique, wrenching ache that you hoard: you go looking for it. Contrary to what so many people try to tell you, people who want to divert you away from the "painful" topic, people who proudly assure you they have "been through it" and "it will get better in time," you want to dwell in its presence, you want to protect it from this heartless, future "time" they promise you is on its way, you want to dwell in the presence of the pain, the mystery of its hold on you.

You feel more at home in the presence of the living mystery than with any strained and false "wisdom." You seek out objects and places that will feed the mystery. A renewed passport that will never be stamped by any immigration official; a thick stand of ivy at a corner from which debris must still be removed, even though there is no cross there anymore; the way the light falls on a study desk at a certain time of day, when you are cleaning out the drawers; the cemetery, with all the dates now filled in, on a certain jointly shared stone, visited faithfully every Sunday.

You become aware of parallels that have the power to bend time into the circle it perhaps is. You court these parallels, or "coincidences": the prophecy of the driver's gray-haired, half-wit sister croaking from a school bus, "THAT MAN . . . HURT!" being fulfilled sixteen years later as Harriet's sharp, vindicating announcement slices the air: "No, you ass. The man is *hurt!*"

And the fact that you lost both of them, Mother, then Father, at this corner. You last laid eyes on each of them, as whole and functioning parents, at the corner of Macon and Church streets. They both last looked on *you* (or, you want to hope they did) at this corner, and both times you weren't looking back.

You don't want the ache to go away, because as long as it's there, so are they. They make a place for themselves in the center of the ache, and you can go on living together that way for quite a while. They can go on living *physically* in you, as long as the ache is physically present.

Another time-bending parallel: I think Daddy did this, too. He did what I am doing now. For sixteen years, he did it for my mother, after she was gone. He hollowed out a place for her and kept it raw and deep with his unanswered questions.

He drew me with him into the living ache, and between us we kept her alive. So that the three of us, in a sense, *did* remain together and go on living in the rectory as a family of sorts for the next sixteen years.

XI: THE WITCH'S CLOSET

I graduated in May. I was physically present for the ceremony, because it would have disappointed Mrs. Dunbar and Professor Stannard if I had just driven home to Romulus and waited for my diploma to arrive in the mail. So for their sakes, I stood in cap and gown on the lawn with my class, and the two of them took me out for dinner at the Old Mill Room in the Boar's Head Inn. The waitresses were colonially attired and the Professor and Mrs. Dunbar were quite debonair with each other. They tried to be both parents and grandparents to me that day, and I colluded with them in their effort, being daughterly and granddaughterly in return.

Down in Chapel Hill, Ben and Nana and the MacGruder parents from Washington watched Harriet stand up with her Bachelor of Science peers, who threw their caps into the air. Harriet got somebody else's cap when they fell down again, and it kept slipping down over her nose during the recessional. But the Nursing graduates stole the show. When *their* group was called, they released into the air a huge balloon man representing a patient in a hospital gown. Up he bobbled into the stratosphere, wide-eyed at his own resurrection. The whole stadium roared with laughter and amazement, Harriet said. The funny thing was, I "remembered" more of Harriet's graduation than I did my own, though I hadn't been in Chapel Hill that day. But then, I'd had much training in putting pictures to other people's descriptions of things. All those old "pictures" of Ruth, doing and saying things far back before I could possibly have registered them, created from my father's stories.

Graduate. From the Latin base-word *gradus,* meaning step. As are also the words "gradation," "gradient," "gradual."

I "graduated." Six weeks ago, the university would not have given me a diploma, yet in what discernible ways was I now more educated? I had put in some more hours in classrooms, hours during which my mind dwelled mostly on other matters. I had made a "Chaucer chart," at the desk in Dee Dee's old bedroom, upstairs at Mrs. Dunbar's, in order to fix in my mind the order of the pilgrims, their status in society and their relations to one another, and who told which story and why, for Professor Stannard. I had turned out the two-short-papers-in-lieu-of-a-final-exam for my Modern Lit. course, one paper on Faulkner's *The Bear* (which I thuddingly endured, but for which I managed to formulate a convincing show of respect: the professor was a Faulkner worshiper), the other on Virginia Woolf's "The Mark on the Wall," in which I competently digressed on "The Organizing Power of the Object." For my American Civ. course, I wrote a paper on the Depression, largely because the word "depression" aroused a feeling of nostalgia in me.

At the same desk, in between the tasks whose completion would turn me into a "graduate," I had burned votive candles, one after another, with a photograph of my father propped between their spritely little flames, and penned thank-you notes to people back in Romulus on the kid finish ecru informals that Mrs. Dunbar kept me supplied with from her stationer's. "I went through all this after my darling Poppy passed, and it's still fresh as yesterday in my mind," she had said. This was after explaining to me gently that I mustn't think of using the ample stock of embossed cards

> To thank you for
> your kindness and sympathy
> at a time when it was
> deeply appreciated

given to me free by the funeral home.

"You can't send cards with a printed message on them, my

darling, even if you *do* write something personal inside. It's just not the custom. I hope you don't mind my butting in, but I feel I must be a sort of stand-in for your dear mother, you know."

I didn't mind her butting in. I loved her for her perfect understanding of my rituals. When she would tiptoe in her high heels into Dee Dee's old room, to bring me a glass of iced tea and a plate of hot Toll-House cookies while I wrote the thank-you notes on the correct stationery, I didn't mind that she saw the votive candles and Daddy's picture and the gold collar stud placed exactly in the center, like a sacred relic, between the flickering flames.

"Such a charming man," she would comment, putting down her offerings on the outskirts of my little altar. "Though I only got to meet him once or twice. And you took that photo of him and even developed it yourself, didn't you?"

"It's kind of grainy, but I like his expression. It was when I was taking a photography course my last year in high school. I waited outside his study until he stopped typing his sermon for Sunday, and then I burst in on him. I caught some of his thoughts still on his face. And I like all those books on the desk. I like to see how many of the titles I can make out and remember what he was reading at the time."

"Do you know what I used to do after Poppy died?"

"What? Please sit down for a minute, Mrs. Dunbar."

"I don't want to take up your time, darling. You have all those notes to write . . ."

"No, no, I've finished all the ones for food; now I'm just answering the letters."

"Bless your heart, you're like I was. You don't *strictly* have to acknowledge the letters, but I wanted to, too. It kept me linked to him."

"What was it you used to do after Mr. Dunbar died?"

"Well, I would go around to all the rooms where he kept his jackets—I told you, he always kept jackets and ties in all the closets, in case a student dropped by to see him—and I would *sniff* each and every jacket. The winter ones and the summer ones. The tweedy ones kept his particular smell on them the longest. It was his absolutely unique smell, a mixture of his pipe tobacco and his aftershave and just *him.* Poppy's skin had an odor sort of like fresh-baked bread. I was very sad when the smell faded away completely from the last jacket."

Dee Dee, who dropped down from Washington in late April
for one of her recriminatory weekends with her mother, offered
me her own style of sympathy after she had sent Mrs. Dunbar out
of the living room in tears: "Look at it this way, Margaret. He
didn't suffer. He didn't linger. He won't have to grow old and rot
and lose his marbles and wet his bed and feel he's a burden to you.
And *you* won't have to lie awake at night feeling guilty as shit
because you're plotting how to drag him off to a nursing home. I
know you don't want to hear this now, but you're in an enviable
position. Unlike *some* of us, you are completely free."

Yes, I was completely free. "Free." A word as dubiously desirable to me as the word "normal."

Every weekend, in that interim after "Easter vacation" and
before "graduation," I drove home from Charlottesville to Romulus. "Home." All these supposedly desirable words had acquired
mocking, or downright sinister, overtones.

Every weekend before the end of my final term, I got in my
Honda Prelude, found for me secondhand by our faithful Ernie
Pasco, and headed west on 64, north on 81, and off, ultimately,
onto the winding country road into Romulus, with the mountains
on my right. The cherry, apple, and redbuds now wore look-alike
green foliage. After crossing the river bridge that rattled and
shook, I never stopped at the Sampson Fish Market. I preferred
the impersonality of the supermarket. I bought frozen dinners
and packaged bread, and cheese and ice cream, and orange juice
made from concentrate. Sometimes, I stopped by the ABC store
and bought a new fifth of Daddy's old Scotch. I bought no beer.

Then I would drive slowly, or not-so-slowly, up Church Street,
depending on the traffic condition of the hour. As of May 1, Mr.
Gaines's $30,000, accepted by our vestry and deposited in Harlan
Buford's bank, would begin earning the best interest rates available for St. Cuthbert's general fund; the bulldozers were due to
arrive at our corner the first of June.

I would park in front of the rectory and be grateful if there
was no one around: no helpful parishioners trimming the boxwood hedge (and butchering it, for no one had Daddy's expertise
with the clippers), or poking around the flower borders, or polishing brass in the sacristy, but with an ear cocked for my arrival,
so they could rush out and "see how I was doing." My father's

maroon Volvo was gone: Ernie Pasco had been able to get a good price for it from his nephew, and the money went into my "fund." The parishioners had also taken up a special collection and so I now had five thousand dollars to assist me in embarking on my "future."

Then I would carry my groceries and my books up to the house and unlock the front door and take a deep breath and step inside. I would put everything down on the floor, and jealously shut the door behind me. The first moments were always the most powerful: there *were* still emanations of him here. His presence seemed to have just gone ahead of me down the shadows of the hall to his study. I would "follow" him to the study, aching in my chest and fingertips as I opened the door. I kept hoping against hope that he would appear to me, swiveling around in his chair from his typewriter, or looking up, bleary-eyed, from too much reading. Wearing his old sweater. After Mrs. Dunbar had told me about Poppy's jackets, I couldn't wait to get home again and sniff the sweater. But Daddy hadn't been a smoker, didn't use after-shave, and hadn't smelled of freshly baked bread. And also, it had been washed so recently. I indulged in a bout of what I knew was unjustified resentment of Ben, for washing the sweater, even though I had been planning to wash it myself. Then I took to wearing it, which was more successful. At night I slipped into the black paisley silk dressing gown I had given him for Christmas. Wearing his clothes, drinking his drink, eating his food: the nearest you can get to "This is my body. Do this in remembrance of me." I wondered if one or two of the more inconsolable disciples hadn't made off with some of Jesus' garments, and put them on in secret after he was gone, and caressed their folds and sniffed the sleeves and felt in the pockets (if there were any pockets) for surprises. Had Jesus, like Mr. Dunbar, had "an absolutely unique smell"? Quite probably he did. Palestine had a hot climate and people didn't bathe all that much. I tried to summon back Daddy's smell—he must have had one—but couldn't. He wasn't a smell sort of person. His voice, however, the cadences of his voice, and, somehow, his *thoughts,* his choice of words and the likely progressions of his mental life, were still very accessible to me, and, remarkably, were to become more so as time went on.

I went through the rectory listening for echoes, alert for visitations of whatever kind might be vouchsafed to me. And then, of course, there were the *real* visitors, some more welcome than others, but, either way, there was no getting out of answering the doorbell whenever it rang. I was still the Rector of St. Cuthbert's daughter. I had certain duties, even if only to honor my father's memory. And, while I often resented the intrusion into my haunted solitude, I also took pleasure in fulfilling the obligations that would very soon be coming to an end. Though everybody was being very tactful about it, my days in the rectory were numbered. "Home" would soon no longer be home. Rectories have to have rectors in them. For the time being, minimal services were being conducted by various supply priests sent by the diocese, but an "interim rector" had been found for the summer—a schoolteacher-priest from Harrisonburg, one of the many priests without a church in our shrinking denomination—and as of June 15, he would be living here.

Not that I would be "homeless." Far from it. People were practically fighting over who was going to get me to move in with them. Mrs. MacGruder took it for granted I belonged to them. In my father's will—an old one, made just after Ruth was killed—he had "left" me to the MacGruders. But though I hadn't out-and-out refused Nan MacGruder yet, I was determined not to unpack my bags in either her town or lakeside house. It would be tantamount to giving up the struggle. It would be a kind of incest. Little brother Ben and I would watch more videos and fall into our old ways. We might even fall into marriage, one of these days. And I did not want to fall into marriage, without falling in love, even if it meant remaining single.

The Major, God help me, had her heart set on a "puh-fect" solution to my homelessness and her encroaching old age. I was to become her "daugh-tah," move in with her, take tennis lessons every day at the Club ("Your mo-thah would have liked that."), and receive a sort of stipend (a very generous one) for being on call to drive her places if the time came when she could no longer drive herself, and do a bit of gardening work ("Your fa-thah was such a devoted gah-den-ah. He would like that."). She broadly hinted that, if I acceded to her perfect solution, I would be compensated with full daughterly status in her will.

"And, of coahse, Mah-garet, it goes without saying: you will have puh-fect freedom to go and come as you like in this house. You will be completely your own puh-son."

Uh-huh.

Meanwhile, Mrs. Dunbar awaited me back in Charlottesville.

She had cajoled me into leaving some boxes behind, "Just . . . you know . . . for good luck's sake, darling. For *my* good luck, I mean. This will always be your home. Even if you decide not to go on to graduate school. Oh, I think it's a shame about that grant. Professor Stannard was so upset about the committee picking that foolish project over your wonderful St. Hilda proposal. I mean, I know we didn't do right by the Indians . . . or 'Native Americans,' I believe we're supposed to call them now, to show that they were here first, but really, who wants to read about . . . I can't even remember the name of that other girl's project, it's so outlandish . . ."

" 'Subversive Feminist Thought in the Oral Tradition of Cherokee Native American Women.' "

"Oh, my goodness me. Will somebody please tell me when those poor women had the *time* for any 'subversive feminist thoughts'? They were too busy having babies, and getting packed up to be forced off their land and onto their Trail of Tears. That *was* the Cherokees, wasn't it, who got banished to Oklahoma? Well, I wish that rich donor and her trendy committee the pleasure of their foolishness. Professor Stannard says there are plenty of other scholarships available . . . maybe not that lucrative, but with your immaculate average . . . ! And I would be able to contribute some. In fact, I've already talked it over with Buddy and Dee Dee. You're just like a daughter, and Poppy and I sent *our* daughter through college and would have continued to support her through graduate school, if that had been her wish. Buddy and Dee Dee are *thrilled* with the prospect of your staying on. Dee Dee, bless her heart, she can be abrasive sometimes, but she really does worry about me . . . she frankly admitted it would be a great load off her mind, to know you were staying on here."

Another offer—of sorts—had come in from an unlikelier quarter. Aunt Con, my mother's sister, now widowed and living in Atlanta, had put in *her* claim—of sorts. I had notified her on Easter weekend, because I thought I ought to, but she surprised everyone by showing up in Romulus late Monday afternoon, the day before the funeral. She had flown to Charlottesville and hired a car and driver to deliver her and her two tapestry suitcases to the front door of the rectory. Then she equally amazed everyone by paying off the driver and sending him back to Charlottesville.

I put her in the downstairs guest room, where she unpacked her voluminous smart outfits, plugged in her hot curlers, and set out her perfumes, her jewelry case, and her Bible on the small desk. Her husband had left her "well off," she said, and recently she had found Jesus. She was appalled to learn there was no full-length mirror in the house. She wept over my father (whom she hadn't liked; he had told me so, and the feeling was mutual), and over her poor sister, and over me. She wept easily, almost in a sociable manner, and changed clothes often. She was handsome, in a bold, overdone sort of way, with her striped hair and heavily made-up, feline-shaped face; I kept stealing glimpses at her, hoping to catch a likeness to the Ruth I remembered. But Aunt Con was a woman in her late forties and Ruth had been twenty-eight when I last saw her.

She made herself at home in the rectory, playing the heavy aunt to me, after having virtually ignored me ever since my mother's funeral. To give her credit, she was helpful. She kept lists, served drinks and food to people, and sent the men on errands and to the liquor store. She had the best time of anyone there. She flirted with Adrian Bonner and asked him when he had found Jesus. Deep into his cold by then, his gray eyes glazed over with fever, he had gazed upon her as he might some wild apparition, and after thinking a minute replied hoarsely that, in his case, it might be more accurate to say that Jesus had found him. Aunt Con simply adored his answer, and would have hugged him, if he hadn't stepped back, politely pleading his cold. Soon after, I heard her ask Nan MacGruder the same question, but Mrs. MacGruder simply replied that she hadn't known Jesus was lost.

She kept her arm possessively draped around me, and boasted to everyone how she was going to "adopt" me, if I'd let her. Perhaps we would take a trip to Egypt and the Holy Land this summer . . . no, summer was too hot over there; better wait till fall. She fingered my hair and face as if I were her doll, and ran her eyes up and down my figure, commenting on my "possibilities." Her best girlfriend in Atlanta ran a designer boutique and together they would take me in hand. She knew, she declared, giving me a little squeeze, just how she was going to "dress" me. She was constantly reminding me, bursting into a fresh shower of tears each time, that her baby sister had been coming to live with her after college, if my father hadn't proposed, and now, if *I* came to Georgia after my graduation, it would be fulfilling an old dream.

Her departure was just as stunning as her arrival had been. On

Wednesday morning, when all the excitement was over, and the two of us might have had to sit down alone in the empty rectory and talk seriously, the same driver magically appeared at our door, and she handed him her tapestry suitcases, then hung back for a flurry of tears and kisses before speeding off to make her connection to Atlanta. "You always know where you can reach me, precious. You are my baby sister's own child, and my home will always be your home. You believe me, don't you? We're going to do fun things together and be *real* close. I was never able to have babies. Endometri—oh, I can never pronounce it, but it means your female parts are all squishy and undependable. Now listen, precious, I *mean* this: you call me *whenever* you need me, I don't care if it's three in the morning. In fact"—laughing through her tears, and glancing quickly at her diamond-studded gold watch— "three in the morning's not a bad time. I'm sure to be home by then, sipping a little nightcap and reading my Bible."

She had called me once, shortly after her return home, to ask me if I would be "a precious" and look around the rectory for a lost earring. I did so, found it under her bed, and mailed it to her, registered, as she'd requested. I didn't hear from her after that, and had yet to call her, at three A.M., or any other time.

But I have to admit that, in a strange way, her bizarre presence during those three days probably kept me going. "Aunt Con" at the rectory was so unlikely, so unreal, that surely all the rest of this had to be, too, and thus I was able to endure it.

The liturgy for the dead, in our church, is an Easter liturgy. It finds its meaning in the Resurrection. It is characterized by joy in the certainty that "neither death, nor life, nor angels, nor principalities, nor powers, nor things present, nor things to come, nor height, nor depth, nor any other creature" shall be able to separate us from the love of God.

The earliest accounts we have of human practices describe rites and ceremonies that filled the time between death and burial. As Dr. Marion Hatchett writes, in his chapter on the burial of the dead in *Commentary on the American Prayer Book,* the rites were created to insure that the dead were, in fact, really dead (and not in a coma or a trance) and that they stayed dead. The rites were also designed to carry the members of the community through their dealings with grief, realign the family structure, and redistribute the property and community responsibilities of the de-

ceased so that the family and community could continue on their
daily rounds.

The rites of burial for the very first Christians were probably
not very different from those of the Jews, who were especially
zealous in the care of their dead; but then, as the number of
Gentile Christians increased, customs derived from pagan practice were incorporated.

Pagan burial customs included the *viaticum*, the last meal for
the dead, or the coin for the ferryman who would carry the dead
across the Styx only if he got paid. They also included the final
kiss; the arranging, washing, anointing, and clothing of the body;
processions with torches, dirges, lamentations, and black clothes.
Before burial, there was the *vale*, or ceremony of farewell, and the
funeral oration. If the body did not go into the ground on the day
of death, a wake, or vigil, was customary.

The early Christians substituted communion for the *viaticum*
and rejected the use of torches in procession because of their
association with the emperor cult. Psalms, hymns, and Alleluias
replaced the lamentations and dirges, and also substituted for the
vale. The early Church fathers, such as St. Cyprian, frowned on
mournful corteges and penitential psalms and the wearing of
black. "Divine summons ought not to be mourned," wrote Cyprian
in his *De Mortalitate*. The dead are not lost, he said, but gone
before us. "While appearing to lose, they have really gained
ground, as travelers and navigators are wont to do." Therefore
Christians should wear white at funerals, said Cyprian, not black
as the heathen do.

But around the year 1000, the attitude of Christians towards
their departed began undergoing a marked change from enthusiasm and glad confidence to an emphasis on God the just and
terrible judge, as well as the lugubrious certainty that just about
everyone was booked for stays of varying lengths of time in Pur-
gatory. Black was reinstated as the de rigueur funeral color, and
the sentiments of the *Dies Irae*, that grisly masterpiece of medieval
religious poetry, replaced Cyprian's happy images of fortunate
travelers and vanguard navigators.

Ironically, it was not until the 1979 prayer book, over which
my father suffered such misgivings, that this joyful attitude to
funerals was fully reinstated. Black palls and chasubles were
stored in mothballs, and white was the preferred color again.

Daddy, being Daddy, had found the somber note of the older rites more attractive, though he did admit that the burial services in the new prayer book *had* restored many beautiful ancient texts and ceremonies that had gotten evicted during the Reformation.

We did all right by him, I think. Compromises were made between present and past. There was a white pall on top of the coffin, along with his white stole and old biretta, but the chasuble he wore inside was purple, the color of sorrow and penitence. Though both bishops who officiated at the funeral (the Bishop of the Diocese, and Charlie Major, who flew back from Arizona) were new prayer book men, he got all his old Sarum medieval favorites at the vigil the night before. Adrian and I saw to that. And Ned Block, who proved to be a mine of helpful liturgical lore as well as a masterful organizer. It was Ned who dug out the six bier lights and polished them himself. It was Ned who set up the all-night chain of prayer among our parishioners, and saw to it that the coffin was correctly placed. (A priest's body is placed in the choir, not the nave, and with his head towards the altar.) What a pity Ned Block hadn't been able to become a deacon. All those years of moving toy soldiers around his empty desk and traveling around the state to reenact old Civil War battles in his antique uniform, when he could have been helping Daddy instead of finding fault.

And when I summoned Adrian to the hospital late Good Friday night, with his Oil Stock and stole, after the neurologist had told the nurses in the Intensive Care Unit that I had permission to stay with my father all through the night, it was the Ancient Western form of Extreme Unction we both agreed Daddy, had he been able to ask for it himself, would have wanted Adrian to use: the form in which *all* seats of the senses are anointed: the eyes, the ears, the nostrils, the lips, the hands (palms of the hands for lay persons, backs of hands for priests), the feet.

It was to Adrian that a more difficult task was presently to fall. Or, rather, he volunteered. Jerry Hope would have done it, but Daddy would rather have had Adrian.

Morticians know a lot; they dress the dead every day. But they prefer to have another priest vest a dead priest. To make sure everything goes on in the right order and that the cincture is knotted correctly, all that kind of thing.

So on Saturday evening I packed Daddy's bag for Adrian, with a brand-new set of Fruit of the Loom underwear bought last Monday at the Mall, after we'd gone to the travel agent's to book our tickets to England; I put in knee-length black socks, his newest pair of Johnston & Murphy black wing-tip shoes, the black trousers from his best suit, a clean clerical shirt, and collar.

I had a moral dilemma over Father Traherne's gold collar stud. Should it be buried with Daddy, or should I keep it? I wanted to keep it, but I wanted to do what he would like.

While Adrian and I were over in the sacristy, selecting the vestments, I asked him what he thought Daddy would have wanted. "Father Traherne was his spiritual father," I explained.

"Yes, I know," Adrian said. "He talked about Father Traherne very often to me."

"But, on the other hand," I said, "I would like to hold on to it. I took it out of his collar for the last time, when we were waiting for the ambulance. His neck was so warm. *It* was warm. I kept in my pocket and touched it a lot during those sixteen hours at the hospital. I thought that maybe if I kept touching it . . . well, you know. It has many old associations. And also, I hope this doesn't sound ghoulish, I value it because his sweat is still somewhere on it."

"It doesn't sound ghoulish," he said gently, with his strange, new hoarse voice from the cold. "Listen, Margaret, would you let me contribute a collar stud of my own? Your father was my Father Traherne. I don't have a gold one, but I'll take this one I'm wearing . . . when I'm at the mortuary, I promise I'll take it from my own warm neck and . . ."

He broke down. He put his hands over his face and, standing quite straight, in the middle of the sacristy, with Daddy's purple chasuble and the other garments already removed and hanging on their hanger, proceeded to sob like a child. I wanted to touch Adrian, and yet I didn't move. Over the past fifteen hours, I had been kissed and hugged and squeezed and patted and cried on by at least seventy or eighty human beings, and my predominant feeling, even towards the ones I cared about, had been one of charitable forbearance: I had to let them do it, because they needed it, and their belief that I needed it, and that they were able to supply it, made them feel better. Yet all the while, the touch I wanted to preserve, the last touch of my father's face against my cheek, his forehead against my lips, moments after his spirit had left his body, was being rubbed away by every intervening kiss; the visceral recall of my last contact with his body became more obscured with every passing touch and breath.

I didn't want to intrude on Adrian, in case he was hoarding some last remembered physical touch of his own.

And so, holding my own shoulders quite straight, letting my hands hang down at my sides, I stood there in the sacristy and let him sob. I drank him in with my eyes, but I did not allow myself to touch him. I imagined him as a boy in that orphanage up on the cold north lakes, on the day it finally dawned on him that he had been abandoned forever. I would bet anything he had stood like this then: defying with his ramrod-straight body the inconsolable truth that was flooding his soul, while he sobbed behind hands pressed flat against his face.

While I waited, I searched for words. I would have to say something, and the right words were so important. As in that long-ago telephone conversation with Ruth, after she had agreed to make the Golden Egg. "It should have something with you in it," I had said, and she had been so pleased.

"I'm sure my father loved you," I said to Adrian Bonner, while his hands still covered his face. "After we got home from your house last Monday night and I gave him the prayer book and he read your inscription, he told me, 'The fact that a man of Adrian Bonner's caliber should treasure my friendship makes it all seem worthwhile.'"

The sobs subsided. "And for what it's worth," I went on, "I want you to know I also love you. For his sake, and also because of what you are."

He took down his hands from his face, which was truly a mess, and held them out to me. I took them. They were wet.

"Oh, Margaret, what are we going to do without him?" he croaked in a hoarse whisper.

"I don't know," I said.

Then he put his arms around me and held me. He held me in a manner no different from the dozens of other sympathetic embracers, but he was the first person whose closeness did not in any way obscure my father's touch. And I savored him for his own sake alone. I felt Adrian Bonner from top to bottom and through and through.

During the many times I have relived that quarter of a minute in the sacristy, an intimation has slowly formed itself in me. An intimation of exactly *what,* I'm not sure, but it goes like this: Is there something in the feeling—however fleeting, or ultimately mistaken, or soon to be disappointed—of *having found the one you love and believing your love might be returned* that may be all we know (or remember) of a better state of being?

I don't know why certain people communicate this possibility, or intimation, to us: some affinity in them, perhaps, some "wave particles" (*pace*, Ben!) that flow from them to us. Often it may be something in them that even they don't recognize. Often they are not all they could be, themselves. But some intensity in them exactly matches some intensity in us. An essentialness in one person meets a similar essentialness in another. Their harmonics, even if only temporarily, coincide. The poets would call it love; the psychologists would call it libido or transference; others would call it just plain old sex. But do any of those words fully embrace it? It's through the body, but it's also beyond the body. The part of us that goes out of us when our body dies, that part I saw *missing* from my father's face, moments after his body died, has a great deal, perhaps everything (despite how we go on about physical appearance) to do with it, though it is bound to express itself through the body. Since we are not ethereal spirits, what other way does it have to express itself?

Certain people pass through our lives and have a gift to give us by arousing intense longings. These longings may last only moments, or they may last years; some people, like Dante, have been know to make them last a lifetime; he passed Beatrice on a bridge and produced great art out of the resulting (unrequited) feelings. But whatever the outcome of these feelings—whether they lead to art, or marriage, or merely an occasional wistful pang—mightn't they also suggest to us the possibility of a union far better than anything we have so far known? Else, why do we *yearn*? If there are yearnings towards something, surely there must be the thing that inspired it: the incomparable essence, sending its waves (or feelings) back to us from somewhere.

I could not imagine the things that Adrian felt at the funeral home later that evening when he did what he went to do. Or no, I could. I could. I followed him right along in my imagination; my "respectful imagination," as Professor Stannard had called it, "which is, to my way of thinking, another definition of empathy."

I didn't ask Adrian about it afterwards. I probably wouldn't have, even if he hadn't gotten so sick and thus effectively managed to remove himself from the scene for the rest of April and well into the middle of May.

"Margaret, I know you're grieving, and also I've turned you off in some way, but I'm worried about you. Every time I come over, you're wearing his old sweater and burning votive candles in his study and drinking Scotch and watching that *tape*. I'm beginning to be sorry I ever made it. I knew you'd probably want to see it, but you're making it into a fetish. Every time I come over, you're watching it."

"Well, maybe you should stop coming over so much. Oh, please, Ben, don't goad me into saying hurtful things."

"It's all right. Say them. At least I hear the sound of your voice. Margaret, it's been almost two months now . . ."

"Seven weeks. Seven weeks ago at four A.M. on Holy Saturday. Tonight is the Eve of Pentecost. And I'm glad you had the foresight to tape the newscast that Friday evening. It was the most thoughtful thing in the world you could have done for me, taping that service. I'll always be grateful to you for it. I *like* watching it. It gives me comfort. I see his face in its last conscious moments, I hear him speaking when he knew what words were. I *hear his last words*, though that bitch cut him off midway through his closing prayer. I see him . . . fall. It's not a fetish, Ben, to want to watch the last fully conscious moments of the person you loved. How many people would give anything for such a tape! I only wish there were more of him in it, and less of the Rabbi and Jerry Hope, and all that panning of faces in the crowd. And why did they keep going back to that man in the wheelchair? What were they hoping for? For him to get up and walk?"

"Yeah, I know what you mean. They had enough of a scoop, as it was. Listen, Margaret, I came over tonight to tell you something that will please you."

"I'd be interested to hear it."

"I just came by to say that if you're holding out on Harriet and Nana about moving into the lake house with them for the summer because I'll be underfoot, that problem is solved. I'm going to summer school. I flunked Physics and I have two incompletes to make up. I won't promise not to come home *some*, but you have my word of honor I will not impose my beastly proximity upon you when I do."

"That's very thoughtful of you, but I still haven't made up my mind about this summer, Ben."

"But you have to live somewhere. They've booked that Father What's-his-name to move in here the fifteenth of June."

"Don't you think I know that? Listen, I'm trying just to live a day at a time, and feel what I feel when I feel it, and do what has to be done before Father What's-his-name moves in. Why can't you let me be? I want to roam around here however I please in the only home I've ever known. What I wear, and what I drink, and the way I spend my time is my business. I want to remember all I can. I want to *absorb* my life, as far as I've gotten with it. And I want to understand the meaning of my father's . . ."

"Your father's death."

"My father's *life*. His completed life. Will you please let me finish my own sentences?"

"I'm getting that familiar feeling that I have overstayed. I guess I'll see you in church tomorrow. I'm serving, though I'm not very enthusiastic about it."

"Who's on tomorrow?"

"Nana says that old retired guy again, who won't look anybody in the eye and is always ten minutes late. Take care of yourself, Margaret. I'm sorry if I hassled you about your future."

"And *I'm* sorry I snarled. Please don't worry about my future, and tell everyone else to stop worrying. If I keep on living, I'm bound to have one. It's just that, well, it's as if I'm *waiting to hear*, or something. And I haven't heard yet."

"Okay, I'll run along. Maybe you'll hear something tonight. After all, if it's the Eve of Pentecost . . ."

As soon as I heard his car drive off, I watched the tape again, all the way through, with no rewinds and replays, or fast forwards. There were only a few glimpses of Adrian; on television, his was the kind of face you'd pass right over. Neither his intensity nor his repose showed through; of course, he had been coming down with his cold.

When my father made his failed effort, during the procession back to the church, to shift Christ's head to his left arm (that was because, I now knew, he had suddenly lost the use of his right arm) and then stumbled and fell, I had to stop myself from pressing the Rewind button and going through it again. This was where I always reproached myself for not having taken better care of him in the days beforehand. If I had only made him go to a doctor *the very next morning* after his "bout of forgetfulness" at Adrian's on Monday night, he might still be alive today. Because, what he'd had that Monday at Adrian's when he completely lost his speech and power of understanding for a moment, the neurologist at the hospital explained to me, had been a warning that a hemispheric stroke was on its way. He'd had something called a TIA (another one of those ominous acronyms), a transient ischemic attack, caused by a temporary impediment of blood flow through certain vessels.

In some cases, surgery was advisable. They could have done the surgery. Sometimes that involved nothing more than cleaning out a fatty deposit and improving the blood flow. In other cases, all they had to do was prescribe the proper anticoagulant. Often, the only preventative needed was two aspirin tablets once a day for the rest of your life. Two aspirin tablets a day for the rest of his life! We had aspirin in all our medicine chests. And a bottle in the kitchen cabinet, next to the spice rack. All that aspirin, already in the house.

"If only I had known, I mean, I could have . . . If I had *known,* I would have . . . he could be . . ." I had babbled to Bishop Major, who had come straight to the rectory from the airport, hustled me off to my father's study, away from the mourners filling the house, and closed the door.

"If I had known what was happening during his talk last Monday night, I could have . . ."

"Now listen here, Margaret. Are you listening?" The big pink man with his patriarchal gray beard and imposing magenta shirt-front seized me by my shoulders and fairly shook me.

"Yes, Bishop Major."

"Are you God, Margaret?"

"No."

"You're sure about that, now?"

"Yes, sir."

"Then step down, and let Him get on with His job. Okay?"

"Okay."

"You know your father loved you, don't you?"

"Yes, sir."

"And you loved him?"

"Well, *yes.*"

"Well, then, if you two puny mortals could feel such love and concern for each other, don't you think God, who thought all this up in the first place, is capable of some love Himself ?"

"Yes, sir." I knew this was not the right time, nor was I with the right person, to bring up any theological quibbles.

Considering the matter closed, he had promptly crushed me to him in a bear hug, and released me. "Trust God to take care of your father, and know what's best for him, and trust *us*, a little, to take care of you. Mother already announced to me when she called Arizona that *she* intends to take care of you, God help you." Then he had winked at me. "As you know, I dearly love my mother, but she goes in a little too much for knowing what's best for others. You'll have to assert yourself, if you understand my point. I'm sure you will take this little confidence in the loving spirit in which it is offered."

"The Reverend Gower was rushed to Memorial Hospital, where he remains in critical condition . . . stay tuned after these messages for more Romulus News Roundup . . . I'm your host, Hartwell Congdon, and we'll be heading in our next segment over to Varnerstown, where the limestone workers are still negotiating for their . . ."

The end of the news on the tape, as far as I was concerned. Press Stop. Rewind. (I knew I'd be watching it again tomorrow.) Turn off the power on the set.

To the kitchen for a cheese sandwich and ice cream. The last meal he had ever made for himself, because I had been up on the parkway. I had seconds on the ice cream, and poured some Scotch over it, as a sort of sauce, also to make the transition to alcohol more palatable. Then I took a glass of Scotch back to the study and started on the middle desk drawer. All those old *Forward Day by Days*. Would Father What's-his-name find them useful? Why should I care whether he would, or not? He would have his own sources and keepsakes, and would expect empty drawers to put them in.

Into the wastebasket, all except for the last one, which I kept as a memento. February through April, 1988, with a lovely reproduction on the cover of the Virgin with a crown of stars, from a stained-glass window in Covington, Kentucky. I flipped through the pages. On March 20, where no saint was listed in the right-hand top space, because the date fell on a Sunday, my father had scribbled in: "Cuthbert!"

Underneath the stack of *Forwards*, as if he had thought it wise to weigh down blasphemy with the little piles of devotionals, was his Madelyn Farley stash: the reviews and interviews clipped for us by Trevor LaFarge, the programs of her "collages" brought back by him from New York, including that first one with its program note about my father's goose feathers.

I reread the loathsome program note. Then I skimmed through some of the interviews, on the alert for the little stabs and pricks certain outrageous statements produced in me. I felt I was feeling them for my father; or perhaps his spirit was feeling them through me. Therefore he lived on.

". . . and don't kid yourself, some of those old images and ceremonies still pack a charge—only . . ." and she laughs her low, sassy Madelyn Farley laugh, ". . . the charges aren't necessarily where the tired old purveyors of dogma like to *think* they are . . ."

". . . He is interested in the *possibilities of his pain in all its variations* . . . and there are people like that, too, you'd better believe it . . ."

I would keep these. Perhaps the day would come, as people kept threatening me it would, when my grief would fade. Then I could take out the clippings and the program and recharge the battery of my father's spirit with the energy of outrage they inspired.

The phone rang.

Please. Let it be.

I had not been strictly truthful with Ben. Concerning my "future," I *was* "waiting to hear," but not from some Pentecostal voice that would light my way with its flaming tongue. I was waiting for a human voice. One particular voice.

"Hello?"

"This is Operator Thirty-nine for Walter Gower."

"Who's calling, please?"

"Operator Thirty-nine," a woman's voice repeated. "From Western Opportunities." She sounded rather defensive for a telephone operator. "For Walter Gower."

"This is Walter Gower," I decided to say.

"I'm speaking to Walter Gower?" She didn't even sound all that amazed.

"Yes, you are," I said sternly. "How can I help you?"

"You have won an award," she said. "Please take down this number. It's your claim number. There are four letters. A as in apple, W as in William, I as in Idaho, B as in boy. Have you got that, Walter?"

"Yes." I wrote the letters on a piece of paper.

"Then there are five numbers. Three-zero-two-two-eight. Would you repeat your claim number back to me, Walter?"

"A as in Adrian, W as in Walter, I as in Idaho, B as in boy. Three, zero, two, two, eight. Look, is this some kind of sales pitch?"

The slightest pause. "You have won an award, Walter. Now if you'll call this number, area code 702, 555-2220, and give them your name and claim number, you will be given further information."

"Where is 702? What state is that?"

Reluctantly she said, "Uh, Nevada, I think."

"And who did you say you were an operator for?"

"Western Opportunities, Walter."

I dialed the number, even though it was not an 800 number and would go on our bill. Another "operator" asked me to repeat my name and claim number. Then I was switched over to a man, who had poor diction and spoke too fast; he sounded as though he was reading from something and had trouble with many of the words. He had no trouble at all either, however, with a female voice being a Walter, and pitched hurriedly into his spiel. *His* name, he said, was Kent Corbin and he had been chosen as my award coordinator.

"In order to receive your award, Walter, your first obligation will be to listen to my presentation. Are you willing to do that?"

I said I was.

Kent Corbin asked me to write down the list of awards I might win. There were five. Was I ready?

Like an obedient schoolgirl, I listed the awards as he rattled them off. 1. A 1988 Buick Riviera. 2. A two-karat sapphire pendant with a fourteen-karat gold chain. 3. A twenty-one-inch Magnavox color TV, with remote control, "and a revolutionary new feature, Walter, that allows you to watch two stations at the same time." 4. A vacation for two in Acapulco. 5. A cash prize of $750.

"Walter? Have you written down the prizes you are entitled to win?"

"Yes, I have."

"Now, Walter, I come to the next part of my presentation. You must answer now, because we're only allowed one call per household. Are you ready for the second part of my presentation?"

I was tempted to remind him that I was paying for this call, but I went ahead and said yes.

"Okay, here we go, Walter. Would you have any objection to sending us two color photographs of yourself and allowing these photographs to appear in national advertising?"

"I don't think I want to go on with this anymore."

"Okay, Walter, thank you, and have a nice evening," said Kent Corbin hurriedly and hung up.

Good night, Western Opportunities. I put Madelyn Farley's blasphemies back in the drawer, for the time being, and placed the February–April 1988 *Forward Day by Day* squarely in the center on top of them, and shut the drawer. Good night, Madelyn Farley. So much for my Pentecostal voices on the eve of Pentecost.

I poured myself another Scotch, went upstairs and undressed, and wandered into Daddy's room in his black paisley dressing gown. He never got to sleep on the clean sheets I had put on his bed on Good Friday morning. On Father Traherne's old bed.

I lay down on top of the white cotton bedspread, and found I was drunk enough to indulge in my childhood practice of spread-eagling myself like the figure inside the wheel of fortune, lying on my back and stretching my arms and legs towards the four posters, and then taking big gulps of air until I felt myself expanding into the household god whose wishes must be granted. The only trouble was, there was no longer anyone in the house to grant them, and also, when I stretched out like this as a grown person, my feet and hands were off the bed and there was no more room for expansion.

I sat up and sipped some more Scotch. I *willed* the phone to ring. As I did so, a memory surfaced. Once, years ago, on the evening of Ruth's departure, I had lain here on Father Traherne's old bed, steeped in the perfume she had left behind, and willing her to be thinking about me, and at that moment she had called from the roadside place in New Jersey, where she and Madelyn had stopped.

I lay down flat on my back again, reassuming the proper magic

position, taking deep breaths, letting them out slowly. *Please call.*
Please call.

Sometime later I awoke feeling chilled, even though it was a
warm night.

That's how Adrian had gotten his cold, which had so conve-
niently turned into acute bronchitis. Jerry Hope's wife had told
me all about it, as we sat in her cheerfully decorated living room
when I had dropped by St. Matthias's rectory to leave my note for
his speedy recovery and a bunch of Daddy's first Siberian irises of
the season. Adrian was recuperating at his rector's house, because,
as Mindy Hope explained, "We *need* him so, and you just can't
trust these bachelors to take care of themselves. They do the
stupidest things. The night he had the Rabbi as his houseguest, he
gave up his bedroom and slept down in his study. But did he think
to take a blanket down with him to cover himself *up* during the
night? Of course not!"

"Well, I won't stay," I said. "I'm sure he's resting, anyway."

I suppose I was expecting her to say, "At least step down to his
room and say hello," but she didn't. She said yes, Adrian slept a
lot—the cough suppressant had a sedative in it—but she would
see that he got my note and the flowers.

"Please tell him that all of us at St. Cuthbert's are wishing him
a speedy recovery. Which is all my note says, really."

But that had been weeks ago. He was home now, seeing patients again on a limited basis. "He's still looking peaky," Jerry
Hope had reported when I ran into him last week in the supermarket. "Mindy has to go by Acacia Street every day like a police-
woman and check on whether he's had his nap. Adrian suffers
from the typical caregiver's hangup. He gives and gives till he
drops. But I think his illness was as protracted as it was because
Adrian was heavily into denial over your father's death. He'd
adopted him as a sort of father."

I drank more Scotch and resisted the urge to dial Adrian's
number. It was almost midnight. Was the satisfaction of hearing
his voice say hello, and then hanging up on him, like some love-
struck teenager, worth waking him up for? Especially when he
was "still peaky"?

I also resisted the temptation to go back downstairs and refill
my glass. One night recently, I had drunk myself into a stupor,
woke and dragged myself to the bathroom to throw up, and had
then fallen asleep by the toilet because I was too dizzy to walk back

to my bed. But unlike Adrian the caregiver, I had remembered to cover myself with a bathtowel.

Before turning out the light and sliding between the sheets in my own bedroom, I opened the closet door wide. Perhaps the witch would come out at last tonight, on the Eve of Pentecost, and we would have our face-off at last. All those years and years of being afraid of her, but now I wanted her to come out.

Ever since Easter weekend, I had waited in vain for my father to appear in a dream. The briefest visitation—a look, a sign, a word, a touch—would have been gratefully seized upon. I had confidently expected that he would waste no time in finding his way to me in the country of the dream; both of us had always had the highest regard for dreams. But so far, not a sign of him. Not one blessed glimpse. Had Adrian had any dreams? How I envied him his illness and fever. Everybody knew you had visions in fevers. Maybe my father had been so busy over at Jerry and Mindy Hope's, keeping Adrian company in his fever, and later over on Acacia Street during the convalescence, that he just hadn't had a chance to get back to the rectory.

And whom did I dream about? I'd been dreaming about the witch who lived in the back of my L-shaped closet, the bane of my childhood darknesses. Only she had undergone a transformation. No longer was she a threat, she was a poor thing, a figure of loneliness and pity. She was a weeper. She wept without hope, the way people do when they know nobody will come and comfort them. I say I dreamed about her, but what I mean is, I dreamed about hearing her weep. That's how the dreams always started: I would hear the weeping, and think to myself, this has gone far enough, I'm grown up and I'm not afraid of her anymore, I'm going to get out of bed and go into that closet and *ask her if she needs anything.* She may be too old and weak to come out. (Although, oddly, the weeping voice was not that of a raspy old crone, but of a young woman.)

But, so far, I hadn't been able to make it out of bed during the dreams. *This is just awful,* I'd lie there and think—or dream that I lay there and thought; *I have got to do something for her. After all, she's had something to do with me all these years. I practically owe it to her.* But I could never bring myself to move.

"Come on out, witch," I now said aloud in the dark bedroom, addressing the open closet door. I knew I sounded drunk and silly, but who, except the witch, was to hear me? "You've been in there too long, the fresh air will do you good. It's a warm spring night, almost summer here in Romulus. It's Pentecost Eve . . . no, it's Pentecost by now. It's the earliest hour of Pentecost. That's when people get messages from the spirit. Tell you what, witchie, I'll be your spirit. Spirits probably need spirits, too. I hope I can bring you better messages than the ones I've had so far tonight. Listen, witch, you'd better get ready for a change. I won't be here much longer. First, Father What's-his-name will be living here temporarily, and he'll undoubtedly take Daddy's bedroom for himself. No telling what kind of junk he'll store in here. He may even block up your passageway, or pile boxes in front of your door. And after he goes, they'll have a new rector. He may have a child for you to haunt, but then again, he may not. So my advice to you is, come out while you can. Come on out, and you can lie here beside me on my bed and tell me what's been the matter all these years. Tell me the story of your life. Tell me what it's like to be you. Surely you can't be all that loathsome. And, anyway, if you are, I can stand it. I can stand anything, because I feel . . . I feel . . . I really do feel, dear witch, that I have nothing to lose."

When I came back from the cemetery on Sunday afternoon, Adrian Bonner's unassuming black Ford Taurus was parked in front of the rectory.

Just like that. It almost seemed like a letdown, after all that agonized yearning.

I went around to the back garden via the old flagstone walk, the way he had come upon us that late afternoon when I had just finished cutting Daddy's hair.

"Margaret." He got up from a wicker chair. The chairs were surprisingly still arranged in the same configuration from the time the three of us had sat here before. He wore a short-sleeved black shirt on this warm day, and his upper arms were very pale. His collar was loose around his neck. He had lost weight.

We shook hands. I was the one who initiated that. Better to be sure of a return handshake than have him step back and plead infection, as he had done with Aunt Con when she tried to hug him.

"I'm glad to see you," I said. "I . . . everybody . . . was worried about you."

"I'm much better, thank you. Just not 'full of beans' as Jerry

would say, but I expect the beans will come back. They'd better."
He smiled, showing the rakish chipped front tooth.

"Please sit down."

"Thank you. I won't stay long. I just wanted to see how *you*
were. And to thank you for your note, and those beautiful irises.
Aren't these more of them?" He indicated the thick stand of purple and blue irises bordering the stone wall. "But that was weeks
ago . . . wasn't it? I seem to have lost all sense of time. Or else they
must have a long growing season."

"No, it's just that there are different varieties with staggered
bloom times. I brought you the earliest varieties."

"What is that navy-blue one? I don't think I've ever seen a
navy-blue flower."

"That one's the Orville Fay. The Orville Fay was Daddy's favorite. And the Sea Shadows he liked a lot, too."

"Such beautiful names, too," he said rather sadly. "I wish I
knew more about flowers."

"Daddy knew a lot. Of course, his mother was a gardener."

"Yes, he told me a little about her. And about the fancy estate
they lived on, and that awful little boy."

We both laughed. Adrian Bonner was not a frequent laugher,
but when he did it was nice to watch him. I remembered how he
had laughed at supper with us, when Daddy had said you never
heard Jesus blaming his parents for the way He had turned out;
and that first afternoon in the garden here, I had made him laugh
with my imitation of Professor Stannard.

I was on the verge of saying, "Daddy told me a little about *your*
childhood, too," but I thought better of it.

We sat without speaking for a few moments. He coughed, and
crossed his right leg over his left knee. His right black shoe needed
a new half sole.

"It's good to—"

"How is—?"

We both had begun nervously at the same time, so then had to
backtrack through the "You first," "No, *you* first" rigmarole.

"I was only going to say, it's good to be in this garden again,"
he said, smiling. "Your turn."

There was just a flicker of intimacy in his tone that conjured
up an image of how we could be, together: sitting in some garden
at the end of a day. Did he remember that I had said I loved him

in the sacristy? Or had all that been wiped out by the fever? Had I been present in any of his fever dreams?

"I was only going to ask how Loretta was," I said. "*She* must have missed you while you were ill."

"Ah, Loretta." He sighed, then fitted his fingertips together in that characteristic way. His blue-gray gaze lifted off into the tree-tops. Once, during an American Civ. lecture, I had attempted to sketch him in this pose, but I was no artist. His hands and eyes were preternaturally large and I couldn't get his mouth to look even human.

"I failed badly with Loretta," he said. "She is institutionalized again, over at Staunton. Her own choice. But I feel partly responsible."

"I'm really sorry. She seemed so fond of you—"

"I'm afraid that was part of the trouble. There were warning signs, but I guess I'm so obtuse. And then when I got sick, she wanted to . . . nurse me at home, and that wouldn't have done at all. I took the coward's way out and fled to Mindy and Jerry's. She showed up there, too, though I never saw her. Now she's back over at Staunton."

"I'm really sorry," I repeated. Thinking: at least it was Loretta that made a fool of herself and not me.

"Interesting you should ask about her. I've been thinking a lot about her myself. It's made me question this whole therapy approach. Though it's a bit late in the game for me to contemplate *another* career change."

"I don't see why one failure should make you want to give up your career. Besides, it's not just your career, it's your vocation, isn't it?"

"My vocation as a priest I haven't a doubt about. It's this concentration on therapy I'm beginning to have serious doubts about. It's a relatively new thing in the church, anyway, these 'specialist clergymen,' like specialist physicians, who do only one thing: plan activities, or arrange liturgies, or—counsel people. We 'therapist clergymen' come into town, invited by a church or some other institution willing to support us, or on our own, if we think there's enough business around, and we hang out our shingle, and offer our fifty-minute hours, just like therapists in Zurich, or New York, or anywhere else. As assistant to Jerry, I get to celebrate Mass once in a while—or Eucharist, as we call it over at St. Matthias's, but it's not the same thing as being a full-time priest. Look at your father, in contrast. He was the old-fashioned variety. The complete parish priest. Did you ever read that French novel *Diary of a Country Priest?*"

"Yes, I did, and I don't think *he's* at all suitable for you to model yourself on just now. He dies of consumption, remember?"

Adrian Bonner laughed again. I had made him laugh.

"Daddy did a lot of counseling," I reminded him. "Why, he's had . . . I mean, he had . . . this one parishioner ever since I was a little girl. She would come once a week . . . twice, if there were 'crises,' and there frequently *were*, and she would read her journal aloud to him."

If I had been hoping to get another laugh out of him, I'd hoped in vain.

"But you see," he said, "that woman was a *parishioner*. She didn't just have your father once a week, or twice a week, to hang on to; she had the Church, she had the sacraments, she had the communal life of the parish. People who don't have those things are likely to try and make God out of their therapist. Or . . . or something else impossible. That's why I say I've begun to question this therapy in a vacuum." He passed a hand slowly backward over his scant hair, frowning. "The problem is," he said, speaking as much to himself as to me, "to be a complete parish priest, you need a parish. And there aren't enough of them to go around."

"Well, St. Cuthbert's is up for grabs—"

"No, no," he said, shocked. "That would be out of the question. I wouldn't even send my résumé to your vestry. I wouldn't feel adequate, trying to fill your father's place. It would be painful to me even to try. And it certainly wouldn't be grateful to Jerry, after all he has done to make it comfortable for me here. I owe him at least another year or two. What have I done so far? I arrive in January, get sick in April, and now it's almost June. And I've sent one patient back to the nuthouse."

"You're too hard on yourself," I said, and before I knew it, it was like old times there in the garden, with me talking a person I loved out of his low estimation of himself. I told him all the nice things those people in the kitchen said about him that Monday night at his house, I reiterated how much he had meant to Daddy, how stimulating my father had found him to talk to. I asked him what he had been reading.

"Eckhart, Sermons Three and Fourteen. Over and over again. An English translation. My brain is still mushy from the illness, I had to give up on my German and Latin texts. But Eckhart comes through in any language; he'd come through in Urdu. I love the way he will stop right in the middle of a sermon and say, 'Now pay attention! I will now say something I have never said before.' And then he does."

He glanced down at his wristwatch. "You're a wonderful listener, Margaret, but I didn't come to talk about myself. How are you doing? What are your plans?"

"I'm doing okay. I still don't understand the mystery of death, but I guess I'm not alone in that."

"That's for sure," he said kindly.

"I'm packing up the rectory, getting rid of things, or storing them in other people's basements. I have to be out of here June fifteenth—"

"Yes, I heard." He uncrossed his legs and sat forward, clasping his hands between his knees, his blue-gray eyes looking directly into mine. "Where will you go?"

"Well, I haven't decided. It's not that I'm going to be homeless, or anything like that. The MacGruders . . ."

"Oh, yes, your best friend. Harriet?"

"That's right. And Mrs. Major wants me to come and live with *her*, which I won't; she's too formidable. And then there's Mrs. Dunbar, the lady whose house I've been sharing in Charlottesville, who wants me to stay with her, whether I go on to graduate school or not . . ." I didn't bother to bring up Aunt Con's fly-by-night offer.

"You've certainly got plenty of offers, haven't you?" he said, smiling.

"Yes, but, you see . . . well, I'm going to be twenty-two in June." Oh, keep your face undemanding and straight, Margaret. You have planned this out, sentence by sentence. Look at this man straight and clear, show your heart in your eyes, but not in a grabby way that might scare him off. "I'd like to start living like an adult as soon as possible. I am an adult. I'm much older than the average person my age, people have always told me that. I want to begin living my own life now. When my mother was my age, she was already the wife of a rector and . . . my mother. I guess what I'm saying is that I don't want to be anyone's daughter anymore. I'm not even sure I want to be a *student* anymore. I want to be a grown woman with a grown woman's responsibilities. I want to take full responsibility for myself . . . and also, if the right person were to come along and want me to, I'd like to share that person's responsibilities."

The silence around us in the garden was like a whirlwind. My carefully rehearsed sentences, now having at last been spoken, unraveled backward into it, coming apart and flying here and there and all around. Though my own face felt numb, I kept looking straight at his, which was attentive, friendly, and (purposely?) *obtuse*. When I saw that absolutely nothing in his countenance had remotely softened or brightened, or become in the slightest degree more personal, I snatched back my dignity before it, too, disappeared into the whirlwind. All this took less than a second.

"Also, I'd like to travel," I said.

"Yes, you certainly should." That he seemed to relax and become a shade more lively at the mention of travel gave me more evidence, if I had needed it, that I had been right to snatch back that little face-saving shred. "It's such a shame about the English trip. Your father was really looking forward to it. Perhaps you might still go?"

"I already sent back both tickets to the travel agent. She has to apply for a refund, because they were those super-saver kind. When the refund comes, it'll show up on Daddy's MasterCard statement as a credit. And then Mr. Winchester . . . he's handling all that sort of thing for me . . . will have to have it transferred into cash."

"Do you have funds of your own, Margaret? If not, I'd be glad to lend you something."

"Thank you, Adrian, I appreciate that. As it happens, I have over five thousand dollars in my own bank account. The parish took up a collection for me. I've also been given a new tennis racket and a journal. I'm a rich woman. Maybe I'll just book myself *another* super-saver and go on to England, and who knows where else. I'm free. I've got my whole life before me, as everyone keeps telling me. I guess my biggest problem, when it comes right down to it, is avoiding the snares of all the fortune hunters who are going to be after me."

Adrian Bonner threw back his head and laughed and laughed.

"Perhaps . . ." he said warmly, when he had stopped laughing—he even ventured to reach over and touch me affectionately on my arm now—"perhaps you could ask your friend Harriet to go with you."

*   *   *

That evening I did not open the bottle of Scotch. I wanted to keep my head clear; also, I needed the company of all my inhibitions. Around dusk, which came late now, I went to Daddy's study and began reading my mother's old letters straight through, in chronological order. What a pity Daddy's had been lost. Why had they been lost? Who had let them get lost? I would have liked to decide for myself just who had wooed whom. He'd claimed he had lured her slowly, with passages from the mystics and the metaphysical poets. (". . . She can always think you meant religion, when all the time you're talking about love.")

But from her end, it certainly seemed she had gone after him with all her wiles. She had blitzed him with letters: had he answered them all? All those pages of mint-green, deckle-edged paper, written on both sides! The heavy-stock paper had held up well; Mrs. Dunbar would have approved of my mother's stationery.

She had drawn him out in just the right unthreatening way, the way an introverted, self-doubting bachelor, already in middle age, would need to be drawn out. Told him her stories of college life, usually finding a spot in each story where she could insert a reminder of her own uncertainties. There was a passage about a classmate, running barefoot downstairs to the front desk to claim a florist's delivery. "I will never forget the vision of the way she ran," Ruth Beauchamp wrote to the Rev. Walter Gower. "So light and sure of herself, so sure of her grace, so sure the flowers would *be from the right person!* I could never have the self-confidence that Sidney does, but I enjoyed just watching her fly."

She had asked his advice: "My sister Con's husband says I should study advertising when I come to live with them . . . he says advertising would provide me with a practical way to use my art. But my art is my *joy*. I don't want to use it to sell *products*. What do you think I should do?"

What if he had written back advising her to travel? She might still be alive now.

But where would my life be?

The letters occupied me until midnight. Slipping the rubber bands back around them in their envelopes, I felt I was finished with something. It was somewhat as Daddy himself had said he felt after rereading Ruth's letters. I felt compassion for the two people concerned, but it was their story.

Where was my story? When was it going to begin? What would I have to go through to get to the beginning of it, or far enough into it to realize it *was* mine?

I was tired but not sleepy. It was going to be another one of those nights. I opened the Scotch after all. The first shot hit the bottom of my empty stomach, bounced up like an acrobat, and transformed itself into a multitude of golden energy messengers leaping upstream through my veins until my brain received the message that I was now up to the dreaded, postponed task of disposing of Daddy's clothes. I carried boxes and plastic bags upstairs, remembering to take along the black felt-tip marker, and in a remarkably short time, or so it seemed, everything was in its proper box and labeled. Ernie Pasco's nephew wore Daddy's size shoe, and wouldn't be too proud to inherit several dozen pairs of perfectly good black cotton socks with reinforced toes. Mrs. Mac-Gruder could get good money for the suits and the jackets and the casual pants at her Republican Women's Next-to-New Shop. The underwear would go to the dump, but out of respect I folded every single piece and laid it carefully in the plastic garbage bag.

Then there were the clerical shirts one didn't sell or give away, and certainly didn't throw away. I folded all these in a box marked LATER—HARRIET'S, which meant I would store it in the MacGruder's basement and face it later. On top of the shirts, I put all the collars, both the new plastic kind and the cloth ones from the old days, which you had to starch. I carried the boxes downstairs, making several trips. My Scotch energy was flagging, so I recharged it.

For the first time there were boxes visible in the hall of the rectory. Up until now, I had maintained a semblance of life as usual. The pictures on the wall were still in their places. No furniture or rugs had been removed. I had been working from the inside out. Now, as of tonight, the "out" had made its first appearance. I was getting ready to go. But where?

I watched the tape again. Went to the kitchen for more Scotch and came back. Pressed Rewind, waited till I heard the click, pressed Start, and settled down in Daddy's chair behind his desk to watch it once more.

There were two glimpses of me, in the panning shots. One was just my back and hair. Harriet was more noticeable, with her arrogantly uptilted chin, her old strategy for distracting people from her short neck. The other shot of me was in profile, during the Rabbi's impressive recitation. A pleasant-enough looking girl, small in stature, low-key, in an unmemorable cotton-knit dress. Her attention was clearly on the speaker, where it properly should be. A well-behaved, low-profile daughter, most probably a clergyman's daughter. One's *ideal* of a clergyman's daughter.

What if my story was to have been simply the story of Father Gower's daughter? What if, without the father, there was no longer any real story? Of course, my life would go on, but anything hereafter would be an echo, or just one more variation, on that old theme. Look at Miriam Stacy. Most people would always think of her, many still referred to her, as "Old Mrs. Stacy's daughter," or, even worse, emphasizing the contrast between child and parent, "You know, the daughter of that *delightful* Rowena Stacy."

I stopped the tape, and didn't bother to rewind it. It was two-fifteen in the morning. I flipped through the TV channels. On one of my recent red-eye vigils, I had been lucky enough to switch right out of Romulus into Thornfield, where Jane had just arrived as governess: the old *Jane Eyre* movie, with Orson Welles as Rochester.

No such luck tonight, so I settled for *Nightowl,* a late-night, or rather early-morning, interview show with an aggressive, rather vain host who specialized in making his guests wriggle in their chairs.

"So they closed you down in Winston-Salem last week," he was saying to whoever his current victim was. "Of course, we all know that's the constituency of the North Carolina Senator in charge of U.S. Morals, but how did it make you feel? Are you getting fed up with being labeled the 'Religion Basher,' the enfant terrible of theater art?"

The camera switched to a lanky woman, wearing a purple shirt and a large jeweled Maltese cross hanging from a gold chain around her neck. She sprawled low in her chair, her legs in their white trousers stuck straight out in front of her. "In the first place," she said slowly, not bothering to adjust her posture or look up at her host, "I am not a 'religion basher.' I am a religious person."

"*You,* Madelyn Farley, a religious person—?"

"Hold it, Carlos." She held up her hand warningly. "Let me

finish my sentence. That's the least you can do after snatching away my powder puff."

"What?" The two of them were on camera now. He looked suddenly very wary of his guest.

"You know what I'm talking about, don't pretend you don't. I got here late because my bloody taxi was stuck in the lunchtime traffic, and it was raining, and your adoring assistant was trying to make me presentable, when you bopped in and snatched the powder puff out of her hand, to get the shine off *your* nose before we went on the air. And then she completely abandoned me to do your Blush-On for you. I call that downright ungallant."

"Oh, come on, now—" Blushing beneath his Blush-On, the host turned on her a smile that would have disarmed most ladies, but this was not a lady.

"As I was saying," she continued. "I am a religious person. More on this in a minute, that is, if I get another minute. For all I know, one of your adoring assistants has already edited me out for my disrespect." Except for a body wave that made her wispy, colorless hair look thicker, she didn't look much different from the morning she had sat in our breakfast nook and undermined me with this same slow nasal barrage. "Now, as for the enfant terrible bit, I have to correct you there, too. I turned fifty this year. Fifty-year-olds can't be enfants, anymore, Carlos. Why, I'm old enough"—her small, hard, metallic gray eyes settled on him at last—"I'm old enough to be your sister."

"We're flexing our talons today, aren't we?" remarked the host lightly, but his eyes narrowed combatively at his guest. "Now, if we *may,* Madelyn Farley, whose provocative theater piece, *Holy Desire,* has become a kind of classic of its genre, let's get back to the closing in Winston-Salem. Why is it that the city fathers—and mothers—down there saw fit to close it before it even had a first performance? What is it about *Holy Desire,* and your earlier pieces, that offends people . . . especially religious people . . . so?"

"Maybe because"—Madelyn Farley flashed him a white smile— "they're scared they'll see the backside of one of their idols . . . and that might lead to an unflattering view of their own backside. As for the 'mothers and fathers' in Winston-Salem, they closed the show completely on hearsay. Not one of them, including the 'Senator in Charge of U.S. Morals,' bothered even to watch the tape of *Holy Desire.*"

"You're not alone in—"

"*Be* a gent, Carlos, and let me finish my sequence, please."

"Sorry, Ms. Farley." Putting on a humble, good old boy act, but with a sarcastic hiss on the "Ms."

"*Thank* you." She made him a little mock bow, and sat up straighter in her chair. "I would like to neutralize this 'religion' buzzword once and for all. As you know, my line of work is not words. It's sound, movement, effects. But I got so sick of being nailed to the wall with the same bloody word in every interview, I was finally driven to the dictionary to defend myself. The word 'religion' can be traced back to Latin and Greek sources meaning simply *to bind together,* or *to pay heed.* Now I'd like to know what I'm doing if I'm not engaged in binding together and paying heed, when I put together my theater pieces."

"Some of us might challenge the bind together bit. Don't you hack apart some of our most cherished—"

"Of course I do. Then I *bind them together* into something new." The big white teeth flashed him another Cheshire-cat grimace.

"And what are you 'paying heed' to?"

"I am paying . . . heed," she enunciated in her slow, mocking nasal voice, "to the *living spirit,* wherever I find it, no matter whose sacred tombstone it is trapped under, no matter whose pomp it is hiding behind. It's in there, and I want it. As long as it's still got charge in it, I want it for my collages."

"But why do you pick on religion . . . excuse me, folks . . . can't use that word anymore. Why do you pick on the Judeo-Christian heritage so relentlessly?"

"Because there's a lot of living spirit trapped in it. It's in little splinters and shards now, but they attract me. I don't know why; it's not my business to know why. I just follow what I call my Hot Wand. I go where it leads me: to a saint's life, to a Gospel, to priestly objects and rituals. My art is my priesthood."

"Yet, you didn't have a religious . . . excuse me, folks . . . conventional church upbringing, did you? How did you first become attracted to all these 'splinters and shards,' Madelyn Farley, creator of the controversial *Holy Desire,* which was closed down last week in Winston-Salem, but is currently running at Kennedy Center here in Washington?"

She plucked at her tinsel-colored body wave. "Actually, I had a muse," she said slowly, in her nasal voice. "A priest. An Episcopal priest. The husband of a late friend of mine. I didn't like him, but I guess there's no rule that says you have to like your muse. I spent a night at their home, 'the rectory,' in a little never-never-land town. This was years ago, I was just a struggling stage designer then, on my way back from summer rep in the boondocks of Virginia. And my friend's husband, this *priest,* informed me that the shirt I was wearing—a costume designer friend had created it for me out of theater scraps—had a piece of altar cloth in it, and that . . . well . . . though he would never have said it so coarsely, I was wearing Christ's personal monogram on my *breast.* This intrigued me. Then, later that night, after my friend and I had stayed up talking, she took me next door and showed me their church. It was like a storehouse full of fascinating props. There was just this one lamp burning over the altar . . . it was all very . . . spooky and numinous. *Then,* the following morning, after the husband had celebrated some weekday Mass, I waylaid him in the sacristy and made him explain the ecclesiastical garments he had just taken off. That's how it all began, though these raw ingredients sometimes take a while to stew in the creative pot. It wasn't for another, oh, eight or ten years, until that encounter in the sacristy was ready to become *Pas de Dieux . . .*"

"With that powerful scene of God being stripped of his ecclesiastical garb at the end . . ." her host broke in. "I see our time's almost up, Madelyn Farley, but in the half minute we've got left, will you tell our faithful night owls watching with us through the wee hours: Where is your 'Hot Wand' headed next? You haven't given us anything since *Holy Desire,* which, by the way, is doing *very well* at Kennedy Center, as a result of the Winston-Salem brouhaha."

"Oh . . ." For the first time Madelyn Farley looked deflated, and suddenly much older. "I may go watch Victor Bannerjee play Christ in the York Festival. See what I can pick up . . . or steal. I may just lie fallow awhile longer. We older people don't have the same pzazz we did as teenagers, eh, Carlos? Also I spent my fiftieth birthday at the deathbed of my choreographer, and it was pretty traumatic."

"Andrew Amstutz. He did *Holy Desire* and *Liturgies,* didn't he?"

"And *Missa Solemnis.*" Either she had let herself sag from sadness or tiredness, or else the cameras had zeroed in mercilessly on a very unflattering angle, because she was suddenly transformed, right there on the screen, into a defenseless, older woman who had been posing as a famous person and had decided the effort wasn't worth it anymore.

"Andrew Amstutz . . ." the host intoned solemnly. "A real loss to the performing arts. Forty-eight years old. One more victim to the tragic scourge of this decade. Madelyn Farley, I won't say it's been exactly *delightful,* but it's been provocative, as it always is with you. And you have my Boy Scout word of honor I am not going to edit out any of your insults. *Nightowl* thrives on insults. So come back and see us, when your Hot Wand strikes again!"

Madelyn Farley was expunged from the screen. The host with his Blush-On cheeks continued to glow and flourish. If anything, he appeared stronger and *younger.* "Later in the week, Nightowlers, we'll be bringing you *another* controversial figure on the Sacred Arts scene: the painter Julian Schnabel. Ever since his retrospective at the Whitney last year, which drew heavily on . . . excuse me, folks . . ." (a winsome smile to his adoring viewers: the nanny is gone, we can play how we like again) ". . . *religious* associations, Schnabel has set the contemporary world abuzz with the question I never got around to asking Madelyn Farley . . . fierce *woman!* What's really going on here, I wanted to ask her. *Is* it a new spirituality you people are 'putting together,' or are all you enfants terribles, excuse me, *aging* enfants terribles on the prowl for spiritual kicks, just like the rest of the New Age crowd? Or, *or,* are you appropriating *religious* . . . oops, the naughty word again . . . imagery simply to shock and provoke—and further your careers?"

Smiling intimately and wisely at his invisible audience, the handsome host paused to caress his boyish haircut; he wore a signet ring on his little finger. "I'm Carlos Wilder. *Nightowl* will be right back to keep you company through the wee hours, after these messages . . ."

When had this program been taped? She said "lunch hour." Did that mean she had been in his studio at lunch hour today? No, of course not, today was Sunday. It must have been a weekday, a working day. A working day how long ago? Was her show still on in Washington? Where was she now? Was it possible she was already back in New York, sharpening her Hot Wand for its next assault? Poor Victor Bannerjee—Daddy and I had watched him in *Passage to India.* Poor York Festival.

Her phone numbers were in Daddy's address book. Under the

"F" tab. There they were, in his writing, *M. Farley,* and the 212 number and the 914 number, along with the respective city and country addresses: the city apartment, or "loft" as an interviewer called it, and the mean old father's place in upstate New York.

I dialed the 212 number, *willing* her to answer. This had gone far enough. I had some things to say, and I wanted to say them. I wanted to say them *NOW.*

Three rings. Another half ring. "Hello." Her voice "You have reached 212–623–3343. I'm out of town, but if you'll leave your number after the tone, I'll get back to you. *Ciao.*"

I waited for the tone, then froze and hung up.

I dialed the 914 number. If the old bastard told me there was "NO Margaret" this time, I was going to tell him to go to Hell, but before he did to please tell me where his daughter could be reached tonight . . . this morning.

An operator's voice came on. "The number you have dialed, 914–845–5010, has been temporarily disconnected."

I redialed four digits of the 212 number, then hung up. Carlos Wilder was now interviewing a politician who had written a best selling memoir about how he had found Jesus in jail. I turned off the set and sat down behind Daddy's desk and on one of his notecards wrote out a little "message."

Then I dialed the 212 number again and, after *her* message, waited impatiently for the tone.

"Hello, Madelyn," I read from my notecard. On a sudden inspiration I had decided to adopt the eerily "familiar" technique of the Western Opportunities people. "Madelyn, this is a Voice from your Past. I have an important message for you. Are you ready to receive the message? Better get a pencil. Okay, Madelyn, here is the message: Your muse is dead. I'm going to repeat that, Madelyn: *Your muse is dead.* Now here is the next part of the message: What has been happening down here in Never-Never-Land far surpasses your theater pieces in two important respects. Write them down, Madelyn. Number *one:* the parts were played by real people acting on their true beliefs. Number *two:* the people were not your creatures, they were God's creatures. 'Pay *heed,*' Madelyn Farley. They were made of real flesh and real blood and they had pumping hearts, not just cutout ones. You touched our lives and changed them, but we weren't just your *sets. Thank* you, Madelyn, and have a nice day . . . if you can."

*　　*　　*

I hung up the phone, sailed the notecard into the wastebasket, snapped off the lamp in Daddy's study, and went up to bed. I was suddenly exquisitely sleepy.

For old times' sake, I left the closet door ajar. But I knew, as you always know such things, that my witch no longer resided there. She had taken my advice and moved on to more haunting territory. I hoped next time she'd find herself a more spacious closet. Perhaps all she had been waiting for, cramped back there in the short part of the L all these years, was for me to invite her out and make friends.

... The great problem of our time is that we don't understand what is happening to the world. We are confronted with the darkness of our soul, the unconscious. It sends up its dark and unrecognizable urges. It hollows out and hacks up the shapes of our culture and its historical dominants. We have no dominants anymore, they are in the future. Our values are shifting, everything loses its certainty, even *sanctissima causalitas* has descended from the throne of the axioma and has become a mere field of probability. Who is the awe-inspiring guest who knocks at our door portentously? Fear precedes him, showing that ultimate values already flow towards him. Our hitherto believed values decay accordingly and our only certainty is that the new world will be something different from what we were used to.

—letter from Dr. C. G. Jung to Sir Herbert Read,
2 September, 1960

XII: Guests and Departures

MONDAY IN WHITSUN WEEK

"Hello, Miss Gower? Oh goodness, it sounds like I woke you up. This is Donald Dabney calling, and I wondered—"

"Excuse me, Donald who?"

"Donald Dabney, up in Harrisonburg. You know, I'm supposed to—"

"Oh, I'm sorry. You're the priest who's going to live here for the summer, right?"

"That's correct. It sounds so good to hear myself called a priest again. For the past six years, I've been teaching high school. I haven't been called a priest since I had my mission at Scudder's Gap. It went under, unfortunately, as a lot of them do, these days. I'm really looking forward to this summer, though let me say, Miss Gower, I'm very sorry about your father. It must have been a shock to everyone. He was greatly loved, I understand."

"Yes, he was. But thank you, anyway."

"Look, the reason I'm calling—and I want you to please just say no if this is inconvenient. It's such a beautiful morning, and I thought I might run down and take a look at the church, and the rectory. Kind of get myself oriented. But if this morning isn't convenient, just please say so."

"No, this morning would be okay. Would you mind making it *late* morning?"

"Not at all. Eleven? Eleven-thirty. I wouldn't stay long. Just to look around, see what I'll need to bring."

"Is there anyone you'd like to meet?"

"Oh, no, no, no. In fact, I'd rather not, today. I'd just like to get the feel of the place, and discuss with you what pots and pans you'll be leaving."

"How about eleven-thirty?"

"Eleven-thirty's perfect. I'm truly grateful. See you then. Oh wait, how do I get to you?"

"You'll be coming down 81. Take exit 59, then follow the sign that says Romulus. After you cross the bridge, you're on Main Street, which takes you through the old downtown, then turn right into Church Street. We're the last church on the street, just past the turnoff into Macon. You'll see St. Cuthbert's. It's old brick with a slate roof and lots of ivy. And the rectory's right next door."

"Wonderful. See you at eleven-thirty, Miss Gower. By the way, you give very succinct directions."

"Thank you, uh . . . Father Dabney. See you then."

It was nine o'clock. He *had* waked me. I had slept dreamless as a stone, after my phone call to Madelyn Farley, and now there was just a little over two hours to pull myself together and make the rectory look presentable. Why should I bother? Because I was still Father Gower's daughter, whatever else I wasn't.

By the time the schoolteacher-priest's beat-up clunker, a two-toned brown Pontiac of early seventies vintage, pulled up in front of the rectory, on the dot of the appointed time, the boxes in the hall had been stacked on top of one another in the guest-room closet, the kitchen floor mopped and smelling of Murphy's oil soap, Daddy's desk cleared, except for a few books and a tall vase of Siberian irises, and another vase of them gracing the mantel-piece in the living room, where I had opened all the windows and scattered some colorful books around, to give a lived-in air to that neglected room.

Donald Dabney was pathetically grateful for everything. He was grateful for my inviting him to come in the front door. He kept reiterating his thanks for allowing him to come at such short notice. He was overwhelmed with gratitude when I urged him to go through the rooms and open whatever cupboards or closets he felt like looking into. I apologized for our shortage of closets, but he seemed to think they were luxuriously plentiful. He looked ecstatic every time I called him Father Dabney, and asked if that would be the general practice here. At the mission, he had just been Donald, or Don, but of course then he was still wet behind the ears from his diaconate, and the congregation hadn't been very High at Scudder's Gap. St. Cuthbert's was Very High, wasn't that correct? He wanted to give them what they expected. He supposed he'd better invest in a few new dog collars and black shirts, and perhaps a new suit. He thought the rectory was charming. He noticed the flowers in both rooms. He went into raptures over Daddy's study with its view of the garden. He examined the titles of the books on the desk, books I had carefully chosen to give him a tacit hint of our "High-ness": he was gratifyingly responsive to every nudge. (*"The Shape of the Liturgy!* Dom Gregory Dix! I could never afford it in seminary, so I just kept checking it out of the library. *The People's Anglican Missal,* now I've got *that* myself. What a pleasure it will be to need to consult it!")

A comical-looking man, he resembled a farm boy whose pituitary gland had failed to shut off when he had reached the optimum height. Father Dabney had to duck when he passed through door frames. He was skinny and awkward, and just above his loose white plastic collar sat the largest Adam's apple I had ever seen. His rumpled black clerical shirt, a winter one, with long sleeves, smelled of mothballs; he had probably taken it out of storage for the drive this morning. But his zeal about his priesthood recalled to me Trollope's Rev. Josiah Crawley, perpetual curate of Hogglestock . . . the *younger* Crawley, that was, in the days before crushing poverty turned him bitter. Father Dabney was poor, but, unlike Crawley, hadn't the consolation of a family. He was a bachelor, but you sensed, even before he told you he was single, that it was not by choice. It was because no woman had come along yet who had looked behind the gangly, unprepossessing appearance, and felt the compensatory affection and respect.

I invited him to stay for lunch—how easy it was to offer hospitality, when you didn't care whether the person said yes or no! I made us cheese sandwiches and lemonade and served it in the garden. We had ice cream for dessert. He said it was the best cheese sandwich he had ever eaten, the best lemonade he had ever drunk, and what brand was the ice cream, he was going to stop off at his supermarket on the way home and buy the very same kind! He kept repeating that he had never seen such a charming rectory and was truly grateful to have the opportunity to live there for the summer. Several times he seemed on the verge of fainting, whether from sweltering in the warm weather inside his winter clerical shirt, or from sheer happiness. I offered him *The Shape of the Liturgy* on extended loan, and ventured to suggest he take the box of Daddy's clerical shirts home and try them for size—there were at least a dozen summer ones. They might just fit him. Daddy had been long-waisted and broader in the chest than Father Dabney, and the difference in proportions might even out. I asked him what subjects he taught at the high school. ("Mathematics, vocational training, and also I'm assistant coach of our swim team. It's some workload they've given me, but I was truly grateful to get the job!")

He insisted on helping me wash the dishes. *And* put them away. Shyly inspecting the pots and pans, he inquired very tentatively if I would be leaving behind a wok, or had he better bring his? He did a lot of stir-frying. There was no wok, I said, but the rectory did have a splendid silver tea service. Perhaps he might give a parish tea party at the rectory. It was usually the custom in mid-summer. He was absolutely overjoyed by this suggestion.

I told him that if any of the parish customs were at *any* time unclear to him, he couldn't do better than take Mrs. Elaine Major as his social guide—she would be the perfect hostess for his tea, for instance—and Mr. Ned Block, a longtime member of St. Cuthbert's vestry, would make an ideal liturgical guide. "Mr. Block's dream was to study for the diaconate," I confided, "but circumstances interfered."

"Ah, yes, circumstances," echoed Father Dabney, his Adam's apple lurching up and down in sympathy.

There turned out to be only one other shortcoming, besides the lack of a wok, in his imminent summer paradise. During our tour of the upstairs, first apologizing for the presumptuous act he was about to perpetrate, the schoolteacher-priest had eased himself onto Father Traherne's old bed, and found he could fit on it only if he maintained a jackknife position. When I suggested he might rent a bed for the summer, the idea of such an expenditure seemed to terrify him. He said he thought he would just tie his mattress on top of his car and transport it down from Harrisonburg. He would sleep on his own mattress on the floor. He could push the four-poster over, and there would be enough room. He was sure there would be enough room, he repeated dubiously, looking around the modest proportions of Daddy's bedroom.

"Actually, I'd planned to give that bed to someone," I said. "By the time you come, on June fifteenth, it will be gone and you'll have plenty of room for your mattress."

Thus it was that the idea came to me that Adrian Bonner should inherit the bed of my father, who had inherited it from Father Traherne.

Finally, I had taken Father Dabney on a tour of the church, where he exclaimed in an admiring whisper over everything from the baptismal font to the carvings on the rood screen, and almost succeeded in beheading himself by forgetting to stoop when following me through the low, Gothic-arched door leading from the chancel into the sacristy. We went downstairs to the crypt, as well, because he wanted to pay a visit to the crucifix whose Reconsecration ceremony, and its sad but dramatic after-math, had been written up in the Harrisonburg paper. The hacked pieces of the little stone Christ, now cleansed and blessed by my father, lay at rest upon two old communion kneelers placed side by side. In the dim light of the crypt, they gave a semblance of wholeness again, all except for the fingers and toes. Just after I had been telling him that our Mr. Ernie Pasco ("he's the one to call if you need anything fixed") was in the process of carpentering a beechwood box to hold these ruins, Father Dabney suddenly dropped awkwardly to his knees on the stone floor and cupped the little figure's chin in his red-knuckled, rawboned hand. I think he said a prayer.

At three-thirty, he departed in a state of bliss, bearing away the cardboard box containing Daddy's shirts and *The Shape of the Liturgy,* and thanking me at least twenty more times for everything.

How easy it was to make people happy, when you didn't want or need anything from them. I sat down in the warm sunshine on the front steps at the end of the church walk, close to the saucer magnolia, feeling mellow and replete from my good deed.

There was certainly something to be said for the *caritas* and *agape* kinds of love over the eros kind. In his *Manual for Priests,* Daddy had always carried a holy card with a quotation from the famous nineteenth-century Notre Dame preacher, Jean Baptiste Lacordaire:

> To live in the midst of the world with no
>   desires for its pleasures;
> To be a member of every family, yet belonging
>   to none;
> To share all suffering;
> To penetrate all secrets;
> To heal all wounds;
> To teach and instruct;
> To pardon and console;
> To bless and be blessed forever; Oh, God, what
>   a life and 'tis thine, O Priest of Jesus
>   Christ.

Plenty of work to do, lots of charity and spontaneous, altruistic love to be given, but no bothersome eros on the agenda. Not a bad life. Of course, Lacordaire had been a Dominican, so eros *couldn't* be on his agenda. That must be the extent of what Adrian Bonner wanted for himself: to be the complete priest, but "obtuse" to eros: to be in on everybody else's secrets, but sworn to secrecy; to be so busy healing other people's wounds and consoling them for their sorrows that you wouldn't have time to brood about your own wounds and sorrows. Would my father have ended up like Adrian Bonner, "a member of every family, yet belonging to none," if Ruth Beauchamp hadn't gone for her conference with the visiting priest in the Green Parlor during St. Mary's Lenten Retreat, and subsequently pursued him from a comfortably safe distance on her green, deckle-edged stationery, until he believed himself to be pursuing her?

A silver-gray Chevrolet with a District of Columbia license tag pulled up in front of the rectory. A woman in a purple sweat suit, but no jeweled cross today, got out and stood in the street, massaging the back of her neck. She looked at the rectory from over the top of the car, uttered a noise somewhere between a snort and a groan, then closed the car door and sauntered slowly in my direction, never taking her eyes off me. How many times in my imagination hadn't I relived that self-satisfied saunter, up our walk and into our lives. Except for the different clothes and the car—though the metallic gray of the big Chevrolet matched her eyes, as the former Mustang had done—sixteen years might never have passed.

Unable to move, I sat on the steps in front of my father's

church and felt time bend itself into a curve, and watched the enemy come.

She stood on the pavement in front of me. Hands shoved gracelessly in the pockets of her sweatpants, she swayed back and forth in her sneakers, looking down at me.

"You are, I presume, 'the Voice from the Past,' who left that devastating message on my answering machine last night," she declared at last in her brusque, mocking twang.

"It was actually this morning. After I saw you on *Nightowl.*"

"Oh, of course." She knocked on her head. "I must be losing it. You would have *had* to watch it to say the things that you did. I was watching it myself in my hotel room. It was taped a week ago. I expected it would be bitchy, but I had no idea he was going to go for blood."

She plopped herself down wearily beside me on the front steps of the church walk. My first impulse was to get up, remove myself from her proximity; it seemed almost sacrilegious to be sitting hip to hip with this person on my father's church steps, within touching distance of where he had fallen on Good Friday.

"But I didn't rent a car and drive down here from Washington to talk about *that* bloody fiasco. Which my ego certainly didn't need just now. Closet bassoons are the worst, they're not at ease with themselves. But I did *not* need Carlos Wilder on my case just now. Even the name of my *rental car* is out to mock me. A 'Celebrity'! See? There it is, written in red letters across the trunk. I didn't need *that*, today, either, but it was the only one they had in the larger sizes, short of their 'luxury' class. I don't drive small cars anymore. Not since . . . that summer in England."

Of all the things she could have said, the mention of that summer in England was the one thing that probably kept me sitting on those steps. This odious person, from whom my spirit revolted, had been my mother's friend. My mother may have loved her. Though I was to undergo more bouts of revulsion against this woman in the days to come, what would keep me glued to her side, then as well as now, was the acceptance of this knowledge: that, and the desire to find out as much as she would reveal about who Ruth Beauchamp Gower had been.

"What," I asked Madelyn Farley, "is a closet bassoon?"

"Oh!" She laughed her snorty laugh. "That's a word my late great friend Andrew thought up. It was our private code word, one of many. He despised the word 'gay,' even though he was—

among other things. The German word for bassoon, you know, the musical instrument, is *fagott,* and the Italian is *fagotto.* Andrew was multilingual. He was multi-everything. He danced, choreographed, acted, directed. He also sang and painted."

"He was the one who died on your fiftieth birthday?"

"He didn't die precisely *on* it, but he was pretty well rubbed out by then. He was blind, and he had tubes in him everywhere, and gauze dressings that had to be changed every hour. He didn't have a clue I was there, but I wanted to be, all the same. I loved him, in my own selfish way. We were once lovers, ages ago. We were even engaged once."

"You were designing the wedding. He and you were going to wear velvet cloaks at midnight in an English forest."

"Jesus, how do you know *that?*"

"My mother told me, the night you spent in the rectory, and I remembered it. You have been part of my life, whether I liked it or not."

"I think I have some idea of how much you liked it. Do I deduce, from that menacing phone message of yours, that your father is dead?"

"He died seven weeks ago this past Saturday."

"Well, I'm sorry, for your sake. I remember how you two couldn't get enough of each other. He and I weren't exactly compatible, but he was an animating force for me."

" 'There's no rule that says you have to like your muse,' " I quoted her own words back to her from the *Nightowl* show.

"You have Ruth's sharp tongue. It's funny. You don't look like her, and you do. But you're not as pretty as she was."

"Thank you very much."

"Don't mention it. I didn't mean you're not pretty. It's just that, on the scale from one to ten, Ruth was a ten, and you are about a . . . seven. You're pretty enough. Depending on what you want to do. What *are* you doing, by the way? I'm sure you haven't been sitting here in front of the church for seven weeks, looking utterly lost, the way you looked when I drove up. Or have you?"

"I wasn't feeling lost, at all. I was feeling pleased with myself. I've spent most of today being nice to the interim priest who's going to take over here this summer. Showing him the church, and the pots and pans in the rectory. I gave him lunch."

"Here we go again."

"What?"

"Nothing. It's none of *my* business. Just my theatrical mind at work. I simply saw the whole pattern repeating itself. The unities and so on. Do you know what they are?"

"Time, place, and action. Aristotle. I just graduated from the university, with a Lit. major. In the case of Father Dabney, there's no danger of my getting stuck in the unity of Romulus, or of repeating my mother's pattern, if that's what you were getting at. Speaking of your business, why exactly *did* you rent a car and drive all the way down here from Washington?"

"Well . . . *Christ.* After that phone call?" Then she must have felt my recoil, because she stopped to apologize, though mockingly ("Sorry if my language offended the preacher's daughter"), before going on. "In the weird state I've been in lately, that call was like . . . a summons. A summons to *what*, I didn't know. I had no idea what I would find when I got here. Among the many possibilities, I saw myself arriving just in time to save you. Or being the one to discover your corpse."

"My *corpse?*"

"Yes, young woman, your corpse. You sounded pretty desperate. Pretty accusing, too, I might add. It was the kind of last phone call suicides sometimes make. You might have inherited Walter's depressive tendencies."

"I never, *ever*, heard my father mention suicide, and I did *not* have any intention of *summoning* you. I didn't even think you'd get the message for several days . . ."

"Well, don't get in an uproar. I'm just trying to answer your question. Whether you *meant* to summon me or not, here I am. Look: be me, for a minute . . ."

The prospect was not an appealing one.

"I'm an artist. I live through my art. I live *for* it. Without it, I'm not very much of anything. And it's three o'clock in the morning, and I've just watched myself being savaged on *Nightowl*. I've been feeling rotten lately . . . no ideas, absolutely no *energy*. But meanwhile, one must put up the front, 'live on one's laurels.' Go around to see my old successes being performed by younger and younger people. Hear myself do the old 'Hot Wand' act on interviews until I feel like puking. My great friend Andrew, the coauthor really, of my best pieces, is dead. My assistant, a funny, savvy, talented young person I spent *hours* with every day, he was almost like my son, just left me to go live with his lover in Brazil. I expect any day to hear that one of them is in the hospital. And so, here I am at three this morning, after watching Carlos stab me in the back the minute I was off the tube and couldn't defend myself against hearing my work being compared to Schnabel. Schnabel! Do you know what he does?"

"I never heard of him before."

"You hadn't? *Jesus!* Sorry . . . excuse me. But it must have been strange growing up down here in *Our Town*."

"I don't know. I haven't anything else to compare it with."

She regarded me with a quirky raise of her eyebrows. "I can't decide if you're an innocent, or just posing as one. Schnabel, for your information, is this painter who will take a big sloppy brush and paint the word 'IGNATIUS' in white paint on an enormous brown tarp cut in the shape of a cross. The rest is left to the beholder. It's cheap, chic, minimalist 'association.' I *loathe* it. And it's *ugly*. I *make* something out of what I appropriate. I create dense, complex, *Byzantine* works. There's a hell of a difference, and I'm damned if I'm going to apologize for saying hell."

"I didn't ask you to."

"You sounded exactly like your father then. That southern gentlemanly modesty, but with its little underlying zap of reproach. You even have some of his singsong way of speaking. Anyway, getting back to three A.M. this morning, I decide to call my number in New York, wait for the tone, and punch in my code, and, you know, see if there's any news . . . perhaps something will be on my machine that might cheer me up. There's one call. Just one call. And it says: 'I have an important message for you, Madelyn. Your muse is dead.' "

"I didn't know you'd been having such a bad time. On the show, you got the better of him. The powder puff . . ."

"I got him that time, but his crew got me back for it. For the last thirty seconds, they selected my most unflattering angles."

"You did look suddenly . . . very tired."

"I looked like a hag, you mean, in your southern code. But listen, my 'Voice from the Past,' what would *you* have felt in my place, if you'd heard that message over the phone? My heart froze. I actually felt it turn to ice. The blood backed up in my veins. I had to lie down. I lay on top of the hotel's quilted bedspread that reeked of stale cigarette smoke, though I was on the No Smoking floor, and examined my life until about eight o'clock this morning. Then, I checked out of the hotel and took a taxi to Hertz and here I am. It didn't take me long to figure out who the

Voice from the Past was. I've been thinking about Ruth a lot lately, and Walter, too. They say as you get older, you live more and more in your past. Anyway . . . where was I? I really am losing it. I can't remember what I was going to say."

"You were examining your life until eight o'clock this morning."

"Oh, right. For the last three years, I've been what we artists call 'lying fallow.' Which is a way of avoiding admitting you're blocked. I've started half a dozen new pieces, then trashed them. I did several sets, including a musical on Broadway, but nothing I'm proud of. And then Andrew, who'd been living in Germany, flew to New York with an inspiration. 'Let's do an evening-length piece on Hildegarde of Bingen,' he says. 'She's tailor-made for you, Madelyn, with all the religious stuff. As for myself,' he says, 'I think I might have *been* Hildegarde in another life. She was a sort of one-woman multi-media show, and a saint to boot. She wrote operas and chants, she was way ahead of her contemporaries in music.' So I read up on her at the library, and looked at her paintings and got excited, but mainly I was excited about doing another piece with Andrew. The Schaubuhne Theater in West Berlin was practically begging us to stage it there. We'd begun to do in-depth research, listened to tapes of her music, which she wrote in the twelfth century, so there would have been no problem with copyrights. I felt alive again for the first time since *Holy Desire*. We'd already got a commitment from this amazing Hungarian dancer who was going to be Hildegarde, and her twelve-year-old daughter, who's a ballerina and a mime, was going to be the young Hildegarde and also stand in, behind a scrim, for Hildegarde's soul through the whole piece . . . you know, the soul of the artist must always remain young. Hildegarde herself lived to be eighty, which took some doing, with all the diseases *they* had.

"Then, while we were over in Rudesheim last spring, really getting into the mind-set of 'The Sibyl of the Rhine,' as she was called, Andrew comes down with pneumonia. They got him over that, the German doctors, and we flew back to New York. He was going to recuperate at my place, so we could continue working. Well, then he notices this funny-looking lesion on the inside of his arm and goes to a dermatologist, who sends him for this *other* test . . . and I'm starting to get very depressed, talking about this. How did you father die? Was it a long illness, or what?"

"He had a stroke during a procession on Good Friday. Our

crucifix at the corner had been vandalized and he was reconsecrating it. It was quite a big affair here in Never-Never-Land. TV even covered it."

"So that's what you meant, about all the theater that's been going on down here. Listen . . . Margaret, I really am sorry."

I couldn't stop myself from flinching when she reached over and touched my arm. If I had ever dreamed of inflicting pain on Madelyn Farley, I had the satisfaction of seeing proof of it in the way her face registered first surprise and then acknowledgment of my repugnance towards her. She looked old, tired, and alone, and now there was something else as well in her face, and I had put it there. She looked like someone who has been used to having her gestures of fondness welcomed by those she chose to bestow them on, and had received the first sign that such welcomes might not always be forthcoming in the future. I suddenly felt sorry for her, in a charitable sort of way, and wished it was in my power, if only because she had once been cherished by my mother, to make her look less gray and defeated.

"Do you still carry that energy stuff in a jar, that has to be refrigerated?"

"You remember *everything*. Uncanny child."

"It was a memorable occasion. Your last visit changed my life."

Madelyn Farley sighed and reached up and massaged the back of her neck with her own hand. I found it a sad gesture, especially after I had refused to be touched by her. Even with the fashionable body wave, you could still see straight through the wispy, tinsel-colored hair to her scalp. She sat slumped forward, a tired, older woman who, acting on a younger woman's impulse, had driven too far in one day. Except for the clothes—no older lady in our parish would wear sweat clothes, outside of a health club—she might have been some older parishioner I had been chatting with on the front steps of my father's church. I suddenly realized with a shock that Madelyn Farley wasn't very different in build or coloring from Miriam Stacy. Well, Madelyn Farley, too, was "an old maid" when it came to that. Only, she had a bolder presence. Also, she was famous and Miriam Stacy wasn't. Madelyn Farley had her art, and Miriam Stacy had her journal.

"Well, that evening changed my life, too, but I don't want to get into any competition with you over whose life was changed most by it. You would undoubtedly win." She continued massaging her neck. "I could use some of that old 'energy gruel,' as Ruth used to call it. When I was younger, I thought nothing of driving fifteen or sixteen hours at a stretch. Now, a few hours on the road, and I'm wiped out."

"Were you two lovers?"

"Your father asked me the same question over in England. Dear Walter, what was the delicate way he put it? Had we been 'Sapphics.' Ruth was very affectionate, but she was straight. So am I, basically, though I won't deny I've had my eras of experimentation. My world is full of the polymorphous perverse. But I've always preferred men when I could get them. The trouble is, I always fall in love with bassoons. But I did love Ruth. And she loved me, too. Even back at that penitentiary for debutantes, Miss Beale's. We'd snuggle up together in my single bed and talk all night. She'd sneak into my room. But we didn't explore each other's nooks and crannies, there was never any of that. There was attraction, I won't deny. Her hair always smelled like Breck, and her skin was so silky and soft . . . and she was as cuddly as a little kitten. And God, could Ruth make you laugh! And she thought I was some fantastic *heroine*. One of the reasons I loved her so much probably, being my selfish self, was because she thought *I* was so wonderful. Her belief in me was like some energy tonic, itself."

"Did you bring luggage?"

"Well, of course. I've been staying in D.C. for a week and a half."

"Is *Holy Desire* still on up there?"

"No, the last performance was Saturday. It did extremely well. The Winston-Salem witch hunt turned out to be a very bankable persecution for me. Why do you ask?"

"I would have liked to see it. To judge for myself. Daddy used to have this friend who saw your pieces up in New York and brought us back the programs and clippings. Do you remember that program note you wrote about Daddy's goose feathers?"

"His goose feathers—? Oh, Christ. Oh, hell. Walter was the last person in the world I ever expected to see that program note."

"Well, he saw it. He kept it in his desk drawer for the rest of his life."

"No wonder you hate me. Oh, poor Walter . . . he probably flagellated himself with it. At the time, I thought that performance was just a . . . neighborhood thing. I didn't think *Pas de Dieux* would ever have another performance after St. Clement's. I certainly never imagined your father would ever hear about it."

"Would you have canceled the performance if you had known he would?"

She gave me a long look. "No," she finally said. "When it comes to my work, I'm as heartless as my own father. He's always put his art before people."

"Finishing his painting on the mountain while your mother was having appendicitis."

"You know, you're starting to give me the creeps with that memory of yours."

"Do you still have that big black portfolio that tied with ribbons, that my mother carried in for you last time?"

"I still have it, but I didn't bring it with me," said Madelyn Farley, "because there are no sketches in it. There haven't been any for some time. Why do you ask?"

"Because," I said, "I was going to offer to carry it into the rectory for you. In memory of my mother."

I saw it dawn on her that she had received an invitation to stay the night, but all she said was a brusque "Ah." I was glad for her lack of effusiveness, however, as I probably couldn't have managed a more gracious invitation.

As we went up the rectory walk together with her bags, she suddenly stopped. "This is so déjà vu," she said, shaking her head as if to clear her vision. "The ivy. The Gothic Revival windows."

I never much noticed what our windows were, came my young mother's vaguely wistful reply. *Except to sometimes wish they let in more light.*

I put her in the guest room, and opened all the windows. After seven weeks, the mingled smell of Aunt Con's perfumes and mousses and hairsprays still lingered. First the unlikely Aunt Con in this room, and now the unlikelier Madelyn. My mother's old connections come back again.

"The same Indian print bedspread," Madelyn was saying, in her déjà vu tone.

"She bought it new for your visit. It's faded a lot since then. I'm sorry about . . . well, this *smell*. My mother's sister was the last person to sleep in here. She came for my father's funeral. I guess she did an awful lot of spraying and atomizing in here."

"Old Connie Roundheels," Madelyn Farley said with a dry laugh.

"You knew her?"

"I never got to meet her, but she paid our airfares the summer Ruth and I went to England."

"Why did she do that?" I was deeply shocked by this revelation.

"Because Ruth and I didn't have any money. Old skinflint Farley wouldn't lend us any, and I had this offer of the job in England. Guildford was too small-time to pay my transatlantic expenses, and I wasn't about to admit I couldn't afford it; they would have thought I was small-time and wouldn't have wanted me. So Ruth called Connie Roundheels. She was tickled pink. She would have done everything in her power to keep Ruth from going back to Walter. She wasn't too fond of your father."

"The feeling was mutual."

"So I gathered."

"But what about my mother's job? Couldn't you have used the money from that?"

"Her job? What job?"

"Didn't she . . . I mean, she taught life drawing for your father. At his art school upstate? She told Daddy about it on the phone. It was her first job, she was so proud."

Madelyn sat down on the faded Indian print bedspread. She was massaging the back of her neck again and looking at me strangely. Then she sighed and declared, in her slow, brusque twang, "Look, I have the uncomfortable feeling I'm going to be breaking down some *illusions,* but you've been asking straight questions and I'm going to give you straight answers. Your mother didn't teach life drawing. She *modeled* for Farley's life-drawing classes. But it *was* the first money she had ever earned, and she felt good about it."

"You mean, naked?"

"That's generally how models model in life-drawing classes, isn't it? We're not talking about the last century. Though Farley *paid* her as though it was the last century. Cheap bastard. What he paid her wouldn't have flown one of us as far as Cape Cod."

I turned away from her and looked out the window. From here I could see the side of the church and the far corner of the wall I had built with Katharine Thrale. "Is your father still alive?" I asked politely, to cover my distress.

"Oh, yes, Farley's still alive. He's got emphysema and hardening of the arteries, he's had cancer twice, and he's senile half the time. But he's still mean as a rattlesnake and he paints every day. His latest economy is not paying the phone bill. Then they cut off his phone and I have to drive up there and check on whether he's died."

I thought of Ruth, standing, or sitting, or whatever she did, in front of a roomful of art students. I had seen her naked out at the MacGruders' lake, when we had changed in that old wooden bathhouse that smelled of Lysol. Her tan stopped several inches below the tops of her thighs and well above the cleavage of her breasts. She also had wide white strapmarks. Many of the women, even the older ladies like Mrs. MacGruder, wore two-piece suits; some of them in the early seventies had worn modified bikinis. But the Rector of St. Cuthbert's wife, who was younger and firmer and shapelier than any of them, had to wear a one-piece suit, with straps as wide as a sundress, and even a little skirt.

"I have to run down to the supermarket, to get a few things. You might like to rest, after your long drive."

"I may do just that."

"Do you still drink white wine?"

"I still drink white wine," she said, unlacing her sneakers and sinking back on the pillows.

When I got back to the rectory, there wasn't a sound to be heard behind her closed door.

I washed the thin slices of liver and coated them lightly in whole wheat flour. We were having liver and spinach, a heavy-duty energy meal I used to fix when Daddy was feeling low. And mashed potatoes. I was glad I hadn't yet packed away my mother's silver and china. I suppose I had been hoping for a "last supper" with Adrian Bonner. I put myself in Daddy's old place and Madelyn on my left, though the place of honor was at the right. But on my left, her back would be to Ruth's honeymoon watercolors of St. Michael's and St. Philip's in Charleston. I didn't want to hear anything more about Ruth's art just at the moment, though I intended eventually to get everything I could out of Madelyn Farley concerning this complex woman who had been my mother.

Outside to the garden for more Siberian irises, which I cut short on their stems and mixed with white daphne growing along

Katharine Thrale's wall. Might as well cut all the flowers I wanted. I hoped that Father Dabney, and whoever came after him, would be good to Daddy's flowers, and know how to care for them.

After I did the centerpiece, I went quietly to the door of the guest room and listened again. Not a sound. The thought crossed my mind, as it had crossed hers in regard to me, that I might be the one to find her dead. Not from suicide, but from sheer exhaustion and a bankrupt spirit. Now that would be a denouement. The enemy expiring in the very house to which she had brought so much pain. But had she brought the pain? Hadn't it already been there? In a sense, she was just the passing angel of release. Perhaps even my father had recognized her as that. Hadn't he urged his wife's old friend to whisk her off on a "little vacation" from himself?

No, Madelyn dying in her sleep in the rectory guest room would not be a satisfactory outcome to the plot at all. There were more knots to be untied, more secrets to be revealed. My houseguest was my captive now. I strained my ear to her door until I had satisfied myself I heard her breathing. "I will not let thee go, except thou bless me": Jacob's words, Jacob's *threat* to the angel with whom he wrestled all through the night till the breaking of day. As Father Gower's daughter, I would probably always be finding Biblical parallels in my life. *I will not let thee go, Madelyn Farley, until you have told me all you know.*

I went outside and sat in the wicker chair in the garden. The long summery day waned. My guest slept on. The sky turned amazing shades of orange and lavender. I realized my fingers had been playing for some time with something that felt like a little swatch of fur, wedged in the whorls of wicker, and upon pulling it out and examining it, I discovered it to be a chunk of my father's hair. It was a chunk that would have pleased him, almost all dark, with just a few strands of white. It must have toppled from his shoulder when I was doing the back of his head, where he was still "young."

I took the lock of hair inside and sealed it in a Ziploc bag and put it with my Priority things upstairs. The things I would take with me wherever I would be going—whether just across town or off on my travels.

As I was mashing the potatoes with a fork, to keep from waking her with the electric beater, I heard the shudder of our downstairs pipes. She was taking a shower. Presently she entered the kitchen, wearing her *Nightowl* outfit: the purple shirt, the white trousers and sneakers, and the jeweled Maltese cross.

"You look a lot better," I said, which was true. There was no suggestion of Miriam Stacy about her now. She had regained command of herself. Her skin was no longer gray. "Your hair looks nice." Which was true, too.

"Why, *thank* you." She made me a courtly bow. "I found this glitzy mousse in your medicine chest and decided to try it."

"It must be Aunt Con's." I sniffed. "Yes, it is. Does that Maltese cross have a story to it?"

"Only that I bought it because I liked the colors in it. They're fake gems. It was very cheap."

"It doesn't look it. And it suits you."

"My image, certainly. The shirt belonged to Andrew. He was greedy about gorgeous shirts and I've kept a lot of them. I like to wear his things. It feels like I'm putting on some of his old magic."

"Before it got too hot, I wore my father's sweater practically day and night."

I lit the candles in the dining room, and served the plates. We sat down and I was in the process of lifting my glass of chilled Vouvray to hers for a hospitable toast.

"Haven't you forgotten something?"

I scanned the table: butter for the potatoes, salt and pepper, even a little cut-glass dish of radishes and carrot sticks I had added in a last-minute panic that there weren't enough items or enough colors in the meal.

"What?"

"Well, the *blessing*," she said in her mocking voice. Flashing her big white teeth at me, she stretched out her hand.

I took it. No one had thanked God for food in this house since my father's death. "Bless, O Lord, this food," I began, going strictly by the book. I was no match for Daddy, with his improvisings to suit the occasion.

At that supper sixteen years ago, when my father and mother and Madelyn Farley and I had held hands around this table, my open eyes had met Madelyn's open ones. Tonight I was surprised to catch her with hers closed.

*   *   *

We talked far into that night, and through the next day and into the next night. We talked in the kitchen and in the garden and even once in the living room.

"What is it about this room," she said. "I noticed it the last time. In the theater we'd call it a stillborn set."

"We never lived much in this room."

"I wonder if it has something to do with its perfectly rectangular shape. It doesn't go anywhere, there are no interesting corners. It's odd, it has a southeast exposure, but the way the architect placed it on the site, he still managed to make it gloomy. I assume it was a he. Ruth and I discussed this room a lot. I had to do a set just after we left here. It was for one of those depressing domestic dramas, I can't even remember the name. The play flopped. But it was Ruth who came up with the idea of using this room. She actually made some of the sketches for that set. It got a few favorable mentions, which was more than the play did."

"Maybe Father Dabney will bring it to life," I said. "He seemed to think it was sheer heaven in here. Maybe the room has simply been waiting for someone to believe in it."

We talked inside the church, sitting in a pew after dark.

"I see you still have that single lamp burning. What is the significance?"

"It means the Sacrament is present." (Nervously wondering if her next set would have a Sanctuary lamp in it.)

"My child would have been twenty-six this year."

"Oh, yes?" I said calmly.

"Ruth told Miss Beale she was going home for the weekend to see her sick mother. But she went with me to have the abortion. In those days it was still illegal. I was lucky mine was clean. The abortionist was a doctor in Danville who'd been disqualified because of drugs or something. Afterwards Ruth and I stayed in the Howard Johnson's, and she spent most of the night holding me in her arms and cheering me up with terrible stories about Connie Roundheels's promiscuity. 'I wonder how many Con's had?' she kept saying. It was Andrew's, but I never told him. He'd already backed out of the engagement. I was too proud to try and win him back with that ancient trick."

"What made him back out?"

"He had fallen in love with somebody else. An actress, that time. After that, he fell for a male dancer. They stayed together for a long time. A long time for Andrew. I was tempted, once or twice when Andrew was dying, to tell him. But what would have been the point? Do you think I was right, not telling him?"

"I think so. I wonder what my mother really wanted out of life?"

"After she married, I think she wanted your father to go on maintaining the illusion of the wise, strong older man she had fallen in love with at that Episcopal college. Then, when he took off his socks and showed her his clay feet, she had second thoughts, I suppose. Or she started remembering the other things that she'd wanted: we talked about them back at Miss Beale's. She wanted to be a sophisticated person and see some of the rest of the world. And she badly wanted to draw and to paint, only she wasn't trained enough to make a go of it in the commercial arts, and she wasn't driven enough to develop the little bit of real talent she had for serious art. I think Ruth was probably a sort of evolutionary fatality. A casualty of her times. In the early seventies, women were throwing off their shackles, realizing it was their right to have it all and trying to make up for lost time. Only a lot of them started running in six directions at once and got dizzy and fell."

Whatever Madelyn's other failings, she seemed to be an adamant truth-teller. I would eventually grow bold enough to ask her anything, though I didn't always enjoy hearing the answer.

"Of course she loved you. She almost went to pieces in Guildford on your seventh birthday. That's when we had our big blowup and she was going to leave. We made up, but a couple of days later she was killed."

"Six days after my birthday. She was killed on June twenty-fourth, the Nativity of John the Baptist. It fell on a Monday that year."

"Ruth was not a thinker, like Walter, Margaret. She didn't slowly come to her decisions by reasoning things out. She acted on her feelings. And, I have to tell you, not only was she a great idolizer of people, but she was an even greater rejecter of those same people. The higher the pedestal she built for you, the farther you had to fall when she pulled it out from under you. She did this with her mother, who never was on a very high pedestal, then with her big sister Connie, who *was*, then with Walter, who was way up there with the seraphim for a while. Then she took up where she'd left off in her hero worship of me back at Miss Beale's. We lasted pretty well through the winter in New York, because I was her excuse not to go back to Walter, and also I was very busy and that was attractive to her. But by the time we got to England, my pedestal already felt like it had a small earthquake under it. I was a lot higher than Connie, at the peak of Ruth's adoration, but distinctly lower than Walter at his peak. It was the way Ruth was. And being a natural rejecter, maybe she found it easy to believe that her own daughter had rejected *her*. Ruth didn't believe you missed her anymore, that's the brutal truth of it. You ask me these things! She thought she'd only open up old wounds if she went back for you, and that it would kill Walter if she tried to take you away from him. She wasn't sure you would even want to go. And, anyway, how was she going to *support* you?"

"Just let me try and understand this," said Harriet grimly. "You are going off with that person? You are going to *Europe* with her?"

The two of us were in the MacGruders' basement. I had just delivered the last of my load of boxes for storage.

"I know it sounds weird. I find it a little so myself."

"Weird! It sounds *deranged*. What am I going to tell Nana, or will you tell her?"

"I'd rather you would, if you don't mind."

"Oh, I'll do it, but I know what she's going to think. Has that woman put some kind of spell on you?"

"Is that you or Nana asking?"

"Me. But she will, too. Nana always thought there was probably more than your father wanted to believe there was between those two."

"Well, they weren't lesbians."

"She told you that?"

"She told me that."

"And you believed her."

"I believe they never explored each other's nooks and crannies. They hugged a lot, it seemed, and they cared for each other. But both of them preferred men. Only Madelyn tends to fall in love with homosexuals."

" 'Madelyn'! You say it as though you'd known her all your life."

"Well, I have, for most of it. She has had something to do with me all these years." Just like the witch in my closet, I had thought suddenly in the MacGruders' basement: those are the same words I thought about *her* in my dreams: *She has had something to do with me all these years.*

Ernie Pasco and his nephew, who was actually wearing a pair of Daddy's shoes (and perhaps a pair of the socks I had given him, as well), came to the rectory and carried away Father Traherne's old four-poster to the house on Acacia Street.

Adrian Bonner came to the house one more time, to tell me how much the bed meant to him. "I had no idea you planned to begin your travels so suddenly," he said, looking rather forsaken. He actually kissed me good-bye, going so far as to brush my lips chastely with his own.

On Wednesday, around noon, Madelyn Farley and I pulled away from the rectory in her rented Celebrity. I had left my Honda Prelude with Ben as a consolation prize. ("At least this way I know you'll have to come back to me, Margaret, even if it's just to pick up your car. And don't forget, I've still got your Golden Egg.") But I had let him kiss me good-bye. After Adrian Bonner's kiss, I could afford to be generous.

As we turned off Church onto Main, I looked over at the woman behind the steering wheel. The mocking, charmless woman whom I had so heartily hated for sixteen years. And I suddenly wondered if Harriet was right: was I deranged?

"I can't believe we are just taking off like this," I couldn't stop myself from saying. "I can't believe I am leaving Romulus with you."

She bared her big white teeth in a grin. She had taken it as an expression of joy on my part. "That is exactly, almost to the very words, what your mother said," Madelyn Farley told me.

It was the twenty-fifth of May. Feast of the Venerable Bede. As Father Gower's daughter, whatever else I was on my way to becoming, I guessed I would always be aware of who was being celebrated, or mourned, or remembered, in the Church Calendar for that day.

My heart teaches me, night after night.

—Psalm 16

EPILOGUE

THE GRACE OF DAILY OBLIGATION

May 29, Trinity Sunday, New York City

Dear Ben,

You shouldn't have sent all these flowers. They must have cost you a fortune. But thank you, anyway. Not only are they lovely, but they're comforting. Especially the delphiniums; Daddy's first delphiniums would be out now. I was here by myself yesterday morning—Madelyn has gone upstate to check on her father, his phone has been disconnected again, he says it interrupts his painting, it is a sort of running battle between them. She fumes and calls him awful things, but I'm sure she really does care for him. Anyway, yesterday morning, the doorbell rang—living in this city is like being inside a fortress. First you have to ask who it is over an intercom, and then if you don't know them, you're not supposed to push the buzzer that lets them in downstairs. I suppose he could have been a murderer announcing himself as a florist's delivery, but I am new to all this and pushed the buzzer, and up he came, a nice young boy with about six earrings through one ear, very sweet, though I couldn't understand half of what he said— and your flowers. He seemed surprised when I tipped him, and even more surprised when I talked to him. He's from the Dominican Republic, but his family lives in the Bronx now. You would have liked him.

All this is so new to me and some of it very strange. The Blimp didn't have to go to India to get freaked out by poverty. What is so disturbing here is the contrast: you look to your right and a flotilla of limousines sails past; you look to your left and there's a man in rags, with one swollen, purple leg eaten half through with sores, sitting on the sidewalk. He's not even begging, just sunning himself. Then you glance in a shop window and see a purse with a $6000 price tag.

I've done a lot of walking this weekend. I walked all the way from Madelyn's place, which is on 17th St., up to the sixties, staying on Fifth Avenue as she told me to. I couldn't begin to describe all the varieties of humanity I saw, but I want to describe this one strange incident. I can't stop thinking about it. I was at about 47th St. when this nice older lady came up to me. She was dressed just like the older ladies at St. Cuthbert's: hat and gloves, even. Only, her gloves and the collar of her yellow linen coat were dirty, and she seemed slightly confused. She asked me if I could possibly spare her a dollar. Someone had stolen her wallet out of her purse, she said, in this very educated voice (she dropped her r's, like the Major), and she needed "carfare" ("cah-fayah") to get home. Of course I gave her the dollar. Then I went on to St. Patrick's Cathedral and wandered around inside for a while. It felt strange, not going to church this morning, so I sat in a pew there for a while, although there was no service at the time, and it was very crowded with noisy tourists, and people were actually selling souvenirs in the nave. Well, when I was leaving, whom should I see in the vestibule but this same lady again! She had just started into her sad, well-spoken explanation about the wallet, but the couple she had approached—they looked like rich South Americans— rebuffed her in midsentence. It didn't seem to faze her at all. She simply began with another person. I stood there and watched her work *the vestibule of St. Patrick's for about fifteen minutes. She took in eight dollars, and . . . this was the interesting part, Ben . . . once, she approached me, opened her mouth to begin her spiel, then,* but without showing the slightest sign of recognition, *lowered her eyes and passed on to the next person.*

Well, I'm somewhat tired, after all my walking. The air is harder to breathe here. Certainly not like that pure Shenandoah air up on the parkway. Dear Ben, take care of yourself, and thank you for taking care of my little Prelude. I will come back for it when we return from England. The things you said on the card were excessive, but then, you are excessive. But the flowers really are special, and make things seem a little less strange.

Fondly,
Margaret

P.S. Tell Harriet I'll be writing her real soon, and love to Nana.

May 29, New York City

Dear Mr. Pasco,
    In my hurry to vacate the rectory, I'm afraid I forgot to turn off the hot water heater in the basement. Would you be so kind as to do it? As Father Dabney won't be moving in until June 15th, that would save the vestry some on electricity. Thank you and your nephew Darrell again for moving Daddy's bed to Father Bonner's on such short notice. I really appreciated it. My mother's friend and I plan to leave for England soon.

Sincerely,
Margaret Gower

Oh, sorry, P.S., one more request. Could you please turn it back on *again the evening before Father Dabney comes? I wouldn't want him to start off without any hot water!*

June 1, New York City

Dear Mrs. Dunbar,
    Please excuse this paper. It's all I could find to write on, and I wanted to say hello. I'm staying with that friend of my mother's, you know, the one in the theater, whom we talked about—I should probably say whom I talked to you ad nauseam about, over the past four years. She is not as bad as I'm afraid I made her out to be. The events of the last week and a half have been a total surprise to me. I look forward to telling you all about them, ad nauseam, when I see you again. Madelyn Farley (that's my mother's friend) is taking me to England. We leave next week. She has insisted on buying my ticket, because my mother bought her *ticket fifteen years ago, and she says it*

appeals to her sense of dramatic shape. She's going for the York Mystery Plays, but first we'll stay in London for a few days, then take a day trip to Guildford (she is going to show me the spot where my mother was killed), and then we'll head north for York. After that, we go to Whitby, so I can see where St. Hilda had her monastery (I haven't given up on the idea of graduate school, but it's on hold for the moment), and then to Northumbria, to visit Lindisfarne, St. Cuthbert's Holy Island. Daddy was so looking forward to taking me there. Then back to London via the Lake District.

I miss you! Will you please, please do this for me? On evenings when you are alone, and I know they won't be many, with all your friends, go and fix yourself a drink, and, when you take your first sip, raise your glass to me and remember our good times. That way you will not be drinking alone. Tell Dee Dee hello, when you next see her, and give my regards to Buddy on his next visit.

Affectionately,
Margaret

June 1, New York City

Dear Miriam,
*   I left town in a rush, and didn't get a chance to say good-bye. I am very conscious of what is probably going on at our corner right this minute, today June 1, and I'm frankly glad I was spared seeing the bulldozers come and rev up their engines and take their first bite. But what I wanted you to know was that, although I took only the minimum of possessions with me—I will be going abroad for a while—I did pack the journal you gave me for graduation. I haven't begun writing in it yet, because I want the first entry to be a momentous opening. But I already have several candidates for that first entry.*
*   God bless you, Miriam, and stay well.*

Sincerely,
Margaret

June 11 (St. Barnabas), London

Dear Adrian,
      This card doesn't do justice to the opening page of the Lindisfarne Gospels, which I saw at the British Library today. But you have no doubt been here yourself and felt the same awe and thanks that this wonderfully intricate work still exists. Eadfrith drew each little animal and painted each color as though he had all eternity, and maybe he did. It gives me comfort and satisfaction, knowing you have my father's bed, and I know it would please him, too. I hope you are fully recovered.

                                                            Margaret Gower

June 11, London

Dear Professor Stannard,
      Am in England with an old friend of my mother's. The British Library is enough to make even an apprentice scholar faint. Bede, *The Lindisfarne Gospels*, Jane Eyre! (C. Bronte wrote so neatly, there is nothing crossed out on the page. G. Eliot was a great crosser-outer and margin-scribbler. Keats has such sweet, large handwriting, Jas. Joyce was just plain slovenly.) I will write again when we get to Whitby.

                                                            Affectionately,
                                                            Margaret Gower

P.S. (*running out of space*) haven't decided about grad school this fall, but am still interested in Hilda. I worry Mrs. Dunbar will get lonely rattling about in that big house. You two were such fun at my graduation dinner.

June 12, London

Dear Mrs. Major,
      Across from our hotel is a very fancy antique shop, and in the window is a Queen Anne ball and claw tea table, with the leaf

carvings, like yours. It made me think of you, and our tea together the day before I left, when you gave me so much thoughtful advice about my future, and such great little sandwiches. I went in and talked to the owner of the shop. He was impressed with my knowledge of tea tables, and I told him I was friends with a lady in Romulus, Virginia, who was an expert on them. He said in his opinion Virginia was the most civilized American state. He said that before the Women's Liberation movement, dealers were able to advise their clients to select a tea table the way a man would choose a wife: begin at the top and work your way down to her ankles and feet. "But that sort of thing won't wash anymore." I thought you would appreciate this story. I am having quite an interesting time so far, though of course it's not the same as it would have been with my father.

As always,
Margaret

June 12, London

Dear Harriet,
   This is my favorite picture in the entire National Portrait Gallery. Only one left in the card shop racks and it had your name on it. Jane Welsh Carlyle was married to the famous, irritable Thomas Carlyle, but she survived and flourished by her tart tongue and her wicked observations about people in her letters. Tomorrow we go to "the place." Madelyn has rented a car with driver. She won't drive in England anymore. More later.

Margaret

Monday, June 13, London
   Well, we went and I saw it. This was to be the momentous first entry in the journal Miriam Stacy gave me, and somehow I had pictured myself overflowing with observations and feelings about it. What did I observe? What did I feel? Did I make the best use of this day? If I can't be honest about it here, what's the point of starting a journal? I certainly don't plan to be reading this aloud to anybody, like Miriam read hers to Daddy all those years.

We were there almost before I got settled in for the drive. M. and I had agreed that we couldn't just tell the driver we wanted to see where someone was killed, so we said we wanted to visit M.'s old haunts around Guildford. He was a very bossy driver and kept telling us what we ought to see, and he could get on the M3 and have us to Winchester in no time . . . he was dying to get on the M3. M. finally got very curt, and the two became enemies for the remainder of the trip. His name was Mr. Nelson. M. wanted to show me the house they'd stayed in but we couldn't find it. This humiliated her and made Mr. Nelson gleeful. We managed to find "the road" after going around in circles for a while and M. having several more go-rounds with Mr. Nelson. He pulled over and she told him to wait in the car, and we started walking off behind a hedgerow. He got out of the car and shouted, "If you ladies wanted to go to the loo, why didn't you say so?" "Why don't you stuff it, Mr. Nelson," M. yelled back. "Now, please: wait in the car."

So M. and I huddled behind the hedgerow ("Let the asshole think we're pee-ing, that way he'll leave us alone"), and then she showed me the spot, as near as she could recall; there have been some new houses built along the road and she had some difficulty orienting herself. "She was coming out of that road, and into this one, it was right over there . . . I think." And I tried to feel something, get some message from my mother through the air after fifteen years, force time to curl into one of its circles again, but . . . nothing. Maybe we ought to have come on the exact date, but I could hardly ask M. to wait around till the 24th, she has commitments back in NY, we have to leave England the 23rd. I got no message; I didn't even notice very much, because I was worried about what Mr. Nelson was thinking about us back in his car. I silently prayed, Rest eternal grant unto her, O Lord. And let light perpetual shine upon her. *I had planned to ask M. to do it with me, I'd do the versicle, she the response, but I chickened out. It seemed hokey. Also her filthy mouth put me out of the mood for sharing it with her.*

Now we're back at the hotel, M.'s taking a nap, she has a headache and feels "exhausted and old," and I can't even remember what trees or flowers were on that road. Daddy's old descriptions of it, and his detailed memories of his bicycle trips and walks in the area, seem more real to me than the place Mr. Nelson drove us to today, just as Harriet's description of the nurses sending up the balloon man in a patient's gown at her graduation seems like something I really saw, and more vivid to me than my own graduation in Charlottesville. We leave for York on the fast train tomorrow.

June 16, York

Dear Harriet,

I saw the place where my mother died. We always discussed what it would be like, when I finally saw it, but it wasn't much of anything. I don't even feel like writing about it. Maybe it would have been better not to have gone. No, I'm glad I went; but it wasn't the kind of day it would have been if Daddy had been with me. Also, we would have gone to his places, too. I am terribly homesick. But how can that be? I have no home. "Well, you could be with us," I can hear you retorting. Yes, I know, I know. Maybe I will come back and stay with you and Nana for the rest of the summer, before heading back to Charlottesville. If I do decide to go straight on to grad school, after all. I've been thinking: maybe I'll do better if I take my "freedom" in small doses. Ben did go off to summer school, didn't he?

And I still haven't been "bewitched," as per our conversation in your basement the day before I left. We share a bedroom, but the only thing I feel guilty about is, she won't let me pay for anything. This friend of hers who died left her a legacy, and she says if I were her daughter she'd be paying my way, and money is for the living to spend. So we are in one of these Prestige hotels that call themselves "Halls" or "Courts" or "Manors"—this one's very posh, with afternoon tea and gardens and old portraits and a library with shelves of leatherbound books, etc. It was once the home of the famous diarist, Lady Mary Wortley Montagu, and she (M., not Lady Mary, who's been dead quite a while) is off with some theater people in town. They all knew the late friend and are having a sort of wake in a pub.

Last night we saw the Mystery Plays, which were held outside, in front of the ruined arches of an old abbey. God was played by a twelve-year-old boy. To create the world, he climbs on a platform high in the arches and bounces down a green rubber beach ball, while the angels, played by other little boys, prepare Paradise for Adam and Eve. All the corrupt people are grown-ups, dressed in fashionable black. Victor Bannerjee was a superb Christ, grave, modest, and haunted. Even my father would have approved of him in the part. But even though M. and I took the requisite blanket and flask of brandy, the evening chill got so penetrating that when Lucifer opens his smoky red doors to admit the damned, Hell looked like the most inviting place to be.

Yesterday morning we took the train to Durham, to see St. Cuthbert's tomb at the Cathedral, and his comb and vestments and other relics down in the treasury. Tomorrow we have a driver for Whitby, and then he'll take us straight on to Northumbria, if M. gets along with him. Otherwise we'll take the train. M. is being very nice to me. She says I am good company and maybe if she follows me to the places my father was going to take me, she can get back some of her lost inspiration.

We fly back to the States on the 23, and I will phone you from N.Y. and see if it's still okay if I creep back to Romulus with my tail between my legs, and gather my strength for the next bout of "freedom." Love to Nana, and don't get too far ahead on your tan at the lake. The sun seems more distant here.

XXX
Margaret

I don't mean to sound whiny or ungrateful. I am enjoying this. But I miss Daddy, and keep wanting to share things with him or say something to him and I'll turn around and he isn't there. Or anywhere. I'm suddenly aware of my own mortality. I am going to die one day, Harriet. So are you. Just think of it!

Friday, June 17, LATE

We are in Bamburgh, at the tip of northern England. In Cuthbert's day, the monks thought nothing of rowing from Lindisfarne to Bamburgh, or from Lindisfarne to tiny Farne Island, where Cuthbert lived as a hermit for many years, except, of course, when his monks rowed over to see him and get "counseling." When M. saw how small our room was, she made the innkeeper give us two. She hasn't been sleeping well. So I am alone, within the sound of the North Sea, and there is actually a castle on a hill outside my window, and a moon, and I'm too tired to write all my impressions and adventures down coherently. I can't believe we were sitting on top of the hill at Whitby among the ruins late this morning and that tomorrow we go to Holy Island (the locals don't call it Lindisfarne; that's what the Danes called it, and the Danes sacked it). The distances of England look bigger on the map than they are. We covered a huge chunk of the English map today, in just a few hours, even though our driver took the scenic route.

M. (sprawled on a bench among the ruins up at Whitby, her hands thrust deep in her trouser pockets, after my "scholarly lecture" on the Abbess Hilda): "If you were an intelligent woman in those days, and wanted some time to yourself, you went to a convent. Or founded one. Then you could read and write and draw . . . okay, and pray . . . as much as you liked, without some man telling you when to blow out the candle so he could roll over on top of you. Nuns were the first professional women."

Joseph Hirst, our driver. M. loved him and kept her language clean, for a change. A wiry, 73-year-old Yorkshireman, who treated her with respect, but also thought a fair amount of himself. Though M. said if she had known how old he was beforehand, she probably wouldn't have got in his car. The rhythm of his speech is still in my ears. He had to go back to York as he has a funeral tomorrow—he drives for the crematorium there—but said he would come back and get us Monday, drive us through the Lake District, and get us to our plane on the 23rd. He told one story after another about accidents and deaths and cremations (a child's body can be cremated free at his place, if it "goes through" with an adult's). But in his accent, it was all oddly cheerful. He also entertained us with riddles. ("Can either of you ladies make a sentence using five 'and's in succession?" We couldn't. "Well, there was this publican, see, and he was having a sign painted for his pub, The Pig and Thistle, and he says to the sign painter, 'Would you put a hyphen between Pig and and, and and and *Thistle?' ")*

Holy Island, June 18

Dear Adrian,
Today is my 22nd birthday, and I am at the place where I most wanted to be on it, but not with the person I had hoped to be with. The taxi driver brought me over the causeway this morning, before the

tides came in, turning Lindisfarne (or Holy Island, as everybody calls it here) into an island, and he'll come back for me late this afternoon, after he brings some children back from a special school in Berwick upon Tweed. He is the taxi service.

The woman I am traveling with didn't feel well enough to come today, and though this sounds uncharitable, I'm glad to be alone. This is a holy place, you can feel it. No wonder it cured your migraines. Those long-ago monks must have led dedicated lives, because eternity is part of the air here. I am sitting on the grass right inside the sandstone ruins of the priory. I brought along stationery from our last hotel for the express purpose of writing to you from here, and I will mail the letter from the post office on the island. Holy Island to Romulus. Well, with a few stops in between, but I am a great believer in rituals like my father was. There is a simple border of flowers all along one wall: yellow gorse, blue veronica, white sea campion, and yarrows in both golden yellow and white. Just three colors, but perfect. Just enough. Daddy would have loved this place. The wind moves through the old walls and arches. The old stones are a glowing pink, buffed and shaped by the elements. I can see a vista of the harbor and the sea, framed by a Gothic arch. There is also a castle I will probably walk to later, if I can tear myself away from this spot, where I am trying to decide how I want to live my life.

I just did a thing you would surely understand. Do you remember the afternoon you came into our garden and I was cutting Daddy's hair? Well, a few days before I left Romulus, I found a piece of his hair from that haircut wedged in the wicker chair. I put it in a Ziploc bag and brought it with me to England, and I have just scattered part of it in the ruins of the presbytery, where Cuthbert was buried for a while, before the Danes became a problem and his faithful monks carried the body to Durham; the other part I have scattered in this simple garden of blues, whites, and yellows. I mixed the hairs in carefully with the soil. Oh, God, I miss him so. But I'm glad I could bring some little part of him here. It makes something feel complete. How he would have loved this hushed and green place, cut off from the mainland for a few hours every day, where the Golden Age of English monasticism once flowered. He always had a yearning for the fresh zeal and lost certainties of those earlier times. I wish I had a few more certainties myself.

I will probably be coming back to Romulus, to pick up my car, and maybe stay with Harriet for some part of the summer, and if I do, I would really like to talk with you, if you can find the time. I don't mean "counseling" or anything like that, though I could use counsel, but as a friend. In fact, it is my hope that we can be friends, and that our friendship will grow, the way I'm sure it would have done if you and Daddy and I could have had more time together.

Margaret G.

P.S. Now it's afternoon. I walked to the castle on the other side of the harbor and it was a disappointment. Dark inside, and only sixteenth century. Some rich man owned it until recently, and brought guests for the weekend who always complained later about how cold they'd been. I was so glad to get back to my priory, and begrudged all the intervening lights and shadows I had missed while I was gone. There is a lovely old church and a cemetery right next to the priory ruins. I walked around the cemetery in the high grass, followed at a suspicious distance by a chicken, who kept giving me beady-eyed yellow side glances. Many of the stones are too old to read. But with others, if you are patient, you can work out entire family histories. Many of the people buried here were once rectors of this church, and their wives; many others were sailors who drowned at sea and there are a lot of children. Here is the verse on the stone of Eleanor Lilburn, who died at age two and a half: "Thou art gone to the grave and we deeply deplore thee/But Christ is thy savior from sorrow and pain./He gave thee, He took thee, and He shall restore thee/And we who so loved thee shall meet thee again." I wish I could wholeheartedly believe that. The sign on the door to the church nave says, "Welcome to this 'Church on the Green' where God has been honored since the 7th century. You will find here a building that speaks of man's love of God, ancient and modern. Please shut these inner doors to prevent birds being trapped in church."

Sunday, June 19, Bamburgh

It might help if I think of writing in this journal as writing a letter. That way, I won't get sloppy or maudlin. Don't I owe myself the same respect and forethought in composition that I owe, say, Adrian? The

*only difference being that I don't have to withhold anything from
myself, or write certain things, or not write certain things, because of
fear of turning people off, or ulterior motives.*

*Today M. felt rested and restored, so we took the boat trip from
Seahouses to Inner Farne, the tiny island where Cuthbert retired to be
a hermit. Our boat had about 20 people on it, mostly birdwatchers,
and a party of schoolchildren from Durham on a weekend trip with
their schoolmaster and his wife. The children, fourth graders, wore
royal blue waterproof smocks, and carried backpacks with the brand*
Puma Young Spirit. *I liked that. If you observed them closely, you
could tell who were the leaders, who were the bullies, who the scapegoat. There was one little loner, neither a leader nor a scapegoat, just
purely himself; I enjoyed watching him stick his attractive little face
out over the side of the boat and think his own thoughts. I tried to
imagine what they might be. The girls wore stonewashed jeans and
some were already pretty, or sexy. They were very conscious of the boys,
more than the boys were of them. Well, it is a moulting age. And girls
are ahead of boys in that sort of thing.*

Madelyn said she was glad we went on the boat called Glad Tidings
and not the St. Cuthbert, *which we saw in the harbor. She joked
about St. Cuthbert being out to get her—she swore she had read in
some guidebook that he hadn't liked women—and that's why he had
made her sick yesterday so she couldn't go to Holy Island and pollute
it with her sacrilegious thoughts . . . or rather what* he *would think
were sacrilegious thoughts. I joked along, saying that today would be
her chance to get him back.*

*"How so?" she wanted to know. "Well, because Cuthbert was the first
human being to live on Inner Farne. Nobody dared go, before, because it was thought to be the preserve of evil spirits. He went to live
there to test himself over the invisible enemy, the way St. Anthony went
off to battle with his temptations. And you know all about St. Anthony, from your* Holy Desire *piece, don't you?" "I still don't see
what you're getting at," she said, looking interested. "Well, if time is
some kind of circle, making it possible for Cuthbert, who lived thirteen
hundred years ago, to make you sick in Bamburgh on June 18, 1988;
then it's equally possible for you to put him through a hell of tempting
and terrible thoughts, alone on his island on June 19, in, oh, say*

683." "Why 683?" "Because in 684, he reluctantly left, to become Bishop of Lindisfarne. King Eafrid rowed out and begged him." "Educated child," she said, ruffling my hair, "and fun to be with, like your mother." When she touched my hair, I was careful not to flinch, though I still feel quite a bit of reserve concerning her. There were probably people on the boat who assumed we were mother and daughter.

First, Glad Tidings anchored at another island, Staple Island, which from a distance looked like cliffs covered in ice or snow. But it was bird droppings, and they sure didn't smell like snow. M. and I sat huddled on a cliff, watching the bird-watchers going about in grim ecstasy with their binoculars, cameras, and camcorders, intruding on the nesting season of black cormorants and kittiwakes and puffins. The screeching din and ammoniac smell of proliferating bird life was almost too much for M. She sat down on a rock, relatively free from droppings, held her hand over her nose and mouth and took deep breaths. Her face got quite gray again.

As the boat approached Inner Farne, many of the bird-watchers put on those yellow hard hats construction workers wear on the job. M. asked one of them why, and he replied, with cryptic superiority, "The terns." The schoolmaster was nicer, explaining to us over the engines that the tern mothers, who built their nests in holes right on the ground, would attack you with their razor-sharp beaks. He had seen people's heads bloodied, on previous excursions. His fourth graders were all unstrapping their backpacks, or taking off their blue waterproofs, to hold over their heads for the perilous descent from Glad Tidings. M. and I took off our jackets, and cowered under them for much of the time we spent on the island. Even if you kept to the paths, up would fly these angry little mothers making a chittering sound like a tiny helicopter, and poke you one with their blood-red beaks. We saw one man's head get bloodied. "Here are your evil spirits," said M., ducking.

It was a pretty island, but hardly soothing during the nesting season of the terns. Probably even Cuthbert had stayed in his hut. M. and I found a bench out of the range of enemy fire, and ate our sandwiches. There was this one unfortunate tern who had made her nest on the most public pathway, and every time a new party of people approached, she had to rev up her little helicopter engine *and fly out at them. "She will probably lose her mind," said M., "or the chick will be stillborn." But M. herself was in a hopeful mood. She had read all the books and pamphlets we picked up at Whitby day before yesterday, and felt she was "on" to something again. Hilda excited her much more than Cuthbert. "It's women, Margaret,* women. *We're our own best hope. Christ had nothing against women; he knew their value, he liked having them around. It was all the women-haters who took over his ideas later, who banished us to purdah. There's a story, you know, that Christ was married to Mary Magdalen. "Oh, poor Cuthbert," I teased her, "he's down there in his hut praying* hard. *The season of the angry mother terns, and as if that's not enough, he hears this evil chirping in the air. He hears a woman's voice from the future saying Christ was married to Mary Magdalen and that women are their own best hope!" "Well, we are. We're* their *best hope, too. It's high time for another incarnation, and this time it's going to be a woman. It has to be."*

It was time to go. I went and said a prayer in Cuthbert's little chapel. "Everybody to the toilet now," said the schoolmaster. "Come, Samantha," said one little girl possessively, taking her friend's hand. Off they went to the toilets, in their leggy, stonewashed jeans. I thought how Harriet had often dragged me off like that when we were children: her own personal property. Three little boys stood in a circle around a tame eider duck, said to be Cuthbert's favorite bird. She had abandoned four eggs and was sitting on a fifth. The schoolmaster explained to the boys that the four eggs were infertile. "That lot's dead," one boy said to another, a pudgy little fellow with wire-rimmed glasses. The pudgy boy put out his hand gently towards the eggs. The patient eider duck gazed up at him trustingly. "Sir? What if I went home and got me 'at and put it over them eggs?" he called to the schoolmaster, who smiled and shook his head sadly. "Everybody to the toilets," he repeated, "and I want no litter at all left. Not a thing do I want to find, do you understand?"

As M. and I were waiting in line to descend under our jackets to the boat, I saw a mother tern fly off, leaving its little brown chick to fend for itself in the campion. At first the chick cried. Tiny little 'eep, 'eep, 'eep's. Then it pulled itself together and wandered down a "hill" that must have seemed vastly steep. It stumbled. It cried again. Then it hurried back up and cowered in a little dirt hollow that matched its color. It cried piteously. "Come on, it's our turn," said M. "No, I can't," I said. "I can't go until I see the mother come back. I have to wait." The little chick was now very still. It had given up hope. I imagined myself missing the boat because I had to see the outcome. But at last, the mother tern wheeled in from the sea, a fish wriggling like a strand of silver spaghetti in her red beak. She defended the fish angrily from another tern mother trying to steal it away at the last moment. She popped it in her chick's mouth. The chick gulped it down, making little satisfied smacking gestures with its tiny beak. The mother flew off once more. The chick cried. Then pulled itself together and marched off down its path again. M. and I were the last ones aboard the boat. When we pulled away from Inner Farne, my eyes were full of tears.

M. went to bed early and had a sandwich and brandy sent up to her room. I think she caught a chill.

Valhalla, N.Y., July 4

Dear Mrs. Dunbar,
  I didn't have a chance to write from England. So much has happened. My mother's friend is here at the Westchester Medical Center, and I am spending Independence Day in a nearby motel. Yesterday she had heart surgery. She might be dead by now, if it hadn't been for our English driver, a knowledgeable old Yorkshireman, who was driving us through the Lake District. She was telling him how, every day, she had less and less energy, and wondered if it could be some kind of low-grade flu. He listened to her symptoms for a while, then said, "Sounds like your valves to me, luv." He told her that only the week before, he had transported a woman (he drives for a crematorium) whose valves gave out. So as soon as we got back to NY, Madelyn saw a doctor and he sent her for some tests and we ended up here, although she said she didn't like the idea of having a triple bypass in a place called Valhalla one bit.

Her convalescence will be long and she isn't allowed to drive for three months. I have offered to stay with her and be her sort of gofer. We will be living with her father in the country upstate. (c/o Farley, Box 946, Overlook, N.Y. 12498.) He is pretty sick himself, but still paints every day. He had a friend drive him down here the day before

Madelyn had surgery. They snarled at each other, and he said she had made him miss a whole day's painting, and not to expect him to coddle her the way he had when she was ten (she had rheumatic fever when she was ten) but I am sure they care for each other.

I wonder if you would do me a favor, since I am too cowardly to do it myself. Would you please call Professor Stannard and tell him I am not going to enter graduate school. I think he has been jealously guarding a financial aid scholarship for me.

I am enclosing the postcard of the Brontes' parsonage I was going to send you. The place itself was frankly a disappointment. Too commercialized now. Joseph Hirst (that was our wise, 73-year-old Yorkshire driver) told us many of his passengers felt that way. I hope you are obeying me and having your evening cocktail.

Love,
Margaret

The General Theological Seminary
175 Ninth Avenue, New York, N.Y. 10011

I am interested in the M.Div. program. Would you please send me information about entrance requirements? My summer address is: c/o Ashmore Farley, Box 946, Overlook, N.Y. 12498.

Sincerely,
Margaret Gower

The School of Theology
The University of the South
Sewanze, Tenn. 37375

I am interested in the M.Div. program. Would you please send me information about entrance requirements? My summer address is: c/o Ashmore Farley, Box 946, Overlook, N.Y. 12498.

Sincerely,
Margaret Gower

P.S. My father, the late Rector of St. Cuthbert's Church in Romulus, Virginia, was a graduate of your School.

July 22, Overlook, N.Y.

Dear Ben,

    This is to acknowledge the receipt of the Golden Egg from the 1973 Easter Egg hunt. It was very fitting that it came in the mail today, the feast of St. Mary Magdalen, bringing with its arrival yet another revelation. I will explain later about the revelation—if I have any energy left after defending myself from all your accusations.

In the first place, I did not ask you to drive my Honda up here from Virginia and fly home. You offered. I thought you had a fairly good time while here. It was my impression you enjoyed our hike and picnic at North Lake. Surely you aren't saying I "used" you because I would not make love that day. If that is your reason, you're being shamefully ungallant.

In the second place, I disagree with you that I am "sacrificing my life" to the "first parent figures I could grab at." Three or four or even six months is not my life. At least I hope it isn't. And if it is, what should I be doing with it instead? Having arguments with you in Romulus or Charlottesville? At least these people need my services. I am good at taking care of older people. I've had some experience, you know. And I am learning valuable things from these two people. Disreputable as you may think they are, I am learning from them how important it is to be doing something you like doing every day until the end of your life, whether it is painting a landscape between coughing fits, or sketching sets for a new theater piece while your ribs mend over brand-new heart valves. And I don't agree with you that Farley is disgusting (except for his language sometimes). You, too, may be missing some teeth and smell a little gamey when you get to be 86.

Let me see, is that everything? Oh, Ben, I wish we could be friends. You have one of the most agile minds of anyone I know, if you would apply it more. You are full of life and lots of fun and very attractive. I have tender feelings for you, but I'm just not in love with you.

Now, about the Golden Egg. I showed it to Madelyn and old Farley, of course, and, in the process, learned something new. I seem to be learning so many new things I am dizzy some days. My mother painted the doves on the outside of the egg, and it's her hair pasted on the Magdalen figure in the little painting inside, but Farley did the actual little painting itself. The two women asked him to do it and he did. They all three worked on the egg, my mother suggested the theme for the picture, but the extraordinary little landscape with the angels and the Magdalen and Christ in the background as gardener, that was Farley's work. I remember my father calling up everybody when that egg arrived—I believe he called Nana first—to tell about how Ruth's talent was growing by leaps and bounds. Funny enough, I don't feel sad or betrayed by this latest revelation about my mother, only increasingly amazed at the mysteries that are other people. Does anyone ever really know anyone else?

I know you sent it as an angry gesture, Ben, but by the time it got here, it became the means for another revelation. So I thank you.

As Always,
Margaret

August 4, Overlook, N.Y.

Dear Harriet,
    Sorry you got the Curmudgeon when you phoned. I was out buying groceries, picking up prescriptions and art supplies for the busy artists, and exchanging my library books. At least he didn't tell you there was NO HARRIET.

Your description of Father Rawbones in my father's vestments was wicked. I don't know what to say about the young man in the wheelchair who comes to church now and is no longer in the wheelchair. Is he saying he was cured by Daddy's service? What is rheumatoid arthritis, exactly? Do you believe he might have gotten better anyway? You didn't make that clear. Your description of the sheared-off corner made me choke up. It will not be easy to see "the cornerless corner," as you put it. But your most cheerfully surprising news was your engagement to the Blimp, and of course you can count on me to come back and be in the Christmas wedding. Is there a chance St. Cuthbert's will have a new rector by then? That Ned Block is being a pain in the ass on the Search Committee doesn't surprise me. I

*only wish he could have felt Daddy was so superior and so irre-
placeable a little sooner. It would have saved us some grief.*

*I'll try and call you one evening, before you leave for medical school.
I think it's very dear that Georgie will go with you and do the domestic
stuff for a while. And of course I don't "look askance at you" for
falling in love with a rich boy. Love is love. I will remind you of this
if I one day surprise you by announcing my love for someone you may
not have expected me to fall in love with. Meanwhile I am perfectly
happy to have you "go first," as you have always done in these matters,
and I look forward to hearing all the details.*

Love (the Best-Friend-ly kind)
Margaret

*P.S. I know Nana must be relieved that Ben finally brought home a
suitable girl for the weekend. Heather is a nice name. What is she
like?*

September 1, Overlook, N.Y.

Dear Mrs. Dunbar,
    *What incredibly wonderful news. And of course I'll accept your
and Professor Stannard's invitation to be your honorary granddaughter. I can't believe this, it's just perfect. I'm flattered to be given the
credit for "playing cupid," but I plead innocent. You two were just right
for each other. I am going to pour myself a drink tonight and toast my
two favorite people in Charlottesville. Please give Professor Stannard
my congratulations and tell him that though I won't be doing a thesis
on Hilda of Whitby, Madelyn Farley has become very inspired by her
and is reading my Bede right now. She will be using quite a bit of the
material for her new theater piece,* **Abbess of Motherwit.** *Wouldn't
it be fun if we could all attend the opening next year in New York? So
everything useful gets used, one way or another, please tell him.*

Much love to you both,
Your Very Pleased
Honorary
Granddaughter

Sept. 13, (St. Cyprian; also Eve of the Holy Cross this year)

Dear Adrian,

I am sorry you were disappointed that I didn't make it back to Romulus this summer, but I also have to admit I am a little happy that you were disappointed. Harriet was right in telling you I am enjoying my present job. I take care of two interesting people who need taking care of, and I read and write and take walks. At the moment I am rereading Middlemarch *(I saw the original ms. in the British Library in June) and* Primary Speech: A Psychology of Prayer, *by Ann & Barry Ulanov (I highly recommend it; they're a married couple, she's a Jungian analyst and teaches at Union Seminary, and he's an English professor; you may even know them, with your Jungian connections) and . . . Meister Eckhart. Sermons Three and Fourteen are worth reading over and over and over. Yes, we need to be out in the world, to learn about the many manifestations of God; and yes, let God be God within you. And I love it at the end of Sermon Three when he says: "If anyone has understood this sermon, I wish him well. If no one had been here, I would have had to preach it to the offering box."*

I found your long letter very interesting and extremely moving. Thank you for entrusting me with so much of your confidence. No, Daddy never went into detail, you are right, he wouldn't, but he did say you had not had an easy time. But you're being too hard on yourself, I think. Things were done to you that shouldn't have been done, and so for a long time you lacked, as you say, the courage to love. Little wonder! The thing is to be able to use what we are given, and you certainly seem to be doing that in your work with others now.

Of course I will see you if you come to New York to visit your old teacher at General. I can come down on the bus, it's only two hours; or maybe I'll drive, if I have the courage to drive in New York. I can stay in Madelyn's loft. I have applied to General myself, and am leaning towards it. Or rather, I am in the process of applying. I wrote to General and to Sewanee. Then I got sidetracked by a requirement on Sewanee's application form. They ask you for "a brief autobiographical sketch, including the major turning points and personal influences that led you to choose the ministry." It's only supposed to be four pages, but I started writing, and I'm already on page 75 and haven't even become a teenager yet. I am liking the act of choosing words, evoking things with words. Bringing back places (like our corner) and people (like my father and mother) who are gone. I would like to be a writer and a priest, just as you are an analyst and a priest, though, on Daddy's account, it still makes me nervous to use the latter word in relation to myself; this is one of the things I'd like to discuss with you: do you think he would have minded terribly? I like to think he would have made an exception in my case, and that would have loosened him up for other cases. Come to think of it, I don't even know how you feel about the idea.

Just drop me a line when your plans are certain and I'll be there. I am very much looking forward to seeing you again, Adrian.

Margaret

P.S. Harriet was right. It's best not to phone here. If I'm not in, it can be embarrassing. I'm very fond of Mr. Farley, when he's behaving himself, but he hates to be interrupted while he's painting, and he's almost always painting.

P.P.S. I remember what you said, about why you admired Daddy. It was a phrase you used. He lives by the grace of daily obligation, you said. I am trying to do that, and I must tell you, it seems to be working most of the time.

September 13

Feast of St. Cyprian, Bishop and Martyr of Carthage, 258, in the Calendar of the Church Year. Today is the sixteenth anniversary of saying good-bye to Ruth at the corner, which is no longer the corner.

Well, Miriam Stacy's journal, you are almost full, what with the "autobiographical statement" that turned into a monster. Soon I will have to replace you with a new volume.

Madelyn, on our walk today (she has color in her skin for the first time):
"Of course you can stay in my loft, but I'm worried about this Adrian."
"Why?"
"Because I'm afraid he's coming to get you, the way Walter came to that college to get Ruth."
"He's not coming to get me. He has lots of problems of his own."

"Yes, but you might be able to talk him out of them, the way Ruth got into the habit of doing with Walter. Well, I can't live your life for you."

"No, you've got your own to live again."

"For which I thank God, or the gods, whoever She, He, or All of Them are. I found a frame for my new piece today; you're nowhere till you've got your frame."

"What is the frame?"

"Hilda's deathbed. I have a bit of experience with deathbeds now. And potential deathbeds. You know that long illness of hers? Well, that's when she'll pass on her wisdom to the young Princess she raised up from a baby, Al—what's her name, the one who will be the next abbess."

"Aelflaed."

"Yes. Then there will be flashbacks in front of the scrim. The flashbacks will be the present of this work, if you follow me."

"I think so."

"It will be a great way to inject some of my hard-earned wisdom. The only trouble is, I'm going to have to break my rule and use words. I'll have to opt for singers. Also this piece cries out for the erotic aspect. There's a strong connection between religion and sex, but so far I haven't been able to work it all the way through in any of my pieces. I wonder about that priest, Paulinus, the one who converted Hilda—I see him as a figure a little like my Andrew. An erotic something between Paulinus and Hilda, maybe. Or Paulinus and Aelflaed. Or maybe with both women. I may have to fiddle around with Bede's chronology a little. It's the symbolism that counts more than the history. And what the hell, it's my piece."

(I wondered if maybe I hadn't been a little premature in inviting the Stannards to come to the opening of Abbess of Motherwit.)

I can't sleep, the night outside my window is too beautiful. Such a clean, young moon, such a night. I can hear my father's voice in it, the exact rhythm and pitch of it, reading Vaughan ("There is in God (some say)/A deep but dazzling darkness . . .") It is a big and spacious night, with room for everything in it: me and all my great desires, an infinity of other things, as well. It is big enough to embrace Madelyn and old Mr. Farley, having one of their typical father-daughter ex-changes below on the porch. "Farley, if you want to stay out here all night and paint the goddamned moon, at least put a f___ blanket *over your legs." "Lap robes are for old men. If I want to paint the moon in my f____ scivvies, it's my affair. You hover just like your mother did. It's not attractive. Your language is not attractive, either." "My language! Where do you think I learned my language?" "All the same, it's coarse in a woman." "Why, you bloody old sexist. Go ahead and freeze them off, then."*

Later: I just finished reading this passage in chapter two ("Prayer and Desire") in the Ulanovs' book: "Surprises happen. We may discover we want more than we thought we dared. In the secret space of prayer, we may reveal to ourselves how much we want truth, beauty, love . . ."

Oh, You. Who are You? What do You want of me? What will I be doing on this day next year? Don't tell me. (You wouldn't anyway, would You?) Do You know, Yourself, or is it left partly to me? Are You withholding my life from me, or unfolding it with me? Are You an eternal parent or are we eternal partners? Are You there for me now? I choose to think so. Otherwise it would just be too lonely.

This is for Your eyes only. Here is what I want. Is it possible to have everything on this list, including the right to serve You?

I warn You, I am going to try for it!